RISKS

RISKS

Patrice Bloom

BANTAM BOOKS
TORONTO · NEW YORK · LONDON · SYDNEY · AUCKLAND

RISKS
A BANTAM BOOK   0 553 17547 5

Originally published in Great Britain by Judy Piatkus (Publishers) Ltd.

PRINTING HISTORY
Piatkus edition published 1987
Bantam edition published 1989

Bantam Books are published by Transworld Publishers Ltd.,
61–63 Uxbridge Road, Ealing, London W5 5SA,
in Australia by Transworld Publishers (Australia) Pty. Ltd.,
15–23 Helles Avenue, Moorebank, NSW 2170, and in New
Zealand by Transworld Publishers (N.Z.) Ltd., Cnr. Moselle
and Waipareira Avenues, Henderson, Auckland.

Printed and bound in Great Britain by
Hazell Watson & Viney Limited
Member of BPCC Limited
Aylesbury, Bucks, England

*For my adored Harry
and
FYM
With special thanks to
my agent, Reid Boates
and
my editor, Pamela Dorman*

Chapter 1

Jessica Martin looked up at the logo stretched across the top floor of the thirty-story high rise: Murchinson Oil. The building was a glare of smoky mirrors. She had often remarked that the whole town was done with mirrors. What Los Angeles needed was one or two gargoyles leering merrily down upon earthquake country.

Entering the elevator, she was unaware of the appreciative glances the male passengers afforded her exquisite face and figure. Her mind and heart were in turmoil.

She was on her way to an appointment with Jeremy Bronson, Corporate Administrative Director of Murchinson Oil, one of her best accounts. She felt both dread and exhilaration. It would be draining professionally, because Bronson wasn't going to like what she had to tell him. And she knew that personally the electricity between them was undeniable—but she was determined to fight it.

She shivered under the sheer silk of her Halston blouse. If she could just be honest with herself, she would admit she really didn't want to fight it. There was precious little personal excitement in her life.

But she also knew she could not allow herself to give in to

1

the attraction. The morals and ethics instilled in her by her late parents, along with her own sense of guilt, ran too deep. To give in to her feelings would cost too much.

Jessica had been sitting in Jeremy's office for fifteen minutes when she recognized the faint aroma of his woodsy cologne.

"Jessica." His voice was welcoming, yet intense.

She swiveled in her chair to return the smile on his ruggedly handsome face. "Jeremy, it's good to see you. It's been too long."

He seated himself behind his desk, a wry grin playing around his eyes and mouth. "You see to that, don't you, Jessica? Always so busy. You're becoming a Hollywood cliché. Part of the we-must-have-lunch crowd." His tone was teasing, but underlined with something deeper.

"Nonsense, Jeremy." Jessica tried to dismiss his remark. "While I admit Murchinson Oil nearly pays my yearly expenses, I do have other clients, never mind a staff to supervise."

Jeremy smiled. "You look beautiful, as always."

She flushed. Beautiful was not a word she would use to describe herself. Handsome, maybe. A woman of some presence, but beautiful? No. Not by today's standards. She did not know how to respond and found she could not meet his gaze.

Jeremy watched her across the desk. Jessica Martin would not think of herself as beautiful, but she was. Her high cheekbones, generous mouth, and slim but feminine figure made her more appealing than all the fashion-plate robots driving the southern California streets. Empty-headed little twits, he thought. But there was something womanly, essential, about Jessica Martin. She *was* beautiful, and if she doubted it, she had only to look into the eyes of any man who saw her for confirmation.

Jessica remained silent. He knew the compliment had distressed rather than pleased her. Jeremy sighed inwardly. She had given him no real indication she felt the same attraction to him, and until she did, he had no right to press

2

his own case. His voice was resigned as he asked, "Have you had time to complete your analysis of our problems?"

Jessica took a deep, relieved breath. She dreaded the day he would voice his feelings—she wasn't sure how she'd handle it. She nodded her head quickly, ready to get down to business. "Yes, the analysis is done, Jeremy." She picked up her briefcase and Jeremy forced his mind away from Jessica the woman to Jessica the professional management consultant.

"Well, it's obvious we have problems. Tell me what miracle Martin Management Consultants has come up with to solve them."

Jessica again felt a surge of relief. For a minute or two, when he'd looked at her with his dark, hungry eyes, she had almost caved in. She pulled the Murchinson papers from her briefcase. "Fresh out of miracles, Jeremy. But I do have some solutions that are viable, *if* you put them into practice." She handed the papers across the desk. "Your personnel people should already have these figures and a copy of this latest Supreme Court decision, but I brought them anyway. And yes, you do have problems, and I doubt you will avoid more lawsuits and bad press unless you correct them."

He rubbed his hand across his forehead. He suddenly looked tired. He had an enormous job for a man of just forty. Murchinson Oil employed some thirty thousand people, and staffing problems were an automatic part of such a giant conglomerate. Like most major oil companies, Murchinson had diversified into every conceivable type of business— agricultural chemicals, farm combines, major construction, mineral exploration, solar energy research, and so on. With so many different products, the conglomerate required nearly as many diverse professionals to make it all work. From corporate management types to geologists, chemists, toxicologists, regulatory attorneys, finance experts, lobbyists, computer analysts, the diversity was staggering, and as Corporate Administrative Director, Jeremy was responsible for seeing that each division was fully staffed and operative. He also had to keep Murchinson current with all the new hiring regulations, an area in which Jessica Martin's management consulting firm had been particularly helpful. He forced a grin. "Okay, let me have it, and don't spare any of the gory details."

"Actually, Jeremy, it's a Catch-22. In determining that minority hiring was a form of reverse discrimination, the courts have placed an even bigger albatross around your neck. The new Supreme Court decision, out of a case filed against Chemi-Co in Texas, has determined you now have to be color-blind in your hiring practices."

His eyebrows rose in an unspoken question.

She continued briskly. "I'm certain your people have already told you all this, but let me go into it for you a step at a time. As you know, the ruling for minority hiring was as follows: You were required to hire a quota or percentage of minorities in direct proportion to the number of minority residents in the community served by your corporation. That quota no longer applies."

A frown creased his forehead. "Elucidate, Jessica. Please."

"It's not over by a long shot," she replied. "The special-interest groups aren't going to buy this cop-out. If the government has chosen to bury its head in the sand for the time being, just because some past quota has been met, the special-interest groups are not."

She leaned forward and continued intently. "They will continue to take their grievances to the media and the courts. You will continue to be subject to suits, class-action and individual, unless something drastic changes and soon. And those suits will get heavy publicity and in the long run severely damage the social-consciousness image your ad agency has been so meticulously building. Stunts like buying a few tables at the Mexican-American Bar Association dinner will not be lobby enough."

He grinned appreciatively. "You do lay it on the line, don't you, Jessica?"

"That's what I'm paid for. I don't accept a fee for telling you what you *want* to hear, Jeremy."

"Okay, where do we go from here?"

"You know very well where we go from here. Or more to the point, where *you* go from here. Straight to the top. That's where your real problem lies."

He groaned. "J. C.?"

Jessica nodded, knowing how much Jeremy would hate it, but also knowing there was no way around it. Jason Carlisle, known affectionately and not-so-affectionately as J. C., was the Chief Executive Officer of Murchinson Oil and headed all its subsidiary companies, whose individual presidents reported directly to him. He was a tyrant with an ego beyond measure. He ran the giant conglomerate as if it were a one-man show and he was that one man. Jason Carlisle believed the old corporate axiom, "A man's staff is a direct reflection of himself." And his staff, particularly at the management level, had to be a mirror of his own impeccable academic and achievement credentials.

Jason Carlisle had been an overachiever as early as potty training, Jessica was certain. Master of Economics from Harvard, the Wharton School of Finance, the London School of Economics . . . and the list went on. He had graduated first in his class from each institution he'd attended. Jason Carlisle was a genius, but also a miserable son of a bitch and passionate bigot.

Jeremy's tone turned serious. "Jessica, you know my position on civil rights and equality. Anything less is intolerable to me. I think you also know I fight for what I believe in. Christ, you know what a battle I had to wage to get J. C. to accept blacks on staff, even in relatively nonvisible positions. But I fought him and I won that battle. I even got two or three Jews into the finance department." He shook his head. "Of course, that was probably just because J. C. secretly believes that all Jews are brilliant with money." He sighed. "Jessica, I do my fighting where I know I can ultimately be effective, within the system! And Murchinson Oil functions under one system—J. C.'s. If I go to him proposing what you're suggesting, on such an immediate scale, there's no way in God's name he'll ever go for it."

Jessica shrugged her shoulders, causing the light lavender

silk of her blouse to ripple sensuously. She knew Jeremy cared about human issues, he was a fair-minded business-man, but facts were facts. "Then if not in the name of God, in the name of the Equal Employment Opportunity Commission, in the name of ERA or civil rights. Put any label on it you wish. But Jason Carlisle is going to have to ease up on his academic requirements if you're going to make any headway in catching up with your obligations. I repeat, the government is backing off for a bit, but the people aren't. You're facing more than lawsuits, you're facing picket lines and nationwide boycotts."

"Is there no way to do this gradually?" he asked.

"Jeremy, you've had my firm on retainer for three years. We've been able to deliver just enough times to keep your fair-employment noses clean. But at this point, I'd lay in a big supply of corporate handkerchiefs, because in addition to pedigree, we have another big problem."

"Jesus, have some mercy, Jessica."

"No mercy, Jeremy. Facts! Never mind that there are only so many minority candidates who walk on academic water and would somewhat appease J. C.'s sense that his private empire has been invaded by mere mortals. I have three counselors working on this full-time. And yes, we have located some viable candidates."

She brought her handbag into her lap as she continued. "But, and it's a big *but,* while my staff has been out beating the bush, your budget people have been living in the Dark Ages. This is California, remember, Jeremy? Land of sunshine, smog, and the three-hundred-thousand-dollar tract house. Getting J. C. to recognize that only so many blacks, hispanics, and women got into Harvard or Yale is only half your problem; you are going to have to come up with a more realistic budget and a blockbuster relocation package. Otherwise, my people's hands are tied." She dug into her purse and came up with a package of cigarettes as she finished. "I'm sorry, Jeremy. But that's the bottom line, as trite as that particular expression has become."

He leaned forward to light the cigarette she'd taken from

the pack, frowning as he did so. "When are you going to give up those damn things?"

Jessica accepted the light, inhaled, and grinned. "When I can go live on a desert island where the air I breathe isn't already worth a two-pack-a-day habit."

He remained leaning across the desk, looking at her. "If you could settle for a long weekend on that island, I could probably arrange for you to use the company villa in St. Croix."

Jeremy restrained himself from adding how much he'd like to join her on that island, but Jessica had seen the desire in his eyes. She fought against a shiver and thought of warm, sensuous sunshine, carefree days, and balmy nights. Jeremy was so damned attractive and she was so hungry for a man's strong arms and body, for tenderness and passion. She was becoming more vulnerable with each day her marriage continued. It would be so good to just let go and deal with her guilt later.

She had to get out of there. She stubbed out the freshly lit cigarette, but not before she saw the look of hope in Jeremy's eyes; he knew she had almost weakened. Instantly, she was in control again. "Thanks, it sounds heavenly, but I couldn't accept. I've got to get back to my office." She slid a manila folder across the desk to him. "Here's my proposal. I feel pretty confident we can deliver if you are successful in getting these concessions from Carlisle." She fastened the catch on her purse, gathered up her briefcase, and stood. "I really must get a move on. I have a minor labor problem in my own office."

Jeremy came around the desk and stood before her. She felt almost physically restrained, although his hands were at his sides. He stared into her eyes and she had to look away. "Call me after you've read my proposal, Jeremy." She left his office on trembling legs, her eyes ready to brim over.

"Damn," she muttered aloud, causing Jeremy's secretary to glance up sharply as Jessica passed her desk. She hurried down the long corridor of the legal department, returning the wave of a young attorney her firm had placed at Murchinson. She couldn't even remember his name, there had been so many of them. So many lives, so many careers.

She reached the reception room, ignoring the smile of the perfect, California-girl receptionist. Jessica knew that everyone thought she was sleeping with Jeremy Bronson, and she grimaced at the irony. She had gotten where she was by hard, determined work and nothing more. She had proven her ability, and it was that ability alone that had earned her the first and only retainer contract ever awarded a management firm by Murchinson Oil. Her beauty had nothing to do with it. But no one in the male-dominated consulting world would believe it.

Chapter 2

Jessica eased her car into the reserved parking space in front of the Martin Management Consultants Building. As always, she took pleasure in the appearance of the building and at her own farsightedness in buying it at yesterday's prices. It was a beautiful little structure, one of the very few like it left in Beverly Hills. In the current real-estate market, she would not have been able to touch it. It was a small house of brick aged to a beautiful patina, in the style of an English cottage, converted into an office building. White smoke plumed from its chimney although it was 60 degrees and still not really winter—or what passed for winter in southern California.

Crisp white shutters shone against lead-glass windows. The effect was one of stability, which was exactly what she had envisioned when she'd first seen it some eight years before, overgrown and neglected. It never failed to please her when she caught sight of it. Sighing deeply, she got out of the car and activated its top-of-the-line burglar alarm.

She entered the building to see the smiling face of her not-California-perfect receptionist, Mary Ann Thomas.

Mary Ann was straight out of Nebraska and had moved to

California to be near her fiancé, who worked in the aerospace industry. She was polite, scrubbed, and dependable. Jessica held her breath every morning for fear Mary Ann would vanish in the night, back to the normalcy of her home state.

"Good morning, Mrs. Martin."

"Hi, Mary Ann. Everything going okay?"

"It's been pretty quiet so far, at least the switchboard has been light."

Jessica frowned. The one thing a consulting firm did not need was a quiet switchboard. "Has the mail arrived?"

"Not yet. Today is the relief man, so I wouldn't expect anything before noon—he's always late."

Jessica made her way through the salmon-and-pearl-gray reception room. "I'll see you later." She went down the corridor to her private office, nodding to her account executives who had their doors open but were on the telephones.

She entered her office and was once again pleased by what she saw. With a tendency to spread out when she worked, Jessica had chosen a large antique dining table as a desk. She'd promised herself that with no drawers to hide things in, all her work would be attended to during a given day and she would come in to a clear desk each morning.

She hadn't quite managed that, but she did love the rich wood grain and massive solidity of the table and the firm yet comfortable upholstered chair that did not swivel, forcing her to turn to her telephone and to rise from her desk rather than lazily roll back. Conscious of how much time she spent at her desk, she was determined to maintain her size-ten figure despite the occupational hazards.

There was also a comfortable sofa, covered in a small beige-and-brown French print, and two chocolate-velvet armchairs fronting the fireplace. Green plants and a limited edition of a Brueghel print caught the sunlight through the lead-glass windows and made her spirits rise. That, along with other whimsical paintings by little-known artists Jessica had spotted early on, completed the setting. The overhead fluorescent lighting had been removed and brass lamps, shaded in linen, cast a soothing glow over her work. The office was a measure of the success for which she'd worked long and hard.

She placed her briefcase on the desk, took her seat, and rang her secretary. Jessica smiled as Carol entered the office. Like Mary Ann, she was a genuine find. No Nebraska innocent by a long shot, Carol was wise and alert, a woman who had what Jessica liked to think of as "a case of the smarts." She had common sense, a dry, ironic humor, and had become as much a friend to Jessica as a secretary.

Carol was loyal, and Jessica trusted her. She was the only person with whom Jessica ever felt free to let down her guard.

"How did it go down at Murchinson?"

"Like a dose of castor oil. Jeremy is realistic, but he wasn't thrilled. I think he'll be able to convince J. C., even though it will leave a few scars." She smiled at her secretary. "Again, Carol. You did a terrific job on that proposal. I know I gave you short notice, but it took longer to draft than I'd imagined."

"No sweat, boss. I'm kinda fond of Murchinson Oil. Especially when my rent comes due. I know we can count on them."

"That retainer does go a long way during cash-flow problems." She motioned for Carol to take a chair before continuing. "Well, what new catastrophes occurred this morning? I didn't have a minute to check in, Jeremy was late, and the meeting ran longer than I anticipated. . . ."

Jessica's voice trailed off uncharacteristically. Carol raised her eyebrows slightly but made no comment. She seated herself and asked, "Do you want it in the order of importance, or sequence?"

Jessica grinned. Very little shook Carol, and she knew that whatever fire had started, Carol would have already dampened some of the flames. "I'll leave that to you."

"Okay." Carol took a breath and began. "Brandon, Brandon, Smythe, and Carson called at nine. Seems they haven't gotten any recent resumés from us and their nose is a bit out of joint. They reminded me they were one of your first accounts, et cetera, et cetera, et cetera."

"Jim's on that account, isn't he?"

"Yes, but I don't think they have much rapport. Jim is just too Brooklyn for the Brandon bunch."

Jessica made a note on her activity sheet. "I'll call them this afternoon and see if I can't soothe their ruffled feathers. I'll also have a talk with Jim." She sighed. "Lord, I've told him aggression is important in this business, but with finesse, with finesse."

"I don't think that word translates into Brooklynese," Carol cracked. She thought a moment, then said, "Let's see, the Beverly Hills Fire Department was here again. Something about checking the chimney flue. Seems they've had a complaint."

Jessica grinned, wondering which developer was trying to get at her precious building this time. "I'll handle that later, too. So far, nothing really tragic, unless you've saved the worst for last."

"Afraid so, boss. Eleanor wants to see you as soon as you can spare a minute." She smiled impishly. "Trouble with Stacey, and this, madame, is a recording."

Jessica had to smile in spite of the news. Carol's sense of humor helped a lot. This was something she'd been expecting. As a matter of fact, it was at least a month late, according to her private calculations. She sighed again, then said, "Okay, tell Eleanor I'll see her in a few minutes. No, wait," she corrected herself. "I'll call her myself. I know she's upset and I don't want her to think I'm not concerned." As Carol rose, preparing to leave, Jessica stopped her with, "Do me a favor. Unless it's something you know can't wait, hold my calls for an hour or so. I have to phone a couple of people and then I'll meet with Eleanor."

"Gotcha!" Carol smiled and left the office, softly closing the door behind her.

Jessica leaned back in her chair and shut her eyes. She had indeed been expecting this request from Eleanor Handler. Eleanor was the third assistant in two years whom Jessica had hired for Stacey Dawson. She grimaced. *Stacey*.

Jessica opened her eyes and automatically reached for the

telephone, ready to dial her home number as she had after the accident, when her eyes fell on the smiling photograph of her husband, framed and resting on the antique table. She snatched back her hand and lit a cigarette instead. She'd learned not to call as she had when Michael had first been released from the hospital. Learned not to smother him with her concern—her private need to assure herself that he was all right, still miraculously alive, that although she could never, ever change what had happened, or forgive herself, he was still alive. He'd hated those calls, finally accused her of checking up on him, denying the fact that, wheelchair or no, he was functioning at least as half a man. And, as much as hearing the sound of his voice reassured her, she did not allow herself the luxury. His coldness at those times was too painful.

"Michael," she breathed to herself, trying to keep her emotions from taking over. They'd had it all—evidently enough to offend the gods. And now, just two years after the accident, they lived in a sort of truce, each terribly conscious of the other's fragility, stepping around one another's feelings, never addressing problems head-on. They lived as though it had not happened, trying to pretend everything was the same between them.

It was only when she was alone, or very tired, that she allowed her feelings to surface. At those times she felt like a madwoman. Frustrated, furious, unable to understand why it had happened to them, unable to forgive the fates.

And how she missed the passion and love they had once shared. The laughter, the love they had made to one another. Now there was almost nothing. And she would have accepted so little—his touch, his warmth, his affection.

She thought back to her parents, now dead. They had had it all figured out for their little princess. Be a good girl, save yourself, you'll see, your Prince Charming will come along and you'll live happily ever after. Lord, they had been so close to right. She had been a *good* girl, she had saved herself, and her Prince Charming had come along, right on schedule. But, Jessica thought bitterly, things don't always go the way you thought they would. The taste of salty tears startled her back to the present.

She sat up in her chair, chiding herself for becoming maudlin, something she swore she would never allow. She had to meet with Eleanor Handler. She shook off her personal problems and tried to concentrate on the business at hand. She knew exactly what she would hear from Eleanor. Carol was right, it could have been a recording. Stacey Dawson was the most consistent producer and best account executive Jessica had ever employed. She was expert in her field of high-level computer sciences. A mathematical natural, she was able to absorb the complexities of the world of computers with ease. Her billings were always in the $150,000 to $200,000 range, figures Jessica could not ignore, no matter how much she disliked Stacey as a person. Even very competent recruiters rarely hit the $100,000 mark. Of course Stacey knew her worth and took full advantage of it. She never pretended otherwise. Still, not a day went by in which Jessica did not wish she could afford to get rid of Stacey.

Eleanor Handler was no dummy. A woman in her late forties, she had returned to the work force after widowhood. Jessica had feared the problems of an older woman taking direct orders from a younger person like Stacey, who made no attempt at diplomacy whatsoever. But Eleanor had been confident she could handle it. And she wanted desperately to get back into the mainstream and start living again.

Jessica faulted herself for hiring Eleanor, but her background as a former math teacher had been perfect for the job, and she seemed mature enough to take Stacey's verbal abuse. Obviously Jessica had been wrong. Stacey never wanted an assistant to succeed. She wanted them to learn only enough to do her drone work, and after that, she was finished with them. An assistant's days were numbered with Stacey the moment she appeared capable of functioning on her own.

Jessica didn't kid herself. That was the reason she had been able to lure Stacey away from one of the big-eight search firms. Here, Stacey was a very big fish in a smaller but quite respectable pond. Eleanor Handler had successfully placed a research computer scientist during Stacey's absence at a convention, and the gauntlet had been thrown. From that point on, Stacey had, Jessica knew, set out to make Eleanor's life impossible.

Well, she couldn't let Stacey go. Jessica was a practical businesswoman and a firm the size of Martin Management Consultants couldn't afford to throw away a six-figure biller. She sighed and pressed the intercom to Eleanor's office.

Eleanor looked like a child who had gotten a bad report card as she sat opposite Jessica in one of the brown velvet chairs. Jessica tried never to talk with an employee while seated behind her desk. Some management experts would say she was making a mistake in not maintaining a more formal atmosphere. But she thought differently. She knew she was in control of her business and while she might appear to be easy, anyone who pushed her very quickly found out otherwise.

"Jessica," Eleanor started, "I think you know why I'm here."

"I can guess, but why don't you tell me anyway?"

Eleanor smiled an ironic smile that only a person who had suffered a great deal would be capable of. "I made a stupid mistake, Jessica. I learned too quickly. I proved I can do this job."

Jessica remained silent but she knew Eleanor was right.

"It's not just being held back, Jessica," Eleanor continued. "I could handle that awhile longer. It's the condescension—I guess I'm a bit long in the tooth for that."

"Eleanor, we've discussed this before. I know Stacey gets a kick out of sounding superior and making others feel like idiots. But as I've said, she only enjoys it if she has an audience. Have you taken my suggestion of not asking her for information in the presence of others?"

"Of course I have. But I'm afraid it has gone beyond that, Jessica. I don't think this is anything new to you. I am, after all, Stacey's third assistant that I'm aware of." She paused for a moment. "You know, it's funny—I don't even take it personally. I just don't want to take it any longer. She really is a bitch and there is no way to pretend otherwise. Nothing is going to change her."

Jessica's silence was confirmation enough. But she had a hard and fast rule—a department head ran his or her own show. She would not interfere unless production was down or ethics breached. She was a woman able to delegate and she knew this was a great part of her success. The computer division was Stacey's baby, and Jessica would not pull rank.

"Eleanor, what about another department? You know there is room in the legal division. Lawyers are no more difficult to place than computer scientists. I'd hate to lose you, and as you say, you learn fast and you've proven you can do the job."

"More's the pity," Eleanor sighed. "I appreciate it, Jessica, but no. I've given my pound of flesh to the consulting world. Next month I was supposed to go off training salary and onto full-account executive pay with commission. I can't expect you to pay me that kind of money while I learn a new field. Besides, the office is too small, and maybe I'm too sensitive, but I just don't think I could go on working here and remain a lady." Eleanor took a deep breath. "I'd like to give you my notice."

Jessica shook her head. She'd known this would be the outcome. Not one of the other assistants had been willing to stay on, even in another field. Stacey wielded her hatchet too well. "I'll accept with great reluctance, Eleanor. Have you thought of what you will do?"

"Yes, I have. I've been thinking about this for weeks. As you may know, since my husband died I've learned to be a survivor. But not at the cost of my personal dignity. And I've learned something in this business: Everyone should keep his options open. Believe it or not, I've been recruited."

Eleanor's laugh was slightly embarrassed and Jessica knew she felt disloyal. She tried to put her at ease and joined in the laughter. "If an account executive does not get recruited, that person is not doing a good job. Tell me, who is the lucky company?"

The relief was obvious as Eleanor leaned forward, her face glowing with pleasure. "I've been offered a job at Data Base Electronics. I can start on Monday or they will wait two weeks if you need that much notice."

Damn, Jessica thought, I really like this woman. She's not only bright, she's a very classy lady. She smiled and said, "I couldn't ask you to stay in an uncomfortable situation, Eleanor. I'm sorry to lose you, but I do understand. Just as I think you understand my position."

Jessica relaxed back into her chair before continuing. "I'm delighted you've found something, and Data Base is lucky to have you. There's no need to stay beyond today, though of course I'll pay you through the week. Why don't you take the rest of this week to regroup before you start your new job on Monday?"

Eleanor rose and smiled at Jessica. "I thought you'd be fair. I owe you a lot, Jessica. You gave me a chance when I desperately needed to feel valuable. I'll never forget you for it."

After Eleanor left her office, Jessica had a quick mental image of Stacey making yet another notch in her Gucci belt. There were times Jessica wondered why she continued to work in such a pressured business. But she never thought about it for long—her sense of accomplishment in building such a successful firm all on her own was too valuable to give up. She'd started with a single desk in a small office and on her own money. She hadn't asked Michael for a dime, and while it had depleted the small insurance money left her by her parents, she had made it.

And now there was a reason far more important than the exhilaration of personal success to keep her working. Now she *had* to continue her career. It wasn't for financial reasons. Michael was still half-owner of his firm and he had inherited a fortune from his parents, so they were quite comfortable financially. She continued working because it was the only thing that kept her whole and sane. She needed the pressure, needed the exhaustion it brought at the end of the day. It was the only way she could cope. She understood it and was grateful for it.

Sighing, she picked up the phone. She would soothe the ruffled feathers of Brandon, Brandon and, as they say in legal circles, all the et als.

Chapter 3

Jeremy Bronson closed the folder on Jessica's proposal. He was, as usual, impressed by the thorough research job she had done. She had the most current figures on management-level people at Murchinson Oil, and she knew to a body how many were ethnic and/or female. She also had comparative figures from other corporations. No doubt about it, Murchinson Oil was way behind the times. They had to catch up, and soon.

There had been enough bad publicity over the latest oil spill and the proposed offshore drilling. The questionable political contributions were on the daily newscasts, and the last thing the company needed now was a discrimination class-action suit filed by yet another special-interest group.

The beginning throb of a headache caused Jeremy to lean back and close his eyes, pondering the problems facing him. There was the dismissal of the accountant in the finance department. The man had turned out to be gay and took his dismissal as a sign of prejudice; worse, he took his claim to an attorney and the press. He had been adamant and any talk of a settlement was out. He had every knee-jerk liberal within earshot fawning all over him. He had decided to come out of the closet in a big way, another media fish to fry. And the worst of it was that it simply wasn't true; no one had even known the man was gay. Jeremy opened his eyes and sat up, musing that there was something wrong in the world when a company could not fire an incompetent because of his sexual preferences.

Jessica was right about their salary scale as well. They were at least five to seven thousand dollars under competitive market, not even allowing for the ridiculous cost of buying or renting a home in California. Murchinson Oil was based in downtown Los Angeles, so nearly everyone who worked for the company commuted. Couple the cost of housing with the steadily increasing cost of gasoline, add that there was virtually no rapid transit in Los Angeles, and their employment package was a joke.

He leaned back in his chair, smiling as he thought how it continued to amaze him that she could have such current facts and figures before his own people had their questionnaires back from the printer. They wasted so much time in studies, covering their asses. The latest salary surveys, the latest cost-of-living surveys. Christ, all they had to do was go to the supermarket, fill their gas tanks, or try to buy a house, to know. Even with their tremendous computer-retrieval systems, by the time the information was compiled, it was already dated.

Jessica used her sources well. She never wasted time, went directly to people who had the answers, and did her own computations. And usually she was right; her few telephone calls were faster and more accurate than any computer service he'd ever seen.

No, Jessica Martin wasted no time. What she wasted was Jessica Martin, a situation Jeremy found tragic.

When she had called his office three years ago requesting an appointment, he had reluctantly agreed. He'd been intrigued by her introductory letter and references even though headhunters were anathema to him. A sometimes necessary evil, but in general an aggressive, pushy bunch

.vith few scruples and even less tact. He had expected a nut-crunching female trying to get by on her sex. He had, in short, expected anything but Jessica Martin. It embarrassed him to remember he'd almost bought into that old saw that intelligence and femininity are incompatible, and had nearly cancelled the meeting. Happily, he had not.

He'd been attracted to her from the day he had met her. It had not just been her beauty, although he could not deny that he had actually caught his breath when he first saw her. It was her style, and most of all her intelligence, to which he warmed instantly. Jeremy could not abide empty-headed people.

Jessica didn't sell, didn't push. She'd asked knowing questions, had done her homework on Murchinson Oil as well as on Jeremy himself. She knew where he had been educated, where he'd worked before Murchinson Oil, how long he'd been with the company. And wonder of wonders, she understood what the position of Corporate Administrative Director entailed.

No, definitely not your run-of-the-mill headhunter. She was a professional, confident of her abilities and the services her firm could render. From that first interview Jeremy had decided to retain her for Murchinson Oil. He hadn't bothered to check her references; most of the names on the list were men and companies known to him. He doubted even the most brazen headhunter would fake such a roster. He'd made his decision some forty minutes into their first meeting and had never regretted it.

At least not professionally. Jessica's firm had served Murchinson Oil in nearly all phases of upper- and middle-level management recruiting. Her work and that of her staff had been satisfying, the retainer fee justified by services rendered. Even under the most delicate circumstance, where a key man had to be replaced, Jessica had been able to carry it off, recruit the right candidate with dignity and confidentiality. Even the great Jason Carlisle had never questioned her retainer fees, which were appreciable.

It was on the personal level that Jeremy almost regretted

meeting Jessica. He could not remember ever having been more drawn to a woman, more completely entranced. Any man would feel it, any man who knew what a woman should be, would recognize Jessica as the real thing. Humor, curiosity, intelligence, warmth, all of that.

Jeremy let his thoughts flow freely. Damned if he didn't think he had fallen in love with her, had probably been falling in love with her for some time. She'd never given him any encouragement, not before and not after her husband's terrible accident. Poor bastard. Except for what he saw in her eyes in unguarded moments, she behaved as a professional colleague. A *married* professional colleague.

He rose and walked to the window wall and stood looking out on the city. He was married himself, that was an undeniable fact of life. No matter that his marriage was not all it should be, he was still married, and the father of two children.

He thought about his marriage at unexpected moments, hard-pressed to define what was wrong with it. His wife tried—she was lovely, an excellent hostess, a wonderful mother. But something important was lacking, there was no sexual intimacy between them now and no desire for it. Maybe they were simply the cliché couple, two decent people who had married too young, experienced too little of life before making a commitment. He'd been so sure she was the kind of woman he wanted and needed in a wife. Perfect for a young punk determined to make it big in the corporate world. And in that regard, she was. There was no denying she had been an asset as a corporate *wife*. But Margaret simply was not, he'd learned too late, what he wanted or needed in a *woman*. And Jessica Martin was.

He wasn't certain just when he'd begun to fall in love with her, not certain when the chemical attraction had become something more. But he had finally admitted it to himself, and further admitted it was probably hopeless.

Jessica just wasn't the type to take a lover. Jeremy couldn't kid himself about that, and in spite of how much he wanted her, he had to admit to himself that an affair with

Jessica Martin would not be enough for him. If she ever gave herself to him, he would want all of her, forever.

Sighing, Jeremy went back to his desk and glanced at his calendar. Four other meetings that day, plus another company dinner party that evening. His fantasies about Jessica would have to wait.

Chapter 4

Stacey Dawson, telephone cupped between her chin and shoulder, stared lovingly at her mink coat hanging on the back of her closed office door. She murmured the usual "Uh, I see," into the receiver, but she was thinking of the luxurious fur against her skin. Not only was the coat wonderfully sensuous, it was the tangible evidence of her success.

Stacey had bought the coat for herself—wholesale to be sure—but nonetheless, she'd bought it with her own money. And she adored it. It was a symbol of many things, not the least of which was the knowledge that she was getting closer and closer to her goal in life. Stacey was determined to be somebody. And mink confirmed that she was truly on her way.

Only half listening to the voice on the other end of the telephone, she shuddered deliciously as she remained fixed on the fur, thinking of later. She would bathe and perfume herself, then spread the coat out over her bed—fur side up—lying nude atop it, her vibrator at the ready. God! It was better than it ever was with a man. Stacey had to be in control—call the shots—and most men simply couldn't function under those conditions.

Aside from her strong personality and subtle ability to let a man feel somehow inferior, men were put off by Stacey's astonishing beauty. There was something almost wild in her flashing turquoise eyes, something dangerous yet intriguing. Even the way her thick mane of blond hair hung around her shoulders had an untamed quality to it. She was a petite young woman, but her body suggested a lushness, from her firm, full breasts to her long, slender legs. She was attractive and frightening at the same time.

Stacey frightened most men, and their weakness disgusted her. A *real* man would know how to handle her—make her feel safe enough to lose control in an intimate situation. But Stacey had not met any *real* men. At least not any she recognized as such.

Once, out of her disdain and impatience with the men she knew, she'd even tried it with a woman. She'd heard enough times that only another woman knew the right buttons to push for total satisfaction. But it had been limited to just once, at a computer convention in Georgia. She'd met an older woman scientist, who'd spent half her life in school huddled over figures and plans for computer designs.

The convention had been disastrous. Stacey had been forced to rent a suite and conduct interviews with prospective candidates in the sitting room. To say nothing of being boring—almost every person there was ancient and the candidates who did want to register for placement in new positions were mostly people Stacey already knew and dismissed as unsuitable. A Marta Kosnovitch had been the last person scheduled for an interview, and when the older woman entered the suite, Stacey groaned inwardly. She had to be in her late forties, dumpy, graying, dressed in a crumpled suit and sensible shoes. Stacey had been tempted to cancel the interview. No way could she market such a lump. The woman would never get through a corporate interview; she was so flustered as to be nearly inarticulate. Yet her credentials were extraordinary and Stacey made the quick decision to attempt to stick her into some think-tank situation requiring little or no public contact, except perhaps with other equally dull scientists.

The voice on the other end of the phone droned on and Stacey half listened while inwardly replaying the scene in the Georgia hotel room. She could remember the dialogue:

"You seem a bit distraught, Doctor—is something wrong?"

The silly old woman had actually blushed, and again Stacey remembered thinking the woman would never make it through an interview.

Marta spoke in an accent that could have been either Polish or Russian. "I have been much surprised, Miss Dawson."

"Surprised?"

"This is truth. When I make appointment—I do not expect you. I expect older woman."

Stacey smiled and relaxed. This was nothing new. She was young to have accomplished so much, to have gained a reputation among a predominantly older group of scientists.

"I'm sure you're being kind, Doctor. I'm not quite as young as I look."

"No," the doctor protested. "You are very young and very beautiful. I think you would be married with babies, not work with computer scientists."

"Well . . ." Stacey said, with a little laugh. "It's not so easy for a girl to get married today. Men haven't changed very much. And a career girl isn't as attractive as a woman willing to stay home and be the adoring wife." She wasn't yet sure if the woman was being sincere or resented her youth.

For the first time the doctor smiled. Her expression softened and an almost imperceptible glint came into her eyes. "This is also truth. Me, too. I said no babies for Marta, I say no to dishes and diapers and men. This I do not regret."

Stacey wasn't sure where the conversation was heading, but she was anxious to get the interview over with. It had been a long day.

"And a wise decision you made, Doctor. You've accomplished so much in your career. You must be very proud."

She shrugged her bulky shoulders, a wry grin softening her heavy face. "Yes, I have pride in my work. I am a good scientist and I like computers. But it is Marta the woman for whom I have the most pride. I did not need Gloria Steinem to be a free woman. I have always been a free woman. I will never need a man in my life."

Stacey had become increasingly confused. What was the woman getting at, and how the hell could Stacey get this interview back on track and concluded? The woman was kind of interesting, but she also seemed a bit nutty.

"That's very interesting, Doctor. You must have been one of the first women's libbers. But we'd best get on with the interview. It's getting late and I have some clients I must meet for dinner."

The doctor stared at Stacey for what seemed a very long time, but was actually only a few minutes. It was as if she were trying to make a decision. Finally, she spoke. "No need to interview. You know my work. You will send me to the best place, a place where I am my own boss, not to answer to a superior. I trust you to do this. I do not care where this place is, I care only to do my work alone."

Stacey had been relieved. Hell, this was easier than stealing. She could place her in a flash; this one would go anywhere in the country.

"Well, of course at your level of experience and with your track record," Stacey said, "there is no reason why you should require supervision. I'm certain if you wanted it, you could head up your own research team."

"No! No team! Marta works alone now. It is time."

For a moment, Stacey thought she had blown it. She knew better as a recruiter to offer more than the candidate asked for. That came later, when it was time to convince the person that some area of objectives could not be met. Then was when a good recruiter held out a different, extra carrot. All recruiters kept an ace up their sleeve. There was just something about this woman that threw Stacey off base.

"Of course," she said hastily. "Whatever you like." She

smiled brightly. "Well, Doctor, it's been a pleasure meeting you. I'll be in touch with you very soon. I'm returning to Los Angeles and I'll make some calls on your behalf."

Again the doctor smiled her strange, slightly sad smile. "Good. The business is done. You will give Marta what she wants. Now Marta will give you what you want."

Confused, Stacey stammered, "I think I have everything I need, Doctor. I can't think of anything else."

"No, you do not yet know what you need—but Marta does."

With that, she rose, removed the papers from Stacey's hands, and lifted her by the shoulders to a standing position. She reached forward and began unbuttoning Stacey's blouse.

At first, Stacey was stunned; she couldn't believe what was happening. She had fought off many a male at conventions; surely she wasn't about to be raped by a woman. She started to protest, but Marta's voice had dropped to a soft, accented drone, almost hypnotic, soothing, assuring, a whisper.

"Is not to be afraid. Marta knows what is good. Marta knows what is needed."

Stacey allowed herself to be led through the sitting room and into the bedroom, Marta's voice never ceasing its hypnotic encouragement. She found herself lying on the bed, watching in astonishment as Marta began expertly to remove her clothing. Not even shedding her own suit jacket, Marta focused solely on Stacey.

And when she was completely nude, Marta began. She was all over Stacey, hands, mouth, tongue. It was incredible—sensations she had never experienced rushed through Stacey's body; she twisted and moaned pleasurably at Marta's administrations, only averting her head when Marta tried to kiss her on the mouth, seeing that strange smile on her heavy face. Stacey did not fight it—far from it—it was a new experience and she was totally caught up in it.

Marta brought Stacey to groaning climax three or four times—Stacey lost count. It was good. Stacey had to admit she had never been made love to with such total concentration and abandon. But her sense of relaxed well-being vanished as Marta, huffing, sweating, and looking anxious, asked:

"It was good for you, yes?"

Stacey sighed inwardly. It was just the same as with a man—the same old insecure question. But it had been an unexpected bonus, a new experience during a dull convention—she'd throw the poor dog a bone.

"Yes, Marta. It was good for me, very good."

"Aaah! Now you will do for Marta."

Stacey could not believe her ears. She had been right in the first place, the woman was crazy. At least she was crazy if she thought Stacey was going to do it. She hadn't thought beyond trying a new experience—but she sure in hell wasn't going to get into it that far. She found the older woman slightly pathetic, staring down at her with loving eyes. But Stacey was also just a little bit afraid of her and of what she might do. She smiled sweetly.

"I—uh—I have to use the bathroom."

She dashed quickly into the bathroom and locked the door. It seemed as if the woman would never get the message, and Stacey wanted a bath and something to eat. She was afraid Marta was going to wait all night. But finally she heard her heavy voice through the locked door.

"You are not good person, Stacey Dawson. You are not good person."

Stacey had not answered and soon she'd heard the front door to the suite open and then firmly close. She waited for some ten minutes to be certain she had not been tricked, then carefully opened the door, saw the bedroom was empty, and raced to double-lock the front door. She went back into the bathroom and drew a hot oil bath. The hell with it, she decided, men or women, they were all a pain in the ass. But she didn't care, she knew she could always get off on her mink coat, and it never made demands.

The voice on the other end of the telephone suddenly caught her full attention. She knew she hadn't been listening and it was a lapse of which she was rarely guilty. She quickly scratched her long red fingernails across the mouthpiece and abruptly hung up the receiver. After only a moment's pause, she dialed the number of the client to whom she had been speaking, and when he came on the line assured him she had no idea what had happened; she had, in fact, not even heard the last part of his conversation, the line had gone dead, then static, then a disconnect. She grinned at the ready acceptance of the recruiters' old trick when their minds had wandered or they didn't have the right answer. She concluded the conversation and quickly hung up the phone.

Okay, Stacey Dawson, she addressed herself silently. Step into the lion's den before lunch. Mustn't keep her highness waiting. She left her office and headed down the hall to answer Jessica's summons.

Jessica looked up as Stacey entered and saw the mink coat. It was sixty degrees outside. "Aren't you rushing the season a bit?"

Stacey smiled. "I'd have left it in my office had I known your fireplace was burning."

Jessica silently awarded her a touché. Stacey seated herself on the sofa, wrapping the mink around her like a duchess. "I suppose this summons is about Eleanor Handler?"

"Eleanor offered me two weeks' notice when I returned from Murchinson Oil. I didn't feel it would be necessary for her to stay. She will be leaving today, if she hasn't already gone."

"Oh, she's already gone, and good riddance too. Honestly, Jessica, for a woman with your business savvy, I will never understand what criteria you base your hiring practices on."

"Present company excluded, I take it." Without waiting for an answer, Jessica continued. "I do seem to recall you also interviewed Eleanor before an offer of employment was extended."

Stacey looked uncomfortable for only a quick second. "Yes, well, I admit I thought she might have had potential. I probably let my charitable instincts get in the way. Poor old thing, a widow and all . . ."

Jessica made a small, impatient movement with her head. "Spare me, Stacey. This has been a long morning. In any event, she is gone and that leaves you without an assistant."

"Well," Stacey said, not bothering to disguise the disdain in her voice, "I'll scarcely know the difference. Honestly, Jessica, I'm so sick of supporting idiots, people who live on my production, my brains, my talent."

"I don't recall you signing any of Eleanor's paychecks, or those of any other assistant for that matter, Stacey."

"It all boils down to the same thing. I waste my valuable time training some nerd, and now I have to start all over again. Eleanor Handler was hopeless, a complete incompetent."

Jessica managed to keep the anger out of her tone as she replied in a controlled voice, "You're forgetting Sam Adelman. It seems she was competent enough to place him with Data Base Electronics."

Stacey shrugged elaborately. "Oh, that. She didn't place him there, Jessica. I admit, I let her take the credit . . ."

"Yes, and you took your cut of the commission as well," Jessica snapped.

"Business is business, Jessica. I'm due a cut of any commission earned by my department. You're damned right I took it. Besides, I did all the work. All she had to do was send out the resumé while I was at the convention in Detroit. She is simply not the caliber assistant I need or want."

"Then you are a fool, Stacey. Eleanor Handler is a very intelligent woman! And Data Base Electronics is a client! Has it occurred to you that in hiring Eleanor Handler, Data Base has made *her* a client as well? She will be recruiting for their computer department. How do you propose to manage that?"

Stacey smiled, unfazed by Jessica's angry outburst. "No problem! The secret of my success is that I *don't* deal with in-house company recruiters. I only talk to people in the position of making decisions. That will certainly not include Eleanor Handler," she concluded smugly.

Jessica suddenly had no stomach for the conversation. She was tired, had a hundred things to do, including a meeting with Jim Steiner that she dreaded almost as much as this conversation with Stacey.

"What *do* you want, Stacey?"

Stacey did not miss the edge of irritation in Jessica's voice. She smiled sweetly, allowing her eyes to become a saucer-sized burlesque of innocent camaraderie. "Well, if you really want to know—I want Martin Management Consultants."

Jessica refused to rise to the bait. "Stacey, if I didn't know your ambitions, I wouldn't have hired you in the first place. Anyone who isn't after my position isn't good enough to be an account executive at Martin Management." Not giving Stacey a chance to respond, Jessica continued quickly, "How heavy is your work load? If you can manage alone for a while, I'll start Carol on the prescreening process for a new assistant."

Stacey was one of the people who knew just how far she could push Jessica, and knew she'd gone the distance. She smiled, all innocence and cooperation. "Oh, don't worry about it today, Jessica. I know you have a lot on your mind. I'll be fine for a week or two, maybe a month. But I do need someone before the Association of Computer Scientists' meeting in Atlanta. That gives you some time."

"Fine," Jessica said. "I'll tell Carol to get on it." She pointedly turned her attention to her desk. "Is there anything else we need to discuss?"

"I don't believe so. I'm running late for my lunch date. I've met the most fascinating man." Stacey rose from the sofa, gathering her mink coat around her casually as she started for the door. She turned back before she left and said with a small smile, "It's wonderful to be in control of your own career. Isn't it, Jessica?"

But Jessica would not rise to the verbal gauntlet. She kept her eyes cool, her voice calm. "I wouldn't have it any other way, Stacey." Jessica did not lower her gaze, nor did she miss the slight tightening of Stacey's lips as she left the office.

* * *

Stacey felt the familiar anger at Jessica's unshakable poise as she headed out of the building for a solo lunch. There was no fascinating man, but she really didn't give a damn. Nor did she mind dining alone. She had a lot to think about. She wasn't in *control* of her career. Not by a long shot. She was successful, as successful as any single recruiter in any field. But she had gone as far as she could go as a single recruiter, and it just wasn't far enough! She wanted it all, and damn it, she was going to get it, one way or another.

Chapter 5

Jessica glanced at her watch. It had been a hectic, alternately frustrating and rewarding day. Meeting challenges and dealing with them gave her satisfaction. It was the work that made her life bearable. She wanted to be exhausted at the end of the day, needed her mind to shut down so that she could get through the evenings with Michael. She had one chore to attend to before heading home to a hot shower and a cold glass of wine.

Jim Steiner knocked and stuck his head into her office. His short, not-quite-overweight body pushed forward at the shoulders, and his head was down, like a bull ready to charge. His silent defenses were all in place, a walking advertisement for body language.

"Sit down, Jim. How was your day?"

He took a seat and frowned at Jessica's cigarette smoke. Jim had just joined a health club and was a convert to clean living. Jessica knew it was inconsiderate of her and she almost stubbed the cigarette out, but she couldn't do it. She really needed it.

"I'll just sit here at my desk, Jim, so the smoke won't reach you."

"It reaches the whole room," Jim complained. "God, didn't you ever hear of a contact high from pot? Cancer could be the same thing, you can probably get it from the air. And forget about cancer," he went on. "You're still a good-looking woman, Jessica—don't you care what it does to your skin?"

Jessica smiled to herself. He was so basic. *Still a good-looking woman*. It reminded her of when she'd first interviewed him. He had been so impressed by her success, and when she had openly admitted to being thirty-five, he'd remarked she was sure well preserved. She hadn't taken offense then, nor did she now. Jim Steiner was twenty-four years old. She knew she must seem ancient to him, compared to the young set he hung out with.

"Let's put my skin on hold for the moment, Jim. You haven't answered my question: How was your day?"

His tone was a challenge. "The day went fine. Lots of action. I got a lot going on. Lots of interviews and I think I'm near a close with the Burke firm. All in all, it was an okay day. Unless you want to count that asshole Brandon."

Jessica winced at the term, but decided not to pursue it. It was more important to explain how he'd offended a valuable client than how his language offended her.

"Jim, you know how long the Brandon firm has been my client. I've explained to you many times that they are an old-line Los Angeles firm. They—"

"Old is the right word, Jessica. Jesus, that creep Tom Brandon is probably mummified."

"Jim, *Mr.* Brandon, *Mr. Thomas* Brandon, not *Tom* Brandon, has one of the finest legal minds in this state. And I assure you, while he is past the age of consent, he is nowhere near being *mummified*. Now, you tell me your version of what happened and why you aren't servicing the account."

Jim took a deep breath and began. "What happened is that I had a perfect candidate for their litigation slot. I called Brandon to discuss it, Christ, I must have called him five times and left messages. He didn't return my calls, so I said to hell with him. I just moved on to other things. The old fart ought to get out of the way if he wants to attract good people. He ought to let the younger partners do the interviewing. After one meeting with him, none of my candidates are interested in the firm anyway. They feel like they've been in a morgue."

Jessica sighed. He was young—she had to remember that. "Jim, Mr. Brandon *is* the firm. The man has set legal precedents. If I were submitting candidates to the firm, I would insist that they be seen by Mr. Brandon."

Ignoring his frown, Jessica lit yet another cigarette, silently vowing it would be her last until she sat down with a glass of wine. "If your candidates have expressed the feelings you've described to me, then I suggest you are not recruiting the proper candidates for the firm. I've told you time and again, just because a person's credentials and experience seem appropriate to a job, that doesn't mean he is right for it. We're not just recruiters, we're also alchemists. There must be a match, the chemistry must be right."

Jim would not go down gracefully. "Okay, okay. The next candidate I send will smell like embalming fluid. That's the only chemical match I can think of."

Jessica's patience was wearing thin, yet she felt sure Jim had potential, so she kept herself in check. If he could just get over the fact that for some reason he felt intimidated by the attorneys he placed—if he could just stop acting like a street fighter—if she could just get him over that hurdle, his innate intelligence would make him an excellent recruiter.

"It's a little late in the day for your particular brand of humor, Jim," she said firmly. "Now, I want you to put everything else aside. I want you to make a concentrated effort to find a litigator for Mr. Brandon's firm." She ignored the look on his face and went on. "And, Jim, I want you to treat Mr. Brandon with the respect he deserves, both in and out of my office. You might be surprised. If you gave him half a chance, you'd find he is really a nice man. You just have to soften your approach."

Jim groaned and jumped up, walking back and forth in front of Jessica's desk.

"What do you want me to do? Ooze-cooze like Stacey

does? I'm just as good as he is—I can't brownnose any-body."

"Okay, Jim. Knock it off!" Jessica said with exasperation. "I've had enough! I spoke to Mr. Brandon today and assured him the reason he hasn't received any recent resumés is due to the fact that you are being particularly selective as befits his fine firm. I expect you to back my words with action."

"Okay, Jessica. Okay, already!" He headed for the door like a man who had just been sentenced to the rock pile. "I'll get on it first thing tomorrow. But if you're finished, I gotta run, got a hot tennis date."

Jessica watched him leave without regret. She couldn't speak to another person before she had that shower and glass of wine. She checked her calendar for the next day, saw it was relatively light, and promised herself that she would take it easy, knowing that she would not. Breathing a large sigh of relief, she left the office and headed toward Bel Air.

Chapter 6

Michael Martin sat facing the walled-in courtyard. The lemon trees were heavy with round yellow fruit, contrasting with the dark green leaves. The old used bricks gave off a warm sheen and the aged, split-oak barrels that Jessica had planted with geraniums and azaleas offered bursts of bloom in contrast to the white patio furniture. But Michael stared at the courtyard unseeingly, his thoughts focused on Jessica and the wreck their lives had become.

The courtyard was her favorite corner of the house, as it had once been his. It was the only area that had not been adapted to suit his condition. Under Jessica's careful supervision and without the aid of Michael's expertise, the contractor had been very cautious in not making the changes appear institutional. The architecture of the old Cape Cod home had scarcely been altered, and although all the ramps were smooth to accommodate the wheels of his chair, they had been skillfully blended to flow into the old brick surrounding the house. Jessica, ever practical but with an eye for aesthetics, had foregone a lawn. The place was beautifully landscaped but everything had been planted in old oak barrels, polished to a golden gleam.

Until the work had been finished, the courtyard was off-limits to Michael. There was simply no way his chair could be maneuvered down the twisting, curved steps from the house. The contractor had come up with plan after plan to adapt it without losing its beauty, but Michael had vetoed every one of them. He knew it confused Jessica, and it had confused him for a long time, until he finally admitted the reason to himself. It hadn't been something he could share with Jessica, it had been too foolish, too juvenile. But for a long time after it had happened, he had fantasized that if the courtyard remained untouched, then the accident had not happened. He had not fallen off the twelfth-story steel girder of a new building he had designed. He wasn't paralyzed, it wasn't permanent, he was still whole. At least he had looked at the untouched courtyard and pretended it had not happened. He had clung to that childish fantasy for a long time before he'd finally let it go.

Had clung to that unrealistic fantasy as he had clung to the fantasy of his marriage. A marriage that neither he nor Jessica was brave enough to admit was over. And he knew that *he* had to be the one to end it, because Jessica never would.

When he had lived in his fantasy, he was still the man he'd once been: strong, muscular, tall, active, vital. Her "Viking," Jessica had always called him. Now he was that man only from the waist up. His upper torso was still muscular and strong from the daily physical therapy, but his lower limbs were thin and atrophied, and no therapy would bring them back.

He had begun to despise himself for clinging to his fantasy and the cruel pretense of a marriage. Jessica had suffered enough, they had both suffered enough. He'd punished her enough that first year after the accident—and she had taken it like a champ. During that first year, he'd been bastard enough to punish everyone on two good legs, Jessica included.

He hadn't been able to adjust that first year when they'd released him from the hospital, sent him home to a house not yet ready for a cripple. With an imbecilic male rehabilitation nurse whose only saving grace was that he did not use the editorial *we* when referring to or speaking to Michael. The nurse had to go, to be replaced again and again until Jessica had finally found Johnny Bridges, a man who would take Michael's abuse and deflect it with his contagious humor. A man who had become Michael's best friend.

Michael had detested himself for the way he'd treated Jessica. And still, she'd stayed.

How much could one woman love a man? He could not reconcile Jessica's devotion, her patience. He'd allowed her no comfort, would not allow her to share his pain, or show any signs of affection or tenderness. He did not allow her to comfort him, and he had made no attempt to comfort her. And still she'd stayed.

When they'd released him from the hospital, it had been an unspoken understanding they would no longer share the same bedroom. Michael needed his male nurse in constant attendance; he had to be lifted in and out of his wheelchair, bathed and dressed like an infant during that first year until he'd learned to do some things on his own. It was something he could not bear to have Jessica witness.

Nor could he bear the thought of lying immobile next to her beautiful and whole body, which he resented in spite of himself. That beautiful body he'd known so intimately and for which he no longer felt any desire. He had known that Jessica would never make demands upon him, that she would gladly have shared his bed just for his physical warmth, his presence. But he could not do it. He could not let her be the loving woman she was willing to be, because he could not be the man she had known. He had paralyzed Jessica along with himself.

He had rejected psychiatric counseling. No amount of talking would ever change the fact that he was dead from the waist down and would forever be so. It was useless, and Michael had no time for lost causes.

And so Jessica suffered. He knew she had needs and he knew he could fulfill them in other ways. Christ, you didn't need a stiff prick to satisfy a woman. A tasting of one another had once been a wonderful part of their lovemaking;

a satisfaction of an almost cannibalistic hunger they'd had for each other. But then it had been a choice, now it was the *only* way, and he could not summon the desire to do it.

Why? He didn't know, couldn't understand it. He only knew that sex had become abhorrent to him. But he knew that Jessica still needed love and sex, and denying her affection and release was just another of his cruelties. Michael slept in his own room, Johnny Bridges always within sound of the intercom, and Jessica went to bed alone. Alone and lonely.

All that had been during the first year following his accident. But today little had changed—Michael still could not handle intimacy, affection, Jessica's love. He no longer behaved like a monster, but he was still unable to bring anything to the marriage. Still unable to give Jessica the sort of relationship she needed—and indeed had a right to.

He prayed that she would go on her own. That she would finally admit there was nothing she could do to save the marriage—that there was nothing of marriage as they had known it to save. And he'd been too cowardly to admit what he already knew—that he would never grow—he would remain an emotional cripple as well as a physical one—if he stayed with her. Their marriage had been the most beautiful union two people could ever have dreamed of—a union so perfect, anything less was unacceptable. Had been—had been—had been! Those words echoed incessantly in Michael's head.

The housekeeper who came every day interrupted his thoughts to ask if she needed anything before she left. He dismissed her and glanced at his watch; Jessica would be home any time now. Michael knew she would be tired and tense, and he could not help but remember the times in the past when he'd been able to make even the most horrific day disappear for her. When he, and only he, could make her laugh, take the tiredness out of her mind and body.

The setting sun glinting off the steel armrest of his chair was a mirror in which he could almost see those times again. Her hair would gleam softly in the dimmed light of the bathroom, her skin would glow rosy and milky from the steam of the tub. Her laughter sparkled like the chilled white wine they drank as they soaked their bodies in the oversize tub she'd insisted on when the house had been remodeled. They would sip their wine and trade stories of the day until their bodies were almost as light as the water itself.

He would then lovingly soap her with her favorite scented sponge, willing the last of the tiredness to leave, wrapping her in the huge terry towels kept warm and soft on the heater rack. He would lift her, still damp from the tub, onto the bed, no longer talking. They would leave their day behind to wash down the drain with the bath water.

Then he would make love to her so it seemed they were both reborn. Satisfied, renewed, they would troop into the kitchen in their old robes, giggling like children, and prepare dinner together. A team, two people, one person.

Michael spun his chair away from the courtyard window. Now only one person and a half, living a life of polite celibacy. Hearing Jessica's key in the door, he made an effort to wipe the sorrow from his face.

She entered the study, the fixed smile on her face, the unspoken question in her eyes—how was his day, what was his mood? Questions she had learned not to ask, knowing full well what the answer would probably be—more of the same. She looked particularly tired this evening, and he forced himself to put a light note in his voice, forced himself to behave as though he hadn't spent the day trying to figure out how to leave her.

"Well, the tycoon returns. How are things in the world of corporate corruption?"

Her smile relaxed as she sat opposite him, crossing her long beautiful legs, looking feminine even in her tailored Dior suit.

"It's days like today that make me wish I'd paid more attention to my high-school French," she said wearily. " 'The more things change, the more they stay the same.' Or something like that—it sounds a lot better in French."

"Rough one?"

"Not any more than usual. Stacey remains the consummate bitch; Jim still thinks he's in New York dodging muggers; Murchinson Oil still thinks Santa Claus will come along with a sleigh full of brilliant minorities who want to work for the thrill of it all; and Carol—thank God or whoever made her—is still Carol."

"Well," Michael offered lightly, "sounds like the French knew what they were talking about." There was a pause, then he said, "I could use a drink, that is if you're buying."

"I happen to be flush this evening," she said, smiling in relief at his apparent good mood. "Just let me get out of my sincere suit and I'll be right with you, sir."

Michael watched her head for the bedroom and the quick shower she would take. No more long soaks in the tub for Jessica. She wanted nothing they had once shared and could share no longer. It was another way in which she denied herself as much as possible. They were killing one another and it had to stop. The lump that came into his throat threatened to strangle him. He had to find a way to free her—free the two of them. She wouldn't go on her own, she had said *for better for worse, in sickness and in health,* and she meant it.

He didn't know how, he wasn't sure just when, but some way, somehow, he would do it. He had to—for both of them.

Chapter 7

Cocktail chatter blended with the soft background music as tuxedo-clad waiters wove unobtrusively through the crowd, wielding their champagne-laden trays.

Drink in hand, Jeremy Bronson stood on the far side of the room observing the guests, his wife in particular. He studied her face—clear, cornflower-blue eyes sparkled against a peaches-and-cream complexion. Ash-blonde hair, swept back in a chic French twist, enhanced her lovely face. She wore a black crepe designer dinner gown, its simple lines silhouetting her slender figure. A strand of opera-length pearls and matching earrings were her only accessories. She looked cool, elegant, untouched.

He sipped his drink. Her smile was alternately brilliant and gentle as she leaned forward raptly while Rosh Hameid made his point, gesturing dramatically for emphasis. Jeremy was amazed. Hameid was normally an extremely private, taciturn man, difficult to engage in conversation. Since Hameid was one of his most difficult clients, Jeremy knew this from personal experience.

Yet with Margaret he was animated, apparently delighted

to be talking to her. Clearly, she made him feel the most interesting man in the world.

Jeremy silently saluted her. She had mastered the art of client relationships. She considered it part of her job, the job of being Mrs. Jeremy Bronson. A client's contentment at a social function was something she considered her responsibility, and Margaret took her duties very seriously.

As another couple joined Hameid and Margaret, Jeremy noted how easily she extended her charm and attention to include them. She was incredibly adaptable, and Jeremy readily acknowledged that her social graces had contributed a great deal to his successful career, if not to his personal happiness. She possessed intelligence, a delightful sense of humor, and the ability to charm almost anyone. Even other executive wives, normally a suspicious and jealous group, protective of their territory, liked Margaret.

He downed his drink and leaned against the wall, his thoughts returning to Jessica Martin. He seemed unable to stop himself from mentally comparing his wife, Margaret Downing Bronson, with his obsession, Jessica Martin. Jessica possessed all of Margaret's attributes, but unlike Margaret, who was, deep down, reserved and cool, devoid of genuine passion, Jessica was warm, outgoing, and earthy. The only real similarity between the two women was quality.

He sighed. No sense going over all that again. Nothing was going to change Margaret; he had tried for years before giving up. She was what she was. The enormous lack in their marriage caused Jeremy a constant sense of loss. Yet he genuinely liked Margaret, respected her, and enjoyed her company, he even loved her. In fact, he had very nearly come to accept the fact that what he had with his wife was all there was going to be—had nearly decided that he could make it enough. But that was before he met Jessica Martin. Once he'd met Jessica, he felt less and less able to settle for the emptiness he felt as a man. He finally admitted to himself that he was hungry, starving in fact, for a woman who would let him feel complete.

He was taken out of his musings by the sound of his wife's voice. He looked up, startled to see her standing before him.

"You look a proper thundercloud, I must say." Her English accent negated any accusation in the comment.

"Do I? I guess I was deep in thought."

"Obviously." She smiled. "And frowning like the very devil, as usual. What were you thinking about?"

"Actually, I was thinking about you," Jeremy said, then noting the question in her eyes, quickly recovered. "How do you get Hameid to open up like that? The man is usually a clam."

She laughed tolerantly. "It isn't so very difficult. I think the poor man might be shy, actually. Or very lonely, I'm not sure which. It's almost as if he has no one to talk with."

"Don't kid yourself, Margaret. The old coot is not *poor*, and he has a harem full of women to talk to. It's your charm that does the trick."

"You flatter me, Jeremy," she protested, but he could see the pleasure in her eyes and he felt a stab of guilt for comparing her to Jessica. "In any case," she continued, "I don't think women in harems are allowed to talk to their masters. Or are they?"

"I couldn't say," Jeremy answered. "I've never been in a harem. What was he bending your ear about?"

"Art. He's a bit of a fanatic—it seems to be his favorite subject. Hasn't he ever discussed it with you?"

Jeremy shook his head. "Our dialogues are pretty limited. We talk dollars—big dollars. That's about the only subject I can get him to respond to."

Margaret smiled sympathetically. "Well, he isn't talking dollars tonight, so you'd best prepare yourself. I've had a peek at the place cards, and Hameid is seated at our table."

Jeremy groaned and placed his empty glass on the tray of a passing waiter.

"It needn't be so bad, Jeremy," she promised. "You just try and look interested. I'll keep him entertained. We haven't quite gotten up through Dadaism yet—that should be good for the first three courses."

Jeremy smiled his appreciation. "I'll try not to stick you with that—you've worked hard enough for one evening."

"Then we'd best head for our table. Try not to look so glum. This is the last Murchinson Oil party for the month."

"Every cloud has a silver lining and all that rot, eh what?"

This time, Margaret groaned at Jeremy's dreadful attempt at an English accent. He offered her his arm and they headed across the room. Vowing to keep thoughts of Jessica Martin out of his head at least for the rest of the evening, he once again reminded himself that his wife was a remarkable woman and a very good sport.

Chapter 8

John Adams stared critically at his reflection in the bathroom mirror. Only two hours before, he had stepped off a plane from Saudi Arabia, and while never a victim of jet lag, he was the victim of a heavy beard that made him appreciate the luxury of the private executive bathroom connected to his massive office.

As president of Amalgamated Enterprises International, John Adams was a very important man. Members of the huge conglomerate spanned the globe with their various products and services. They constructed and staffed hospitals in the Middle East. They developed and marketed the most sophisticated medical equipment in the world. They were pioneers in laser surgery, CAT-scanning equipment, X-ray technology. There was scarcely an arena of interest to medical science in which Amalgamated was not heavily and successfully involved. Yes, as its president, John Adams was a very important man indeed. And he knew how to use that importance to the fullest.

His craggy and handsome face had benefited from his sixty-two years. He was a virile man who enjoyed every day of his busy life. Women, food, work—he loved it all. His voice was pitched loud enough for Marshall MacAbee, his general counsel and head of all legal matters for Amalgamated, to hear above the running water.

"Hell, Marshall, those pricks are so rich they pee oil every time they take a leak! I know they're a pain in the ass, but that division makes us a pisspot full of money and we're not about to lose it because of some incompetent fool." He guided the old-fashioned razor confidently across one cheek as he continued. "You just have to know how the Saudis think. Number one, they have the attention span of a moron with a toy that has more than one moving part. What you have to do is let them have their information fast and make fucking well sure it's accurate."

He paused to lean his face closer to the mirror before tackling the chin and delicate lip area. He slathered on more shaving cream before saying, "See, the thing is, they don't want to hear the same information twice. Once you make your proposal, you better damn well be able to live with it, because there sure as hell ain't no going back. Now, back home in Texas, we admire a man like that—we expect that in Texas. A Texan deals like that 'cause he knows what the hell he's doing. Those buggers over there are still cutting their baby teeth when it comes to negotiation. That's why I don't understand this latest foul-up."

John Adams's voice was slightly distorted as he pursed his mouth to shave around his chin, but his tone never lost its condemnation: "The man you sent over there must be a jackass. And I'm frankly surprised at your judgment. All the numbers were worked out before he left, how the hell could he have screwed up? This is a big contract we're talking about, and even though I've been able to put out this particular fire myself, there are still some hot coals smoldering. We already have ten hospitals operating in the Middle East, and this contract could be for ten or twenty more. That's not just building the hospitals, mind you, that's also staffing them. That's fucking megabucks."

"As if there isn't enough trouble over there already. Hell, Marshall, you know the rules as well as I do. We are allowed to have company compounds in the Middle East to house our workers and their families *if*, and that is the biggest *if* you're ever going to hear, *if* we operate strictly by the book. Booze is a no-no, it's against their religion. Women seen bareheaded off the compound are considered a direct insult. Damn it, you know the list as well as I do, I don't have to read you the whole damn thing." His voice deepened in anger. "Yet what do I find when I go over there? Not only booze being sneaked into lunch pails and taken on the site to sneak a nip every hour or so, I also find so much wife swapping going on to break the monotony that we could be facing a major scandal, aside from being completely ousted and our assets being seized by the government."

He tried to calm down. Marshall MacAbee was a good man, he would get it straightened out. "We have to replace the project manager in Riyadh. He is an absolute incompetent. Christ Almighty, we pay those suckers enough money, it shouldn't be so hard to get someone to earn it!

"But that's not your department; I digress. I want you to get me a lawyer over there who is also a politician—a diplomat. Hell, those sheiks are getting their sons back home with Harvard educations. Now mind you, Marshall, Harvard hasn't made a goddamned one of them any smarter, but the thing is, they think it has. They still think like their daddies, but they want to be talked to as if they had a brain in their heads. Why is that so hard? The President addresses the people of the United States on that level every day!

"We need a man who can speak the language like a native," Adams went on without pausing. "A man who can eat their damned buffalo cheese and goat's milk, all their indigestible food, without a drop of whiskey to wash it down. What I want, Marshall, is a lawyer who is going to go over there and come back with those contracts in his pocket."

He daubed on a little more shaving cream under his nose. "So far this whole damned project has been run like the federal government, and that just won't do. We can't afford to fuck up like the government. I don't want to go into the next board meeting with any more problems about the

Middle Eastern operations. I want it straightened out, and I want it done fast!

"And I don't want a family man! I'm not about to have any pillow talk distract our boy's attention. I want a healthy, ambitious, smart young son of a bitch and you can promise him the moon and stars if he will commit to a two-year stint. We'll give him plenty of R & R time and plenty of pussy even while he's in Riyadh."

He paused reflectively and washed the excess lather from his face. As he rubbed the generous bath towel over his smooth cheeks, his voice was muffled as well as quizzical. "Never could understand why they call it 'pussy.' Cats are so damned cold and aloof, but a woman's cunt . . . Anyway, our boy won't have to worry about pimples, you can promise him that. And we'll pay him real heavy money, and hide half of it from the IRS. All we want is two good years out of his young life. You find me a boy who is a killer, one who wants to go right to the top! That's the man we need."

John Adams was accustomed to talking at great length without interruption, but he suddenly realized that Marshall MacAbee hadn't made one comment. He called out, "Marshall? Am I going too fast for you? Is the water too loud?"

Receiving no reply, Adams stuck his head around the corner of the door. For a second, which seemed an eternity, he could only stare. Marshall MacAbee was sitting straight up in his chair, his legs still neatly crossed so as not to muss the crease in his Savile Row suit, his yellow legal pad beside his hand on the conference table. His eyes were staring straight at the bathroom door.

Only they weren't seeing anything.

Marshall MacAbee's eyes were glassy and dazed, his mouth twisted to one side, hanging open, a stream of spittle trickling down his chin.

John Adams raced to his intercom, punched the button hard, and screamed into the box, "Get an ambulance here, quick!"

His next call was to the corporate medical director, who arrived in minutes to determine that Marshall MacAbee had suffered a massive stroke. He'd heard perhaps half of Adams's dialogue according to the few notations on his legal pad. From a cursory examination, the doctor determined MacAbee had probably suffered the initial stages of the stroke sometime before their meeting.

In less than half an hour the ambulance had arrived and rushed MacAbee to the hospital, leaving a shaken John Adams staring after it, crusted remnants of shaving cream clinging to one earlobe.

That had all been four weeks ago, and John Adams now sat at his desk with almost the same look of shock and disbelief etched upon his craggy face. Marshall MacAbee would not be solving any legal problems again.

The president of Amalgamated Enterprises International felt a dual sense of loss. He had liked and respected MacAbee as a friend, and he had trusted him as one of his most reliable executives. Now he was as good as dead, and it was a tough pill to swallow. Yet swallow it he must. He had a corporation to run and the associate general counsel was not capable of taking over for MacAbee.

John Adams punched the intercom. "Get Jessica Martin on the phone," he instructed his secretary. It was just past noon in New York, but already he felt as if he had put in a full day's work.

Chapter 9

Carol Lane had come to work for Jessica Martin before the ink was dry on her divorce papers. She had not worked for nearly a year in an attempt to save her marriage, but it had been to no avail, had in fact driven her ex-husband and her even further apart.

Not that it had ever been really good between them; after the honeymoon hangover had cleared, she'd had a good, hard look at the man she'd married. She could blame only herself for giving in to the antiquated belief that a woman of twenty-nine had better get married before the big Three-0h or her chances were pretty much nil. She had married her husband because he'd been the last one to ask in a long time, and she was feeling the onslaught of thirty with the same apprehension of a skier who hears the first faint rumblings of an avalanche.

And he tried; she couldn't fault him on that. They just hadn't been right for one another. Maybe opposites do attract—and maybe that's all they should do. Living together on a day-to-day basis with nothing in common hadn't worked out. Carol was basically a free spirit who liked living to the utmost. Her ex-husband felt life was to be lived on a timetable. He was incapable of being spontaneous. Everything had a time, including sex.

His military background had never really left him. He believed that sharing household chores when both parties worked was time-effective. But as Carol had once remarked drily, when she made the bed, she made the bed. When he made the bed, he made a production.

And so they divorced. Carol returned to the work force and her current position as assistant to Jessica Martin. She loved her work, had long since passed the big Three-0h, and found that she valued nothing as much as her freedom and a bed that she always made up, but upon which one could never bounce a quarter.

She sat at her desk awaiting the arrival of Jessica Martin. Carol was always in the office a half hour before normal business hours to prepare for the day's work. Jessica never arrived before 10 A.M., starting her day from her home at 6:30 in the morning in order to reach her East Coast clients, adjusting for the three-hour time difference. Carol held down the fort and fielded incoming calls until Jessica arrived. Carol Lane was very good at her job and she truly admired Jessica Martin, both as a friend and a boss. But she dreaded what this morning's messages would do to Jessica's facade of calm serenity.

Carol creased her brow as she shuffled the notes, putting them in order of importance. She knew how Jessica would react to the one on top.

The message was from John Adams, president of Amalgamated Enterprises International, the New York–based conglomerate for which Jessica had recruited Marshall Mac-Abee as general counsel some four years before. The poor man had suffered a stroke and would need to be replaced.

John Adams wanted Jessica to come to New York to discuss the replacement candidates and to meet several new people in the company who would be working with Mac-Abee's replacement. Jessica had always traveled for her clients, making whatever trips were necessary to screen potential applicants.

Jessica believed that when she visited candidates at home on their turf, they felt freer about discussing career options without being seen meeting with a "headhunter." Seeing the way in which a candidate lived and interacted with his or her family often gave her insight into what that person was really like.

Carol thought that Jessica's willingness to go the extra mile was the mark of a true professional, and Jessica was professional to the core. At least, that was how she'd always conducted business before Michael's accident. She hadn't traveled at all the first year after his fall. Carol had certainly found that understandable. The physical therapy had been extremely painful, and Michael's adjustment was difficult. But as the second year came and went, and Jessica still found reasons not to travel, Carol became more and more concerned.

Jessica had managed to avoid traveling by using her vast resources and friends in the right places. But Amalgamated was an important client, and its president had been responsible for numerous referrals to Martin Management. She could not refuse John Adams, yet Carol knew Jessica would find some way not to go. A search assignment of this magnitude would require at least a week in New York and possibly other trips if suitable candidates were not located in or around Manhattan. Carol felt a mixture of sadness and anger.

Michael's accident was going to wreck everything for which Jessica had worked so hard. Damn it! Carol wasn't going to let it happen. Even if she risked losing her job, she was going to convince Jessica to make this trip. It would serve two purposes—it would keep John Adams happy and it would give Jessica a break from the terrible burden she'd carried since the accident. This time, Carol decided, she would speak her mind and take whatever consequences it brought. What the hell were friends for?

She sighed as her buzzer rang. Jessica had arrived, and Carol scooped up the messages as she headed for her office.

* * *

"Morning, boss." Carol purposefully kept her voice light. "Ready for the deluge?"

Jessica seemed relaxed enough as she glanced at the sheaf of notes in Carol's hand. "It's only ten-fifteen. Could so much have happened so early?"

"Yep," Carol grinned. "Like they say, the joint is open for business."

Jessica returned the smile. "Okay, get some coffee and let's get at it."

Carol reshuffled the messages and slipped them into her notebook, then poured herself a cup of the steaming Blue Mountain coffee and said, "First off, your friend Larry Wiggins is in for a shock. He's about to lose ten—count 'em—ten partners and a whole slew of associates." She allowed the shock to register for a moment, hoping it would not be enough to warrant turning down Amalgamated.

"Ten partners? What have you heard? Who called?"

"Mitchell Dodd. He didn't have much time to talk, and he couldn't speak too freely from the office in any case. He knows how closely we work together and asked me to fill you in." She took a sip of her coffee, then continued, "It seems it's been in the works for some time now. The younger partners feel Larry Wiggins is dead weight. They think of themselves as movers and shakers, don't agree with how he wants the office managed, and worse"—she paused for effect—"it looks as if they will be taking a hefty chunk of business with them."

"Good Lord!" There was genuine concern in Jessica's eyes. "Does Larry know?"

"That's the worst part. According to Mitchell, he doesn't think the man has a clue. Mitchell wanted you to know because of Rebecca, and because he knows how fond you are of Larry Wiggins." Carol sat across from Jessica. "Incidentally, he said for you not to worry about him, he's going to stick with Larry. But he couldn't speak for Rebecca. He doesn't think she knows yet either."

Rebecca Weinstein had been a junior partner in the firm of Loventhal and Kramer when Jessica had recruited her to join Larry Wiggins's firm as a tax partner. This would come as a devastating blow to her. She had left a good firm because of the reputation and clientele of Larry Wiggins. There hadn't been a hint of a spin-off.

Jessica's head whirled. "How did Mitchell get this information?"

"He wouldn't say. But he's certain it's gospel. No doubt whatsoever."

"God! It's times like this when I hate being on both sides of the desk." Jessica sighed. "Do you realize I am powerless to even warn Larry or Rebecca? I can't even prepare them for the shock."

"Not unless you breach Mitchell's confidence. Of course, since Mitchell is sticking with Larry, he might give you some leave."

"Certainly I won't breach his confidence," Jessica stated firmly. "But you're right, maybe if I talk to him, he'll okay it. I have to find a way to tell Larry what's going on and start our efforts to save him. My Lord! This could destroy Larry."

Larry Wiggins was one of those men who had stepped into a vacuum. From the day he'd passed the bar, practicing law had been his life—he'd taken the enormous plunge of opening his own shop while other young men were taking the safe and secure route of joining established law firms. Larry had worked to make his practice a success, worked at it to the exclusion of all else. He'd felt there would be time for marriage and a home. But of course there had never been enough time. He had sacrificed it all for his firm, making it one of the most successful in Los Angeles. Now in his late sixties, if he lost the firm, he lost everything. It was all he had.

Carol watched as Jessica's mind raced, trying to figure a way to help her friend. She knew Jessica was also thinking of Rebecca Weinstein and the unfortunate position in which Jessica had inadvertently placed her. Even though she couldn't have anticipated this, Jessica would feel responsible.

"Well obviously," Jessica said, "I'll stand by Rebecca, too. I'll talk to Mitchell and get the details, then I'll find replacements for the firm."

"No easy task. You know how quickly rats desert a sinking ship. They don't board them any faster."

Jessica's tone was firm. "Larry Wiggins's firm is *not* a sinking ship."

"Well, you may know that and I may know that, and you may even pull it off, but that's still how it will be perceived in the legal community once the news hits the streets."

Jessica looked thoughtful. "Yes, you're right, of course. But I've put out bigger fires than this one. No matter how bad it seems now, I'll be able to help." Jessica put aside the information she'd just been given. "What else happened?"

Carol referred to her notes. "We've got a little problem at O'Brien and Kelly. Mr. Stuart really has his hackles up."

"What's troubling Bob? He's only been on board two months."

"Yeah, well, I guess it only took him that long to find out what's going on over there. As they say in old detective movies, it seems the accountant has absconded with the funds; they can't even pay the stationer for Bob's business cards. They're only paying pressing bills like payroll, rent, phones, et cetera."

Jessica shook her head in wonder. "Has the whole legal community gone mad today? Surely that shouldn't concern Bob? I can't imagine the man wasn't bonded."

"I don't know and Bob didn't say," Carol responded. "Anyway, the cash-flow problems aren't Bob's big concern. They're making payroll and their client base is sound. Bob is more concerned with the bar association."

"Why, in heaven's name?"

"It's that attorney they brought in from Atlanta. Seems she failed to pass the California Bar Exam."

"Well," Jessica offered, "that's a shame, but it's happened before—California has the toughest bar exam in the system. Surely the firm will give her another chance."

"Oh yes, that's no problem. She'll sit for the next exam. But in the meantime, she's not California Bar."

Jessica was beginning to wish Carol would get to the point. With a hint of impatience she said, "She's not a litigator as I recall; she isn't going into court. What's the problem? Why is Bob so upset?"

"Because she is listed on their letterhead as an attorney with the firm. Not only that, but she is sending out work with her signature as an attorney with the firm."

Jessica's impatience was replaced by shock. That was a definite no-no. It was true an attorney from another state could be employed by a California firm without being a member of the bar, but all work sent out had to state that fact, and if the attorney's name was listed on the letterhead, it had to be accompanied by an asterisk to indicate the person was not a California State Bar member.

In short, Bob Stuart's concern was well founded. O'Brien and Kelly were asking for real trouble. Not only from the bar association but from any client who had been billed for the attorney's time and who found out she was not a bar member. California had no reciprocity with any other state bar, she was not recognized as an attorney in California, and if she made a mistake, the client could sue the hell out of the firm.

Anger showed in Jessica's voice. "What on earth are they thinking of?"

"Beats me, boss. But what Bob is thinking of is his keester. And I don't blame him—after all, he's been an attorney in this town for four years without a mark against his record. He thinks she's sleeping with O'Brien and he isn't about to risk his reputation being with a firm carrying on such shenanigans."

"Nor should he," Jessica said. "How did you leave it with him?"

"I told him you'd get back to him. Dave O'Brien hasn't a clue anyone outside the firm knows about this—if you call him on it, he'd have to know it came from Bob. And Bob expects you to do something—we placed him there, so I guess we owe him."

"Yes, we do. Even though it's something beyond our control." Jessica leaned back in her chair, a sudden spasm of pain darting across her forehead. "Damn this business, it's always the candidate who is at risk. I have to figure out a way to approach O'Brien and still protect Bob."

"It's a hot potato—but we've got another one potentially as bad. David Clarendon's last placement with World Vision Pharmaceuticals looks shaky. I don't have all the details, but I know David was upset. I heard him on the telephone and it sounded pretty ominous." She grinned at Jessica. "I don't know why you aren't gray-haired by now."

"Neither do I." Jessica sighed. "Well, it's been quite a morning."

Carol took a deep breath, then said, "It's not over yet, boss."

Jessica's head snapped up at the change in Carol's tone.

Slowly, Carol said, "John Adams called this morning."

Jessica relaxed a bit. She truly liked and admired John Adams and was ever mindful of his help with her career. Like Jeremy Bronson, he'd granted her one of her early retainers, confirming Martin Management as a recognized search firm.

"What did he want?"

Carol's expression looked dark. "It's Marshall MacAbee. He's had a stroke."

"Oh no!" Jessica cried, immediately concerned. "When? How bad?"

"A few weeks ago and very bad, I'm afraid. The prognosis for recovery is dismal. The doctors told John not even to hope for any normal activity to return."

A familiar sickness gathered in Jessica's stomach. Not exactly the same words she'd heard from Michael's doctors, but so close as to make it seem a relived nightmare. "Oh dear God! This is terrible. Marshall is such a kind and gentle man, as well as a brilliant attorney. Poor John, they'd become really good friends in the bargain. He must be devastated."

"He is. But he's also the president of Amalgamated and

business goes on as usual." Carol paused for the briefest moment before saying, "He wants you to come to New York, Jessica."

She saw Jessica's body stiffen, saw the protective veil descend over her green-flecked eyes.

"That's not possible. With everything that needs my attention here—Larry Wiggins—I've got to find a way to help him, and the Bob Stuart mess. There are a hundred things that are bound to come up and if David's placement at World Vision falls through, well, you know how impossible he is about replacing a candidate. No, it just isn't possible. . . ."

Carol remained silent. She'd known Jessica would jump at the bones of the various office problems, and they *were* serious. But there was very little meat on those bones compared to Amalgamated. She knew Jessica was aware of just how lame her excuses were next to what she owed John Adams. Still, Carol wasn't ready to jump in with both feet, not just yet.

"No." Jessica shook her head. "I can't go. Surely I will be able to deal with this by phone?" Her tone was a plea.

Now Carol was ready. She kept her voice soft but firm. "You know you can't handle this without going to New York, Jessica. John would never expect or accept that from you. His call wasn't put as a request—he was leaving for Europe this morning but he'll be back in three days. He wants you to telephone when he returns and arrange your schedule."

There was both surprise and reprieve written on Jessica's face. Surprise at Carol's statement and reprieve that she would have three days in which to come up with something. "Yes, well, of course I'll call just as soon as he returns. I'm sure I can work something out. John is a reasonable man."

Carol had already overstepped her bounds, and she felt she might as well go all the way. "He's reasonable all right. But what excuse can you give him that he can consider reasonable, Jessica?"

"Why—the problems I have here. John knows he isn't my only client."

Carol had to push. "Jessica, Michael will be all right. He has his nurse full-time. I'll check in on him for you. You *have* to make this trip."

"Michael? What does Michael have to do with all this?" There was panic in her eyes. "It's the other problems— I . . ." She could not continue. There was no anger in her voice, and suddenly Carol realized Jessica probably had not talked to anyone since the accident about the state of her marriage. Carol decided to volunteer.

"Jessica," she said softly, "isn't it about time you talked about it? I'm not blind. I've worked for you for years. I've seen what these past two years have done to you. You can't continue like this—it isn't normal, you're only human. You are going to destroy yourself and your company along with you."

Jessica felt the panic rise. Her throat threatened to close, and her breathing felt labored. It was all too much. But she couldn't confide in Carol, couldn't confide in anyone. It was too hurtful, too personal. She forced a deep breath into her lungs and calm into her voice.

"Carol, you're a wonderful friend, but really, this is not something I can talk about. Not now. I wonder if you would do me a favor?"

"Anything." Carol knew the conversation would go no further. The curtain was still drawn tightly around Jessica.

Jessica frantically searched her mind for something for Carol to do for her. "Uh, I've had a headache all morning. I seem to be out of aspirin. Would you try to rustle some up?"

"Right away." Carol wasn't about to push it. Jessica wasn't out of aspirin. Carol personally kept her office medicine cabinet well stocked. But if Jessica wanted time alone, she would have it. She turned to leave the office. Jessica's voice halted her at the door.

"Would you also hold my calls until I tell you to put them through? Maybe after this headache eases I'll be able to concentrate."

"Sure, boss. Take all the time you need."

Jessica nodded dully and Carol left the office without another word. Jessica knew she had seen through her ruse and would not return with the aspirin, and she was once again grateful for Carol's sensitivity as the tears she had been holding back spilled down her cheeks. She felt so tired, so tired and so damned alone.

Chapter 10

Stacey lay back on the bed listening to the sound of the shower and his off-key singing. She grimaced. He was completely refreshed after their "matinee" as he referred to their lunchtime meetings. Stacey thought of them as convenient fucks. At least they were certainly convenient for him. They always met during the lunch hour. *He* never lost any time away from his business. Weekends were mostly allocated to work or travel and he never asked her to accompany him on his trips. She hadn't quite figured that one out yet. Eric Radner seemed the kind of man who would want a sexy woman on his arm at all times. Something didn't add up, but she'd find out in due time. Their affair had only been going on for five months and as quick a study as she was with men, there was much about Radner that did not fit the norm.

After a scuffle in bed, Eric always headed immediately for the shower, as he did today, even washing his hair and carefully styling it, using the blow-dryer he kept at her place. She wondered occasionally if perhaps he privately thought sex was dirty. He certainly couldn't wait to wash the earthy smell away. But at least he wasn't kinky; she was grateful for that. Stacey enjoyed sex, but she wasn't into any weird trips. The most he'd ever asked was that she suck him off, and that wasn't kinky—even though he'd never return the favor. With him it was strictly a man-woman fuck with no frills. Never mind. Her plans for Eric Radner did not include love and passion. She didn't care that he was a boring, mechanical lover, totally predictable, although he thought of himself as a super stud. An illusion that Stacey was careful to nurture.

The affair had begun mostly to flout Jessica's rules about not getting involved with a client. And while Stacey privately agreed it was best not to mix business with pleasure, she shivered with delight knowing what Jessica would say if she found out about them. In truth, it was the chance for a private little joke on Jessica that had prompted Stacey to accept Eric Radner's offer of lunch and bed, in that order. But Jessica had nothing to do with why she stayed with Eric. She had been quick to recognize what Eric Radner could mean to her future. Stacey needed clout, and Eric Radner was a perfect means of gaining it. She planned on becoming Mrs. Eric Radner, and once that was accomplished, she'd have everything she needed to become just as big and important as Jessica Martin.

Eric Radner was the sole owner of the enormous Radner Enterprises. They manufactured sophisticated machinery for the world of communications. Conservatively, he was worth about forty million dollars, give or take a million. A man sworn to bachelorhood for reasons he would never articulate. Not that Stacey ever pressed the issue; she was far too clever for that. Instead, she carefully perpetuated the image of an independent career girl, with no strings.

She knew she fascinated him, kept him intrigued, which was just as she intended. She was wild, adventuresome, and sophisticated—talents not lost on Radner. She was also very savvy and knew he liked that she could discuss megabuck deals with him and understand nearly as much about the deals he plotted as he did.

Stacey knew he liked her because she was smart, sexy, beautiful, and as far as he could tell, totally undemanding. She seemingly wanted nothing from him but the joy of a couple of hours in the hay several times a week. From his point of view, she was clever, listened to him, encouraged him to talk business, to preen and pose for her. He never realized that she was cleverer than he imagined; that she was carefully preparing Eric to consider her the perfect candidate with whom to end his bachelorhood.

Stacey Dawson intended to become Mrs. Eric Radner, and he would think it had all been his idea. To hell with the fact that he bored her in bed. She always had her mink and vibrator. Of course, she grinned to herself, if things went according to plan—and she didn't doubt her plan for a minute—she would be exchanging the mink for sable. Yes, sir. She had plans for Eric Radner. He was going to give her the one thing in life she had never known and craved above all else: He and his millions would give her *power*. And power made a person safe.

Eric came out of the bathroom, dressed, combed, and looking as if he hadn't spent five minutes, let alone a full two hours, in bed. As he poured his customary brandy from a decanter on the end table, he smiled at Stacey, who stretched lazily. "Look pretty satisfied with yourself, Missy."

Ignoring the corny remark, she grinned lasciviously at him. "That should be my line to you, Tiger. You continue to amaze me."

He lapped it up, looking smug. His slightly thinning hair allowed an occasional glimpse of scalp to shine through the hair spray. His short, stout body was not aided by the five-hundred-dollar suit and pure silk shirt. He was a small man, but there was a suggestion of power. On occasion, when discussing a particular deal he wished to make, a small company he wanted to acquire or just a competitor he wanted to best, she'd seen a hint of cold cruelty in his narrow gray eyes. But he'd never been rough with her, and after all, she could be cold and cruel in business herself.

His voice was amused as he took a seat in the chair facing the bed, rolling the brandy glass back and forth between his palms. "I wonder what Jessica would say if she knew you and I had just had a sensational fuck?"

"*What!* is exactly what Jessica would say. I don't think she knows what a sensational fuck is."

He laughed. "Do I detect a meow or two? I've known Jessica for years and I've always had a hunch there's a lot of fire under all that prim and proper ice."

"No cigar, sweetie. What you see is what you get. I'd take any odds that Jessica was a virgin when she married, and I guarantee she's been as boringly faithful as a Catholic housewife." Stacey smiled seductively. "You're the one who says marital sex has nothing to do with sensational fucking. Anyway," she concluded, "who wants to talk about Jessica Martin?"

She was determined not to let his curiosity about Jessica become part of the conversation. Since Michael's accident, she knew a lot of men showed interest in how Jessica was handling it. She knew further that more than one man fantasized about Jessica's past two years with a cripple and just how they could make it up to her. Eric Radner was Stacey's property and she had no intention of letting him get sidetracked.

He smiled. "I don't particularly want to talk about Jessica. I just thought about her as I was looking at you stretching like a lazy alley cat, because I have to make an appointment with her."

Stacey frowned. She didn't want Jessica to know about them, not until she had him completely locked up. But she quickly erased the frown. She was sure Eric wouldn't say anything; he was a very private man. "Why are you seeing Jessica? What's up?"

"I plan on doing some reorganization. I'll need several key men, both here and in our foreign office." His voice took on a confidential tone as he continued. "I was saving this as a surprise, but this afternoon was sensational so I'll give you a little bonus and tell you now. Of course," he cautioned, "this is strictly private information."

Stacey's mind raced with curiosity, but she remained silent.

"You know how hard and long I've worked to build my

little empire. But there's no more challenge, the deals are too damned easy to accomplish. I'm bored with it and I'm fifty-five years old. It's time I had me some fun, made some changes in my life."

Stacey's head jerked up, and he caught the movement.

"Not to worry, sweet thing. I'm not planning on changing things where you're concerned." There was a cold, slight narrowing of the pupils of his eyes. "That is, not as long as you behave yourself."

It was just a quick flicker, anyone not as alert to their prey as Stacey would have missed it, but she saw it. As he continued to speak, she dismissed what she'd seen as her own anxiety over what he might be about to tell her.

"What I'm changing is my life-style," Eric said. "I want a key man to take over for me, run the business—not that it can't practically run itself the way I've got it set up." He leaned toward Stacey. "But here's the big surprise, baby girl. I'm going to buy me a really big toy. The biggest damn toy a man could have." He paused for a moment, then resumed in a far-off tone, "I'm going to fulfill a dream—a dream I've had ever since I was a kid hanging around the playground." His voice became joyful. "I'm going to buy me a baseball team! Can you imagine it? My own baseball team!" He rubbed his hands together in glee. "My own, full-fledged, fucking major-league baseball team! With my name emblazoned on the back of every player, and someday on the World Championship Pennant! What do you think about that?"

"A baseball team?" Stacey could not keep the surprise from registering on her face.

"You got it, honey—I'm going to have some fun with the rest of my life. And if you're a good girl, I'll give you a lifetime box seat, right behind home plate." He laughed and took out a cigar.

Stacey could hardly believe what she'd just heard. Jesus! His own personal baseball team. It would cost millions and he talked as if he were buying a Tinkertoy set! She actually felt herself getting damp. "Eric Radner, you devil! I never figured you for a closet jock." She shook her head wonderingly. "A baseball team. That's the most fabulous, sexy thing I've ever heard of."

"It's pretty sexy all right," he agreed smugly. "Not many men could make that statement. But it's all in the works. I'm having a firm in Century City handle it—a specialty firm, only dealing with sports law." He grunted in distaste. "Although they are trying to make a big deal out of it—like I was acquiring AT&T or something. Bunch of asses is what they are—practically want my life history to present to the franchise board." He chuckled. "Hell, let 'em have all the information they want. I've already given the most important data—my financial statement! That's all any deal ever comes down to—the money."

Stacey nodded her head in agreement as he continued, "That's why I gotta see Jessica. I need her help."

"What kind of help? Maybe I can help you."

"Now, don't you worry your pretty little head about that. You've taken damned good care of my company. Thanks to you, I have the best computer minds in the country who right this minute are figuring out new ways to make me more millions so I can spend afternoon hours here with you." He pinched her lightly. "No, the kind of people I need fall into Jessica's category."

Stacey seethed inwardly. It was just another example of the fact she had reached a plateau in her career. Without the kind of clout Jessica Martin had, Stacey would remain relegated to the one field in which she had proven herself. It infuriated her. She could recruit anyone Jessica could—there was no reason to limit herself to computer scientists. But she kept her anger to herself. Her day was coming and she didn't want Eric to think she was jealous of Jessica, or of any woman, for that matter. "Good," she said with conviction. "Let Jessica handle it. I certainly don't want to waste our time together talking recruiting."

She deliberately shifted her position on the bed into an inviting pose, saying, "Look at you, stingy bastard. Sitting clear across the room, already dressed and ready to leave.

All this talk about baseball teams and jocks has gotten me horny again. Can't I tempt you with seconds?" It was exactly the right thing to have said to him.

He laughed, a quick ruddy flush darkening his health-club tan. "You're a greedy little girl and you know I love it. But I have to go. Got another meeting with my lawyers. Got to watch over them so they don't fuck this up. Can I make it up to you next time?"

Stacey forced a sexy purr into her voice. "You just try to get out of it, Tiger, you just try."

Taking no risk with his carefully groomed hair, Eric grinned, blew her a noisy kiss, and started for the door. "I can see myself out. You just lie there and rest up for our next go-round."

Stacey lay back on the satin sheets, her mind racing. What a setup. An enormous corporation, millions of dollars, and now a major-league baseball team. She'd have even more power than she'd dreamed of. She rolled over to the night-stand and took a joint from the drawer. Before lighting it, she called the office to say she had a migraine. She was too pleased with herself and the turn of events to go back to work.

She lit up and inhaled deeply, holding the smoke inside her lungs; it was good stuff and she felt a jolt immediately. Stacey hardly ever used drugs—she wanted to keep her wits about her all the time. But occasionally a joint was just what she needed and she was particularly enjoying this one. She stretched, tossing the covers aside, and grinned at her reflection in the mirrored canopy above the bed, the only kinky accessory in an otherwise tastefully furnished, country-French hillside home.

She knew she had never looked better. Her skin had the exact glow of the inside of a peach. It drove men crazy without their ever realizing why. Stacey's skin made her look edible. She ran her hands around the high, firm contours of her lush breasts, the nipples erect and rosy red with excitement. Her shapely legs, unusually long for her height, still gleamed with the sweat of sex. Her turquoise eyes were shining and the deep gold of her long, thick blonde hair spread out over the pale blue satin sheets was magnificent. And she knew it. She smiled up at her image.

A baseball team, she mused. What in the world ever gave him the idea? Eric was an industrialist, and while baseball was big business, it just didn't seem to fit him. She shook her head, her thoughts going at full tilt. Who does he think he is? Jerry Buss? Does he think buying a team will turn him into a jock? She giggled. Jerry Buss didn't need to buy teams to be a jock. He was already tall and sexy and powerful. Sorry, Eric my boy, if that's what you hope for, you'd better lower your sights. Think more in terms of George Steinbrenner, he's more your speed.

Giggling again, Stacey made a mental note to find out all there was to know about owning a major-league baseball team. She wasn't about to let Eric Radner catch her napping.

She blew a little billow of smoke up toward her reflection. Aloud she said, "We'll be another Georgia Rosenbloom-Fronterie." She laughed, the pot really taking effect. She spoke to herself in the mirror with genuine affection. "Only we'll do a better job of it, won't we, sweetheart?"

Chapter 11

Michael sat in his wheelchair, waiting for Jessica. He felt a mixture of panic and relief. This was it. The first honest confrontation. Neither he nor Jessica had instigated it. This time, the hand of fate had intervened.

He hoped with a terrible desperation that he would handle it well. Hoped he could be a man from the waist up, but he still felt as if someone had poured ice water down his spine when he heard her key in the front door.

"Michael?" she called. "Where are you?"

"In the study," he answered. "Reading some blueprints. Why don't you get comfortable and bring us a drink? Make it martinis, okay? I'll be just about finished by then."

He heard her high heels click across the parquet floor of the entry hall, then the sound of her bedroom door opening and closing. He spread the blueprints out on his desk, trying to make it appear as if he had actually been working. But the truth was that all day his thoughts kept coming back to the fact that tonight there would be no way of avoiding what had to be done. He corrected himself. He could avoid it, he didn't have to bring it up, and he'd make book that Jessica wouldn't. But he refused to be that kind of coward—he no longer had the stomach for it.

He took a deep breath as she entered the room carrying a pitcher of martinis and two frosted glasses. Her smile was brave, but her face showed the strain of a day he knew had been rough. She looked so vulnerable he felt his resolve weakening, but he caught himself.

"Busy day?" he asked.

Jessica sat across from him in the big Eames chair he used to love. Stretching her long legs out onto the ottoman accentuated the outline of her figure under the thin silk caftan. "I'll say. It was the proverbial madhouse. I sometimes feel my office should be a padded cell. Can the whole world possibly be this crazy?"

He forced his laugh to sound normal, although the tension in her beautiful eyes caused his throat to ache with sorrow. "That bad, huh?"

"Oh, not bad. More chaotic. It was just a very busy day and there are a few problems—but, uh—they can be handled." Her voice was somewhat unsteady. "I'm just feeling sorry for myself." She smiled, and he recognized the effort it cost her. "How about yourself? Looks like you've been hitting the old blueprint trail. Something exciting?"

The note of hope in her voice hurt nearly as much as what he knew he had to do. She so wanted him to become involved in his work again, to have the passion for architecture that had always consumed him. He didn't think it would return, not the way it had been. Michael Martin had not just designed buildings. He'd seen them through to their completion, down to the last detail. Which meant climbing up on narrow steel girders twelve stories off the ground. It meant getting right down into the foundation as it was being dug. It meant getting to know the laborers and instilling in them the same sense of pride in their work on his building as he felt over its design. Most of all, it meant *not* being in a wheelchair. But Michael was determined not to let her know how he felt—especially now.

"Actually," he said, forcing a false note of enthusiasm into his voice, "it is kind of exciting. Ben Hobard has come up with a beautiful site for a new town-house project. It's got all the potential you could hope for, scenic view, actual land space for each unit. On multilevel lots—there's a chance for privacy, for individual dwellings. I've just been kicking around some ideas," he finished, hoping he'd managed to fool her.

"Michael, that's wonderful. Really—a sense of privacy? In a town-house complex?" Jessica's enthusiasm was genuine. "Will you think of solar energy?—Murchinson Oil forgive me," she went on. "Tell me all about it."

He saw the hope leap into her tawny eyes, causing the green flecks to sparkle like emeralds. But he didn't want to go too far, didn't want her calling Ben Hobard to tell him how excited she was. Not until Michael could call Ben and explain, get Ben to cover for him. There wasn't any complex.

"Whoa, slow down! I just got the layout today. It's only a rough idea of the terrain and locale. Ben sent it over by messenger, but I must admit at first glance I thought it might be fun to design." He had a hard time meeting her eyes. "I haven't made a commitment yet." He saw the subtle change in her eyes, but knew she wouldn't push. He could be certain of that. She'd let him take the lead.

"I'm sorry, Michael," Jessica said. "You know how carried away I get when you have a new concept. It's funny— only the other day I was thinking how truly dull and unimaginative most new buildings seem to be. Your ideas always thrill me." Her eyes twinkled. "Just promise there won't be one mirrored facade and I'll go quietly."

He forced a grin. "Not even a reflecting pool, all right?" He looked away from her, down at the papers on his desk. "As a matter of fact, I plan on making some preliminary sketches tomorrow, then I want to start figuring the scale and technical details. I have to wait for the soil analysis of the hillside before I know what structures it will support through rain, mud slides, and all the other California goodies." He took a deep breath before continuing. "But it will give me plenty to do while you're in New York."

There! He'd done it! It was as if a bomb had been thrown into her lap and she had recoiled from the direct hit. Her skin paled, and she leaned forward, a bit too casually, trying for control. She took a sip of her drink, then raised her eyebrows. "New York? Who said anything about going to New York?"

Okay, he had his answer. She wasn't going to face it. He would have to force the issue. "John Adams for one. Surely he reached you at the office?" He knew she was going to deny it, he could see her mind racing.

"Oh, John," she said casually. "Actually no, he didn't reach me at the office. I missed his call and he's off to Europe. Nothing important," she hedged, "I'm sure. I didn't speak with him, he left a message with Carol."

"I'm sure he did, Jessica. Probably the same message he left with me."

"With you?" There was fear in her eyes.

Michael steeled himself to continue. "Yes, you'd just left the house when he called, a little past nine. He thought he'd catch you before you left since he was leaving for the airport himself."

"Yes, well, as I said, I missed his call," she replied, not looking at Michael. "But I'm sure it was nothing important."

Here we go, Michael thought, it's now or never. "I'd say that Marshall MacAbee's having a stroke from which he is not expected to recover would come under the heading of important."

Jessica said nothing, merely sat with eyes downcast, scarcely breathing. She'd never lied to him and he knew it must hurt now to have done so. Still, she would not help; he would have to do it all.

"So when do you leave, Jessica?"

"Leave?" she asked hollowly. "I'm not leaving, Michael. I can't get away now—it's impossible. But I'm not worried. I'm sorry I didn't tell you, but really, I can handle it from here. I can't just jump on a plane to New York."

"You mean that *I* can't just jump on a plane to New York, don't you, Jessica?"

She stared at him, wide-eyed, unable or unwilling to speak. He would never get on a plane in that chair, yet she couldn't be the one to say it.

"Jessica." He indicated the wheelchair. "I'm the one who is grounded, not you."

"Michael." Her voice was a plea. "Michael, please . . ."

"No, Jessica! *You please!* You please answer me. You always traveled for your clients before my accident, and you will travel for them now. You can't let John Adams down."

"I won't let him down, Michael. I have an excellent file of candidates to present to John. I don't have to go to New York to do that."

"Have you met those candidates, Jessica?" When she didn't answer, he continued, "Of course you haven't. Jessica, you've never recommended anyone you haven't met personally, not in your whole career."

"That's not true, Michael," she said lamely.

"All right, maybe at the junior level, when you were first starting out in the search business. But never, ever have you presented someone you haven't met at this level. You've earned every fee you've collected. Are you going to start cheating now? And with John Adams, of all people?"

Jessica knew the truth of his words, and he saw the terrible pain she was feeling. Torn in two directions. He had to help her. For once since the accident he was forgetting his own troubles long enough to think of this magnificent woman whom he'd loved for some twelve years. Someone whom he must now let go before it was too late for both of them. John Adams's telephone call had given him the courage—and the excuse—he'd been searching for.

"Michael," she said, "please try to understand. It isn't because of you, I promise. Of course I don't intend to cheat John Adams, or any other client for that matter." She looked away from him. "But I simply can't get away now. There are problems at the office, problems I haven't told you about. I must deal with them. It's the timing . . ." she finished. "The timing is all wrong."

"It's a shame Marshall MacAbee didn't consider your schedule when he decided to have a stroke," Michael said coldly.

"Michael!" Her tone was shocked. "That's a terrible thing to say to me!"

"And lying is a terrible thing to do to me, Jessica. I don't know what other problems have cropped up, but I do know you can handle them, and that a week in New York to meet your obligations isn't going to matter that much."

Jessica squared her shoulders. "Michael, I won't let John down. I'm sure he'll understand. I just can't go to New York—if that's a requisite of this search assignment, I just can't accept it."

"Jessica," he said firmly, "listen to yourself. Can't, can't, can't! What you can't do is admit the truth. Would you like it to go to a Korn Ferry? To one of the big-eight search firms? Would you like to throw this in their laps? After all the years you've spent proving you are as good as they are? What the hell were those years for?"

She wasn't budging. He allowed his voice to slide into the old sarcasm that had immediately followed the accident and the diagnosis he'd never be a whole man again. The taunting, accusing tone he'd used for the first year. "What are you really afraid of, Jessica? That I'll do myself in if you're gone for a few days? That I won't be able to handle it without your cheerful face around to remind me life is worth living? Is that it, Jessica?" He wheeled his chair over closer to her before continuing. "Or is it you're afraid you'll enjoy some freedom, some space? Maybe meet a whole man, maybe get laid and feel like a woman again instead of the full-time baby-sitter to a piece of stone?"

Her cry was torn from the deepest part of her soul. "Michael, how can you talk to me like this? How can you be so cruel?"

"I'm no more cruel to you than you are to yourself, Jessica. I've known all along that you feel sorry for me."

"No!" she cried. "Guilty! I feel guilty!" She could not stop herself. "I put you in that chair! It's my fault you can't walk! If I hadn't gone to Chicago for World Vision, we'd have been on our vacation—you wouldn't have gone out to the site on a Sunday. . . ." Her words were suddenly choked off. She had never intended to let him know the burden of guilt she carried.

Michael put his face in his hands, his groan that of a

wounded bear. His stomach began to churn with nausea. "Oh, Jesus! Oh, Jesus! Is that why you've stayed? Oh, sweet Jesus, this is even sicker than I thought."

They were both silent. It had never occurred to him that she carried that inside her. He became more resolved than ever. His voice dripped acid.

"Well, my long-suffering wife, you have my absolution! I hereby forgive you for leaving a grown man all alone in the big city without your protection." He saw the pain in her eyes deepen. His own guts were churning with this new hurt, but he wouldn't stop now. "Besides, the accident is ancient history. Don't you think it's time you let go of it? Let go of me? Do you think I enjoy your martyrdom? Do you think just because we pussyfoot around that I don't know what it's been like for you?" He wheeled the chair even closer to her. "Well, I do—goddamn it! And it is beginning to smother me. Get out of here! Go to New York! Save your business! Save your credibility! Save your life! And for Christ's sake let me breathe!"

"Michael . . ." Her whisper came from a throat gone raw. "Do you really know what you're saying? You can't possibly mean what you're suggesting. Dear God, you don't know what you're saying."

"Of course I know what I'm saying!" he roared, causing her to jump back in startled alarm. "It's my cock that's paralyzed, not my brain! We can't go on like this—it *is* smothering me. You smother me with your goddamned unfailing good humor! Your goddamned strength! Your goddamned patience! You've been robbed, baby, *robbed!* When are you going to act like a victim?"

Sweat beaded on his forehead, and his heart raced, but he forced himself to go on. "When are you going to kick and scream? When are you going to act like the woman I knew? When are you going to let me up and start living again?" He put his face directly in front of hers, staring into her eyes.

Jessica gripped her glass, her hands white at the knuckles, her eyes huge and wounded.

"Well, Jessica?" Michael pressed.

She was silent for a moment, but Michael could see some

sign of her old dignity returning. Oh, she'd think about it later, think he was just having an emotional tantrum, but he wouldn't let her out of it. He'd keep at her until she was on the fucking plane—that would be phase one.

She rose in one fluid movement. He stared at the grace of her body and ached, wishing to feel something again. But he kept his eyes cold.

"All right, Michael." Her voice was cool. "I'll make my reservations in the morning." She left the study without a backward glance.

Michael allowed his exhausted upper torso to sink back against the chair. He'd done it—he'd set her on the road to freedom. He picked up his drink and toasted the air around him. "To Michael. He did not distinguish himself in battle, but at least he didn't turn tail."

Ignoring the tears that unexpectedly slid down his face, he downed his martini in a single gulp, then wheeled his chair over to the table to take the nearly full pitcher back to his desk where he proceeded to get quietly, thoroughly drunk.

Chapter 12

Jim Steiner poured himself a cup of coffee and grinned at Carol, who stood waiting for the water to boil for herbal tea. "What are you so mad about anyway? All I said was that Jessica looked like a zombie at the staff meeting. She sounded like one, too," he went on. "What's with her? Is she afraid of mutiny if she's gone for a week?"

"Only if we let you out of your cage," Carol said bitingly. He gave her a Bronx cheer.

"Boy, you'd think she was a sacred cow or something. Can't you loosen up? Don't you have a sense of humor?"

"Why? Are you planning on saying something funny, Jim?"

Jim was never quite sure of himself with Carol. He didn't think she disliked him. It had never occurred to Jim's healthy ego that *anyone* would dislike him, especially a woman. It was just that he was never too sure about Carol. She should know that he wasn't really knocking Jessica Martin. He liked and respected her as much as he could any woman who was also his boss. Jim was all for women's lib in the sex department, but it didn't go much beyond that. Still, for some reason, he wanted Carol to like him.

"Cute, Carol, real cute. But I'm serious. What the hell's wrong with her?"

"It's none of your business. But, if I didn't already know you were as dense as concrete, I might try to explain it to you."

"Don't tax your beady little brain, Carol," he retorted quickly. "Anyway, what I really want to know is who's in charge while Jessica is away?"

"I am, buster! And I've been to Brooklyn; I've made New York cab drivers tremble. So don't think you're going to get away with anything."

"The thought never entered my mind." He grinned. "I'm just glad to hear it's you and not our little Miss Stacey-Mary Poppins-whip-and-chains Dawson."

Carol tried to hide her amusement but Jim was too observant and pounced on it eagerly. "Aha! Caught you. You ain't too fond of the broad yourself."

"Never mind, Jim."

"Never mind, my ass! Listen, oh great terror of the cabbie set, you'd better stop worrying about me goofing off and keep your eyes on our resident ball breaker. She won't miss a trick while Jessica is gone, and I warn you now, if she starts in on me, I'll cream her."

"Jim," Carol sighed, "you're always looking for a fight. Why should Stacey bother you?"

"You can't be serious? That woman is a menace. She's after me, I tell you."

Carol laughed. "Your worries are over, Jim. You're not even in her league. Stacey has bigger fish to fry."

"Oh yeah? I got news for you, bubbie. She just about raped me and I'm telling you she *is* after me."

Carol was interested, Jim could tell, but she wouldn't admit it. He smiled to himself. She was okay, a little too stuffy when it came to Jessica, but okay. He'd give her the bit of gossip she wanted to hear but wouldn't ask about. Hurriedly, he continued. "You remember that hot romance she had going with that aerospace guy? Remember the explosion? When he finally came to his senses and told her he planned to keep his nuts in their original shell? Jesus, you could hear her rimming him out on the telephone all over the office." He grinned, remembering the scene. "Anyway," he went on, "she asked me to have a drink with her that night. She said she needed someone to talk to."

He had Carol's full attention and was enjoying it. "Anyhow, I agreed to go with her for a drink and after she'd cried on my shoulder about how men are always taking advantage of her, she invited me to go home with her and have dinner. I was still on training salary and practically existing on handouts, so I said sure, why not?"

He paused to sip his coffee, amused at the interest in Carol's usually noncommittal eyes. "Turns out, the dinner she had to offer was herself. Jesus, what a broad. I had her number from day one, a real ball breaker, and I sure in hell wasn't going to get involved with her."

Carol, totally caught up in the story, couldn't help herself. "What happened?"

Jim laughed. "Want to see the scars? I got out of there, but just barely."

Carol remembered Stacey had suddenly taken a strong dislike to Jim Steiner, but she had put it down to Stacey's usual bitchiness when a new recruiter showed promise. She wanted to know the rest. "But *how* did you get out of there?" she pushed.

"With my pants still zipped, but not with the finesse Jessica is always harping on. Look, Stacey offered herself up on a platter for a reason I'll never understand, but I had enough sense to back off. Besides," he grinned, "I really was hungry. I just told her to go fuck herself since she was having so much trouble getting me or anyone else to do it."

"God, Jim. I know Stacey can be a pain, but don't you think you were a little rough?"

"Me, rough? I offered to show you my scars, didn't I? Here, I still will. . . ." He started to undo his belt.

Carol quickly stopped him, laughing in spite of herself. "I'll just take your word for it. But tell me, honestly, how *have* you managed to continue working here? I mean, Stacey is hardly famous for her forgiving nature."

"No shit, Sherlock!" His eyes filled with so much mischief that Carol found herself grinning in anticipation. "I'll admit once I had a chance to think about what I'd said, I was a bit edgy. She's the big cheese around here, and I was still a rookie. I really wanted a chance at this business," he said earnestly. "So, after hiding out from her for a couple of days, I asked if I could buy her a drink."

"And she accepted?"

"Like a shot! I think she thought I was going to give her a mercy hump. Anyway, I took her for a drink and confessed my big secret. I told her I'm gay."

Carol gasped, her eyes filled with the question she couldn't ask.

"No," he laughed. "No faggots allowed in Brooklyn, didn't you know that? I'm as straight as Orange County. But *she* bought it. I told her I'd reacted as I did because I was scared. I told her I couldn't get it up for a woman and I didn't want Jessica to find out and lose my job. I got her to believe it's the reason I always act so tough, so no one will guess."

"Jim," Carol laughed, tears rolling down her cheeks, "you are a monster, an absolute monster."

"This is true, very true. But you gotta fight fire with fire. Anyway, just like I figured, my confession made her come better than my balling her would have. I imagine it will all come out one of these days when she wants to convince Jessica I don't belong here. When she wants to get rid of me like she did Eleanor Handler."

Carol suddenly took another look at Jim Steiner. Maybe he was a little too aggressive and defensive, but he certainly wasn't stupid. Stacey *would* savor that information and use it in any way that suited her. She'd disguise her pleasure in telling Jessica she had a faggot on board and that she'd heard from a very reliable source that he'd actually made a pass at a candidate. It wasn't too hard to figure out what Stacey would do. She would use it, no doubt about it. "Well, your secret is safe with me."

"I kinda thought it would be. And I'm safe with Martin Management, just so long as you don't leave here while the viper is around. I might need a character witness."

"I'm glad you told me, Jim. If Stacey ever tries to pull that stunt, you can be sure I'll tell Jessica just what did happen."

"I'm gonna count on it." He smiled at her. "Sure you don't want to see my scars?"

"I'll pass this time. Now get on back to work. I've got a million things to do, one of which is to see that Jessica makes her plane."

Chapter 13

The pages of *Forbes*, *Fortune*, and even *The Wall Street Journal* blurred before her eyes. Nor could she concentrate on the film, some inane Burt Reynolds car chase. The headsets for music made her temples ache. There was nothing to do during the entire flight from Los Angeles but confront her feelings and try to put them into perspective before she arrived at Amalgamated.

She was bewildered and confused by Michael's attack. What had happened to him, to them? How could he believe she thought it was all his fault? If anyone was to blame, it was her—her ambition that had caused his accident, had nearly caused his death. He'd never have gone to the site on a Sunday if she had been in town. But she had tried to make up for it—had tried to make his life bearable. Or *had* she done it all wrong? She wasn't a saint and she wasn't a psychiatrist. She had only wanted desperately to save their marriage.

She shuddered and the memory of his outburst came back like a slap in the face. How long had he been living a lie? How long had he resented her, felt smothered by her? Could he even bear the sight of her? Did he even *know* her? How could he think she was afraid to leave him because she might be tempted to have an affair? The irony of it brought a bitter taste to her mouth. She didn't have to leave the city to have an affair, and Michael had to be aware of that. To fling such an accusation at her was unforgivably cruel. She could easily have had an affair had she wanted to. Jeremy was there, handsome, exciting, the electricity between them obvious. Yet she'd resisted him, gone without tenderness and sex for two years out of loyalty to Michael.

Or was it all loyalty? Did she deny herself out of guilt? She still felt responsible. *Was* it her way of punishing herself? No! She loved Michael. You don't just stop loving someone . . . or do you? It was obvious Michael had stopped loving her. She ached with hurt and confusion.

Tears of frustration stung her eyes. She couldn't deny the truth to herself anymore. She *was* hungry, and not just for the release of sex, she was hungry for warmth, for tenderness, for intimacy. She felt so weary, so damned alone. Michael could have used any number of reasons to get her to go to New York. He could have worn her down with arguments about her professional responsibilities.

But Michael hadn't worn her down with reasoning, he had deliberately berated and humiliated her. Mocked their marriage, mocked her genuine efforts to make his life bearable. It was over, he'd made that clear enough. But he needn't have ended it with ugliness and accusation.

Her tears turned to anger. For the first time since the accident, Jessica allowed her own feelings to come first. She didn't think she could ever forgive Michael. She latched on to the anger, let it grow inside her rapidly beating heart. It was the only emotion she wanted to feel just then, the only emotion she felt she could handle.

By the time Jessica arrived for her appointment at Amalgamated, she was in control as usual, certain John Adams would detect nothing. She was shown immediately into his executive dining room.

Deep burgundy carpet covered the floor, carpet so thick

her balance was threatened as her high heels sank into its depth. The walls were covered in pearl gray silk. A Renaissance portrait of a Medici prince was lit by antique pewter lamps.

The chairs were upholstered a pale olive and burgundy French print. The dining table, set with china and crystal, was of rosewood. It was an imposing yet comfortable room, a statement of John Adams's importance as president of Amalgamated. Heads of state dined in this room, and Jessica appreciated John's courtesy in affording her equal importance.

His hearty voice returned her to reality. "Jessica, let's have a look at you."

Jessica extended her cheek for his fatherly kiss, and smiled. "John, I'm so glad to see you."

"As you'd better be. It's been too long." He scrutinized her carefully. "You're as beautiful as ever—too beautiful to be a working woman. 'Course that's just the old Texas country boy talking. Come, sit down and have a drink."

Although Jessica had not seen him so much as raise an eyebrow, the door opened and a waiter appeared with a silver tray upon which sat two drinks. A bourbon on the rocks for John and a tall crystal glass of Pouilly-Fuissé for Jessica. He never forgot a thing. She accepted the glass of her favorite wine with a smile.

They took seats in the big wing chairs and settled themselves before Jessica began. "I wish I were here under happier circumstances, John. This has been a terrible shock."

"Yes," he replied. "Bad business, very bad. Marshall was a good man. . . ." His words trailed off. "It's hard to speak of him in the past tense, yet that's the way things are. And as you know, Jessica, I am a man who always faces facts." His voice took on a lighter tone. "And one fact I'm prepared to face right now is that somehow a very beautiful woman has fallen into my clutches and my chef has prepared a sumptuous meal. We can talk business later."

Through cocktails and lunch John kept the conversation

light, amusing her with corporate anecdotes and New York horror stories. When they'd eaten, the waiter set up coffee and Jessica knew that lunch was officially over.

"Jessica," John said, "our problem is immediate. The legal ramifications of Amalgamated's vast enterprises are enormous, and we will have to replace Marshall as soon as possible. Naturally, I expect you to make this your number-one priority. Our retainer contract will be the same as always and we will, of course, pay your expenses while you are here in New York or anywhere you have to go to interview candidates. I've already set up a schedule of sorts." He picked up the folder which had somehow been placed next to his wing chair without Jessica having noticed it.

Opening the folder, John looked at her and said. "This contains the spec sheets, plus the new salary level, as well as additional benefits packages over the past two years. Not much has changed since Marshall came on board, but there have been some cost-of-living increases and the life insurance is a lot higher. Those are things you can go over later. The stock-option plan is the same, but we've increased our relocation package considerably, especially at the executive level."

He pulled some sheets from the folder and gave them a glance. He knew exactly what they contained. "We can now offer a thirty-year, very low interest mortgage loan, plus, if necessary, the company will purchase the existing home of a candidate from out of state. We will pay whatever is fair market for a profit in the area. The thing we need," he went on, "is a good man, and we need him yesterday, so we are ready to deal."

He placed the papers back in the file and handed it to Jessica. "The duties remain the same as when you recruited Marshall, so we don't have to go over that again. There is one addition, however. I will need an attorney for the Middle East. Those specs are in the folder as well. Marshall would have called you on this." He sighed and continued, "All the requisites are listed. I would only add that the situation with our hospital division there is a mess. We not only need an international attorney who understands their laws, we need a diplomat who understands their culture."

His tone changed, wrapping up with his usual thoroughness. "There is really no need for us to discuss this further. You can read a job requisite better than I, so you can go over this on your own. I've arranged several meetings for you this afternoon. There are some new people who moved here with our acquisition of Worldwide Shipping whom you haven't met. They'll be reporting to the new man, so you'll want to get a personality fix. It's all set and should see you through six or six-thirty. Okay with you?"

"Of course, John," she replied. "I have a few men in mind already. Men whose backgrounds are quite similar to Marshall's. In fact, two very good men are right here in New York. That would eliminate the need to relocate. I have meetings scheduled with them for tomorrow and the next day."

"Good girl," he beamed. "I figured you'd do your homework when I left the message with Carol." He sipped his coffee. "That's what I like about you, Jessica. You're a success now, your company is doing extremely well. I keep tabs, make no mistake—but you still work as hard as you did when you were starting out. That's why I know I can count on you. Any questions?"

His rapid-fire instructions were not new to Jessica and she had indeed done her homework. There was no need to tax his overburdened time. The folder would be complete, and she could begin work at once. But as he finished his coffee and prepared to end the meeting, she stopped him with, "John, I'd like to talk about Marshall for a minute." Her voice softened. It was painful for him, and she had a lump in her own throat. "I know it's hard, but I have to know. Is he in pain? Does he know what has happened to him?"

John thought for a moment, then said, "I'll have to answer that yes and no. No, he isn't in pain, at least his doctors assure me he isn't. Yes, to your second question. Yes! He does know what's happened to him. He can't speak, or even move, but his eyes are very much alive. Yes, he knows what's happened to him, I'm sure of it."

They were both silent for a moment before Jessica asked, "When can I see him, John? Is he allowed visitors?"

John Adams frowned. "Jessica, I don't think that's such a good idea. He's allowed visitors, but can you imagine what it must be like for him? What it would be for him to let you see him? Don't forget, you knew him as a virile, vital man. I don't think Marshall or any man for that matter could bear to have a beautiful woman he'd once known see him as a helpless—" He broke off in midsentence as he saw the quick, unexpected tears spring into Jessica's eyes. Silently he cursed himself—he was a man who rarely spoke without thinking first.

He cleared his throat, drank some more of his now-cold coffee, giving her a chance to compose herself. Then he reached out and took her hand in his. "Jessica, forgive me. For a man *Fortune* magazine once called brilliant, I can be a pretty dumb jackass. Please try to forgive me. Of course you know how Marshall must feel, you've already been there."

Jessica squeezed his hand. "There's nothing to forgive, John." Her voice was dry but her eyes were still shining with unshed tears. "I overreacted and it was stupid of me to suggest seeing Marshall. I'm the one who should apologize."

"Of course it wasn't stupid. I wouldn't expect less of you. I know you've always like him and it took guts to offer to see him. I'm an ignorant clod, I know, but not so ignorant I can't recognize genuine distress when I see it."

He paused, then asked gently, "Are things worse with your husband? Is there anything I can do?"

Jessica tried to get a grip on her emotions. She never brought her personal problems into her business relationships, yet John did seem genuinely concerned, and she was tempted to ask his sage and mature advice. But she resolved not to; he had his own problems. She forced a smile. "John, of course you're not ignorant. Things could be better with Michael, but there is nothing you could do to help. I was just reacting to Marshall and the thought of his being so helpless. Maybe for a minute there it brought back some painful memories, but I'm fine, really. I promise."

John didn't believe her. But he admired her courage and

professionalism and vowed to mind his own business. Liking her as much as he did really didn't give him license to pry into her personal affairs. With a smile, he summoned his secretary to escort Jessica to the first of her meetings.

John had been on the nose, as usual. His timing was exact, and at six-thirty Jessica left Amalgamated, tired but pleased. It would be an exciting assignment and it would require at least a week in New York.

Michael's cruelty was still in her heart. But she admitted that perhaps it would be a good thing to be apart until they could deal with their anger and pain. They both needed time to think.

Chapter 14

Jessica looked up, startled, as the waiter placed a fresh martini on the table in front of her. She rarely had more than one drink, and she did not remember ordering another. Too embarrassed to question him, she picked it up and sipped slowly. Looking around at the elegantly dressed people, she wondered if they, like herself, were sitting in the Palm Court drinking cocktails they did not want rather than face the emptiness of a hotel room.

It was a new feeling. On past business trips, after a day of meetings, the only thing she'd wanted was to go to her room, have a long soak in the tub, one drink, then place a call to Michael before bed. Of course, that was all in the past, before the accident, before Michael's bitter tirade. Tonight, she could not face being completely alone.

She'd opted for the Palm Court and the company of strangers with whom she would not converse. She planned on having one drink, two maximum, then going to her room and ordering room service.

"Alone at last, my beauty."

Jessica lifted her head, expecting to see some conventioneer, prepared to shrug him off. Instead, before her was the mischievous, grinning face of Jeremy Bronson. She was disconcerted, not sure if she was glad to see him or not. Her laughter seemed unnatural to her own ears. "I would hardly call the Palm Court of the Plaza Hotel alone." As Jeremy sat down without asking permission, she asked, "What are you doing here?"

"I could say waiting for you, which wouldn't be a lie since I've been doing just that for three years," Jeremy teased. "But actually, I'm here on business."

"At the Plaza? I thought Murchinson Oil had acquired the Havermore Inn chain. Are you patronizing the competition? That's not the old corporate spirit."

Jeremy groaned in mock fear. "You've got the goods on me. What is the price for your silence?"

Jessica laughed and was startled at how good it felt. "My sanity! Surely I've done my homework properly? You did acquire Havermore Inns, didn't you?"

"Jesus, woman! Don't you ever stop thinking about business?" He signaled the waiter. "Yes, you've done your homework, so take that stricken look off your face. We did acquire the Havermore chain. 'Close to convention centers, the airport, and the downtown business district.' *Not* having to stay at a Havermore Inn is one of my executive percs. Now, it's my turn," he said. "What are you doing here?"

Jessica grinned, appreciating his candor. "The same as you—business."

"Good," Jeremy responded with glee. "Because I fall into that category. We'll have a drink first and discuss who gets to deduct the whole thing over dinner."

Jessica hesitated for a moment, her head already light from the martinis. The prospect of eating alone was dismal in her present mood, but she wasn't sure she was up to dining with Jeremy—she didn't have all her wits about her. "Oh, Jeremy, it's a lovely offer, but I've already had a drink. One and a half actually. I planned on just ordering room service," she continued, "and getting to bed early. I have a rough schedule tomorrow."

"You're going to finish your drink and you're going to have dinner with me. Room service? In New York? Ridiculous! Besides," he went on, "I want to share a corporate secret with you. It's a secret because the stockholders in Poughkeepsie would think it outrageous. But since you aren't a stockholder, I'll trust you." He leaned forward, lowering his voice conspiratorially. "Murchinson Oil retains an apartment at the Plaza year-round. And that apartment comes with a full staff of servants, including the best French chef this side of Paris."

The waiter approached and Jessica saw with dismay that still another martini had been placed before her, along with a double scotch for Jeremy. She looked up to see Jeremy staring intently, his appraisal thorough and appreciative. His gaze made her slightly uncomfortable and she renewed her resolve to be on guard.

"You look absolutely stunning. You must have driven half of New York crazy today."

"Jeremy," she chided. "You promised to stop this flattery. You must know by now that it embarrasses me."

"And you must know by now that I don't flatter," he countered. "I never say anything I don't mean. You are beautiful, it's as simple as that."

Keep it impersonal, Jessica reminded herself. "Well now," she began, "tell me about this expensive French chef you keep secret from your stockholders. I admit I'm famished. What do you suggest we have him prepare?"

"We suggest nothing. Maurice has the most uncanny ability I've ever witnessed. He can tell just by looking at a person exactly what foods will please them."

"Come on, Jeremy," she laughed. "You can't be serious."

"But I am. I've seen him do it a hundred times, and he's never been wrong. You'll see for yourself. By the way," Jeremy cautioned, "he's cooked for royalty and the meal will take hours. He will not allow one bite of his culinary genius to be rushed. Each course must await the clearing of the palate in order that one may fully appreciate the next."

"It sounds wonderful," she sighed. "I don't think I'm capable of making any decisions tonight—including what to eat." Suddenly she realized she'd accepted his dinner invitation when it had been her absolute intention to refuse.

Jeremy studied her face, then frowned. "Rough day?"

"Rough week is more like it." What was she doing? And with Jeremy of all people! She hadn't wanted him to know she was upset.

"Want to talk about it?"

Jessica paused before answering, finding to her surprise she was once again tempted to confide in someone. After keeping everything bottled up for two years, it seemed she suddenly wanted to talk to anyone willing to listen. Maybe a man could help her understand Michael's attitude, but she couldn't talk to Jeremy about it, especially after two martinis. Her smile had a tinge of regret that did not go unnoticed by Jeremy. Her voice was soft. "It's very tempting, Jeremy, but no, I don't think so."

He looked at her for a long moment. Then, as if coming to some sort of decision, he spoke. "I thought, business aside, that we were friends, Jessica. Friends can talk to one another. Or are you afraid I have ulterior motives?"

"I'll admit that's probably part of it," Jessica answered honestly. "But really, it's just that I'm not ready to discuss it yet. I don't quite understand the problem myself."

"Nor are you likely to unless you do talk about it," he encouraged. "Michael's a man, I'm a man, I might be able to give you a little masculine insight. And I can, I assure you, put my personal motives on hold. You are obviously in pain. I'm your friend. I'd like to help."

She was flustered. How could Jeremy have concluded the problem was Michael? "Am I that transparent, Jeremy? I could have meant a rough week of work, you know."

"No way, Jessica," he retorted. "A business problem would have you stimulated, have all your juices flowing. We're two of a kind in that regard. We love business problems, thrive on challenge. The only thing to make you have more than one martini, and too tired to be decisive, would have to be personal." He went on firmly, "Now, I repeat, if you want to talk about it—and I think it's time you did—I'm here to listen."

Jessica returned his penetrating gaze. She wanted so much to accept his offer, to get it off her chest, to find some answers. But she wasn't sure about discussing Michael with Jeremy. It would seem like a betrayal to strip him bare to another man, especially a man to whom, she admitted to herself, she was attracted. Yet Jeremy seemed so sincere. "Maybe later," she hedged. "I admit the problem is with Michael, but I've had too much to drink. I don't think I can think. . . . There! That's proof. You know I am never redundant. I just don't think that now is the time."

"Now is the time, Jessica," Jeremy pushed. "And having had too much to drink is probably just what you need to let down those defenses." He relaxed in his chair. "But I'll tell you what—first we'll enjoy Maurice's culinary sins, then we'll have cognac in the properly chaperoned apartment and talk. There's one musty old bottle of Courvoisier that is guaranteed to hold the solution to any of mankind's problems."

Jessica no longer had the energy to resist. She smiled at him. "I am completely in your hands, good sir."

She rose unsteadily from the table and Jeremy joined her, taking her by the arm, emitting a soft chuckle as he spoke. "Would that you were, my lovely, would that you were."

Chapter 15

Jessica was no stranger to luxury and corporate excesses but as the elevator door opened to reveal the foyer of the Murchinson Oil apartment, she was astounded to realize it took up an entire floor of the Plaza Hotel. A crisply uniformed maid admitted them into the living room and Jessica stood still, marveling at the elegant perfection.

Walnut floors were strewn with oriental rugs, and a beveled mirror hung above the antique carved fireplace, which was the color of pale honey. Paintings adorned the amber, silk-covered walls and Lalique crystal sconces offered the softness of candlelight. Porcelain vases were filled with exquisite flowers perfuming the air.

The room was divided into conversational areas, and the upholstered sofas were masterpieces. Old damask and velvet in tones of honey, cinnamon, and amber gave the room a soft antique patina. The furnishings in the living room were worth a fortune, and Jessica dared not think of what the rest of the place must have cost.

"Well," Jeremy grinned, "what do you think?"

"I think it's beautiful. And I also think it is absolutely decadent."

Jeremy frowned, feigning panic. "My God! You *are* a stockholder."

Jessica laughed. "No, I'm not a stockholder. But this is incredible. It must have cost a fortune."

"You're darn right it did. We make some pretty big deals in here."

Jessica frowned in mock disapproval. "I'm sure you do. But I have to tell you, Jeremy, after seeing this, and I've only seen one room, it's going to be tough keeping a straight face when you cry to me about your personnel budget."

"Oh no, you don't, my lovely headhuntress. No business talk tonight."

The double doors at the end of the room opened and a tall man in a chef's toque entered. Silently observing Jessica and Jeremy, he nodded affirmatively and announced the first course.

Jeremy took Jessica by the arm, leading her across the room. He kept his voice low. "Maurice has decided on your favorite foods. Let's not keep him waiting."

Jessica looked up at Jeremy and grinned. "You know I don't believe a word of this so-called secret talent."

When she turned her head away from him, she could not restrain the laughter that spilled from her throat. The dining room was as lavish as the living room. The table could easily have accommodated sixty people, and the other appointments were as rare as museum pieces.

"Jeremy, this is too much. And to think I have to keep it a secret."

"That you do, my lovely," he responded. "Don't forget Murchinson Oil is the company that cares. Spending its profits in search of new energy sources and all that."

Jessica grinned. "No one would believe me anyway. I may feel guilty as hell in the morning, but I'm going to enjoy all this decadence tonight."

The table had been set up so that Jessica and Jeremy were seated together at one end. Her doubts about Maurice's uncanny secret ability dissolved as one after another of her favorite French foods were placed before her.

The meal began with a delicate leek and celery broth,

served in elegant Sèvres bowls, followed by blanquette de veau à l'ancienne, her absolute favorite French veal dish. The accompanying tissue-thin noodles and red Bordeaux-Médoc wine were the best she had ever tasted.

Jeremy kept their conversation light and impersonal, and Jessica found herself relaxing. As Maurice presented the crowning glory of the meal, a peach tart in a pastry shell so delicate it was almost translucent, Jessica mused that if things had been different, the evening would have been like a dream. Beautiful surroundings, gourmet food, and a rugged, handsome, attentive man by her side.

After dinner they returned to the living room, where brandy snifters rested in individual silver warmers, the promised old bottle of cognac open and breathing. The fireplace glowed and Jessica at last felt released from knots and inhibitions. When Jeremy leaned back against the sofa and asked if she was ready to talk about what was bothering her, she didn't hesitate.

Jessica was amazed at how calm her voice sounded, how easily she opened up, letting go of two years' pain, frustration, confusion, and guilt. She told him everything, sparing neither Michael nor herself.

Jeremy listened without interruption. When she was finished, Jessica sank back exhausted, but feeling lighter than she had in years. Jeremy was silent, his handsome face set in deep concentration. For a quick second, Jessica feared she'd made a mistake, that he was regretting inviting such personal revelations—perhaps he hadn't wanted that much intimacy. Nervously she took a cigarette. Jeremy leaned forward to light it before he spoke.

"Your husband is quite a man, Jessica." His voice was remote, as if he were speaking to himself.

She wasn't sure she'd heard him correctly. Was he being sarcastic? Sympathetic? Surely he wasn't being complimentary? Not after all she'd told him.

"Not the reaction you expected, is it, Jessica?"

"I—I'm not sure. That is, I'm not sure how you mean it."

"It's not the reaction I expected from myself. Hell, Jessica, we aren't kids—I think my attraction to you has been pretty apparent. Naturally I've speculated about you and your marriage these past two years—I thought I had it all figured out."

He sipped his brandy, a rueful expression in his eyes. "I sensed that you were attracted to me as well, even though you never gave me any encouragement. The electricity was always there, and I could only think of one solid reason you denied us the pleasure and comfort we could give to one another. I blamed your husband—it was the only answer. I was convinced he played on your sympathies. I thought that was how he kept you." He shook his head. "I never pictured *two* people who were making their lives hell. I pictured a frightened, helpless cripple selfishly holding on to the only thing left in his life. Now I see just how *un*selfish he is trying to be—for both of you."

Tears stung Jessica's eyes. She didn't understand. What was so unselfish in the cruel way Michael had treated her?

"Just what are you trying to tell me?"

"That I understand why he behaved as he did. And I am going to try to make you understand it. Then, I am going to take you back to your room before I lose sight of my own principles."

Suddenly, Jessica felt angry. If Jeremy's sympathies were with Michael, if he couldn't see her pain, she didn't want to discuss it anymore.

"Jeremy, I don't want to talk about it anymore. Just forget it—I'll handle it myself."

"You can't handle it yourself, Jessica. You don't even understand his motives."

"*I* don't understand? All of a sudden you're an expert on my husband's motives?"

Jeremy's response was gentle. "Jessica, I'm a man who has wanted you all these years. Wanted you to the point of madness at times, and I couldn't have you any more than your husband could. I understand his motives because when it comes to you, I've been as paralyzed as Michael."

He kept bringing it back to Michael. Michael and Jeremy. *Their* deprivation. What about *her* deprivation? Jessica felt furious. "Well, you needn't feel paralyzed any longer," she announced bitterly. "You even have his approval. I told you he wanted me to get laid."

She sprang from the sofa, unbuttoning her blouse, her breasts rising and falling with her rapid breathing, her dark hair falling across her face. Angry tears streamed from her eyes. Jeremy rose and removed her hands, rebuttoning the blouse, gently but firmly forcing her back onto the sofa.

"Jessica, do you think me that much of a bastard? I want to love you, not lay you. But I want you when you're ready to come to me, come to me because you want me, too. Not because you are hurt and angry."

"Pretty speech, Jeremy," she said bitterly. "But why not be honest? It's because you can suddenly visualize Michael sitting in his wheelchair, isn't that it? Now he's suddenly real to you, not some vaguely imagined man keeping me out of your bed. You've suddenly developed morals. It's *honor among men* time."

"That's rubbish!" he retorted. "I'll always want you, Jessica. Nothing will change that. But I want you whole and happy—I want you free. And Michael is trying to set you free."

"Then what's the problem? Or don't free women turn you on?"

"Jessica, listen to me. Michael had to be cruel. It was the only way to make you face the situation—to start living again. You wrongly blamed yourself for his accident and you crawled right into that chair with him. It wasn't your fault! It was a rotten twist of fate, but it wasn't your fault! Michael knows that—that's why he—"

"Michael thinks I've been acting like a martyr! He has ended our marriage! It's over. I don't have to understand anything!"

"Yes, you do!" he insisted. "Your marriage *is* over. Michael has accepted that and so must you. You have to start living again."

She was dizzy with emotions: confusion, lingering anger, self-pity, and worst of all, fear. Fear that what he was saying could be true. That her marriage was truly over.

"Jeremy, if it had been me, Michael would never have left me—never!"

"But it's different with a man, Jessica. No matter what you say, men and women are different. A man could have made the necessary adjustment if it had been his wife in that wheelchair. A man could have taken his physical release when he needed it and totally separated it from his love for his wife. But women just don't take sex that casually. They need something more, something meaningful."

Her eyes widened. What he was saying made sense finally, at least part of it. She could never take sex casually, never.

"All I ever wanted to do was make it up to him—be there for him."

Jeremy knew he had finally gotten through to her. "And you were, Jessica. You gave up almost everything for Michael, and in the process, gave up yourself. That's a lot of giving for one man to take. Let him go, Jessica."

The flood finally came. Jessica crouched back against the sofa cushions, her body heaving with grief and the knowledge that it was over—totally and completely over. Jeremy let her cry it out, and when she was finally quiet, gently guided her to the bathroom to wash her face with cool water and regain her poise.

As he needed to regain his own. His insides were churning like a whirlpool. It had taken every ounce of strength he possessed not to take her into his arms and comfort her. But he didn't trust himself. He was in love with her. If he'd taken her when she'd thrown herself at him in anger, it would have been finished. Jessica was not a one-night stand.

Jessica returned to the living room a bit calmer and took a seat on the sofa. Jeremy handed her a snifter of brandy and a cigarette.

"Feel better?" he asked, and at her tentative nod added "You've needed that for a long time."

Jessica attempted a smile, took a sip of brandy, and inhaled deeply on her cigarette. "God, I've made so many mistakes, Jeremy. So damned many stupid mistakes."

"Hey, I thought we were going to let up on the self-flagellation. You have to quit beating yourself, Jessica."

Jessica did not reply. Her thoughts were suddenly carried back, back to World Vision Pharmaceuticals, a major company whose account she had courted vigorously. The call from Chester Lawford, head of all recruitment contracts for World Vision, had come in on an early Thursday morning. He had decided her proposal to act as their exclusive management consulting company was viable. He was ready to sign the contracts *if* she would personally come to Chicago and meet with himself and other top departmental heads.

She remembered her turmoil. The call could not have come at a worse time. She and Michael were scheduled to depart the very next morning for their first vacation in two years. A lovely romantic trip to Barbados, where they would bask in the sun, drink exotic drinks, make delicious love, and forget the world of business existed.

Yet the World Vision account could be the one that finally made her company the enormous success she had worked so long and hard for. She *had* to make the trip—she couldn't bring herself to let such a plum elude her.

And so she had asked Michael to postpone their vacation. To reschedule it for the Monday following her return. He had agreed, pleased for her, proud of her success. And she had made the trip in happy anticipation. It had seemed the world was hers.

And for the two days of meetings, it appeared that she was right. She had impressed the department heads *and* Chester Lawford. The meetings concluded late Saturday, when the contracts were signed at a celebratory dinner in one of Chicago's finest restaurants.

She had her plane tickets for her return to Los Angeles on the red-eye flight. But when she had telephoned Michael to inform him of her exact arrival time, he'd suggested she sounded tired and ought to take a flight out on Sunday. She *had* felt tired, elated, but tired, and to her eternal regret, she agreed with Michael and rescheduled her flight for noon on Sunday.

She shuddered involuntarily, remembering. While Jessica soared high in the air in a TWA jet, Michael had tumbled to the earth below.

He had decided to go to the site of a building under construction to check one final detail before he and Jessica left for their trip. But while standing on a steel girder, he somehow lost his balance and fell twelve stories to the ground.

When Jessica arrived at her Bel Air home, Carol was waiting for her with the horrible news. Jessica's life had been filled with agony and guilt from that moment on.

Jeremy brought her back to the moment. "Let it go now," he said gently. "Let it go."

Jessica nodded sadly. "Yes, yes I have to, I know that now. It's just so much to digest all at once. I never thought my marriage would end, not ever. Even after the accident, I thought we'd work things out eventually. Now it's over, I have to begin a new life, and I don't know how. I don't even know *where* to begin."

Jeremy sat beside her on the sofa and took her hand in his. "You begin with a good night's sleep. And tomorrow you call Michael. You tell him you understand. Tell him you recognize what he is trying to do. Don't forget, he's going through this same hell right now."

Her voice was soft and shy, her green-flecked eyes deep and misty. "And then?"

Jeremy felt his heart constrict. She was so beautiful. "And then, tomorrow night you have dinner with me. We'll talk. The worst is over. You can deal with this, Jessica, and I'll be right there to help."

Jessica could not meet his gaze. Suddenly she wanted him to hold her. Wanted to lean on his strength. Her mind raced. How ironic that it should be Jeremy Bronson who made her see the truth about her relationship with Michael. That it should be Jeremy who was beginning to make her see that she wasn't to blame for the accident. She flushed, remembering, her eyes involuntarily going to the buttons on her blouse. She looked at Jeremy, embarrassed, unable to voice her thoughts.

He smiled, and when he spoke his voice was husky with desire. "Don't be embarrassed, Jessica. Don't ever be embarrassed over what we feel for one another. We'll take this one step at a time."

He rose, still holding her hand, and helped her up from the sofa. "Come on now, I'm taking you back to your room. You've had a hell of a day and you've got a big one tomorrow."

Jessica had never before felt like a helpless woman, but she certainly felt like one at that moment. She allowed herself to be led from the apartment like a docile child.

Once in her own room, she barely managed to undress before falling into a deep, sound sleep.

Chapter 16

Michael Martin hung up the telephone and frantically wheeled his chair into the bathroom adjoining the study. He barely made it to the sink before his stomach heaved. Over and over, seemingly endless dry spasms shook his upper torso, causing him to feel so dizzy he feared his chair would not hold him. There was little to bring up—he'd scarcely eaten since his tirade had convinced Jessica to leave for New York.

He sat staring at the washbasin, perspiration pouring down his face. By sheer willpower and deep breathing, he was finally able to calm his stomach. His throat burned raw.

At last, somewhat calmer, he rinsed the basin clean with hot water, then turned on the cold tap, drenched a washcloth, and mopped his sweating face, rinsing and mopping again and again until he felt able to wheel himself back into the study.

He sat by the window, looking out without seeing, his phone conversation with Jessica replaying in his head. Her voice had been calm, the anger gone, but it had been sad, so terribly sad. She had finally accepted the truth.

Jesus God! Make his heart stop racing—make his mind stop racing. He'd finally done it! It had to be done and he'd done it! He'd finally quit being an emotional crybaby and freed them both from a life of guilt and denial. But now what? He felt no real surprise at the panic engulfing him—he hadn't thought everything out. Wasn't sure of his next move, and she would only be in New York for a week or so.

His emotions ran the gamut: he was glad for Jessica, but he was hurting all the same. Their love had once been everything to him, and he had done what he'd done out of the memory of that love. He knew he'd had no choice—they couldn't go on as they had been—*he* couldn't go on as they had been. But, God, it hurt. He hadn't counted on how much it would hurt. And it wasn't over yet.

He pounded his fist against his unfeeling legs. But to what would he turn? He had only the vaguest kind of plan in mind, just something he'd read about in an architectural trade magazine, something he hadn't really investigated thoroughly. But as vague as it was, he had to prepare for phase two, and he only had a short time to do it. He'd have to risk it.

"Time to separate the men from the boys, Michael!" he reminded himself.

With renewed resolve, he wheeled his chair to his desk and punched the intercom button that would summon his nurse-companion of the past two years. Johnny Bridges's cheerful voice responded at once and Michael took his first deep breath.

"What's up, Mike?" Johnny asked as he entered the study, his boyish face set in its customary pleasant expression. He sincerely liked Michael Martin, and the two men had become good friends. Johnny knew that something heavy had gone down with Jessica and Michael—it was impossible to live so closely with two people and not be aware of the problems. Still, Michael had not volunteered anything, and Johnny never pried into other people's affairs.

Michael studied the face of his friend for a long moment before answering. "I'm—uh—I'm leaving, Johnny."

Johnny Bridges did not miss the pain in Michael's eyes, but did not want to probe too deeply. Instead he asked, "Leaving as on a vacation?"

Michael felt uncomfortable under his steady gaze. He hadn't really thought everything through, and he had no idea what Johnny's reaction to his vague plan would be.

"No." He shook his head. "Not a vacation, not exactly." He knew he was saying it all wrong, but he was uncertain of the best approach. Finally he blurted out, "I don't suppose you've ever considered leaving L.A.?"

Johnny frowned, then shrugged. "I haven't really thought about it. I mean at least not for the last two years. I've liked my job with you and Los Angeles is okay."

"I see," Michael said, his disappointment evident.

Johnny was quick to pick up on it. "But that doesn't mean my feet are in cement, either. I'm not a native, and there is plenty of the country I haven't seen. Maybe you'd better be more specific."

Michael grinned wryly. "I'm having a little trouble with that, Johnny. I mean, I can't be very specific, not just yet."

"I'd like to say I understand, but damned if I do."

"Let's put it this way for the time being. Are you a man of adventure, Johnny?"

"Hell, that's my middle name. You suggesting an adventure?"

"It could be, at least it could be for me. I can't guarantee it would turn out the same for you."

"Let me get this straight. Are you offering to continue my employment in new surroundings?"

"I am."

"Where we headed to?"

Michael took another deep breath before answering, "Deliverance."

"Deliverance?" Johnny laughed. "What in hell's Deliverance?"

Michael stared at him, then found himself smiling. "Maybe just what the name implies. Are you game?"

"Is this all you're gonna tell me about it?"

"For the time being, it's all I know to tell you. But if you agree to go with me while I find out, I promise I won't try to keep you with me, if it turns out not to be for you."

Johnny thought about Michael's enigmatic statement for

several minutes. He *did* like the man, and he *wasn't* that hung up on Los Angeles, and Michael really didn't have anyone else. . . . "Oh, what the hell." He grinned. "I'll start packing."

With grateful eyes, Michael watched him leave the room. For the first time, he felt he could really do it.

"By God," he said out loud, "I *will* do it."

Chapter 17

Carol had spent an anxious morning awaiting Jessica's return to the office after her trip. She hadn't known what to expect but Jessica greeted her as usual and suggested they get right to work. And now, two hours into the day, while Carol was concentrating on what Jessica was dictating, her mind was racing with questions she felt she could not ask. She sensed something was amiss—Jessica had not said a word about what had finally convinced her to make the trip, and Carol's curiosity was working overtime.

Jessica looked marvelous, more relaxed than she had in ages. She glowed with vitality. Carol recognized the excitement of the Amalgamated search assignment; what Jessica had dictated to her represented a tremendous retainer fee. Yet there seemed to be something more. Nothing she could put her finger on, but Carol knew Jessica well, and *something* was different. Whatever it was, Jessica looked great, and if something wonderful had happened while she was in New York, hallelujah!

"Carol," Jessica asked, "why on earth are you staring at me like that?"

"Sorry, boss. You just look different—rested. I didn't

think anyone could come back from a hectic week in the Big Apple and look that good."

Jessica smiled. "Do I look rested? Thank you for saying so. It *was* a hectic week, but exciting as well. A great deal was accomplished. . . ." Her voice trailed off and she looked past Carol, her eyes remote, ". . . a great deal."

Something was definitely up. "Well, even though I hounded you to go, I'm certainly glad you're back."

Jessica smiled fondly. "Carol, you didn't hound me. You were right to insist I make the trip."

"Given the circumstances, I won't say it was my pleasure. But I'm glad if it helped—you can call on me anytime."

"Thanks, Carol. I know that and I won't forget it. Now tell me, what's been going on?" Jessica was glad that Carol nodded her head and did not try to pursue the conversation. Jessica wasn't ready to talk about everything, not yet.

"Plenty! I know your clients are loyal to you, but whew, talk about dependent! You'd have thought the world was coming to an end just because you were away for a week. Although I think it does them good to have to wait for you."

"Mmmm, music to my ears. But you've handled everything beautifully, as usual." Jessica glanced at her watch. "And I've been working you to death for two hours. I'm sure you could use a break."

"No sweat, boss. It feels good to be back in action. Anyway, we've nearly caught up. The only thing left to schedule is a meeting with Eric Radner. He had the biggest fit of all when I told him you'd be away for a week."

"I wonder what's going on?" Jessica mused. "Eric is usually very much in control. Did he mention trouble at Radner Enterprises?"

"No. In fact, he didn't sound upset exactly, more like he was excited. As if something very big was going to happen and couldn't until he talked to you."

"Well," Jessica said, glancing at her appointment book. "My calendar is clear for tomorrow. I'll call him and set something up. With Eric Radner, you never know what to expect."

"Then that covers it." Carol closed her steno pad and

prepared to return to her office. "Things really went pretty well while you were away. Even Jim Steiner is shaping up. He's actually got two interviews scheduled with the Brandon firm."

"Wonderful. I knew he had the makings of a good recruiter. He just needs a little seasoning." As Carol stood, Jessica asked, "What about Stacey, any problems there?"

Carol made a gesture of helplessness before saying, "Nothing major. Oh, she's being impossible about her new assistant. I got lots of resumés in, but she keeps adding more and more requisites to the qualifications. I have a few interviews scheduled and one candidate should be interesting as hell. . . ." Carol laughed. "A man answered the ad. Can you imagine a man taking orders from Stacey?"

"Good God, no!" Jessica said. "That would never work out, never."

"That's what I thought." Carol shrugged. "But Stacey wants to interview him and he wants to be interviewed. What should I do?"

Jessica laughed. There was no end to Stacey's nonsense. In every other way she was a thoroughly professional recruiter, but she seemed unable to resist making problems. "Schedule him, Carol. Ten to one he'll be the person she insists be hired. But it will never work out."

"None of them ever work anyway, boss. So I guess it doesn't matter." Carol headed for the door, then stopped casually. "Since we're all caught up, tell me about New York. How was everything?" She leaned her back against the door, waiting. And her antennae rose as she saw a slight, almost undetectable change in Jessica's expression: a sudden darkening of the eyes, a subtle shift in her position.

"Oh," she replied, "you know New York, Carol."

She hadn't imagined it. Carol knew something was up.

"The city itself is always exhilarating after laid-back L.A.," Jessica continued. "John Adams is still wonderful, considerate, demanding, decisive. I didn't see Marshall MacAbee—John felt it would be too much for him—but I did meet the new people at Amalgamated and I don't anticipate any trouble filling the slots." Her words came out in a rush.

"The two men I had lined up in New York will be interviewing this and next week and they are both extremely qualified and interested. The Middle Eastern thing will take a bit more doing, and I have to make it a priority. God knows people are jumpy about going over there in these times. I'll probably put Jim on it with me. An international assignment is always exciting and it might encourage him. It was a good trip really. I'm glad I went after all."

Carol sensed there was something Jessica still hadn't told her.

Jessica continued, almost as an afterthought. "Oh, I almost forgot. I ran into Jeremy Bronson. He was also staying at the Plaza. I was able to talk over the proposal with him."

As Jessica lit a cigarette, Carol felt something click inside her head. Something *had* happened in New York, and maybe that something was Jeremy Bronson. Carol could certainly understand it if it was. The one time she'd met him she'd nearly passed out. But Jeremy Bronson and Jessica? That would be a shocker. What about Michael? What the hell was going on? But then why the hell not? Jesus, Jessica was only human—God knew she could use some excitement in her life.

"Well, what did he say?" Carol asked, carefully masking her curiosity.

Jessica seemed to have drifted away. She looked at Carol with a question in her eyes. "I'm sorry, Carol, my mind must have wandered. What did who say?"

"Jeremy Bronson. What did he say about the proposal?" There! She hadn't imagined the flush that came to Jessica's face, nor the nervous way she crushed out her freshly lit cigarette.

"Oh, uh—well, I don't think there will be a problem." Jessica was practically stammering. "Jason Carlisle is reviewing it now. I, uhm, I think we'll get the relocation package and the salaries upgraded, but I don't think he'll budge on the academics. Jeremy actually seemed confident enough . . ." Her voice trailed off and suddenly, she didn't seem quite so radiant and rested anymore.

Carol wasn't going to push it. Her fierce loyalty to Jessica and her genuine concern for her happiness were more important than satisfying her meddling curiosity. "That's great, boss. Good old Murchinson is going to come through again."

As the door closed behind Carol, Jessica sat back in her chair and closed her eyes. She felt good. She felt somehow back in control of her life. New York had been exactly the respite she'd needed. Jeremy's strength and understanding had enabled her to believe she could be happy again.

Chapter 18

David Clarendon grimaced as the aspirin melted against his tongue and threatened to lodge somewhere in his throat. He could never remember to fill the water carafe on his desk, and thanks to women's lib he could no longer ask a secretary to perform such a menial task. He tried to squeeze forth enough saliva to keep from choking and massaged the sides of his temples to move the pain around. His headache had been pounding for hours, and now Mack Johnson was on the phone, mad as hell and not letting David get a word in edgewise.

Damn it anyway, he'd worked his tail off on that assignment and had actually celebrated when he'd successfully filled the position with Dr. Sol Bernstein. It had been a big fat fee and now it looked as if he'd have to earn it twice.

But first he would stall for time, talk to Jessica about it, see if they were really obligated under these circumstances. He knew the "office telegraph," as he privately referred to Carol, had informed Jessica of a potential problem. Jessica would expect him to approach her for a possible solution. But in the meantime, he had to calm Mack Johnson down.

"Listen, Mack," he said into the receiver, "I hear what

you're saying, even though it's damned hard to believe. I mean, it's just weird, you know?"

Mack continued his harangue on the other end of the line as if David hadn't said a word, and David found his own patience wearing thin as he cut in. "Of course I checked him out thoroughly. Jesus, man, you know the position he held at Chem-Tran. Getting him to leave and move to Chicago was a coup. And Chem-Tran practically has a contract out on my life for stealing him. I tell you there wasn't a hint of instability about Dr. Bernstein."

The answering voice of Mack Johnson was a roar, causing David to hold the phone away from his ear for a moment. "Mack, I am *not* trying to cop out! Hell, Martin Management has served World Vision Pharmaceuticals for two years, I'm not going to let you down. I only brought up Chem-Tran because of how well they thought of him." He closed his eyes, trying to force the pain away, saying, "I met with him myself at great length. What you're telling me just doesn't add up. Okay?" He waited for assurance from the other end of the line. "Good, I'm sure there is a logical explanation, I just have to find out what it is. I'll be back in touch with you the minute I have something."

David quickly hung up the phone and headed for Jessica's office.

"David, how are you? I'm sorry I haven't been in to see you yet. I haven't been in to see anyone yet. I just finished dictation with Carol."

David took the chair in front of the fireplace, pulled out his ever-filled pipe, and lit up, knowing Jessica wouldn't mind. "You're looking very well, Jessica. The trip to New York must have been successful."

"Very, but I'm glad to be back. Now tell me, how are things in the medical division. How are you?"

"Worried," he replied. "Worried and confused. We've got a real weird one on our hands this time, and I'm not sure what our obligation is."

Jessica wasn't certain of her feelings about David Clarendon. He was an excellent recruiter, and well respected in the field of industrial medicine. But as a person, he was somewhat self-centered and extremely impatient. David liked to take the easy route whenever possible. Not such a terrible trait, Jessica had to admit, but still a trait she found somehow unattractive. She shrugged off her speculations. "What's wrong?"

"Do you remember about eight months ago I placed Dr. Sol Bernstein at World Vision Pharmaceuticals?"

Jessica's stomach tightened involuntarily. Just the mention of World Vision always brought back that feeling of guilt. But she steeled herself, determined not to lapse back into old memories. "Yes, of course," she replied quickly. "He's a toxicologist, isn't he?"

"Right, and one of the most respected in his field. He's also our problem."

"What's his complaint? As I recall it was a pretty hefty fee, so the salary must have been good. Doesn't he like Chicago?"

"Evidently not! It seems that Dr. Bernstein has disappeared."

"Disappeared?" Jessica asked in amazement. "You don't mean literally disappeared?"

"So it would seem. I just got off the phone with Mack Johnson, head of medical recruitment for World Vision. Anyway," he went on, "it seems that Dr. Bernstein has been acting pretty weird of late. Not turning in reports, not available, that sort of thing. Then last week he just didn't turn up at all."

"I know this is a stupid question, David, but have they talked to his wife? Someone in the family?"

"Not such a stupid question. I asked Mack the same thing. Seems the family disappeared right along with him. When Mack couldn't get an answer by telephone, he sent a letter by messenger. The apartment manager said he hadn't seen them for a week."

"What did Mack do next?"

"Well, nothing actually, because the apartment manager called the office as Mack had asked him to do if Dr. Bernstein showed up. Well, he didn't show up, and the apartment

117

manager became suspicious, so he went into the apartment with a passkey." David paused and let out a rush of breath before continuing. "The apartment was completely cleaned out. It was a furnished place; they still hadn't found a house they wanted to buy. All their clothes and personal belongings were gone. They left without a trace, not even a forwarding address."

"But that's bizarre!" Jessica said. "A whole family just up and disappears? Has Mack notified the police?"

"No, he hasn't. And he doesn't intend to. After all, the rent on the apartment was paid up, Bernstein didn't exactly skip town, and besides, Mack doesn't want to get involved—doesn't want World Vision involved. He figures that's up to us. Or at least it's up to us to contact other relatives if we can locate some. Let them file a missing-persons report. What Mack wants is another toxicologist. He thinks I sold him a real looney-tunes."

Jessica remained silent, trying to digest the information. Nothing like this had ever happened to her before. Of course they would have to do something. "Well," she said, "I'm sure there is a rational explanation for this. Unless he really did go off the deep end—but that seems unlikely. I mean, why would his whole family disappear?" She frowned. "Something doesn't smell right."

"Yeah, my commission check, that's what doesn't smell right. That job was a tough slot to fill. I had to work my buns off on it."

"You know you don't have to worry about your commission," she reassured him. "We never refund fees. But you will have to replace him. Our guarantee is for one year, whatever the reason for termination or resignation." She thought for a moment. "I assume he's officially off the payroll?"

"Yep," David replied. "As of today. He has some money coming and they will hold it in escrow until we find him." David's confusion showed in his voice as he asked, "What should I do about Bernstein? I'd swear he was as mentally sound as the dollar used to be. Do you think I should try to track down a relative?"

"By all means," Jessica responded. "I think we're obligated to find out where he went and why. It will be important in replacing him—we need to know the facts. Do you have any ideas?"

"I seem to recall he mentioned a brother who is also a physician. A sole practitioner somewhere in Arizona, I think. Shouldn't be too hard to find him. I'll get on it first thing tomorrow."

Jessica nodded. "Good. And again, I'm certain there will be some explanation to satisfy Mack Johnson that you did your job properly—there has to be."

David rose and headed for the door. He turned back to smile at Jessica. "I sure in hell hope so. You know how hard I worked to convince Mack Johnson I'm the wunderkind of medical recruiters. I'd hate like hell to blow it because of some nut."

Jessica stared into space after David left the office. What a strange thing. Was World Vision a curse to everyone? Why on earth would a respected scientist simply disappear like that? Well, nothing could be done until David did some groundwork. It would take a few days. She prayed that nothing terrible had happened to the Bernsteins, and decided to talk about it with Michael. He adored mysteries and it would be something to break the ice with, take the immediate strain off her homecoming. She had come directly to her office from the airport and had not yet spoken to Michael.

Chapter 19

The moment she stepped through the front door, Jessica sensed a stillness in the house, as if it had been vacant for a long time. She felt rooted to the parquet flooring in the entry hall, her luggage resting at her feet. She tried to call out Michael's name, but it stuck in her throat. She knew he wasn't there. She didn't know how she knew, but she *knew*, and her heart began to race.

The den door was closed. Her ears strained, but there was nothing but silence. She took a tentative step forward, then veered toward her bedroom. She would shower and change—Michael wasn't gone, the den door was closed because he was working on something. Of course, that was it; he was working. She turned back, retrieved her luggage, and walked resolutely to her bedroom door. It opened silently. Everything was in place.

She undressed with deliberation and took an extra-long shower. Donning a caftan she reentered her bedroom and spied the suitcase resting as she had left it on the bed. She moved forward and unfastened the catches. Carefully she removed the clothing and placed it in the closet, her movements slow and deliberate.

Finally, everything unpacked, she walked to the bedroom door and out into the center hallway. The stillness remained heavy in the air. She took a deep breath and forced herself to walk to the den doorway. Her hand was trembling when she grasped the brass knob. She turned it slowly. The door swung open. She let out a little moan.

It was all gone. Everything of Michael's had been removed. His books, the design awards, his drafting equipment.

She saw the envelope, propped against the telephone on the cleared desktop. She turned away sharply and headed for the bar in the living room. Taking a brandy snifter from the shelf, she poured a hefty amount of brandy into it, spilling a few drops on the marble countertop. Then she turned and went back to the den, picked up the envelope, and sat down in the Eames chair.

She stared at her name scrawled across the face of the envelope, Michael's bold handwriting a neon beacon. She sipped at the brandy, turning the envelope over, then returning it face up, staring blankly at her name. She knew she had to open it, had to know what the thick, pale gray linen stock contained.

She rose from the chair and placed the envelope back against the telephone, adjusting it so that it would be in the exact same position in which she had found it. She lit a cigarette and left the den.

She walked from one room of the house to another. There was no trace of Michael anywhere. She stepped into his bedroom, and although she knew what she would find, she opened his closet doors—empty. She walked into his dressing room. Something in the corner caught her eye and she bent down to retrieve a single crumpled sock, obviously missed in the haste of packing. She stared at it: a sock, one lone crumpled sock, all that was left of twelve years.

She fled, clutching the sock in her hand, and returned to the den. Gingerly she lifted the envelope from the desktop and resumed her seat, smoothing the crumpled sock across her lap. She slid a fingernail under the back flap, grateful for the small delay caused by the tight seal of the glue. Slowly she pulled out the crisply folded linen pages and opened the folds to the top page and Michael's familiar greeting:

My dearest Jessica,

I pray this is the last cowardly act I ever commit. To face you with what I have to say in this letter would have required more courage than I possess.

By now you understand why I had to treat you so cruelly. I had to stun you into shock to get you to take that first step, but you must know it was done out of love for you and for what we once had. Love that will always be in my heart and soul. I pray you will understand that as well.

Darling Jessica. How terrible I feel to know your misplaced sense of guilt kept you in a lifeless marriage, in which I couldn't even offer you warmth and companionship. How I regret that I didn't recognize the source of your torment and free you from it. I am no longer a whole man—a condition I finally know I must accept. I can only do that alone. It may still smack of self-indulgence, but that's the truth of it. I must learn to accept my limitations and I must do it on my own. I cannot bear the continued look of hope in your eyes—a hope that can never be realized.

I don't know if I will ever design again, Jessica. All the love I had for it seems part of another life, which in a sense, it was. We've been together long enough for you to know I can't do anything halfway. Just designing a building and not getting physically involved with it seems unbearable to me. Like a fighting marine assigned to a desk job in Washington. I've never been able to be a spectator, not in my work and not in my life. And I can't bear seeing you live as a mere spectator in your own life. You must *live* your life, Jessica, live it! It's too precious, and as everyone knows, far too short.

We shared wonderful years, Jessica. But that life is gone now and we can never bring it back. I will treasure what we had as long as I live.

Please, Jessica, accept it now as that—a wonderful,

glorious memory. If my future happiness is important to you, and I know in my heart that it is, please find someone new. Find a strong, loving man to share your life. Go to him freely, without guilt, without looking back. Don't ever look back.

I'm going away, Jessica. It's something I have to do, something that is right for me if I am ever to get on with the business of living. And after the initial hurt, you will see that it is right for you as well.

Don't fear for me, Jessica. I'm not going to do myself any harm. I wrestled with those demons long ago and found myself far too cowardly for such an act. I'm not yet sure of my plans, but I am going to search for something to do, something that will give my life, as I must now lead it, some meaning.

Please don't try to find me. I have made financial arrangements; you will be able to draw on our funds without limitations.

Once I've found what I want to do with the rest of my life, after enough time has passed for this terrible pain to subside and for your new life to have begun, I'll let you know where I am.

Johnny Bridges is going with me and Ben Hobard will be able to reach me should any emergency occur, but please don't pressure him for my whereabouts as it is a heavy burden I have asked him to carry out of friendship. When next you and I speak, it will be as two wonderful old friends.

Letting go will be very hard for both of us. But please, we both must, and finally, I have. Be happy, my darling, be successful, be alive.

Thank you for all of the laughter, forgive me for all of the tears.

> Love and farewell for now,
> Michael

Jessica sat very still, straightening the creases in the crumpled sock. The silence of the empty house roared in her ears.

Chapter 20

Sol Bernstein drew his finger through the ring of moisture his glass had deposited on the bar top. His brow creased in a concentrated frown, and he startled as Paul Mellon slapped him across the shoulders.

"Why so deep in thought, Sol? You look like you're a million miles from here."

Sol turned to the regulatory attorney for World Vision Pharmaceuticals and made an effort to return his smile. "Hello, Paul. No, don't sit down. Let's get a booth where we can talk."

Paul's eyebrows inched upward. "Sounds serious, Sol," he said playfully. "But okay, I have a little pull in here. I'll get us a nice table while you settle your bar tab."

Paul walked away toward the hostess as Sol placed money on the bar, then followed him toward the back of the cocktail lounge where the hostess waited to seat them.

Once their drink orders were taken, Paul leaned forward. "Now, what's up?" he asked. "Got trouble at home? Listen, it's always tough on the little woman when she's been moved across country. She's probably still a little lonely—why don't I have my wife give her a call and—"

Sol interrupted him in a voice heavy with concern. "There's no trouble at home, Paul. But there is trouble at World Vision. That's why I asked you to meet me."

The waitress arrived with their drinks, and Sol motioned for silence until they'd been served and she was out of earshot.

Paul took a small taste of his drink, then said, "You sound pretty ominous, Sol. What the hell's up?"

"My dander for one thing." Sol paused for a moment, then took a deep breath and said, "Paul, World Vision has falsified test results on the two new drugs Analil-2 and Baromide-7."

There was the briefest of pauses as Paul shook his head from side to side, a smile on his face. "Sol, I think you've flipped your cookies. World Vision wouldn't do a thing like that." He set down his drink before going on. "I reviewed the documents that went to the FDA myself. I saw all the test results. There was some trouble during the initial research and development stages, but those kinks were worked out." Before Sol could interrupt, Paul said quickly, "You're mistaken. Those drugs are the greatest thing to hit the market in years. They'll not only help a lot of people, but with our stock options, they're going to make us rich. So relax and enjoy your drink."

Sol sighed. Paul Mellon was not one of his favorite people at World Vision—too much the 'slap 'em on the back' salesman type. But he *was* a regulatory attorney, and Sol had to make him aware of what was going on and get his advice on how to handle it. "Paul, I am not mistaken. I have the proof. Those drugs will have severe, long-range toxic effects."

The smile on Paul Mellon's face vanished and his normally perky tone was suddenly lawyer-serious. "What kind of proof do you have, Sol? And where did you get it?"

At last, Sol thought, the man was going to take him seriously. "All the research done in the labs is fed into a master computer for storage and retrieval. But it seems my predecessor, Dr. Abrahams, kept a private file of his own. I came upon it quite by accident when I was looking for a particular textbook. The file was hidden behind a row of medical books." Sol took a sip of his drink. "I think he meant for me to find it."

"Rubbish!" Paul shook his head. "How could he? He died of a sudden heart attack—how could he have known he wouldn't be with World Vision?"

Sol rubbed his forehead wearily. Maybe he was being overly dramatic. What Paul was saying made sense. "Okay, I suppose you're right about that, Paul. Perhaps he didn't intend for me to find it. But that doesn't alter the fact the file does exist. And that it proves those drugs *cannot* be released on the market."

Mellon shook his head emphatically. He wasn't going to buy it. "Sol, we've waited years for the FDA clearance on those two drugs. They've been tested, retested, and tested again. On animals, on humans. We even did the placebo tests. There were no problems of any kind," he finished conclusively. "The drugs are effective and safe."

Sol leaned toward Paul urgently, saying, "Paul, naturally I don't expect you to believe me without proof. And you may not even understand that proof when you see it. Toxicology is pretty complex stuff; it might mean as little to you as a legal brief would to me. But I'll put it into lay terms for you, okay?"

Mellon nodded in reluctant agreement.

"The test results *you* saw were correct," Sol began. "There were no toxic effects on the studies using guinea pigs and rats. And there were no adverse effects on the humans who agreed to try the drugs. But, and here's the whole thing, if the humans actually got the drugs and weren't given straight placebos, the toxic effects wouldn't show up for several years, possibly not until the next generation, like the DES situation."

Sol paused for a moment to let Mellon digest the information. Then he quickly continued, "So the information you reviewed before submitting it to the FDA was all correct. But you didn't get to review *all* the information because it wasn't included." He tried to keep the panic out of his voice as he said, "Paul, Dr. Abraham's file shows severe toxic effects were evident in the testing of the drugs on larger animals—rabbits and dogs. And those effects were extremely hazardous."

Mellon was becoming quite nervous. He signaled the waitress for another round of drinks, although Sol had scarcely touched his. He waited until they were served, then spoke in a voice now strained and cautious. "What were those toxic effects, Sol? How were they manifested in the rabbits and dogs?"

Sol experienced the tiniest feeling of relief. At least Mellon was listening, paying attention. "Analil-2 can cause ulceration under the skin. In rabbits and dogs it ate downward to the bone, causing irreversible calcium and marrow loss. Baromide-7 will be life-threatening to diabetics, especially undiagnosed diabetics. There is a lot more, but it's very scientific and would take too long to explain. Just believe me, the proof is in the file. I don't mean to talk down to you, Paul, I only want to save time. The next step is up to you."

"What do you mean, up to me?" Mellon's voice raised slightly, but he quickly lowered it. "I don't have anything to do with this."

"What do I mean?" Sol repeated, thunderstruck. "Of course you have something to do with it. You're a regulatory attorney for World Vision. You have to give me direction. I don't know who to go to first."

"Well, you don't go to me! In fact, I'm damned pissed that I let you tell me this much!" Paul snapped, his face a study in anger and exasperation. "I don't want any part of this whole damned thing. And you'd better do some serious thinking about your own involvement in it."

Sol Bernstein couldn't believe what he was hearing. Ever since he'd realized the truth about the two drugs, to his way of thinking he'd had no choice but to bring the facts to light. He'd counted on Paul Mellon's help, and now here was Mellon turning his back. "Paul," he implored, "perhaps you don't fully realize the importance—the seriousness—of the situation. Those drugs are dangerous! You *have* to get involved. I don't know who falsified the information to the

FDA, but now the bureau must be informed. World Vision has to voluntarily withdraw the drugs for further testing. As an attorney—"

"As an attorney," Paul interjected harshly, "I've learned to mind my own business, and I'd advise you to do the same. There are millions of dollars involved here, Sol, millions and millions. Drop this thing—drop it right now!"

"Drop it?" Sol said, the disbelief evident in his voice. "I can't drop it! And neither can you. We're talking about people's lives here. Whoever is guilty of falsifying the results will have to face the consequences. But good God, man, we can't let it happen. We have to do something!"

Paul took a long pull on his drink. He looked long and hard at the man sitting opposite him. The damned fool was thinking like a scientist, probably reciting the Hippocratic oath inside his head that very minute. What the hell did he know about the real world? He'd spent his whole damned life in some basement laboratory. Well, it was time Sol Bernstein came out of the lab and into the real world.

"Sol," Paul began in a quiet, intense voice. "You'd better start learning the facts of life. You say with scientific innocence that the 'guilty party' will simply have to face the consequences." He paused, then added, "Sol, who is the guilty party?"

Sol could only stare at him in silence. He had no idea who was actually guilty.

Mellon leaned back against the booth, striking a lawyerly pose, his voice now calm and confident. "I think you are beginning to get my message. If what you say is true, more than one person is involved. This is big, big business, Sol— and these are the big, big boys." He paused again, then using his best fatherly manner said, "You don't want to take them on, trust me. What you want to do is forget all about this. Just do your job and keep your mouth shut. That is my advice to you."

"But I can't do that! These drugs can kill! I've told you, these are people's lives we're talking about!"

"And it's your life and mine I'm talking about." He lowered his voice. "Ever hear of the corporate Mafia, Sol?"

Sol shook his head, his eyes large with shock.

Paul continued, "Well, there is such an animal—and I'm telling you, you don't want to mess with it. Now, what you do is destroy that file and leave those people's lives up to the Lord, if you believe in him."

Sol simply could not accept what he was hearing. Corporate Mafia? Was Paul serious? "Paul, you sound threatening. What are you really trying to tell me?"

"I'm trying to tell you exactly what you think I'm telling you. If the file is correct, then believe me, the fix goes all the way to the FDA." He waited for this information to sink in, then continued, "Now, do we forget all about this?"

"I can't," Sol said helplessly. "I'm a doctor! I can't allow this to happen. And you're an attorney—you have an obligation to—"

"I have an obligation to survive. For my wife, my kids, and for myself. And you have the same obligation!"

Sol shook his head sadly. "I'm afraid I can't live that way—I just can't."

"Okay," Mellon said, finality in his tone. "It's your funeral. But don't try to involve me. I'll swear I never had this conversation with you. I'll swear I never heard about any file—I'll make you look like a crazy, overzealous scientist. I'll do whatever is necessary if you get me into this thing. I mean it, Sol!"

Sol was incredulous. "You mean to say you'd go on working at World Vision knowing what they're trying to get away with?"

"I would if I felt personally safe," Paul responded, "but thanks to your little revelation, I don't feel safe any longer, not knowing about something this volatile." Paul finished off his drink before adding, "I'll be resigning as soon as possible. As a matter of fact, I'll relocate to another state. I want no further dealing with you or World Vision. It's too hot to handle."

Paul stood up from the table and watched Sol put his head in his hands. Placing a bill on the table, he said quietly, "You'd better think about what I've said, Sol. It isn't too late. Think about it long and hard. You're on your own, you know—there won't be anyone to back you up. Destroy that file while you still can."

With that, he turned and headed out of the cocktail lounge, leaving Sol seated before his untouched second drink.

Sol's mind raced with possible scenarios, none of them pleasant. He sighed, sat upright again, and took a long swallow of his now-watery drink. Well, he thought, Mellon hadn't solved his problem. Jesus, Paul Mellon was frightened enough to resign from a good job—he had to have meant what he'd said to Sol.

He was doubly glad now that he'd chosen to disappear from work. If the company lawyer turned his back on the situation, what could Sol expect from the higher-ups? What was he going to do? He was becoming more and more alarmed himself. He couldn't keep his wife and kids holed up in the small motel on the outskirts of Chicago any longer—they had to go somewhere, and they could never be told of the information Sol had discovered. If he was in danger, he would at least see to it that they were not jeopardized.

He rubbed his hand across his forehead, trying to ease the sudden throbbing pain in his temples. He had one more avenue open to him for help—at least for some temporary type of help.

Chapter 21

It had been three days since Jessica had returned home to find Michael gone. She felt weary to her very bones, work being the only thing keeping her from falling completely apart. She hadn't told anyone about Michael leaving her—she couldn't talk about it. She made excuses for her tiredness as a low-grade virus. Everyone seemed to accept it except Carol. She could see the doubt in Carol's eyes, but blessed her for not pushing it.

Jessica was attempting to finish all her calls before her meeting with Eric Radner. She was way behind schedule and it was with annoyance she heard a knock on her office door.

There was no time to spare this morning. But when David Clarendon entered, the look on his face told her she'd have to make the time.

"You don't look as if you have good news for me, David," she said tiredly.

David sat down and lit his pipe before answering. His methodical mannerisms, usually comforting to Jessica, were annoying today. She had so damned much to do.

Finally comfortable, David spoke. "No, I do not have

good news, Jessica. As a matter of fact, you're not going to like what I have to say at all."

"I gather you reached Dr. Bernstein's brother?"

"No. I didn't have a chance. Dr. Bernstein reached me."

Jessica exhaled with relief. "So far what you're saying is reassuring. He's all right, then?"

"For the time being. But the proverbial you-know-what is going to hit the fan. That is, unless you can think of some way to put a lid on it." He paused for a moment, then said, "I think you'd better have Carol put your calls on hold for a bit, Jessica."

Something in his tone made her very alert. Not questioning him, she buzzed Carol to hold all calls. David was a calm man and if something had happened to rattle him, it must be important.

"Okay, David, I'm all ears," she said as she sat back in her chair and gave him her full attention. "Where is Dr. Bernstein and what did he say?"

"Where he is is still a mystery," David began. "I don't know where he was calling from and as of now he doesn't intend to say. He wants our assurance that we're going to help him."

"Is he in some sort of trouble?"

"He thinks so," David replied. "He thinks he's in big trouble."

Jessica sighed. She was in no mood for melodramatics, and David had an annoying habit of dragging things out.

"David, get to the point. What trouble? And why is Dr. Bernstein being so secretive?"

David took a deep drag on his pipe before plunging in. As he began to relate the events as he knew them, Jessica became more and more amazed. What David was telling her didn't seem possible. It was like a bad movie.

"David," she interrupted, "has Dr. Bernstein checked out any of these allegations with his predecessor?"

"He can't," David replied. "The reason the job opened up was Dr. Abrahams died of a sudden massive coronary."

"Your tone sounds ominous, David." Jessica frowned.

"I'm only using the same tone Sol used with me," David sighed. He began pacing the room, filling in the blanks as best he could remember.

Jessica shook her head, unable to accept what she was hearing.

David stopped pacing and took a seat on the couch. His voice was tired as he continued, "Anyway, before Sol pulled out, he checked with new products and the packaging department. The campaign for the drugs is already under way. The regulatory attorney resigned without notice, made some excuse about a family emergency."

"Does Dr. Bernstein have possession of the file?"

"Yes," David answered. "He felt he had to take it for his own protection. World Vision doesn't know it exists."

"Well, that was clever of him," Jessica said. "He'll need it when he goes to the authorities."

There was a pause and then David said, "He's not going to the authorities. He's frightened—all he wants is out. That's why he called us. He wants our help."

Jessica was silent, her mind racing, trying to find some means of solving Sol Bernstein's problem. But what could she do to help?

David interrupted her thoughts with, "Jessica, Sol doesn't think the company attorney was kidding about Mafia involvement with the company. He's taking it very seriously. He's got four kids and a wife to think about and what they think right now is that he's gone looney. He didn't tell them about the file because he is afraid for them."

Jessica was startled at the mention of the Mafia. It was too frightening even to contemplate. "But, David," she protested, "Sol Bernstein is a scientist, a dedicated man, from what you've said. If those drugs are released on the market—it's unthinkable. He *must* go to the authorities. How else can he live with himself?"

David shrugged. "All in one piece, I guess. You tell *him* to go to the authorities. Tell *me* how we're going to handle this."

Jessica thought for a long moment before replying. "Dr.

Bernstein has every right to be upset. The mere thought of falsifying test information that could do physical damage to human beings is too horrible to consider." She frowned. "But not reporting it because of supposed Mafia involvement in World Vision is totally unacceptable."

David frowned. "Sol sure as hell doesn't think so. The mob is into legitimate business—why not pharmaceuticals? It's a perfect cover for drug traffic. Who really knows what's in those colorful little vials produced overseas? Customs inspectors can't open every shipment," he finished.

Jessica laughed a little hollowly. "You're beginning to sound as paranoid as Dr. Bernstein, David." She paused, then said, "Look, I'll talk with him. Somehow we have to convince him to tell the FDA; we can't be a party to this knowledge and do nothing."

"Whoa, Jessica," David responded firmly. "Maybe *you* can't sit back and do nothing, but I sure as hell can! I'm a recruiter, not Ralph Nader. Sol didn't sound all that paranoid to me. And what World Vision does is their business. I want no part of it. Like Sol's friend the attorney, I've already forgotten the conversation."

David studied Jessica for a long moment before continuing. She returned his gaze with the expression of someone firmly convinced of being in the right.

"Jessica," David asked softly, "think for a minute. Do you really want to take responsibility for this? Say you do convince Sol—say he spills the beans. Are you willing to accept what could happen? Another sudden massive coronary? Dr. Abrahams had no record of heart trouble, he . . ." David's voice trailed off.

Jessica remained silent.

"You know how these things work," David continued confidently. "It could take years before any side effects manifest themselves. The company knows that. And they also know just how many millions of dollars will flow in before any suspicion arises." David tapped his pipe on the edge of a marble ashtray. "Then come the lawsuits, the appeals. Hell, Jessica, they probably know down to the last day how long they have before detection. And even if they are caught, the appeals process takes years. Even then, no victim will ever be awarded anywhere near the amount of profit the company will have made on the drugs."

There was continued silence from Jessica as she gazed accusingly into his eyes. David sighed deeply. Jessica Martin was one stubborn woman, and he'd worked for Martin Management long enough to know about her principles.

"Well," he said finally, "you can be a one-woman crusade, but as far as I'm concerned, I've never heard of Sol Bernstein or World Vision."

"Are you serious, David?" Jessica broke her silence. "Are you that much of a coward?"

His eyes crinkled in amusement; David Clarendon didn't insult easily. He rolled with the punches and usually came out a winner.

"I'm that much of a survivor," he answered. "Look, I don't appreciate Bernstein making me privy to this information any more than the attorney did. In fact, aside from the fact he was a little hysterical, I can't imagine why he told me anything! All he had to do was tell me he wanted out of World Vision. He isn't acting rationally, and I don't want any part of it. I'd like a leave of absence, Jessica, until this thing blows over."

Jessica's eyes turned cold. Her disgust and disappointment were stamped on her features. "And you'd do that, David? Take a leave of absence, abandon Dr. Bernstein, and dump the whole thing in my lap? I think you'd better make that leave of absence a permanent one."

"Now it's my turn," he said. "Aren't you overreacting? Maybe this low-grade virus you have is making you unreasonable. You know how easily I can get a job with another search firm." He smiled. "How easily can you replace me as a recruiter?"

"A lot easier than I could work with you when I've lost respect for you."

The smile remained on David's face as he moved closer to her desk. He felt no rancor; he was a realist, Jessica was not.

Simple as that. He reached into his pants pocket, extracted a key ring, and removed the first key, placing it on her desk.

"As you like, Jessica. Here's my key to your kingdom. I'll just clear out some personal things and be on my way."

David walked to the door, turning back to say, "You should think about this, Jessica. This is above and beyond the call of duty. There's no way you can help the man, and you needn't get involved. But if you are determined, have Carol transfer his next call to you. I'll leave the hardcover file of his background on my desk. His master file is in the computer."

Still smiling, he opened the door and left the office.

Jessica sighed and impatiently tapped out a cigarette from the pack. As she lit it she thought, what the hell am I going to do? If she couldn't convince Sol Bernstein to go to the authorities, should she go herself? Report what Sol had told David? But then, David would deny any knowledge of it, as would the regulatory attorney. And there was the damnable aspect of confidentiality. Without Sol Bernstein's okay, she couldn't repeat a word of what he'd said to anyone.

She had no idea what her next move should be, and she wasn't given further time to think about it. Carol buzzed, announcing that Eric Radner had arrived for their meeting.

Chapter 22

Stacey paced angrily back and forth in her office, a frown marring her beautiful face. Things simply were not moving at the pace she had counted on. Eric Radner was so caught up in his baseball team negotiations he was paying less and less attention to her, and she seemed no closer to getting him to ask her to marry him than she had been several months before. Her anger boiled as she thought of the meeting going on between Jessica and Eric this very minute. Stacey knew the nature of the conversation; it was, after all, information he'd given her in the privacy of her own bedroom. Still, she hated the thought that Jessica would receive such an enormous retainer fee for recruiting executives to take over Radner Enterprises. Stacey already thought of Radner's money as her own, and the thought of Jessica getting one cent galled her. But then, she tried unsuccessfully to console herself, she would get it all back when she put Jessica Martin out of business. These things didn't happen all that fast.

Stacey's hatred of Jessica Martin was not personal. Jessica herself had never done anything to harm Stacey. It was what Jessica represented that Stacey hated: security, breeding, class, money, a husband. Jessica was safe. And Stacey was vulnerable, always had been vulnerable, her beauty and brains her only weapons against the cold, competitive world. She had no one, no family, no real friends, only her work and her determination to marry Eric Radner at any price. She had risen as high in the search business as she could on her ability alone. She needed backing to make the quantum leap to superstardom, and Eric Radner's money could help her make that leap. His money would make her safe.

Stacey didn't know who her father had been and her mother had never bothered to find out—just some casual date in some dingy bar. Stacey knew she had been born instead of aborted only as a means of additional welfare money with which to buy more booze. She'd had to bear the condescension of social workers and the kids at school who had nice clothes and good homes. Kids like Jessica must have been. Secure, safe, and loved. Above all, loved.

Secure people intimidated her in spite of the success she'd made of her career. People whose lives were full, who had loved ones and the respect of the community, brought back all the pain of her youth and erased any self-confidence she had achieved as an adult. Jessica Martin was a natural target for Stacey's frustrated wrath. Stacey knew in her gut that as a child Jessica had never suffered the humiliations that had been a daily part of Stacey's growing up.

She was certain Jessica had never sat in a crowded classroom, in a dress shoplifted from a Goodwill bin, bearing the laughter of the other children and the glare of the teacher as her young stomach growled loudly in protest of constant hunger. But Stacey had.

Damn, damn, damn. It was so unfair. Had always been so unfair. Stacey was as good as anyone. She had a right to have it all. And she was determined to get it! She had to speed up her plans, her time was getting short. Radner *had* to come around.

As Jessica accepted Eric Radner's outstretched hand, she once again experienced an odd feeling of discomfort. She couldn't exactly put her finger on it, but something about the man disquieted her. She mentally shrugged it off as only her personal reaction to his coarseness. Jessica could never quite understand why manners and class seemed incompatible in some self-made men.

"Eric," she said, "I'm delighted to see you. I'd have been happy to come to your office—this must be an imposition on a man as busy as yourself."

Eric lit a cigar and, uninvited, took a seat before the fireplace. Jessica took the chair opposite him, keeping her smile in place, although she winced at his words.

"No problem, little lady. I was in the neighborhood, as the saying goes."

"Well, I repeat, it's very nice to see you. It's been some time. How can I help you?"

A broad grin stretched out his slightly puffy face. For a moment all the hardness seemed to leave his eyes, and Jessica could barely wait to hear what had him as excited as a young boy.

"Jessica, I'm stepping down from Radner Enterprises. That is, I'm stepping down in a manner of speaking."

She couldn't keep the surprise from registering on her face. Radner Enterprises *was* Eric Radner. Had he told her the Russians had landed on Rodeo Drive, she could not have been more shocked.

His grin broadened and he continued, "Yeah, I know, it's a big surprise. But wait, there's a lot more. The reason I was able to come to your office today is because I was in Century City with my attorneys."

"Century City?" Again Jessica was surprised. Radner Enterprises had always been represented by Lawton, Foster, and Schaeffer, a downtown, old-line-conservative law firm. "Have I slipped up somewhere? Has the Lawton firm moved to the West Side?"

Eric laughed. "Boy, I gotta hand it to you, you're a real hot one. You keep track of everything, don't you?" He took a big puff of his cigar before saying, "No, the Lawton bunch haven't moved. And yes, they still represent Radner Enterprises. But for the deal I'm working on now, I needed a specialist—had to come to the West Side for that."

"You're being very mysterious, Eric. But I won't pry.

Suppose you tell me exactly what you mean by stepping down and how I can assist you?"

"Right, bottom-line time," Eric said decisively. "Jessica," he went on, "I want you to find me a man to head up Radner Enterprises in the States, and a man to handle our European operations. He'll be based in our London office."

Jessica sat forward in her chair. This was truly an astounding announcement—and a fabulous search assignment. She could barely believe what he was saying.

"Now, the kind of man I need for the States," Radner continued, "has to be a proven commodity. I don't want any rumors floating around that I'm in any kind of trouble, because I'm not. In fact, Radner Enterprises has been branching out considerably. We now not only have just about a legal monopoly on the manufacture of communications equipment, we are beginning to make a dent in the big boys' playground. I'm in negotiations right now for a major contract to supply certain parts and new technology to NASA. I don't have to tell you what a coup that would be—Lockheed is shivering in their boots. Yessir! Radner Enterprises is as sound as money in the bank. This new man has to be able to step right into my shoes, run Radner Enterprises under my direction, and be respected by the business world as a whole." Flicking some ash into a nearby tray, Radner said, "The man for Europe has to be tops too, we're making inroads abroad that even have the Japanese worried. The man I have there now is too limited in his thinking—can't see beyond his nose. I will remain Chairman of the Board. The new man will come on as President. The man for Europe will be Senior Vice-President in charge of European affairs."

Jessica found it hard to accept what she was hearing. "Just how much control will the new man have, Eric? You say he'll run Radner Enterprises under your direction. But the kind of man you're describing isn't likely to be a yes-man."

"A yes-man!" Radner snorted with contempt. "I haven't hired a yes-man in all my years of business. That's another reason I want you to get me a proven commodity. You're going to have to raid the giants of industry. I want Radner

Enterprises to run pretty much as it always has, but hell, I also want a man as smart as I am. I'm open to new ideas, new concepts. I'm not looking for a toady, I just want it understood that no major policy changes will occur without my prior consent."

Jessica was filled with curiosity. He hadn't even hinted at what had brought him to this decision. "Okay, Eric," she said, "I think I get the picture. What's your time frame?"

"I want you to move on this as soon as possible. Naturally I'll wait for the right man, but I'm anxious to get it settled." He puffed harder on the cigar. "Now, tell me what all this is going to cost me."

"Well," Jessica said coolly, in her element with this type of assignment, "you are a privately held company, so you'll have to come up with more in the way of a base salary to compensate for lack of stock options. I assume you still have no intention of going public?" At his emphatic nod, she continued, "I'd say you are looking at a six-hundred-thousand base, plus bonus and some sort of profit sharing. That's for the slot in the States. In Europe, you're looking at around three-hundred-thousand plus bonus, cost-of-living differential, which incidentally is appreciable in London, and again, some sort of profit sharing."

He was silent but Jessica was unfazed. She knew his financial worth and she knew further that he was a man who spent his money when it was necessary.

"You'll have to include the usual executive benefits," she continued. "Life insurance, club memberships, limousine, possibly a helicopter, and certainly an employment contract. The usual. Then figure my fee and expenses and you've got your cost."

He puffed silently on the cigar, mentally calculating the figures she'd given him—they coincided with his own. He grinned. "You've got yourself a search assignment, Jessica. And if you deliver fast, you can count on a healthy bonus."

"That's very generous, Eric," she said, "but you know I don't accept bonuses. I do my job and you pay me for it." She softened her tone. "But I do appreciate the thought."

"Okay." His grin had not lessened. "No bonus. But

maybe I can figure out something extra that you won't object to." His eyes glittered as he asked, "You a sports fan, Jessica?"

She cringed inside. She had been—God, what a sports fan—before the accident. When Michael could look at the healthy body of an athlete without hatred or envy, before he had—*before*—it seemed her private thoughts always began with the word *before*. She forced a smile to her lips. "Afraid not, Eric. Why do you ask?"

"I ask because I am now going to satisfy your curiosity." The words tumbled out happily. "Jessica, the reason I am stepping down at Radner Enterprises is because I'm buying a baseball team! And I figured as an extra bonus you might like a lifetime pass."

"Eric," Jessica said incredulously, "am I hearing you correctly? You're buying a baseball team? You mean like the Dodgers—the Yankees? A real baseball team?"

His enjoyment was etched on his face. Everyone reacted in the same manner. And no wonder. How many men could make that kind of statement? "You got it, sweetheart," he laughed. "A major-league baseball team. I want to have me some fun with the rest of my life. And I can't think of a better toy, can you?"

"I certainly can't," she replied. "Which team are you acquiring?"

"I'm not at liberty to say just yet. The lawyers in Century City are in the midst of negotiations right now. A real specialty firm; they only deal with sports and entertainment stuff. That's why the Lawton bunch couldn't handle this deal." He leaned back, satisfied, adding, "Mind you, this whole conversation has to be kept quiet."

"Of course, Eric," Jessica assured him. "I wouldn't dream of breaching your confidence. I'd like to congratulate you though. It's very exciting—what a challenge to start in a whole new field."

"Yeah, that's the way I figure it," he replied. "And speaking of that, maybe you'd better start getting interested in sports. You know, toy or not, baseball is big business. I'll probably be needing some key people there as well."

Jessica's head was reeling. With the two assignments he'd already given her, the fees would exceed two hundred and seventy thousand dollars. And that didn't include the fee based on the first-year bonus. And he was talking still more executives. She shivered with excitement. It wasn't the money, it was the acceptance, the accomplishment. Martin Management Consultants was in the big leagues. And since she was alone it was her anchor; it was quite simply, as Michael had said, all she had.

She smiled and said, "Consider your needs a number-one priority, Eric. I'll have Carol call your secretary; she can fill her in on what data I need to share with my candidates. And," she continued, "I'll need particular information on these new growth arenas—the new product lines, and so forth."

"I'll get a package together right away," he agreed. He rose and offered his hand to seal their agreement. Jessica took it and smiled as he said, "Don't forget, Jessica. This is top-secret information. I can't have anything leak while I'm negotiating. I don't want any foul-ups. I *want* this team."

Chapter 23

Jessica's spine was still tingling with the excitement of the Radner search when Carol announced that Jeremy Bronson was on the line. Her hands began to shake. They'd neither seen nor spoken to each other since that night three weeks ago in the Murchinson Oil apartment at the Plaza Hotel. The very next morning Jeremy had been called back to Los Angeles for an emergency meeting that had necessitated his immediate departure for London.

Jessica had both anticipated and dreaded their first conversation. Jeremy still did not know that Michael had left her. She felt awkward, not sure what to say to him, how to begin. Shakily she forced a deep breath and reached for the receiver.

She decided to play it safe. "Welcome home. How was jolly old England?"

"Cold, damp, and lonely," he replied with his usual candor. "How are you, Jessica? And that is not a casual question. I mean how are you *really?*"

So he wasn't going to play games. Well, she wouldn't either. "I'm okay, Jeremy. Better than I thought I'd be." She paused for a moment, then said, "Michael has left me, Jeremy. He was gone when I returned from New York."

There was silence on the other end of the line. But finally, Jeremy spoke. "We have to talk," he said. "When can I see you?"

Jessica began to tremble. Could she see Jeremy and just talk? She didn't want to toy with Jeremy, she felt he would expect her to be ready for him if she agreed to see him. And she wasn't at all sure she was ready. Michael was still very much in her mind and heart.

"I don't know, Jeremy," she began. "I—"

"Jessica, we have to talk! This has to have been monstrous for you. I should have been here to help you. Now again, when can I see you?"

Jessica quit fighting. "I have a five o'clock meeting downtown. That should take me till nearly seven."

"Perfect," he said, the relief evident in his voice. "I keep a small apartment in town for nights when I work late and don't want to drive all the way to the Palisades. I'll be waiting for you."

Jessica took down the address and quickly concealed it in her wallet. She recognized it as a furtive gesture and mentally shook herself.

She sighed and looked at her watch: nearly four-thirty. Just time enough to freshen up and get to Larry Wiggins's office. She checked her makeup, ran a comb through her thick dark hair, and sprayed on a mist of Balenciaga's Quadrille perfume. She gathered up her purse and briefcase, left the office, and headed for her car.

As she guided the Jaguar XKL through traffic she ran over again in her mind her scheduled meeting with Larry Wiggins. She'd thought long and hard about how she would approach her old friend with the idea of a merger. She'd lined up two very good small firms, both of which had been receptive to her suggestion. Now the trick would be to get Larry interested before he found out about the impending defection of his ten partners and several associates.

He was on his feet, standing before his desk as his secretary of some fifteen years ushered Jessica into his office.

145

"Larry," she said, coming to greet him affectionately. "I'm so glad to see you. You look wonderful! We should be ashamed, it's been months and months."

"So it has," he answered, "but the months have been kind to you. You're a sight for these sore old eyes. Sit down, please." He indicated a chair and asked, "Can I offer you a drink? A glass of wine, perhaps?"

Jessica rarely drank during business hours, but this promised to be a hard few hours. "A glass of wine would be lovely, Larry. Thank you."

Larry Wiggins crossed to a paneled wall and pushed a button; the panel slid silently to one side to reveal a fully stocked bar. He poured the wine into two tall crystal glasses, and as Jessica watched him, she prayed the merger idea would be sufficient balm for the bad news he would soon face.

Once seated, drinks in hand, they smiled at one another and Larry Wiggins spoke. "Now tell me, what is this big deal you have to discuss with me?"

"Well," she began, "this might surprise you, Larry, coming from me. I know the rules and a firm the size of yours rarely ever considers what I have to propose, but here goes: Larry, what would be your reaction to a merger?"

Something changed in his face. His eyes twinkled and he looked as if he had a secret he was bursting to tell. But he kept his tone noncommittal. "A merger? Well, that's an interesting thought," he said slowly. "You're quite right, our firm is pretty big as it is. What made you bring such a proposal to me?"

"I've found two excellent small firms, absolute quality corporate and securities work. I checked them out very carefully. They have some very good institutional clients and I saw a CPA audit of their books." She stopped for a moment, searching his face for some reaction, but he merely sat there twinkling at her.

Taking a short breath, she continued, "Both firms are solid and enjoy good reputations in the legal community. All told, it would involve absorbing fifteen people, but their client base more than covers the expense of bringing them on board. They're interested in a firm such as yours, in a founding partner with the kind of reputation you enjoy. So I came to you," she finished.

Larry sipped his wine. "That's very interesting. Institutional clients, you say? About fifteen people?"

Jessica nodded. He was up to something, she was sure, but she couldn't figure out what.

"That would be just about the right number of people to replace the ten partners and four associates I'm about to lose, wouldn't it?"

"Larry," she gasped. "You old devil! How long have you known?"

There was no anger at her ruse; he was genuinely enjoying the shocked expression on her face. "Quite a bit longer than you have, I'd venture," he said, then chuckled. "I wondered how long it would take before you came riding to my rescue."

"Well, I'd have been here a lot sooner if you'd told me. Why didn't you call me?" she scolded. "You know I'd have dropped everything."

"Because it doesn't really matter, Jessica," he answered. "Oh, I know what you think," he went on, "what everyone thinks: that this law firm is my whole life. That Larry Wiggins without his law firm would be a duck out of water." He grinned conspiratorially. "Well, maybe at one time that would have been the truth. Sure, I poured my heart and soul into this firm and made it one of the most respected in town. But I had another side to my life, Jessica, a side that I kept hidden by necessity." His face combined relief with joy as he continued, "But I don't have to hide it any longer. That's why the news of the defections didn't come as the devastating blow you'd anticipated."

Jessica was dying of curiosity, but she knew he wanted to tell it in his own way, so she did not interrupt.

"I've known what my ten young partners have been up to almost from the first day they started talking about it amongst themselves," Larry explained. "Funny, how the young think they can pull the wool over anyone's eyes who is past thirty. They think I'm deadweight, too old-fashioned, too conservative for today's world."

He paused for a reflective moment, then said, "And you know something? They just might be partly right. I *am* conservative and old-fashioned. What I am not is deadweight. I've given plenty to this firm over the years and I could give plenty more if I chose to. But the thing is, I no longer choose to." He smiled at her before saying, "I'm going to retire, Jessica. I'm going to take my portion of what's coming to me and I'm never going to pick up a law book again for as long as I live. So you see, there is no longer any reason for my young partners to defect—they have changed their minds."

Jessica was stunned. The very thought of Larry Wiggins giving up the practice of law was unthinkable. Was it a cover-up for the terrible hurt? Surely he wasn't serious? "Changed their minds?" she asked slowly. "Larry, you don't mean you've already resigned?"

"That I have," he answered. "And with a few exceptions, a happier group of lawyers you'll never meet. This way they get to keep the whole ball game: the goodwill that goes with the name Larry Wiggins and the right to run the firm in any way they see fit."

"I don't know what to say, Larry," Jessica murmured. "Do I congratulate you? Say I'm sorry?"

His smile was merry, his eyes still twinkled, and Jessica knew there was something more. "Congratulate me, by all means. I've had it good, Jessica, better than most men. Forty satisfying years in a profession I loved and respected." His voice was full of affection and sincerity as he continued, "A profession that enabled me to meet people such as yourself, quality people who have become my friends. I expected your visit, Jessica. I knew you'd hear of this plan through your sources and I knew you'd try to save my rusty old hide." He smiled warmly at her. "I only hope you know how much I appreciate you for it."

Jessica rose and walked to Larry's chair. He stood and they embraced warmly, as two very good friends will do when an unexpected tragedy has been averted. His eyes misted slightly for a moment, then that odd twinkle reappeared.

Jessica asked, "You haven't told me everything yet, have you?"

"Perceptive as ever, aren't you?" He chuckled. "You're right. I haven't told you everything. But I am about to. First, let me open a split of champagne. I want you to toast me." He returned to the bar and expertly uncorked a split of iced champagne, pouring them each a glass.

"And just how am I to propose a toast," Jessica asked, "when I don't know what it is I'm toasting?"

"You are toasting my forthcoming marriage."

Jessica could not contain her gasp. Larry Wiggins married? Larry Wiggins had always been married to the law.

"Surprised you pretty good, didn't I, Jessica?" He gave a short, warm laugh before continuing. "I know what everyone's always thought. Hell, some people even believed I wasn't quite normal—if you know what I mean. The monastic, workaholic Larry Wiggins." He handed her a glass of champagne before continuing. "But I had my other life. I just had to keep it a secret. I've been in love with my fiancée for thirty years. We couldn't marry because she's a Catholic and from a very prominent family. And although she and her husband were separated when I met her, she's a very *strict* Catholic and divorce was out of the question." He sighed, remembering all the years of waiting. "Her estranged husband died some six months ago. Now there's no reason for us to be apart." He couldn't keep the happiness from his voice as he said, "We're getting married next month and sailing for Europe and the longest honeymoon in history."

Tears sprang to Jessica's eyes and once again she embraced her old friend. What a wonderful story—what a romantically wonderful story. And to think how he'd fooled everyone all those years. Who would have believed that Larry Wiggins, *the* Larry Wiggins, upright conservative counselor to the mighty, had had a secret love for the past thirty years?

Larry smiled shyly, saying, "You can see why it had to be

kept secret, Jessica. As I say, my fiancée is from a very prominent family—there could be no scandal. And I couldn't build a successful conservative downtown Los Angeles law firm and have it known I was the lover of a married woman. People weren't as tolerant in those days." He paused for a moment in memory, then added, "At my age, I don't know if they would be as tolerant of it today."

"Of course I understand," Jessica quickly assured him. "Oh, Larry, this is wonderful news—I can't tell you how happy I am for both of you. When do I meet her? I can't wait—what a lucky woman."

"I'm the lucky one—and you'll meet her at the wedding," Larry grinned. "I've decided to shock hell out of the whole town. We're going to do it up brown, as the saying goes. The Beverly Hills Hotel, the whole works. Hell, I'm inviting everybody, I can't wait to see their faces. Other than my senior partners, you're the only one I've told," he finished gleefully. He laughed and downed the rest of his champagne.

Jessica put down her glass and kissed his leathery old cheek. "Larry, this meeting has been weighing so heavily on my mind. I was so worried about how you would take the news. What a wonderful happy ending."

"A happy ending for me, that's for certain," he replied. "But what about your two law firms? What will you do for them?"

"Don't you worry about that, Larry. You're out of the law business, remember? I'll find the right firm for them, believe me." She reached for her briefcase and started for the door, saying, "And now, I have to go. I've got a seven o'clock meeting and I'll be late."

"Jessica," Larry detained her, "I'm out of the law business, that's true. But for you—if there is ever anything you need, anything I can do for you . . ."

"Thank you, Larry," Jessica said. "I'll remember that. And don't you forget my wedding invitation. I really can't wait to meet your lady."

Jessica left the office with a lightened heart.

Chapter 24

Jessica sat in her car for ten minutes, trying to work up her courage. The address Jeremy had given her was one of the high-rise apartments in a newly developed section of downtown Los Angeles. She had felt so confident when she left her office, so sure she could unscramble her emotions and put her feelings for Jeremy into perspective.

Yet there she sat, her mind racing. Was she really ready for this? It was the twentieth century, but she was acting like a Victorian maiden. It was ridiculous. She either had to accept her attraction to Jeremy or walk away from him. Period.

She forced herself to leave her car and enter the building. She took the elevator, grateful it was empty, to the fifteenth floor.

She found his apartment and rang the bell.

Jeremy answered at once and she quickly stepped inside and walked to the center of the room. It was comfortable, but sparsely furnished, and Jessica knew it was used for the exact purpose Jeremy had described—merely a place to sleep when he worked late. There was nothing remotely seductive about it.

She turned to find Jeremy standing directly behind her, his eyes questioning. It was difficult to begin. "Jeremy, do you suppose I could have a drink?"

He nodded silently and Jessica seated herself on the sofa as Jeremy expertly mixed a pitcher of martinis. This was a Jeremy she had never seen: The usual three-piece business suit was gone, and in its place he wore a thick Irish knit sweater and casual flannel slacks. He looked more attractive than ever.

Handing her a beaded glass, he took the chair opposite the sofa. Jessica realized with relief that he was not going to rush her. His voice was husky. "Are you ready to talk about it?"

She shook her head. "I don't think talking will help. I almost didn't come up here, but I couldn't just leave you waiting. I felt I should explain . . ."

Jeremy sipped his martini, the creamy white of the Irish sweater making his brooding eyes darker. She said softly, "I think the worst is over. It's just the house, I guess. It's just so empty—as if he had never been there. Yet it's still so full of him. Can you understand?"

Jeremy nodded but volunteered nothing. She knew he wanted her to come to him a grown woman making her own decision.

"Now that Michael's gone, I guess I have finally accepted that my marriage is over."

"I think you really started to accept that in New York, Jessica." There was gentle encouragement in his tone. "You have to get on with your life now, a life I hope to be a part of." His eyes darkened. "You can't hurt Michael now, Jessica. He's made his move."

"I know I can't hurt Michael now, Jeremy. But what about your wife? Do you realize we have never spoken of her? Surely she is someone whom I could hurt?"

Jeremy rose and returned to the bar, saying, "No, we haven't spoken of my wife." He added to his drink, returned, and sat opposite her. "Maybe it's time we did."

There was genuine regret in his tone as he began. "Dammit, Jessica, I wish I could give you one of the stock explanations. The dull hausfrau who didn't grow with her husband—the nagging wife—isn't that the most common scenario? Of course, one usually adds that she doesn't understand me. That would probably help, wouldn't it, Jessica?" His dark eyes were intense, and Jessica found she had to look away as he went on. "Well, that isn't true. As a matter of fact, she is a beautiful, talented woman. Very intelligent, brilliant in social-business situations, and a truly superb mother to our children."

Jessica's confusion mounted. If his wife was all that, why did he want her?

"I wish I could speak ill of her, Jessica, because somehow I think it would make it easier for you to accept what we feel for one another—but I can't. What might help is if I tell you how we met and what our marriage has been."

He rose and walked to the windows, addressing the view, his voice slightly remote.

"I was on my first important assignment for Murchinson Oil. Just your average full-of-piss-and-vinegar young junior executive, impressed as hell at being sent to London, determined to make a good showing and accelerate my rise up the corporate ladder."

He shook his head wryly and Jessica found herself sitting forward, her spine rigid, her shoulders tense.

"Margaret, my wife," he continued, "then Margaret Downing, came to the London office to visit a friend who happened to be the English secretary assigned to me. They invited the young 'Yank' to tea and quite frankly, I was fascinated by Margaret. She is quite lovely, as I've told you. Very like a piece of fine porcelain, and I was more than a little taken by her poise and English reserve. She was so different from the American girls I had known."

Jeremy paused to take a long swallow of his drink. There was amused irony in his voice.

"It was all pretty heady stuff to me—an international assignment and the company of a young English beauty." He turned to face Jessica, his eyes intense. "It seemed so perfect—we got so caught up in it, did all the romantic things, picnics on the Thames, long walks in the English countryside, browsing through antique shops, dinner dancing . . ." His words trailed off for a moment, then he continued. "My imagination was working overtime, projecting the future. I knew where I wanted to go with my life and my career and egotistical young ass that I was, I had a pretty definite idea of the kind of wife I wanted to share it with. Margaret seemed the epitome of all I thought my wife should be."

He left the window and returned to the chair opposite Jessica. "I wasn't as callous as this might sound, Jessica. I really thought we were in love. I think we *were* in love. Or in love with what we had created in our own minds. For Margaret, I was the dashing young American offering a fairy-tale future. For me, Margaret was the perfect English princess to inhabit that fairy tale." He shook his head. "Hell, I could envision it all, the perfect, successful young couple. It would be ideal—I'd become a major executive and Margaret would be the perfect, loving wife. Evenings spent before the fireplace in our perfect home, Margaret working at some fancy needlepoint, me sipping after-dinner brandy, reading *The Wall Street Journal*. Just like in the movies.

"Margaret liked the picture as much as I did. I courted her with an intensity that would have turned the head of any young girl. And we were both young. This was over sixteen years ago and after a three-week courtship, and against the wishes of her very proper English parents, we were married, and I brought my young bride to Los Angeles."

He rose and walked to the bar to freshen his drink. Jessica had a hundred questions but waited for Jeremy to go on. He put the fresh drink on the bar untouched and returned to stare out the windows.

"It was everything I had envisioned. For quite a few years. Margaret *was* the perfect wife for a corporate man. She did it all—entertaining, charities, ran a perfect home. Everything by the book."

His voice was tense and Jessica bit her lip.

"Even the children came right on schedule, one of each. That's Margaret's way—everything must be done perfectly."

There was genuine pain in his voice and Jessica found herself almost wishing he would not continue.

"I don't know when I began to realize I could do with a little *less* perfection. It had been part of our lives from the beginning. You see, to Margaret *perfection* is simply *good form*—the way things are done." He rubbed his hand across his eyes, and Jessica knew he was unearthing long suppressed feelings. "But for me, the perfection became oppressive, her lack of spontaneity burdensome, like a lack of fresh air. A man can't relax with so much perfection. That vital *something* so essential between a man and a woman was missing."

He turned to face Jessica. "I wanted our marriage to work, I wanted that very badly, but I knew it couldn't. And Margaret didn't even think anything was wrong, because for her, nothing was. Our life was secure, orderly, proper. Everything her background had prepared her for." He shrugged his shoulders in resignation. "It was my fault, all of it. It was *my* unhappiness, *my* need, *my* craving for that bonding, that complete surrender of one person to the other. But that just isn't Margaret's way—a proper Englishwoman does not allow vulgar displays of emotion. A proper lady stays in control of herself in all situations, private and otherwise."

Jeremy again faced Jessica, his eyes pleading for understanding. "I finally decided to accept things as they were, and for a long time, I did. But it just wasn't enough, finally."

He began to pace the room, his voice falling into the soft cadence of a person addressing himself.

"I'm not very good at pretense, Jessica. I began to view our marriage as a sham, our love life a polite coupling of two people going through the motions." He sighed deeply. "It just didn't work for me. After the birth of our second child, I just stopped going to her bed. It's an agreement Margaret finds perfectly reasonable."

Tears filled Jessica's eyes, but Jeremy did not notice.

"I was no saint, Jessica. I'm not going to try and paint a pretty or noble picture of myself. As unreasonable as it was,

I felt cheated, rejected somehow, and for a time, angry. I looked elsewhere for my needs, not often—there were a couple of affairs, but they offered me no more fulfillment than my marriage. I still felt empty. I didn't want an affair, Jessica. I wanted a commitment—I wanted to give and receive a hundred percent from a relationship." His tone deepened. "I was discreet—I didn't want to hurt Margaret. But I'm certain she knew."

Jeremy crossed the room and took Jessica's hands in his as he seated himself beside her.

"I'm not trying to describe a life of misery, Jessica. Margaret and I lead a very civilized life. She's had what she wants—marriage to an executive, two beautiful children, a lovely home, social standing in the community. You'll just have to take my word for it—it has been enough for Margaret."

This time Jessica had to voice her thoughts. "But it's not enough for you, Jeremy?"

He shook his head. "Not anymore, Jessica. I had just about decided it would have to be enough. That my marriage was probably the norm, my expectations of Margaret unrealistic. And then I met you, Jessica. I met you and I knew there *was* more, I knew what I craved in a relationship was indeed possible between a man and a woman. I fell in love with you. I didn't plan it, but it has happened, and there is nothing I can or want to do about it."

"Jeremy"—she made her tone as gentle as possible—"what about your children?"

His face showed his concern. "My children are wonderful, Jessica. I love them as deeply as anyone could imagine."

"Then you must have thought about how falling in love with another woman could hurt them. They could wind up hating you, Jeremy."

"No!" He shook his head. "I could never believe that."

"Jeremy, we aren't talking about a casual affair here, we're talking about love. You've said you are in love with me."

"And I *am*," he declared. Suddenly he realized there was something Jessica *wasn't* saying. "Jessica, you said we

156

aren't talking about a casual affair. Are you saying that you are falling in love with me, too?"

She didn't answer at once. "I don't know if I am or not, Jeremy. I haven't healed from my own emotional wounds sufficiently to know for sure. Maybe I am falling in love with you, but right now, I just can't handle it."

"And you can't change it. It isn't something you can just turn on and off."

"That's true. But it is something I'm going to have to be very, very sure of before I can commit to it."

"What are you so afraid of?"

"Of ruining your family, Jeremy. Of taking my happiness at their expense."

"You haven't been listening. I've told you, I don't have a marriage to ruin."

"You can't be sure of that, Jeremy. Your wife may be content with her life as it is. Maybe security and social position are enough for her to close her eyes to a casual affair. But not to love, Jeremy. No woman is stoic enough to ignore that."

Jessica began gathering up her things. She turned to face Jeremy. "Forgive me. I was wrong to come here tonight. I should have taken more time to work my feelings out. I don't want to play games with you, and I don't want to step from one emotional nightmare into another. I can't take being hurt again. We both have a lot of thinking to do." She headed for the door, turning back to find that Jeremy had followed her, his eyes pleading. "You said you only wanted me when I was ready to come to you. Do you still mean that?"

Jeremy returned her gaze for a long moment, then took her quickly into his arms. His kiss was tender, warm, and loving, but could not conceal his desire for her. Jessica felt her legs turning liquid as she responded with a long-denied passion of her own. She knew she wanted him, could finally admit it to herself, but she had to be certain of her feelings, had to be certain it really was love she was feeling. Otherwise there were simply too many people whose lives could be ruined, herself included.

When he finally lifted his lips from hers, she could not

catch her breath. His voice was deep, urgent. "I still mean it, Jessica. I love you. I'll wait as long as it takes."

"I won't come back unless I'm truly ready, Jeremy. I promise."

She opened the door and quickly left the apartment, the touch of his lips still hot on her own.

Chapter 25

Jim Steiner frowned as Carol ordered an extra-dry martini. He asked for a bottle of beer and leaned forward. "Christ, Carol. You're as bad as Jessica with her cigarettes. Don't you know what hard liquor does to a woman's looks? It all adds up at your age, you know."

Carol grinned. "Forty is not exactly Methuselah, buster. And a martini after a long day is good for my hardening arteries. I'll bring you a note from my gerontologist if it will ease your mind."

The two of them had become buddies and often lunched together. They liked to call themselves the Harold and Maude of the recruiting world.

Jim began munching on a breadstick. Carol chided, "You're a fine one to talk. Do you know how much sodium is in that innocent little Italian breadstick?"

Jim dropped the stick onto his butter plate as if it were a live snake.

Carol laughed. "Why don't you come right out with whatever is bothering you? You didn't invite me for a drink on a Friday evening for the pleasure of my company, unless you've got a late date with one of your disco bunnies."

He didn't respond. Carol prodded. "Hey, pal, this is me, good old Carol. You can talk to me."

Jim took a sip of his beer. His normally mischievous eyes were serious and his forehead was creased into a deep frown. "Carol, I'm Jewish!" he blurted out.

Carol wasn't sure how she was supposed to respond. "So?" she managed. "You're Jewish, the Pope's Polish, and I've forgotten what the hell I am. What's this all about?"

"I'm about to be canned from Martin Management."

"What?" she retorted incredulously. "Because you're Jewish? That's ridiculous. Jessica doesn't even know how to spell prejudice."

He shook his head impatiently. "I know she isn't prejudiced—she knows I'm Jewish! But I have to turn down a big search assignment, one that is very important to her. We have a big rush on this one and she's not gonna be too happy about it."

"Wait, back up a minute," Carol said firmly. "You have to turn down an important assignment because you're Jewish? Which assignment?"

"The Amalgamated search for an attorney for the Middle East," he replied. "I can't work on that order."

Carol was beginning to get the picture. "You want to talk about it?" she asked quietly.

He was silent for a moment, then looked directly into her eyes. Earnestly, he said, "Yeah! Yeah, I guess I do want to talk about it. It's a little complicated—do you have the time?"

She was about to make a flippant remark about her dance card scarcely being filled at her age, but something in his eyes stopped her. "All the time in the world, Jim."

He signaled the waiter for refills and sat forward, his voice pitched low. "I'm not religious, Carol. I never have been. I don't go to temple—my folks do, but it's more of a social thing than religion."

She sat quietly, waiting for him to continue.

"I went to Hebrew school," he went on, "and of course I was bar mitzvahed, but that's about the size of it." He drank some of his beer, his eyes focused somewhere in the past.

"If anyone was really religious in the family, it was my grandfather. He was a terrific old guy—very proper, always dressed sharp with a high polish on his shoes." He smiled in memory. "Pop Pop, we called him. But even Pop Pop wasn't religious in the usual way. He was against organized religion. He even left the temple because of his beliefs, and that was something few Jews ever did. But he was a free-thinker and he stood up for his beliefs."

Jim took another breadstick and began crumbling it absently as he continued. "He didn't push religion, his version or the Torah. What Pop Pop pushed was Zionism. Israel. A country for our people. Pride in our heritage." There was a small pile of crumbs in front of him and he pushed them into a V-shaped mound as he spoke. "Funny, I never thought I paid that much attention to him, but I guess I absorbed a lot more than I realized." He looked up at her. "What I'm trying to tell you, Carol, is that while I am *not* religious, I *am* Jewish. Do you understand what I mean?"

She nodded. "I think so, Jim. But go on."

"Hell, I guess that's it! I mean, I guess Pop Pop really got through to me. I'm Jewish and I care—deep in my guts, I care. I can't forget my heritage." He stopped, then said with difficulty, "I can't recruit for a bunch of Arabs."

"Jim," Carol said, "you make the Arabs sound like Hitler's Nazis."

"Why the hell not?" he shot back. "They want to destroy Israel."

Carol felt a little out of her depth. She'd never been that politically involved. She felt it would all go on with or without her two cents' worth. She knew the PLO wanted Israel destroyed, but she'd pretty much lumped the rest of the Arab world with men like the late Sadat, who would welcome peace. Still, she had to try to help Jim. "The Amalgamated assignment isn't recruiting for Arabs. It's an American company," she offered.

"An American company doing business with Arabs!" he retorted angrily. "It amounts to the same thing if I recruit for them. Don't you see, Carol?" he asked. "In order to fill this assignment, I have to discriminate against my own people. I have to do all those shitty little things to figure out whether or not a candidate is a Jew."

There was genuine pain mixed with the anger in his voice, and it cut into Carol's heart, but there was nothing she could say to him.

"I have to go on a fuckin' witch-hunt!" he ranted. "Make sure the candidates have blond hair and blue eyes. I practically have to ask them to drop their pants to prove they aren't circumcised. I have to spy on them," he said, his voice tight. "Use trick recruiter questions. Can't ask them outright if they are Jewish, just have to make certain they aren't."

Suddenly he brushed the little pile of crumbs off the table with an angry wave of his hand. "It's a fuckin' betrayal, of my people and of my grandfather. If I find a non-Jew to go with those bastards, then I'm just as bad as they are."

Carol wasn't sure what to say. She was one of those blue-eyed blondes who have never known the pain of prejudice. But she understood how deeply upset he was.

He leaned forward intently. "Every time one person says yes to another act of prejudice it's as if a thousand people said yes. Every time a recruiter sends a Gentile who is acceptable to the Arabs, it's a thousand people sanctioning their hatred. A thousand people putting their stamp of approval on the destruction of an entire country." He lowered his voice before he finished, "If I do it, as a Jew, if I do it and for profit, hell, Carol, I just couldn't live with that."

"Have you talked it over with Jessica?"

"Not yet," he answered slowly. "At first I thought, what the hell, just grab the files of candidates you know aren't Jewish. Fill the slot, take your commission, and laugh all the way to temple." He sighed, leaned back in his chair, and said, "But when I started going through the files, when I actually saw my own hands quickly flip past a name like Meyers because I *wasn't* sure, and Rosenberg because I *was* sure, then I knew I couldn't do it." He paused, then said, "Carol, I'm going to tell Jessica on Monday. That'll do it for me with Martin Management. She's in a bind on this one and needs the help bad. We're short two recruiters in legal, so it's a bitch. But I just can't do it."

"Jim," Carol said, her tone soothing, "you're wrong about Jessica, dead wrong! I don't know when you're going to realize what kind of person she is. You're right, with two recruiters on vacation, it'll be a tight squeeze. But she'll understand. The main reason she assigned you was because it's an international search and all recruiters love those." She smiled, saying, "You won't be fired. She'll switch the assignment to another recruiter, you'll just switch job orders."

For the first time since they'd sat down, Carol saw some of the tension leave Jim's face. He looked at her hopefully. "Do you really think so? I mean," he went on, "do you really think she'll understand? After all, I didn't have the balls to tell her right out front that I didn't want the assignment. Do *you* really understand?"

"Jim," Carol said quietly, "asking me if I really understand your feelings is like my being asked by a black person if I really understand what it is to be black. Of course I can't feel this as deeply as you do. But I admire your principles, and so will Jessica." She put her hand on the back of his. "If you didn't always act as if the word sensitivity wasn't in your vocabulary, Jessica probably would have thought twice about giving you the assignment. But believe me, she will understand."

Jim put his hand over hers, squeezing it gently, gratitude and friendship in his eyes. A sudden mischievous grin played around his mouth. "Aaah, Carol. If you were only twenty years younger."

She returned his smile. "Aaah, Jim. If you were only twenty years *older*." They both laughed.

"If I *were* twenty years younger," Carol said, "I'd be out having a ball instead of sitting across from some young punk who constantly reminds me I'm about ready for Medicare!" She pulled her hand from between his and reached for her drink. Taking a last swallow, she asked, "Now, how about buying me some dinner to soak up those two martinis?"

Chapter 26

Jessica sat at her desk, not yet ready to begin her day, her mind focused on the past weekend. She had read and reread Michael's letter, searching for a false note, something, *anything,* to make her doubt the sincerity of his words. She found nothing. Slowly over those two days, she had come to accept his decision, finally believing that he wanted the marriage to end as much for himself as for her. Only once was she tempted to call his partner Ben Hobard to plead with him to tell her where Michael had gone. In the end, after reading his letter yet one more time, she realized Michael was right—a clean break was the best for both of them. She vowed to leave him alone to start his new life.

As she needed to start her own. Her mind drifted back to her meeting with Jeremy, to his kiss. She had come to no final conclusion about him, except to admit that she did indeed have deep feelings for him, maybe even love. But, like Jeremy, she did not want a casual affair, she needed the same commitment Jeremy did—and that could certainly destroy his wife and children.

It was a very sobering thought. She didn't know how they could work things out, but she would not allow herself to rush into something she would later regret.

She forced her mind back to the day ahead. Jim Steiner had requested a meeting, and she had to begin the search for Eric Radner and follow through on the men interviewing at Amalgamated International. Perhaps, she thought, that was why Jim wanted to see her. It wasn't going to be easy to get a man to go to the Middle East with things as unsettled as they were over there. Still, they had to put on a big push; John Adams was in a hurry on this one. She thanked God for her work; she could throw herself into it and keep her personal troubles in check.

Determined, Jessica was about to go into the computer room to program the specs on the Radner assignment when Carol buzzed to announce that Dr. Bernstein was calling for David Clarendon. Jessica took a deep breath and picked up the receiver. "Dr. Bernstein, this is Jessica Martin. We haven't had the pleasure of speaking before."

His answering voice was wary. "No, we haven't. And I'm not sure why we're speaking now. I placed this call to David Clarendon," he said shortly.

"Yes, Doctor, I know you did," Jessica replied calmly. "But David is no longer with Martin Management. I will be handling your file personally from now on."

"My file?" Bernstein exploded. "What kind of file? Listen, where can I reach Clarendon? He got me into this mess, and I expect him to get me out of it!"

Jessica recognized the strain in his tone. "Actually, Doctor, I don't know where you can reach David," she said. "I don't know if he has joined another search firm or not. But I'll be more than happy to handle your file—it only contains your resumé and background information. I'm certain I can assist you."

He did not respond for a few moments, and when he did, his voice was once again wary. "Just how much do you know about my—situation, Mrs. Martin?"

"I think David filled me in on just about everything, Dr. Bernstein. It's shocking and I know what you must be going through. I want to help you in any way I can."

"If you know all the facts, you also know that it won't be easy to help me. By taking the job at World Vision, I may have ended my career in the corporate medical field," he finished bitterly.

"Nonsense, Doctor," Jessica reassured him. "A man with your credentials will always be welcome in any area of medicine. The very act of going to the authorities will distinguish you as one of the most ethical men in the field. You—"

"Wait just a minute, Mrs. Martin!" Bernstein interrupted. "Who said anything about going to the authorities? I'm not going to the FDA!" His voice took on a tone of near hysteria. "Maybe Clarendon didn't tell you everything. I am not going to put my family in jeopardy."

Jessica knew she had to handle this very carefully. There was genuine fear in his voice. He'd have to be guaranteed protection, but those drugs could not be allowed to go on the market. "David told me of your concern about Mafia involvement at World Vision," she started cautiously. "I find that impossible to accept. What the company is planning to do is unthinkable, but I believe you are overreacting to think there might be Mafia involvement."

His laughter was bitter, his voice sharp. "Can't accept it, can you? You aren't very clever then, Mrs. Martin. At least not as clever as you are reputed to be. I mention Mafia and you immediately think of Al Capone. I'm not talking about that kind of gangster. I'm talking about the corporate Mafia—big-business men who will stop at nothing for profit."

"Corporate Mafia?" Jessica echoed. "Dr. Bernstein, you're not serious? There is no such thing as a corporate Mafia."

"And there was no young girl named Karen Silkwood, was there, Mrs. Martin?"

Jessica was stunned by the comparison. Karen Silkwood's death had been ruled accidental, but the files she allegedly had in her car were never found. Good God! Surely he was wrong! Surely there weren't cold-blooded killers in the upper echelons of Corporate America?

"Dr. Bernstein," Jessica said carefully, "if you are right, then more than ever you have to consider this. The government will protect you and your family."

His voice was cold. "There won't be any need for their protection, because I'm not going to the FDA. I want you to find me a job, someplace small and remote."

"But have you thought this through?" Jessica pressed. "You have the proof—what makes you think you'll be safe as long as you have the proof?"

"Because only you, Clarendon, and myself know I have the proof. The company doesn't know it exists."

"You're forgetting the attorney," she reminded him. "You told the company attorney."

He snorted. "That young punk ran for the hills as fast as I did. He reviewed those documents for the FDA. He had his own hide to save. He's no threat to me." He paused, then said, "My only concern is you and Clarendon. I still can't believe I was fool enough to tell him the reason I left."

"You had to talk to someone, Doctor," Jessica replied. "And you can trust David not to say anything." She had to fight to keep the distaste out of her voice. "His reaction was the same as the attorney's. He wants no part of this."

"Why did he leave your firm?"

"He requested a leave of absence until this is over. I made it permanent," Jessica responded. "I can't work with people for whom I have no respect."

"Then it doesn't seem likely you'll be able to help me, does it?"

Jessica was at a loss for a moment. It was different with the doctor, he was fearful for his life and his family's safety. "Doctor, there is a difference here. I'm obligated to you as a candidate of this firm. Anything you've said to me or one of my recruiters is confidential information and will remain confidential."

"A stupid bout of hysteria and I couldn't think straight. Otherwise, I'd never have told anyone." His voice was tired, and Jessica knew how much he was suffering. "These are the big, big boys, Mrs. Martin. And I'm just a little toxicologist. I'll have to take your word that I can trust you. I have no other choice." He paused, then asked, "What's our next step?"

"Well," Jessica said slowly, "you have money coming

from World Vision. They have it in escrow for you. If you'll give me power of attorney, I'll contact them and have it released to you."

"No!" he said quickly. "Let them keep their money. I don't want them to know where I am. I need you to find me a job in some small, remote place, maybe a think tank. A place where I can go into hiding."

"Dr. Bernstein," Jessica said firmly, "listen to yourself. You're much too well known in corporate medicine to go into hiding on a job. If you're in danger, there's only one place to go." She softened her tone. "Please, won't you come to my office so we can talk in person? Or I'll come to you. You know you can't live with this secret—it will destroy you. . . ."

The line went dead. Jessica called his name two or three times, but knew it was useless. He didn't trust her, and she had no way of calling him back, no idea where he was.

The whole thing had slipped through her fingers. She had handled it badly. She needed advice, but to whom could she turn? She needed to talk with someone who would counsel her without making her reveal more than she should. But who?

Suddenly, she knew. "If there is ever anything I can do, if you ever need me, Jessica . . ."

She picked up the phone to call Larry Wiggins.

Chapter 27

Jessica was crushed when she learned Larry Wiggins was out of town. He and his fiancée had flown to New Mexico, where they intended to retire. They would be house hunting, and while he might be checking in for messages, his secretary couldn't say just when. Jessica declined to leave a message; she needed some answers immediately.

She hadn't known where else to turn. She needed to talk it out and thought she might even require legal advice. But with Larry away, to whom could she go? She needed someone who understood the corporate world at the highest level. Someone who would know if there was such a thing as a corporate Mafia and just what it entailed if it did exist. Suddenly she realized that Jeremy was that person. She could trust him implicitly, and he knew the corporate world inside out.

She dialed his private line and felt immediately better at the sound of his voice. They arranged to meet for cocktails. Forcing herself to concentrate on other things, she went into the computer room and resolutely fed the requisites for the Radner search into the machine.

* * *

She plowed through her work for the rest of the day and when she arrived at the El Padrino Room of the Beverly Wilshire Hotel, Jeremy was waiting for her in a quiet back booth.

Rising, Jeremy noted the worry in Jessica's eyes. "Sit down, Jessica. I've ordered you a drink. You look pretty serious."

She took a sip of the martini. "Jeremy, something has happened that I've never encountered in my career and I don't know how to handle it," she began. "I need your advice—but I don't want to get you involved."

Jeremy was instantly attentive. "If it concerns you, Jessica, I want to be involved."

She smiled gratefully, but said, "No, Jeremy. Although I thank you for that, I don't want—can't let you get involved." The smile left her face and she lowered her voice. "I need your advice, but you have to promise that you won't press for details. I can only tell you so much."

He nodded his head reluctantly.

"Jeremy, have you ever heard of a corporate Mafia?" Jessica blurted out.

His eyes darkened, and he frowned before speaking. Jessica felt fear in the pit of her stomach. He hadn't laughed at her question and that in itself was very frightening.

"Just what do you mean by a corporate Mafia?" he asked guardedly.

Jessica shrugged her shoulders in frustration. "I'm not sure what I mean, or even if it exists. Perhaps I'd better tell you what happened first; maybe you can put it into some perspective for me." She took a deep breath. "Through my office, I've become privy to some rather startling information. Information that is frightening and, frankly, hard to believe."

"Tell me what you can, Jessica."

"What would you say if I told you a major pharmaceutical house has falsified test results on two new drugs to the FDA? Drugs that are about to be released on the market. Drugs that have severe, long-term toxic side effects."

There was a quick flash in Jeremy's eyes, but he did not interrupt.

Jessica continued rapidly, eager to get it all out. "This information came to me secondhand at first, but I've since had what I consider confirmation from the party involved." She paused to light a cigarette and take a sip of her drink. "In any case, the party who has proof of this information, or so he says, is nearly hysterical with fear. He refuses to go to the FDA and insists there is a corporate Mafia and that as long as he keeps quiet, he's safe."

She rushed on, "I tried to reason with the person, but it was no use. He's really hung up on this Mafia idea and even brought up the Karen Silkwood case. I tried to get him to go to the FDA for his own safety, but he hung up on me." She sighed deeply. "My only contact with him has been by telephone and I don't have a clue as to where he is hiding or what I should do next."

Jessica watched Jeremy intently. "Are either of these drugs likely to cause death?" he asked.

Jessica nodded her head. "I didn't get the specifics, he didn't want to talk to me about it. There are only three people aware of this information, and I'm one of them. If any of them talks . . ." She shook her head. "I'm afraid of what could happen."

Jessica searched Jeremy's face for a clue as to what he was thinking.

"Jeremy," she asked, "why would a company knowingly put bad drugs on the market? Someone suggested that they'd do it for the profit alone, but I just can't accept that."

"I don't know which company you are referring to, but I'd venture there could be many reasons in addition to the profit motive. Is the company in trouble? When was the last time they had a major breakthrough? Are they desperate for a new and revolutionary product? Are they facing a take-over?" His brow creased in concentration. "There is no way to evaluate the benefit a pharmaceutical company would reap from a couple of new 'wonder drugs.' People tend to think of corporations as faceless entities. That just isn't the case. Corporations are run by *people*. And people need to succeed—need to produce—need to protect themselves and their existence." He smiled and shrugged. "I don't know if that answers your question or not, Jessica. There are just too many reasons decisions are made—good and bad."

He leaned across the table in order to speak in a lowered voice, his smile replaced by a frown.

"This could be a very bad business, Jessica. Obviously the drugs have to be kept off the market if what you've been told is true." He paused for emphasis. "But, Jessica, hear me well—you must be very careful. You may be involved in something way over your head. Frankly, it could be dangerous," he finished strongly.

The knot in Jessica's stomach began to grow. Jeremy was frightened for her, she could see it in his eyes, hear it in his tone. "Jeremy, are you saying there *is* a corporate Mafia? That the doctor could be in real jeopardy if this got out?"

Jeremy's head snapped up. "Again, corporations are run by people and people often do dreadful things, it doesn't matter how you label them." He captured her gaze and held it with a compelling look. "Jessica, I'm sure you didn't mean to tell me this, but confirm it now that you have—is there a doctor involved in all this?"

Jessica bit her lip—she hadn't meant to let that slip. She said nothing and Jeremy continued in a tone that indicated he would come back to that point.

"Let me put it to you this way, Jessica. There are a lot of unscrupulous actions taken by major corporate officers who for their own reasons value nothing more than profit. I wouldn't be surprised if that included human life as well. This person—this doctor—could be in serious danger. That's my answer to you."

"But what do I do?" Jessica pleaded, trying to keep panic from overtaking her. "Yes, there is a doctor involved, but I can't reveal the man's identity, nor can I repeat any more of what he has told my office." She frowned. "I'm way out of line in having told you this much, but I felt sure you'd know if I'm right to be worried."

"I'm afraid your instincts are right on target, Jessica," Jeremy replied, making no attempt to soft-pedal anything.

"I'm not going to go into specifics, nor cite any incidents, but yes—after all my years in the corporate world, I think I would consider your fears valid."

Jessica's shoulders slumped. "Then it's up to me. I have to go to the FDA and tell them what I've learned without revealing my source."

"You're not thinking straight, Jessica. You said yourself, your information came to you secondhand. I gather this doctor is too afraid to come forward. You have nothing to take to the FDA. Without the main source, your information is useless. Not only could the doctor deny your charges, he could sue you."

Jeremy could see he wasn't getting through to her and he strengthened the conviction of his tone. "Not only could the doctor sue you, if this became known, but the pharmaceutical house could sue you as well. No!" he said forcefully. "You cannot go to the FDA, not on your own."

"But if I don't, then the drugs will go on the market."

"Yes," he replied heavily, "that's a possibility—unless this doctor comes to his senses and goes to the authorities himself. He's the only one who can lodge such a charge and make it stick." He raised his shoulders in resignation. "I'm sorry, Jessica, but at this point your hands are tied. It's up to the doctor. If he decides he can live with this, if he lodges no complaint, there is really nothing you can do."

"He won't, Jeremy. He's too afraid."

"And he may very well be right to be afraid," he replied. "But listen to me, Jessica. I believe people are basically decent. This man is a doctor—he won't be able to keep it inside himself. When the panic eases a bit, he'll come to his senses, and the FDA will protect him."

He leaned forward, his voice urgent. "Jessica, all this seems to have happened very fast; the man hasn't had time to realize the hell his life would be, living with this kind of knowledge. I believe he'll come around, and he will report it. If he wasn't a decent man, a man of ethics, he'd never have come to you in the first place, he'd have deep-sixed the whole thing."

What Jeremy said made some sense, but Jessica still felt

her heart sink. Dr. Bernstein's voice hadn't sounded as though he were anywhere near coming around. Her hands were tied and it sickened her.

Jeremy reached across the table and took her hand. "It gets evil out there sometimes, Jessica." He caressed her hand. "This sounds like a particularly ugly mess and I know how deeply you feel about it. But again, you must give me your word you'll take my counsel. You can't do anything without the doctor."

Jessica gazed at his hand, but said nothing for a moment. Maybe he didn't fully understand what she'd told him— she'd had to leave out so many important details. She'd have to wait until she heard from the doctor again before making a final decision. She smiled sadly at Jeremy. "I promise, at least I promise not to do anything rash. Maybe I can reason with him, handle it better next time he calls. If he calls," she finished glumly.

Jeremy squeezed her hand. "He'll call you, Jessica. Or he'll call the FDA. He's a doctor. He won't be able to live with this."

She looked into his eyes and Jeremy saw trust and faith and the beginnings of something more. She made him feel like a giant, and he ached for the wanting of her. Ached waiting for her. But he'd made his promise; he would not push her. He released her hand and picked up his drink. She would come to him soon, just as she'd turned to him in this crisis. He loved her enough to wait.

Chapter 28

At the "Right to Know" production offices, Ed Franklin sat across the desk from the show's producer, Carlton Brenner. "Right to Know" was the hottest television news and exposé show on the air and Ed's reportorial nose was itching—this assignment intrigued the hell out of him.

Brenner spoke. "This could be one dynamite segment, Ed, but it requires careful investigation. World Vision Pharmaceuticals is a biggie, an international conglomerate. We don't want to step into any quicksand—and all we are working on is an anonymous tip."

Ed Franklin nodded his curly red head in agreement, his boyish face serious, his blue eyes intent. He looked like a kid fresh out of college, enthusiastic and innocent. In fact, he was in his mid-thirties and one of the best investigative reporters in the business. Ed was a behind-the-scene reporter. His perennially juvenile freckled face made people trust him on sight. They told him things they had no intention of revealing.

"Couldn't agree with you more, Carlton. And I think our tipster's advice is a good approach. I've pretty much narrowed down the best management consultant firms who

175

work in the health-science field," he said. "In fact, I think I know who the firm is."

"Who's your source?"

"I contacted the Society of Toxicology," Franklin replied. "Told them I was a toxicologist and wanted to make a job change. I asked them for a list of firms they recommend." He smiled. "There aren't that many. I think our firm is Martin Management Consultants. They're based on the West Coast in Beverly Hills."

"How did you arrive at that conclusion?" Brenner asked skeptically, tapping his pencil absentmindedly on the desk.

Ed grinned. "I guess I can share my secrets with you, boss. I had my secretary call and say her boss was interested in opening a string of diagnostic laboratories. He'd be in need of medical people to staff them. She asked all the legit questions about fees and refunds. The girl at Martin Management bought it and was only too happy to give a list of references." He finished with a grin. "World Vision Pharmaceuticals was one of them."

Brenner stopped tapping his pencil. But before he could frame his question, Ed had the answer.

"You got it. When we pulled the same ruse with World Vision to confirm the reference, we were told that Martin Management Consultants had the exclusive for their medical staffing needs and had served them in that capacity for over two years."

A smile spread slowly across Brenner's face. "That was fast work. How do you propose we proceed?"

"I think the first step is to get inside Martin Management," Ed answered. "I suggest we approach them on the basis of doing a segment on executive search firms and how they earn their fees, et cetera. You know all the bits—hell, if what I'm told is true, all headhunters love publicity. It should be a snap to get an interview," he concluded.

"Agreed," Brenner said. "But how do we get around to this doctor and the false test results given to the FDA?"

"Well," Ed answered thoughtfully, "my approach will depend pretty much on how this Jessica Martin strikes me. She has an excellent reputation among both clients and candidates. Her company is solid," he went on, "and we didn't get a single negative about her on both performance and confidentiality." Franklin smiled wryly. "Actually, she comes across as a paragon of ethics—the type I usually don't trust—but if she is, I don't think she would keep something like this covered up. But if she does know and isn't going to pop, we may have to take a different approach." His tone hardened. "I want the name of this doctor. I may have to start poking around World Vision."

Brenner shook his head. "Not until we absolutely have to. We don't even know who our tipster is. Maybe someone directly involved in the mess, someone who is running scared and wants it stopped before it's too late. The thing is, we just don't know *who* and exactly *what* we are dealing with at this point. This could be a real biggie, but we can't afford to step on any toes until we have absolute proof."

"I hear you," Ed agreed. "I'm leaving for the Coast right after we finish this meeting. I'll start with Jessica Martin and report back to you before I make any other moves."

"All right, Ed," Brenner said. "We'll try this route first. Our tipster said the person who placed this doctor knows all about this. If your Jessica Martin won't breach confidentiality, we'll go the other route." He paused, then continued, "Be careful, Ed. If this is true, I really want to expose those bastards. But if it isn't, I don't want to risk a lawsuit."

Ed Franklin nodded and left the office. He collected his notes, which he stuffed into his battered briefcase. He pulled on a worn sports jacket, which along with the battered briefcase was a carefully studied effect, and headed for his car and the airport.

Like Carlton Brenner, he smelled a big one in this story.

Chapter 29

When Ed Franklin was ushered into Jessica's office, he was almost sorry they weren't actually doing a segment on search firms. She was a beauty and would look great on camera. He put on his best little-boy grin and extended his hand. "Boy, I didn't think I'd ever get inside this office," he said ingenuously. "I haven't had a third degree like that since I was a kid and Mom found out I'd ditched school."

"Carol is very protective of my time," Jessica said, maintaining a cordial but distant manner. She accepted his handshake, and indicated the chair in front of her desk. "Please sit down. I think Carol has already told you I'm not fond of publicity and doubt very much I'd want to do your program, excellent as it is."

"She did tell me you were reluctant," he replied. "May I ask why?"

"It's not very mysterious," Jessica answered. "We're often called upon to recruit under delicate circumstances. It's better for us to maintain a low profile."

Ed laughed, keeping his boyish demeanor. "That's sure a different attitude from the other search firms we've contacted. They can't wait to be interviewed."

"Yes, well," Jessica replied in a contained manner, "we all have our own methods of doing business. Mine is very low-keyed. I really don't think there's anything I can contribute to your program." When he didn't acknowledge this, she continued, "I do not discuss my clients or candidates outside this office. That's why Carol tried to discourage you. This is surely a waste of your valuable time."

Jessica lit a cigarette and leaned back in her chair. She was a quick study and something about Ed Franklin bothered her. She scrutinized him carefully. "But I am curious—why come all the way to California? Why my firm? Surely you could have found a suitable firm in New York?"

Ed was impressed. She was sharp; he'd have to go very carefully. "Actually, you're right; we could have settled for a firm in New York, and we will be talking to others, but we came to you because in the course of our inquiries your firm was highly recommended." He smiled. "You'll be pleased to know that you received an extremely high rating."

Jessica remained polite but there was a slight frostiness in her tone. "I'm quite aware of the reputation of my firm, Mr. Franklin. But thank you for confirming it. I'm sorry not to be more cooperative, but I really would not be interested in appearing on your program."

Ed made a mental note that flattery definitely was not the right approach with Jessica Martin. "I'm sorry to hear that," he said, giving it just the right touch of sincerity. "The search business has become big business. Your own operation, for example, is very impressive." He leaned forward, saying, "Our purpose in doing a segment on search firms is to expose those that are unethical; those who do not live up to their agreements with clients and candidates."

"And you came here expecting me to name such firms?" Jessica replied coldly. "I repeat, Mr. Franklin, you have wasted your time."

This lady wasn't going to be easy, Ed decided. If necessary, he would discontinue the sham of the search-firm segment. She was bright and very secure.

Not many people would turn down an opportunity to appear on the show. He switched gears. "I don't expect anything of the kind, Mrs. Martin. We have our sources for that sort of information. What I need to know from you is the extent to which that sort of activity goes on."

"Mr. Franklin," Jessica retorted sharply, "you didn't come all the way to California to ask me that kind of question." She looked him directly in the eyes and said, "There's something about this entire interview that doesn't smell right to me."

Ed abandoned the charade. "Okay, Mrs. Martin, you're right. We're not doing a segment on search firms," he leveled with her. "I'm here to speak with you about an entirely different story. I think you have information that would be very helpful, information about one of your clients and a candidate." He smiled. "I apologize for the ruse, but I had to get in the door."

Jessica's voice was icy, matching the stony anger in her eyes. "As well you should apologize!" she said. "You are here under false pretenses and I resent it greatly. Besides which you have wasted my time. I've already told you I do not discuss my clients." She rose, saying, "You'd better leave now."

"Aren't you overreacting just a bit?" he asked, remaining seated. "Surely in your business you have to be devious at times."

Jessica sat back down. "The most devious thing we ever need to do as recruiters is to use a false name to contact a candidate, and that is for his or her protection."

Ed started to respond but Jessica cut him off angrily. "There is nothing more to discuss, Mr. Franklin. I don't know what story you are working on and I don't want to know." She picked up some papers on her desk. "You'll have to excuse me now."

"Look, Mrs. Martin," he said firmly, "I'm going to do this story with or without your help. But I think before you make so rash a decision as to have me tossed out bodily, you should at least know which of your clients I'm referring to."

He paused for a moment and Jessica could not hide her curiosity. He said softly, "I think the name World Vision Pharmaceuticals might get you to reconsider."

There! He had his answer. A less experienced reporter might have missed it. But Ed caught the subtle change in her expression—the darkening of the green flecks in her eyes. She knew—Jessica Martin knew!

Her voice remained calm and poised. "Mr. Franklin, I repeat, I do not discuss my clients."

"Then you admit World Vision is a client?"

"I admit nothing and I think you'd better leave."

"Look," he said matter-of-factly. "We already know they're your clients. We know about the toxicologist your firm placed there. And we know the reason he left the company. We're aware of the circumstances." He shrugged lightly. "You can make this easy or difficult, but you can't just walk away from it. It's no longer a secret," he finished.

Jessica felt a pang of apprehension, but covered it, saying, "Mr. Franklin, I am a woman of great patience, but I'm losing it fast. I have no idea what you're talking about, and if I did, I reiterate, I would never discuss a client or a candidate with you."

Ed Franklin hadn't become tops in his field by giving up easily. This woman could save him a lot of time tracking down the doctor—he wasn't going to let her off the hook now. "Mrs. Martin, surely you realize the seriousness of this situation? I can appreciate your quandary—your reluctance to breach confidentiality." He raised his voice slightly. "We know! The doctor is in hiding for fear of his safety. There's only one way he can reveal what he knows and remain safe, and that is to go public! To go public in a big way! 'Right to Know' is about as big as you can get." He added an irrefutable argument. "Once we go public with this, no one would dare touch him or his family."

He had her attention now. She was listening intently. He continued hurriedly, "Look, the FDA will cooperate with us, and we'll guarantee him protection. He'll be perfectly safe, we'll see to that. And those bastards, excuse my language, won't get away with it."

He softened his tone, saying, "You needn't be involved; anything you tell me can be kept off-the-record—nothing you say will be used for attribution. We protect our sources." He leaned toward her again. "Just tell me where the doctor is hiding, give me his name, and I'll take it from there."

Jessica's mind raced. What should she do? Was he right? Would going public be the safest thing to do? How did she know she could even trust this Ed Franklin? How did she know he was even who he said he was? She couldn't tell him—she couldn't tell anyone, not before she talked to Sol Bernstein once more.

Her tone was even, concealing the uncertainty. "I'm sorry, Mr. Franklin, I can't help you. I really do not know what you are talking about."

He looked at her with a mixture of sadness and contempt. Jessica felt his disgust and cringed inwardly. He must think her an unfeeling monster, someone unconcerned about the harm those drugs could do to people. But she had to protect Bernstein; she had given her word. She would try to find him, convince him to go to Franklin himself, but she would not tell Ed Franklin anything.

Ed tucked his reporter's pad into his breast pocket. "As I said, you could make it easy, Mrs. Martin. Eventually I'll find him—we mean him no harm, we want to help him." He stood up. "Someone tipped us about this, so someone besides yourself and the doctor knows. That's a pretty heavy burden for you to carry, don't you think?"

He turned and walked to the door of the office, where he put his hand on the doorknob, then faced her again. "You'll force me to start asking questions at World Vision."

Jessica remained silent. He took one last shot. "I'll be at the Beverly Hilton, if you should change your mind. Again, your name need never be mentioned."

He waited a moment, but Jessica's face remained impassive. Jessica Martin knew all about it, even though she hadn't cracked. Her eyes told it all.

Chapter 30

As soon as Ed Franklin made his exit, Jessica's legs began to shake. She felt her heart beating against her chest and it took three tries before her hands would stop trembling long enough to light a cigarette.

Who could have talked? And what the hell did she do now? Sol Bernstein still hadn't called her back, and with the "Right to Know" people snooping around, his life could be in even more danger.

This was too big to handle on her own. She reached out to dial Jeremy's number, but stopped herself. She couldn't start running to him with everything that happened; she was already sorry she'd told him as much as she had. No one else should have to get involved in this.

She had to clear her head. When wrestling with a problem, she always made a list of the components. In this case, the people who knew about the file: there was Dr. Bernstein, the attorney who had left World Vision, herself, and David Clarendon. The doctor certainly couldn't have talked, or Ed Franklin would know his whereabouts.

She hadn't revealed that much to Jeremy, and it was inconceivable to her that he would have breached her confidence, unless—unless his fear for her was so great—but no! Impossible. That only left the attorney and David Clarendon. She couldn't imagine that David was the one, he'd been adamant about not getting involved and that meant complete silence on his part.

Perhaps Dr. Bernstein had been wrong—perhaps the attorney had been unable to live with it; maybe he had a conscience after all.

If it was him, the next step was contacting the attorney, letting him know what a dangerous situation he had created for Dr. Bernstein, and trying to get him to tell her where she could reach the doctor to warn him. She had to get to Sol Bernstein and convince him to talk to Franklin. But how? She didn't even know the attorney's name.

She wasn't using her head, she chided herself. She could find the name, she was an excellent recruiter. She took the Corporate Counsel Directory from her shelf. It broke down all attorneys within a corporation according to their area of law. World Vision would not have that many regulatory attorneys on staff. She would have to use an old recruiter trick to find out which lawyer was the right one, but it wouldn't be that difficult.

Quickly she scanned the list. There were five of them. Dr. Bernstein had referred to him as a "young punk." Jessica looked up the credentials of the five attorneys listed; three of the five were very senior. So she had only to make her call based on the two younger men.

She dialed World Vision's number and asked for the legal department. If she was lucky, she'd get his name with one phone call. It was either Jonathan Cabbot or Paul Mellon.

When the legal department answered she used a recruit name so as not to be recognized. "This is Marla Adams. Is Jonathan Cabbot in the office?"

The girl said she would ring his extension. Bingo! Jessica had her man. It wasn't Cabbot. The man she wanted was Paul Mellon.

"Mr. Cabbot's office."

"Oh, I'm sorry," Jessica said quickly. "I guess I've been

given the wrong extension. I was calling Paul Mellon. Could you get the operator to transfer my call?"

"I'd have your call transferred," the girl said politely, "but Mr. Mellon no longer works for World Vision."

It was time for recruiter trick number two. "Oh dear, when did he leave?" she asked, allowing a note of distress to enter her voice. "I mean, I'm an old friend from law school. I've been in Europe the past two years. I didn't know he'd changed jobs."

"Europe? How lucky can you get," the girl said. "I'd sure like a couple of years in Europe."

Jessica didn't want to alienate the girl, she wanted information. Reining in her impatience, she said, "You wouldn't want two years there as a lawyer, believe me. I hardly saw a thing, just work, work, work." She took a deep breath and said as nonchalantly as she could, "Listen, do you have any idea where Paul is now? I'm really anxious to reach him—I haven't seen him in a long time."

"Well," the girl hesitated, "we aren't supposed to give out that kind of information, but what the heck, if you are old friends . . . he's working at Carlton Chemicals in New Jersey."

Jessica quickly thanked the girl and terminated the call. She looked up the number for Carlton Chemicals, glancing at her watch as she dialed. It was four-thirty in the East. He should still be in his office.

The phone rang several times and she waited nervously before the operator came on and rang his extension. "Paul Mellon," he answered in a harassed voice.

Relieved, she said quickly, "Mr. Mellon, this is Jessica Martin of Martin Management Consultants in Beverly Hills. Have you a moment to talk with me?"

"Look, Mrs. Martin," he answered impatiently, "you've caught me at a bad time. My secretary is out ill and my desk looks like the remains of the *Titanic*. Besides, I'm not interested in talking to any headhunters. I've just made a job change and I'm quite happy here."

"Mr. Mellon," Jessica interjected quickly, "I'm not calling to discuss a career change. I'm calling to discuss Dr. Sol Bernstein."

There was silence on the line and Jessica could almost smell the fear in the man.

"Can you wait a minute?" he asked, his voice tight. "I want to close my office door." There was a long pause and when he came back on the line, his voice was falsely jovial and cooperative. "Now, what do you need? A character reference? I can't tell you very much—I did work at World Vision, and of course I met Sol a few times, but I really didn't get to know him."

Jessica was not surprised he'd try to fake it out, but she knew just the mention of Bernstein's name had distressed Mellon. "Mr. Mellon," she said, "I'm not doing a reference check. My firm placed Sol Bernstein at World Vision. I'm calling to discuss his reason for leaving the company."

"Well," Mellon said expansively, "I'm afraid I can't help you out there, either. I don't know why he left. In fact, I didn't know that he had left."

"Please, Mr. Mellon," Jessica insisted, "let's not play verbal chess. You do know why he left; it was you who suggested he leave." She could hear his quick intake of breath over the line. She continued, "And it is for that reason that I've called you." She paused a moment, then said, "Someone else knows the reason he left. And that someone talked to an investigative reporter about it. I'm calling to find out if that person was yourself, and if you know where Dr. Bernstein can be reached. I don't think I have to tell you how serious this situation is."

"Look, I don't have the slightest idea of what you're talking about! I don't even know where Sol Bernstein is, I haven't even spoken his name since I last saw him at World Vision." Belligerently he added, "I don't know what you're up to, but you'd better not try to involve me in anything!"

"Mr. Mellon," Jessica said, "I'm not trying to involve you. But if what Dr. Bernstein says is true, you're already involved. If you know where he is, you must tell me."

"I don't have to tell you anything!" He was practically shouting. "I don't even have to talk with you! I will say it once more and once only: I know nothing about him or his reason for leaving World Vision! I don't know where he is and I don't want to know! Don't call me again!" And with that, he slammed down the phone.

Angry tears of frustration filled Jessica's eyes. It was obvious that Mellon hadn't been the one to tip Ed Franklin. The man was much too frightened. He wouldn't have talked to anyone about it.

That left her with David Clarendon, and she didn't expect any more cooperation from him than from Mellon. She buzzed her bookkeeper on the intercom to ask if David had filed for unemployment insurance. In minutes the bookkeeper was back on the line to state that he had and was still collecting. Jessica asked for his home phone number from the file card, hung up the intercom, and dialed it.

Clarendon answered on the fourth ring, sounding a bit out of breath.

"David," she said, "it's Jessica. You sound a little winded. Are you all right?"

"Sure," he answered. "I'm fine. I was out by the pool."

"Well, I'm sorry to take you away from the sun, but I have to talk with you."

There was a pause, then, "Had a change of heart? If you're willing to forgive and forget, so am I." He chuckled. "Although I must admit, I'm enjoying this time off. But if you're calling to ask me back, I'm all yours."

"I'm sorry, David," she replied, "but that is not the reason I'm calling. I want to know if you've heard anything from Sol Bernstein."

His voice was wary as he said, "Not a word. Why would I?"

"You know very well why you *might* have heard from him," Jessica said sharply. "All right, you say you haven't. Then has anyone contacted you to inquire about him?"

"No, Jessica," he replied, honestly perplexed. "Why should anyone contact me? What the hell is going on?"

Jessica believed him. It was absolutely necessary to make some connection with Sol Bernstein, and if David couldn't help her, where else could she go? She had to level with him.

"David, someone has talked about what Sol Bernstein told us. There's an investigative reporter asking questions about him and World Vision."

David whistled. "Listen, Jessica, forget what I said. At least until all of this has blown over. I'm not ready to come back to work."

Jessica had hit another brick wall. "Okay, David. I understand what you're saying," she replied. "You haven't changed your mind and you still won't get involved. But there is one thing you can do that won't involve you—you can give me some idea where I can locate him. I have to let him know what's going on." She waited for a response but he was silent. "David, he could be in real danger."

"I tried to tell you that, Jessica—I'm glad you are beginning to believe me. I haven't the faintest idea where he is," David said. "But I can give you a suggestion—just for old times' sake. Remember I mentioned he had a brother who's a physician in sole practice in Arizona? In fact, he comes from a long line of physicians, most of whom practice in Arizona. A recruiter with your talent ought to be able to locate a brother."

It wasn't much, but it was better than nothing. "Thank you, David. I'd forgotten about his brother. I'll try that route. Do you know what kind of medical practice he has and where in Arizona?"

"Sorry, Jessica," he answered, "that's all I know. But if you're really bright, you'll stay out of this. There's no reason for you to be involved—neither of us can be connected to this mess."

"One of us already is, David. *I* was the person the investigative reporter interviewed." This time, Jessica hung up the phone. Let the coward stew over *that* for a while.

She was no closer to Bernstein now than she had been. But at least she had a lead. What she had to do was track down Bernstein's brother. That would involve another recruiter call to his former employer, Chem-Tran. She wasn't sure what ruse she would use for that one, but she'd think of something. She'd find the brother and surely *he'd* know where Bernstein was hiding.

Chapter 31

Ed Franklin was thoughtful as he hung up the telephone. The anonymous tipster had called Carlton Brenner again, had given him additional information about World Vision and had given him the name of the doctor Ed was searching for.

It was dynamite information, a terrific lead, exactly what he had hoped he would get from Jessica Martin. But she had refused to cooperate. And if what the tipster had told Carlton Brenner was true, it all began to make sense. Ed Franklin had felt sure Jessica Martin was hiding something, but he hadn't imagined anything like their anonymous caller suspected. That Jessica Martin wouldn't help Ed Franklin because she was trying to get to Bernstein to warn him to destroy the file. That Jessica Martin would be in league with and would protect her client, World Vision.

Somehow, it just didn't figure—Jessica Martin's concern had seemed to be with breaching the confidentiality of a candidate. He hadn't taken her for the type of person who would condone the placement of bad drugs on the market. Still, you never knew. Under all that class and poise, maybe she was an ambitious cookie, out for the bucks.

But something had rankled Carlton Brenner as well, and

he had cautioned Ed to proceed very carefully. In Brenner's opinion, the caller had not sounded like the average anonymous tipster. Usually a tip would be given once and once only, the caller afraid of detection by repeat contact. This tipster seemed desperate to get the information to Brenner. And desperate people could spell real trouble to their kind of investigative reporting, throw all sorts of red herrings into the pot, innocently or as a means of being taken seriously.

Ed intended to be careful; he knew in his gut that this story had merit. He'd seen that in Jessica Martin's eyes. He had to go on the assumption that the tip was genuine; that was his job.

So far, all he had was the name of the doctor. It was thin, especially if the man was in hiding, but it was better than nothing. In the meantime, he had already decided to check out Jessica Martin. He had to know if she was being protective of the doctor, her candidate, or of World Vision.

The gloomy overcast morning mirrored Jessica's feelings as she closed and locked the door behind her, making certain she had hit the combination to activate the elaborate alarm system Michael had installed in the house.

She got into her car, started the motor, and slipped into gear. Her head ached dully. She was spent, emotionally and physically. Wearily she backed out of the garage and into the circular driveway. Changing gears, she headed for the entrance to the main road down the hill and out of the Bel Air gates. She drove without thinking, and when she reached the gates leading onto Sunset Boulevard, instead of making her customary left turn toward Beverly Hills, she found to her surprise she had turned right, onto Sunset, headed toward the Pacific Coast highway.

"What the hell am I doing?" she asked herself. "I should be getting to the office—there's so much to be done. What if Sol Bernstein calls again and I'm not there?" But she continued along Sunset, taking the curves with care, unconsciously holding her breath until she caught sight of the ocean, beautiful to her even on such a gray and cloudy morning. There had always been something soothing about the vast expanse of water. She could not go to the office this morning—she had to clear her head.

She turned right onto the Pacific Coast highway and accelerated to a comfortable speed, the ocean on her left, craggy hillside on her right. She now knew where she was headed, and she knew instinctively that it was somehow the right thing to do.

She drove steadily for over an hour before reaching the turnoff for the nearly concealed private road. Bumpy, narrow, steep, and to someone who had never driven it before, a bit frightening. But Jessica knew every rut, every bend, and drove it with confidence. Her body felt the slight incline as the narrow road began to climb the rocky hill, and she could see in her mind's eye the vista that awaited her some five hundred yards ahead. Already she began to feel calmer. She crested the hill and parked carefully, setting the emergency brake, feasting her eyes on the sight before her.

The ocean appeared endless, the gray clouds beginning to lift as the sun penetrated their layers. Gulls swooped and cried out. The waves lapped with rhythmic consistency, making Jessica breathe regularly for the first time in days. She sat inside a few more minutes, then got out of the car and stood at the very edge of the plateau, looking down at the stretch of beach, the blue and white water, the smog-free sky. This was to have been the site of their dream home— hers and Michael's.

Carefully she stepped over the edge of the plateau onto the makeshift stairs of rocks and wooden planks. It was a steep descent, but she could have made it with her eyes closed, so often had she and Michael come there to plan the house. Dirt clods flew as she climbed down, grasping the skimpy railing Michael had built. When she reached the bottom she blinked, trying to see through the tears that had blurred her vision.

They were still there. The slender little spikes, the rotted yellow ropes, the patchwork design that Michael had staked out as the basic plan for the various rooms—all had miraculously survived the elements.

She stumbled over to what would have been the entry and

began walking through the roped-off squares, circles and L-shapes. Just to her right was the area which would have been the kitchen—a complete circle of glass in which she could cook and see sky, ocean, and nature. And there, to her left, the L-shaped room—Michael's studio. She walked farther into the lot, careful not to disturb anything. Directly in front of her would have been the octagonal living room. It was also glass enclosed, housing an open fireplace in the center of the room with a view of what Michael had always called infinity. They had made love within those octagonal-shaped spikes. Right there on the moist beach, pretending the fireplace was roaring, ignoring the cold against their bare bodies, the scratchiness of the gritty sand. All of this reminded her inexorably of Michael.

She no longer tried to stop the tears. They flowed freely down her cheeks, mingling with the fine mist of the ocean air. She hadn't been there since the accident, hadn't been able to bear the thought that Michael would be unable to make the descent from the plateau to the tiny cove upon which they had planned to build. It was something they never discussed—neither she nor Michael had ever admitted that this particular dream was as lost to them as the use of Michael's legs. Like so many things, they simply pretended it no longer existed. They never spoke of selling the land—never spoke of it at all. But Jessica had never stopped thinking of it. It was to have been more than their dream house, their escape, their hideaway. It was to have been Michael's most unusual architectural concept, his crowning achievement as an artist.

She stepped outside the roped-off plans and walked to the water's edge. She saw a beautiful chunk of driftwood and almost picked it up—Michael had collected driftwood the way others collected antiques and fine art. She stared at the wood for a long moment. No reason to collect it now. Michael would not be there to appreciate it.

She hugged her waist, sobbing unrestrainedly. Why was she torturing herself? There was nothing to be done for it, nothing would change their situation, and Michael had been right to leave. She knew he was no longer the man he had been; he had finally decided to find out what he could become.

Still, the hard lump of pain between her ribs, over her heart, tore at her, cutting off her breath.

Her eyes swept the horizon with its indescribable view. It had always made Jessica feel she had come back to her true home. But not today. What she was feeling now was anything but peace. She felt pain, only pain. *Why* had she come here!

And then, as if the answer had been there all the time, waiting for her, on their private beach, she knew. She couldn't come to grips with her emotions because she hadn't really said good-bye to Michael. Not in her heart, and until she said good-bye, she could not go forward.

And that was what had unconsciously driven her to come to their cove. It was the last bit of the dream, and she had known at some deep level of her heart that until she said good-bye to that place, to the last of their dreams, she could not say good-bye to Michael.

He had said in his parting letter, "The next time we meet, it will be as two very dear old friends." She shivered. Michael had finally accepted what life had cruelly dished out to them, had accepted the past as a beautiful memory.

And as if he had actually spoken, Jessica heard Michael's voice telling her, "And so must you, Jessica. So must you."

With the imagined sound of his voice came a calm, a stillness inside Jessica. She took a deep breath and a last look at the roped-off pegs. She felt a smile touch her lips and her back straightened of its own accord. She reached into her shoulder bag and extracted a handkerchief and her compact. She flicked it open, preparing to dry her tears, when she saw the man behind her.

The sun, now shining directly into her eyes, created a halo around the man. She could not distinguish his features, but reflected in the small round mirror, he stood there atop the plateau, staring down at her. Her heart began to race.

Her palms damp, she nearly lost her grip on the compact. She didn't think he knew she'd seen him. Instinct made her stand perfectly still. Sheer willpower kept her from turning her head. She was completely alone in the isolated cove.

Pretending to fix her makeup, she held the compact at eye level. He just stood there, looking down. Who was he?

Should she confront him? This was private property, as the sign off the coast highway clearly indicated. He had to have seen it. Yet maybe he was just a tourist, someone wanting to get a closer look at the ocean. Or maybe a real-estate agent scouting for properties. Or he could be—a killer—a maniac.

"Stop it!" she silently ordered herself.

She took a deep breath, slipped the compact back into her purse, and swept her eyes down the beach. There was no place to go. The ocean was before her and the man on the plateau above and behind her. She caught sight of the driftwood again. It was a large chunk, and if it came down to it, it would make a good weapon of sorts. On shaky legs she walked back to the water's edge and bent as if to examine the wood. Out of her peripheral vision, she could see the shadowy form still standing above her. Slowly, she lifted the chunk of wood and made a great show of turning it, first to one side, then the other, as if examining its shape. She then reached into her jacket pocket and extracted her handkerchief. She wiped at the sand while she kept him in her line of sight. How long could she stand there holding the wood? Where could she run if she had to?

A sudden movement caught her eye and made her heart pound even faster. Was he coming after her? She gripped the wood firmly between both hands—if he was, she would put up one hell of a fight. She turned to meet her fate, only to see the empty plateau. There was no one there—no one. She stared, adjusting her vision out of the direct glare of the sun. Nothing. All she could see were the front wheels of her car.

Had she imagined it? She racked her brain. Had she heard a car before she became aware of him? She couldn't be sure; the sound of the waves could have blotted out the sound of a car engine. But she couldn't have imagined it. There had been someone there—a man had been watching her. Hadn't he?

She shivered. She couldn't stay there forever, had to

climb those rocky steps and reach the safety of her car.

Nervous but determined, she began to walk slowly back to the steps. She looked up, straining her ears. She heard nothing and could see only the jagged underside of the plateau. She would not know what, if anything, awaited her until she reached the top of the steps.

Saying a silent prayer, she put her foot on the first step, paused, heard nothing, then continued, one shaky step at a time. As she neared the top, she stopped to slow her breathing. The next two steps would bring her head above the plateau, and she would be immediately visible.

She forced her feet to move and mount the final two steps. She balanced herself with one hand on the spindly railing, clutching the driftwood tightly in her other hand.

She climbed the remaining two steps and dashed to her car, grateful for once that she had been too upset to remember to lock the doors. She quickly checked the backseat to be certain no one was hiding inside, dropped the driftwood to the ground, and jumped inside the car, locking the doors.

It took several minutes before she could breathe normally. She forced herself to calm down. She saw not a trace of the man as she drove, faster than she should have, along the narrow bumpy road. She reached the entrance to the coast highway and spun her wheels as she made the turn onto the road.

She drove for nearly ten minutes, keeping a wary eye on her rearview mirror. No one seemed to be following her and she again began to wonder if she had imagined the entire episode. Had the sunlight played tricks on her? Why would anyone be following her? But if it hadn't been her imagination, if it had been just a tourist, an ocean lover, why hadn't he called out to her? That's what beach people did. But then, she hadn't called out to him either.

She shook her head. It made no difference now. She was safe, on her way to her office. Surprisingly, Jessica felt almost serene. Now that her fright had passed, her earlier sense of calm and inner stillness had returned. She had confronted her personal demons, and at last felt ready to face the future on her own. It was a big step forward.

Chapter 32

Paul Mellon's shirt clung to his back under his suit jacket. He'd been going in and out of cold sweats ever since Jessica's telephone call. Christ! He couldn't risk being involved in this mess, and if it went public, he'd be involved, no way around it. He could be disbarred, lose all the years he'd put into the law, lose everything—career, family; hell, his wife was just barely hanging in there as it was. She was still ticked about his leaving World Vision and moving her away from Chicago and her family. She'd be on the first plane out of town if this went public.

He himself had not falsified the documents given to the FDA, but he could still be prosecuted as an accessory. He'd been informed of the file and had advised Bernstein to stonewall it. If that came out it would make him as guilty as World Vision, and he knew there'd be no way he could beat the rap.

Sol Bernstein had to be stopped, persuaded not to give that file to anyone. World Vision would have to shelve the drugs if Bernstein made waves, but even that would be too late for Paul Mellon. The only thing Paul could do was talk to World Vision. But who at World? The head of the legal department? No, he had no power to pull the drugs. Besides, the fewer people involved in this mess the better. Mellon would have to go directly to the top—to George Williams, president of World Vision.

His palms were sweaty and the receiver was slippery in his hand as he waited to be connected to Williams's office. When the secretary asked the usual and in this case maddening question as to the nature of the call, Paul almost hung up. He couldn't tell her. He insisted that it was confidential and urgent, reiterated he was formerly an attorney with the company and was certain George Williams would want to talk with him. She finally agreed and put Mellon on hold.

George Williams's smooth, Ivy League voice grated against Mellon's taut nerves. "Mr. Mellon, this is George Williams. I don't believe we met while you were on our legal staff."

"No, sir. I never had the pleasure." Mellon detested the deference in his tone. It was habit, but dammit, he didn't work for this man any longer, he didn't have to grovel!

"Well, what can I do for you, Mr. Mellon?" Williams said, just a hint of impatience in his voice. "My secretary tells me you feel some urgency in speaking with me."

"It is urgent, sir," Mellon said quickly. "That's why I came directly to you." He took a deep breath, then began. "It's about your two new drugs, Analil-2 and Baromide-7."

George Williams's voice was a hearty boom. "The wonder drugs of the ages," he said. "Yes, sir, an absolute medical breakthrough. Why do you want to talk about them?"

"Mr. Williams, are we speaking on a secure line?" Mellon asked cautiously. "I mean, could anyone listen in?"

There was only a slight pause before Williams responded, "Why don't you give me a number and I'll call you back on my private line."

It took very little time before Williams called back. His voice was wary this time, the Ivy League facade shelved. "Now, Mr. Mellon, just what is so urgent about our new drugs that requires a secure telephone line?"

Paul jumped right in, told Williams of the call from Jessica Martin, of the file Sol Bernstein had told him about, and his

own advice to the doctor that he destroy the file and leave
World Vision.

Williams did not interrupt, but after Mellon had finished,
he had a few questions. "You say this file is in the possession
of Dr. Bernstein? And that no one knows where the good
doctor is?"

"That's the best information I have, Mr. Williams," Paul
responded. "This Jessica Martin thought I'd know—she
thought I might have been the one to talk to the reporter."

"Well . . ." Williams's voice was thoughtful. "Of course
you realize this is all a dreadful mistake. Maybe there were
some toxic side effects in the early testing, but they were all
worked out." The Ivy League smoothness returned. "This
file you refer to must have been old material. There's nothing wrong with those drugs, Mellon, not a thing wrong."

Mellon did not know how to respond. For a moment he
breathed a sigh of relief, but then he remembered Sol's face
and how upset he'd been and the memory overrode what
Williams was telling him. He knew the file was accurate. But
he wasn't going to say that to the man on the other end of the
line; Paul Mellon was scared.

"Well, I was sure of that, sir. That's why I advised Sol to
forget about it." He made his tone a match to the president's. "The thing to do is find him and convince him there's
no problem. I don't know where he is, and from the way the
Martin woman talked, I don't think she does either. Of
course Bernstein might contact her again, I couldn't say. I
also don't know who the investigative reporter is, but it
wouldn't be in World Vision's best interest to have even the
hint of a problem get out."

"I quite agree with you, Mr. Mellon," Williams replied.
"Now, you just relax. We shouldn't have too much trouble
locating Dr. Bernstein. . . ." He paused and the silence
roared in Mellon's ears, before Williams continued in a
remote voice. "Or anyone else we need to have a talk with.
We are not without our own resources, you know." Confident again, he continued, "We'll be able to reason with the
doctor, show him he's wrong." Williams's voice was con-
spiratorial. "You did the right thing by calling me. You're a

good man, Mellon. I don't exactly know why you left us, but should you ever wish to come back to Chicago, just give me a call."

Mellon was about to thank him when Williams added one last thing:

"And by the way—I don't think it would be wise of you to talk about this to anyone else." The warning was implicit in his next words. "And if anyone calls you, I think you'd just better plead ignorance of the whole affair, don't you agree?" Without waiting for a response, he finished "We'll handle *everything*. Good-bye, Mr. Mellon." And the line went dead.

Paul Mellon didn't know if he felt better or worse. He knew now that Sol Bernstein had been absolutely right about that file. There was something in the tone of George Williams's voice, something in the way Williams had said "We'll handle *everything*" that made his blood run cold.

Those were the big boys, just as he'd warned Sol. Well, he'd shown them he was on their side, that he'd tried to dissuade Sol, and that the minute he had any information he'd gone directly to them with it. The way Paul figured it, that meant they owed him. In fact, Williams's offer to return to the company proved that. The big boys took care of their own.

He decided he felt better. He could forget about the whole thing; they'd handle it. After a while, maybe he would call Williams, maybe he'd take him up on his offer. It would get his wife off his back and maybe because he'd shown them he was a corporate man there might even be a good raise or promotion in it.

Maybe he'd come out of this thing smelling like a rose.

Chapter 33

Sol Bernstein stared unseeingly at the orange-blooming cacti lining the long dirt road that led to his brother's ranch house. The Arizona heat was intense but the air was dry. The endless stretch of desert was quiet and beautiful, but Sol was too tortured to appreciate the scenery.

As a scientist, as a human being, he felt enormously guilty in not having gone to the authorities. He knew he was a coward and knew just how much human suffering those drugs could cause. He was aware of his duty as a scientist and as a man. But what of his duties as a husband and father?

Maybe the FDA could protect their lives, but he would be finished in industrial medicine. The corporate network would go into full swing and no company would ever hire him if he blew the whistle on World Vision. And industrial medicine was all he knew; the only way he could support his family, educate his children. Still, maybe the FDA would find him a place in government.

He sighed. Why in hell had he given in to the panic and told Clarendon? Why in hell had he told Paul Mellon? He was an idealistic old fool. He'd believed Mellon would have been as outraged as himself. Still—if he'd only left it with

Mellon. Hell, he could have invented a million excuses to Clarendon for wanting a new job. He'd acted like an hysterical idiot.

He was honest by nature, but panic had taken the place of his better judgment. And if he was to believe the Martin woman, Clarendon had turned tail as fast as Mellon. Neither man worried Sol, but Jessica Martin did. She'd pushed too hard for him to go to the FDA. But still, what could she do? She was honor-bound not to breach confidentiality, and if she went to the FDA herself it would mean nothing without Sol's testimony and the file.

"Water under the bridge," he thought wryly. He was wasting time trying to explain his actions to himself when he should be thinking of his options. He'd planned to lie low for a while, take some time to think things over calmly, come to his own decision as to what he should do. Maybe figure a way to get the file to the FDA anonymously, without it being traced back to him. Could he do that?

Something caught his peripheral vision. He turned his head, his eyes scanning the long, twisting dirt road. A car was approaching, at a speed that indicated the driver had not traversed this road before. The isolated ranch was his brother's retreat from the heavy demands of his medical practice. Whoever was coming down that road did not belong there, and Sol felt the beads of perspiration gather on his forehead.

His first thought was to go inside and lock up the house. He was alone, having sent his wife and the children to stay with relatives. His brother wouldn't be coming to the ranch until the weekend. What should he do? Wait to see who it was? Go inside and call someone? But even if he knew what to tell the sheriff, it would take him an hour to get there.

There was nothing to do but wait it out. He judged the car was still a good five minutes away, so he quickly went inside and got the automatic pistol his brother kept to scare off coyotes. Tucking it out of sight under his sweatshirt, he grabbed an extra drinking glass, returned to the porch, and sat down, wondering if he'd have the courage to use the gun.

As the car neared the front porch, he could see through the dusty windshield that the driver was alone. He appeared to be a young man with red hair. He looked like a college kid, probably a nature-loving tourist who'd lost his way. Still, Sol did not speak as the man stepped out of the car, mopping his brow.

Ed Franklin grinned. "Whew! This desert heat is really something."

Sol nodded his head, thinking he was probably right, a lost tourist. But he volunteered nothing.

Ed continued, "Mind if I come up on the porch for some shade?"

Sol felt the reassuring cold steel of the pistol under his shirt. No reason to be inhospitable, not yet. "Suit yourself," he said. "You must be lost—not many people live around here. I guess I know them all. Haven't seen you before."

Ed grinned again, stepped up onto the porch, and took the chair Sol indicated. "I've never been to Arizona before, but it sure is one beautiful state."

"This ranch is pretty far off the beaten path for a tourist," Sol stated. "What brought you way out here? One of those nature trails?"

As with Jessica Martin, Ed decided not to play any games. He'd tell Sol Bernstein why he was there, throw him off guard immediately. "I'm not a tourist. My name is Ed Franklin and I'm an investigative reporter for the 'Right to Know' production team." He paused for the barest moment before saying, "And you must be Dr. Sol Bernstein."

Sol's panic returned. How had they found him? He'd have to pretend he didn't know why the man was here, try to play the unsophisticated country doctor.

He covered his anxiety with what he hoped was an innocent demeanor. " 'Right to Know'? That's a TV show, isn't it? What on earth are you doing way out here? And how did you know my name?"

"I came here specifically to see you." Ed spoke slowly and carefully. "We're doing a story on World Vision Pharmaceuticals. That's why I want to talk to you."

Sol wasn't going to offer anything. "I'm no longer with World Vision, Mr. Franklin. So I'm afraid you've had a long, hot drive for nothing."

Ed smiled wryly. "Seems like everyone I talk with tells me I'm wasting my time when I bring up World Vision. I know you are no longer with the company, Doctor. That's why I want to talk to you."

"Doing a show on the pharmaceutical industry? Might be of interest to some people, I suppose." Sol added, "But again, I'm afraid you've wasted a trip if you came to talk to me. I wasn't with the company long enough to help you. I came out of the chemical industry, pharmaceuticals were a bit too tame for me." He smiled. "Now if you wanted to talk chemicals, I might be your man."

Sol indicated the pitcher of lemonade on a tray by the chairs. "It's a shame, such a long, hot drive. But look, help yourself to a glass of lemonade; I put out an extra glass when I heard you coming." He kept his voice calm. "Have a nice cold drink before you head back. You don't want to be driving the desert at night unless you know your way."

Ed recognized the man's fear. Bernstein was trying to be cagey, but his folksy charm wasn't working. The man was sharp and Ed knew it. "Dr. Bernstein, it's much too hot to play games. We know about the file and why you left World Vision."

Sol's color paled. Who else knew? How long before World Vision knew? Or did they already know? Was this man really who he said he was, or was he with World Vision? He moved in his chair as if to adjust his posture, and with the same movement, pulled the gun from beneath his shirt and pointed it directly at Ed Franklin.

Ed was startled, but he didn't panic. He didn't like looking down the barrel of a gun, but realized Sol was terrified. He wouldn't shoot unless he was pushed.

Sol's own voice betrayed his discomfort. "Okay, Mr. Franklin—if that is your name—just who are you, and what do you want?"

"Ed Franklin *is* my name," Ed said firmly. "And I *am* with 'Right to Know.' " He softened his tone. "You can put the gun away. You've got nothing to fear from us, we want to help you." Sol said nothing and Ed continued, "I just want to talk to you about World Vision and the toxic effects of the two new drugs they intend to release on the market. Drugs called Analil-2 and Baromide-7."

Now Sol was certain the man was a fraud. The names of those drugs had not been made public; only the FDA and World Vision knew the drug names. He didn't know who the hell this kid was, but he was going to be damn careful with what he said. "I think I heard those names mentioned when I was with World Vision," Sol began, "but I'm curious as to how you'd know them; they haven't been announced to the public yet."

"I told you," Franklin said calmly, "I'm an investigative reporter. I have my sources. It wasn't difficult to find out the names of the drugs." He paused, then continued with some urgency, "Look, Dr. Bernstein, you can trust me. I think you know you've got to trust someone. You're hiding out of fear for yourself and your family. We know all about it."

Ed reached into his pocket and carefully withdrew his wallet, keeping his eye on the gun. "I have identification if you'd care to see it."

Sol snorted. "A press card is easy to come by, Mr. Franklin." He kept the gun pointed at Ed. "Now, you tell me who you really are and how you found me. I've told no one where I am. Not even my wife and children know. Who told you?"

Franklin sighed. "As I said, we have our sources. But to put your mind at ease, I'll tell you how I found you. I talked to Dr. Roberts—the man who took your place at Chem-Tran. He's a great admirer of yours, told me you had trained him and even recommended him as your replacement."

So far his information was correct. Sol had trained and recommended Dr. Roberts. He relaxed his grip on the gun a little.

Ed continued, "I told Dr. Roberts you were one of several men in toxicology we wanted to do a feature on. I told him you were on vacation from World Vision and that no one knew where you'd gone. I convinced him that time was important to this segment, otherwise we wouldn't interrupt your vacation." He took another sip of lemonade, noting that Bernstein had relaxed slightly. "Roberts was delighted that your work would be recognized, so he was very cooperative. He suggested you'd probably go to your brother's ranch in Arizona." Ed smiled and shrugged his shoulders. "Getting information is really quite simple, Doctor. People don't realize how simple it is."

For the first time, Sol began to believe Ed Franklin might be who he said he was. Dr. Roberts knew how much Sol loved the ranch and the peaceful desert. He *would* have suggested it as the place Sol would most likely go. Still, why "Right to Know"? That was the part that didn't make sense. "Let's say for a minute that you and I might have something to talk about, Mr. Franklin. Something like the file you refer to," Sol said carefully. "Let's say there are drugs known as Analil-2 and Baromide-7. Why would your program be interested in them? And how—if they do exist—did your program become aware of them?"

"Exposing consumer rip-offs is the thrust of our show," Ed explained. "And particularly when people can be physically harmed. As to how we found out—we were tipped, the same way we find out about a lot of bad news." He looked Sol straight in the eyes. "A simple anonymous phone call with just enough information to put us onto you."

Sol's panic returned unabated. A tip! Who the hell would do that? And why a TV show? Why not the FDA? "I suppose asking who your source is would be useless?" he asked.

Ed nodded. "Even if we knew the source, we wouldn't tell you. But in this case we don't know. We've checked into this carefully, however, and feel it has validity. We want to help you."

Sol sagged in his chair, the gun now held limply in his lap. They knew. He couldn't fool this man who was not, he realized, the naive young kid he'd first taken him to be. "This tip—they used my name. They knew what was in the file?"

Ed decided the best thing was to tell him everything as it had happened, so he'd cooperate. "No, at least not during the first phone call. They told us about the toxic effects of the drugs. But from there on, we were working blind, using our usual methods of following through on a potential story."

"But how did you get to me?"

"We have our methods—not nearly as glamorous as most people think. The point is, we did get your name and I'm here. The next move is up to you."

Sol knew the next move *was* his, but he wasn't ready to make it yet. He needed to know more, much more, before he committed himself.

"I'd like you to tell me everything, from the very beginning," Sol said.

Ed poured another glass of lemonade. His throat was dry from the heat and excitement. He was onto something big. He eyed Sol over the rim of his glass. He took a deep breath and began from the first phone call. Sol listened in silence, his suspicions of Jessica Martin growing. She *had* to be the one who had given Franklin his name. She had broken her word. The so-called tipster had been Jessica Martin.

"You don't have to continue, Mr. Franklin," he interrupted, his voice heavy with anger and resignation. "I know it must have been the Martin woman. She gave you my name, didn't she?"

"Hardly!" Ed sputtered. "I couldn't get that lady to give me the time of day!"

Sol looked suspicious, but Ed continued persuasively, "Look, I already told you we don't know who tipped us, but I do know it wasn't Jessica Martin. The second time our tipster called it was suggested that we get to you in a hurry because Jessica Martin would be working for World Vision's interest. That she would try to find you and persuade you to destroy the file."

Sol frowned. Maybe he was wrong about Jessica Martin. Something sure didn't add up. "But Jessica Martin was insistent I go to the FDA," he said, bewildered.

The two men were silent for a moment, each busy with his own thoughts.

Sol's fears mounted. Maybe the reason Jessica Martin had been so insistent he come to her office to meet with her personally was not to convince him to go to the FDA, but to get her hands on that file and help World Vision get Sol Bernstein.

Ed remembered his initial reaction to Jessica. He just didn't believe the tipster about her—yet the caller had been so adamant. He sighed, hoping he could find the right words to convince Sol Bernstein that his only safe bet was using the TV show to go public.

"Look, Dr. Bernstein, I don't know yet if the Martin woman is involved. But I do know there is only one way you can handle this: go public and go big! And 'Right to Know' is about as big as you can get," he said strongly. "The FDA will work with us and we'll protect your family. Once this story is on the air and the whole nation knows what World Vision tried to get away with, no one would dare harm you or your family."

"What about Karen Silkwood?" Sol exploded. He could not get the girl out of his mind. "Somebody got to her, didn't they?"

Ed sighed. "Her death was determined to be an accident, Dr. Bernstein." Ed pulled his chair a bit closer to Sol. "But just suppose it wasn't—that proves my point. Miss Silkwood was *not* on her way to the 'Right to Know' offices. I tell you we can protect you. You have my word on it *and* the word of the network."

Sol thought for a moment. Maybe this man was right. In any case, what other out did he have? "Just how would you do all this?" he asked cautiously.

"We'll send your family on an extended cruise trip, guarded and protected twenty-four hours a day. They can enjoy a vacation at the same time. You will come to New York with me. We'll begin putting the information together. We'll bring in top government toxicologists to assist you and we'll have all of your tests documented. That will verify what you found in the file. You'll be guarded around the clock. You'll put World Vision out of business."

"Not to mention putting myself onto a permanent unemployment line," Sol said bitterly. "There won't be a corporation in the country who will hire me after I blow the whistle."

Ed laughed. "Dr. Bernstein, you need a little education about the impact of television. After we get through with the segment, after the world finds out what a courageous and dedicated doctor you are, there won't be a company in the world that isn't *begging* to have you on staff."

The look on Sol's face was less skeptical and Ed continued hurriedly. "Look, not all companies are corrupt. You'll be a national hero, and aside from your excellence as a scientist, any company would jump at the chance to have you on board. What better endorsement of corporate integrity could a company offer its stockholders than that of a man who risked his life and career to ensure the public's safety?"

It made sense. Things were looking a little brighter. "When would all this take place?" Sol asked.

"You can leave with me tonight, right now," Ed said. "Is the file here?"

Sol was too cautious for that one; he wasn't going to blindly follow this man into a possible trap. He kept his voice calm. "No, the file isn't here. I wouldn't keep anything that hot with me. I'll have to get the file. I'll meet you in New York."

Ed Franklin frowned. "Dr. Bernstein, I can only guarantee your protection if you are with me. Let me go with you to get the file, then we'll go to New York together."

His words made sense, but Sol still didn't trust him completely. He patted the gun he was still holding in his right hand. "I can take care of myself until I get to New York," Sol said. "No one knows about the file except you, the Martin woman, and two other men who are too terrified to get involved. I'll get the file and bring it to you in New York."

Ed hesitated for a second. He sure as hell didn't want to scare him off, but he also didn't want to run the risk of Bernstein disappearing on him. "I understand, Doctor. You still aren't sure of me. But I swear to you I am who I represent myself to be. Maybe you are convinced about those other two men, but what if our caller is correct and Jessica Martin is involved in this? What about her?"

"She doesn't know where I am, not yet anyway," Sol replied. "I'll be gone before she finds out."

"Okay, Doctor. But you'd better make it soon. I think she's a pretty sharp cookie, and I'm sure she'll get to Dr. Roberts the same as I did." He finished his lemonade and rose, saying, "Be extra careful until you get to us. Once you're actually in New York and under our care, you'll have nothing to worry about." He extracted his card from his wallet and handed it to Sol. "Here's where you can reach me. Can I count on you?"

Sol nodded and the two men shook hands solemnly.

Ed walked down the porch steps, got into his car, and in a moment was driving down the dirt road toward the main highway. He had mixed feelings—he was elated over what promised to be the biggest story of his career, and worried sick about letting Sol Bernstein out of his sight until everything was wrapped up. He shook his head. There was nothing he could do about it—the man had been adamant.

Sol waited some forty minutes before going inside and removing the file from its hiding place. He then called his brother to say he'd be leaving that night and would be able to explain everything to him soon. He packed his few things, drove into town, and boarded the first plane to Newark, Delaware, where his wife and children were staying with relatives. He would have to tell his wife what was going on—he could think of no other way to convince her to take the extended cruise Ed Franklin had offered. But his Bess was a brave and sensible woman. Now, with a solution at hand, it would be safe to tell her everything.

Chapter 34

Jessica hung up the phone dejectedly, a sense of relief mixed with failure. Ed Franklin would have made an excellent recruiter. He'd gotten to Dr. Roberts at Chem-Tran way ahead of her and was already en route to Arizona and Sol Bernstein. There was no way she could intercept Sol and prepare him for Franklin's arrival. It would be up to Franklin to convince Dr. Bernstein to go public with the file. From there it would be up to the "Right to Know" people to protect him. Jessica had tried; she'd maintained confidentiality, and now she could get back to her other clients.

She was about to buzz Carol on the intercom when the door to her office burst open and Stacey stormed in like a whirlwind. Her eyes were flashing and her usually perfect hair was in total disarray.

"Stacey!" Jessica exclaimed. "What on earth? Haven't you ever heard of knocking?"

Stacey slammed the door shut and stormed over to stand before Jessica's desk. She slapped her hands down hard on the surface, causing the heavy crystal ashtray on the top to shudder. Her voice was filled with fury. "Jessica, I want you to fire that little prick and I want you to do it this minute."

Jessica was in no mood for one of Stacey's tantrums. "Stacey, please take your hands off my desk and lower your voice. I do not appreciate your barging in here unannounced and uninvited and I particularly do not appreciate you shouting orders at me." She forced herself to calm down. "If there is something on your mind that you wish to discuss with me, take a seat and we will do so."

Stacey glared at Jessica, but she removed her hands from the desk and took a seat by the fireplace.

"Stacey," Jessica asked wearily, "who is it you want fired this time?"

Stacey's tone was a study in controlled fury. "The little prick. Tom Jason."

Jessica sighed. This was a record. She'd known how tough it would be for a man to take orders from Stacey, but Tom Jason had only been on board a couple of weeks. What could he have done in so short a time? "Stacey," Jessica began, "I warned you that having a male assistant would take careful handling. What happened?"

"That little bastard went to one of my clients behind my back!" The control was now gone. "He presented a candidate to one of my very best clients. He didn't even check with me first! I'm goddamned pissed about it!"

"That doesn't sound bad enough to warrant this strong a reaction," Jessica commented. "Unless the candidate was inappropriate, the client annoyed?"

"No!" Stacey spat back. "The candidate was fine. In fact they want to interview him. He didn't make a mistake in the choice of a candidate, but he did not check with me!" Her cheeks were flushed bright red, her eyes still blazing. Had Jessica not been so annoyed by Stacey's tantrum, she'd have been fascinated by this totally out-of-control display. "How dare he do such a thing? Just who the hell does he think he is?"

Jessica kept her voice noncommittal. "I rather imagine he thinks he's a person doing his job. He was hired to assist you," she continued. "By arranging an interview I would suggest that he's doing his job rather well."

Stacey lit a cigarette, the smoke streaming from her

nostrils, giving her the appearance of an angry dragon. "His job is to *assist me*, period! He is not to contact my clients! No one contacts my clients! No one!"

Jessica felt her own anger mount. Coolly, she said, "Stacey, I think there is something you're forgetting here. The clients you refer to are clients of this firm. Of *my* firm. They are the accounts you are assigned to, but they are the clients of Martin Management Consultants." She confronted Stacey directly. "I'm afraid you lose sight of that fact."

"The hell I do!" Stacey shot back. "You can call them *your* clients if you want to—if you get off on playing the boss lady, be my guest. But let me tell you something—those clients are mine, I don't care what label you put on it." She leaned forward and clenched her hands into tight fists. "If I left this firm every damned one of them would follow, wherever I go. So let's get this straight—I won't have anyone contacting *my* people. And I want that prick fired."

Jessica was furious with Stacey's presumption. "Stacey, I'm going to have Carol hold my calls, and then you and I are going to have a long overdue chat."

Jessica sat down behind her desk and buzzed Carol. This would not be one of the times Jessica sat opposite an employee by the fireplace. She would conduct this meeting from behind her desk as head of her company.

"Stacey," she began, "there is no question you've been a valuable employee. But you seem to have trouble maintaining your perspective. You seem to forget that you *are* an employee." She paused for emphasis. "*I* own Martin Management Consultants. I like to give my department heads free rein, but there is a limit to what I will tolerate."

Stacey calmly took a cigarette and lit it before replying. "I'm the most valuable recruiter you have here, and you and I both know it. I've brought in damn near as many retainer contracts as you have." Her manner was cold, determined. "You'd like to run this place like one big happy family. The Waltons at work and play. Well, that's bullshit. This is a business and I make my living from it." She took a deep drag on the cigarette and added, "I will not be told who to have in my department. I want Tom Jason fired. He has to go."

"Tom Jason will go if and when *I* decide he has committed a big enough error to warrant dismissal. I think there is more to this than his merely contacting a client."

"There's more all right. We had such a row over this the entire office heard us. But closed up here in your ivory tower, you missed all the goodies." Stacey's sarcasm was replaced by renewed anger. "I called Tom on the carpet for having gone over my head and I warned him if it happened again he'd be out the door in two seconds flat!" Stacey crushed out her cigarette and immediately lit another.

Jessica stared at Stacey. She'd never seen her this angry.

"And that little bastard," Stacey ranted, "that ball-less little prick of a bastard dared laugh at me. In front of everyone, he laughed in my face."

"In front of everyone? Just where did this confrontation take place?"

"In the coffee room—what the hell difference does that make?" Stacey answered bitterly. "I warned him," she hissed, "that if he didn't stop laughing he'd be wearing his coffee instead of drinking it. And he only laughed harder." Stacey's voice rose again. "You would not believe the nerve!" Pulling herself somewhat together, she continued, "Anyway, I told him to forget about it happening again. I told him he'd just laughed himself out of a job. I told him he was fired!"

Stacey angrily crushed out the half-smoked cigarette. "He just laughed and said, 'I was hired by Mrs. Martin. If I'm fired it will be by Mrs. Martin. I'm going to be the best damned recruiter in the business and no broad with penis envy is going to hold me back.' " Stacey paused to catch her breath, her eyes full of hatred. "Can you believe that? Penis envy!"

Jessica had the exact lead she needed. "It would appear," she said quietly, "that his choice of descriptive was as unfortunate as your choice of a site for the meeting." Ignoring Stacey's protest, she went on, "You showed very poor judgment, Stacey. Tom is a man and I'm sure he has his pride. You should have seen him in the privacy of your office. That way you could have avoided this ugly scene. I don't see that you left him any choice but to respond as he did." She continued, "You're going to have to lose your appetite for an audience, Stacey. It may make you feel good to sound superior, but it's very degrading—and you see the results it brings."

Stacey could be contained no longer. "Oh, when the hell are you going to come down off that ladylike high horse?" she exploded. "I don't care if he's a man or a billy goat! He works for me! I'll talk to him anywhere I find convenient!"

Jessica would not be sidetracked. "You bring me back. Tom Jason does not work for you—Tom Jason is in *my* employ. As *you* are in my employ. That is what you continue to lose sight of." Her voice was steely as she continued, "It's a shame you waste so much energy making trouble, Stacey. You could use that energy to gain loyalty from the people in your department. Your methods only alienate everyone. If your ambition is to someday have your own agency, you should start learning how to handle people with dignity and persuasion."

"I will have my own firm anytime I want, Jessica. And I'll run it a hell of a lot better than you run this one." She spat the words out. "Fortunately, I have other things in my life to fulfill me. I don't have to submerge myself in a business."

It was yet another cheap shot, but Jessica wouldn't rise to the bait. "Since you do not want your own firm at this time, I assume you wish to continue as an employee of Martin Management. That's fine with me—as you say, you are an excellent recruiter." Her eyes flashed. "But only if you remember who owns this company."

When Stacey did not respond, Jessica continued, "That includes Tom Jason. I'll have a talk with him. It's obvious that the two of you can no longer work together, but he's shown considerable promise and I'm going to give him the option of transferring to another department. It will be up to him whether he stays or leaves." She paused, then asked coldly, "Is that clear, Stacey?"

Stacey was seething. "One thing about you, Jessica, you are always very good at making yourself clear." She rose from her chair and stood looking intently at Jessica. "I'm no slouch in that department myself so I'm sure you'll understand me when I say, if you intend to keep Tom Jason on board, then you'd also better take great pains to keep him out of my way!"

With that, Stacey turned on her heel and left the office, slamming the door behind her.

Stacey was a hard case. She seemed so determined to alienate those around her. It was something Jessica had never been able to understand.

She sighed. Stacey might be her most valuable recruiter, but billings or no, Jessica was just about fed up with Stacey Dawson.

Chapter 35

Jessica had been working extremely hard over the past three weeks; she was dead tired and it was now well past 11 P.M. as she turned into the driveway of her Bel Air home. Her dinner meeting with the Eastern law firm for which she was attempting a merger had gone on much later than she had anticipated.

It would be difficult to get all the senior partners of both firms to agree to all terms, she realized, still so deep in thought she at first didn't realize something was wrong. The lights were not on, not in the garage, not in the house, and not around the grounds. And the garage door was open.

She braked to a quiet halt, half in and half out of the garage. The lighting system was automatic and worked off a timer that controlled both the lights and the alarm system. Normally, the electric eye automatically closed the garage door as the car was backed in or out; something was wrong.

Her pulse began to race. "Stay calm," she silently cautioned herself. "It was probably a brief power failure—some freaky thing that set the electronic gadgets off. That's why the lights aren't on. Probably just a power failure."

But that comforting thought was quickly dispelled by the

memory of the backup generator Michael had had installed for just such a situation. Their house was located high atop a hill and frequent high winds meant that power failures were a constant annoyance. No, even had there been a power failure, the backup generator would have gone on and automatically reactivated the lights and the alarm system.

The headlights of her car illuminated the space directly in front of her, but it was a large, four-car garage, and the darkened corners suggested all sorts of terrifying possibilities.

"You can't just sit here," she said aloud. Resolutely, she forced a few deep breaths. "The flashlight, of course." She leaned to her right and fumbled with the catch of the glove compartment door. When it finally sprang open, the click was magnified in the stillness. She extracted the two-celled battery flash, but it did little good as she swept it quickly around the expanse of the garage. She needed the high-powered flashlight in the trunk of the car, but she didn't quite have the courage to get out and retrieve it.

"Come on, Jessica," she said, taking false comfort in the sound of her voice. "You're a big girl now."

With determination, she slowly and carefully panned the garage interior with the flashlight. She saw nothing out of the ordinary. The garage held the usual summer patio furniture neatly stacked at the rear, a few garden tools hung in place on the right wall, and three or four storage cartons, the contents of which she suddenly could not remember.

So far, so good. Slowly, she rotated the beam of light to the left wall and was unable to suppress a gasp when she saw that the inner door to the house was slightly ajar.

Mentally, she retraced her steps of the morning. Could she have forgotten to lock the door and activate the alarm when she left for the office? She had been in a rush. "Think, Jessica. Think," she whispered. But she knew she hadn't forgotten. She had always been compulsive about such things, often coming all the way back up the hill to double-check that she had locked up. She was the same about the gas burners on the kitchen range. She couldn't have forgotten—in fact, since Michael had left and she was alone in the house, she'd become more cautious than ever. Someone must have broken in.

She began to breathe a little easier. It must have been a burglar. A burglar who knew how to disconnect the alarm system. That had to be it—didn't the police say that most burglars hit a house during the daytime when people were away at work or shopping?

She had dismissed the daily housekeeper when Michael had left. Someone could have been watching her movements, could know the house now sat empty all day long except for the three times a week the new cleaning service came in. A professional could have been watching the house and figured out the schedules.

But if a burglar could learn her schedule, he would know she was living there alone, that she would be alone now. What if he was inside, waiting for her? What if she hadn't imagined the man at the cove two weeks ago? What if someone had been watching her, stalking her, was waiting for her right that minute?

Her heart pounded as she tossed the flashlight onto the passenger seat and put the car into reverse. She backed out of the driveway and headed quickly down the hill to the guardhouse at the Bel Air entrance gates.

Her breathing had not quite returned to normal when she reached the guard's station. She had an eerie feeling of having been pursued down the hill, though she'd seen no car lights behind her.

She pulled alongside the kiosk and rolled down her window. Recognizing her, the guard was instantly concerned. "Something wrong, Mrs. Martin?"

Jessica nodded and fumbled for a cigarette. The guard reached into his vest pocket and extracted an ancient Zippo lighter, which he held steady until Jessica's cigarette ignited and she took a deep, relaxing drag.

Jessica smiled nervously. "I may be overreacting, Mr. Baker, but when I drove up to my garage, the door was open and the lights were all out and the door to the house was ajar."

He kept his voice calm, but his eyes were intense. "Is anyone supposed to be at home, Mrs. Martin?"

"No, no one. I'm certain I locked up this morning *and* put on the alarm system. But it seems to be off as well."

The guard glanced at his watch. "The patrol made their sweep about half an hour ago. They didn't report anything unusual. Of course, at this hour of the night they wouldn't necessarily expect to see lights on."

"No," Jessica agreed. "I do think someone has broken in. I know that door was locked."

"Then you didn't go inside?" Jessica shook her head. "Good for you. A lot of folks would have and it's a dumb thing to do." He put the Zippo back into his vest pocket. "You just try to calm yourself—have your cigarette. I'll get the patrol car on the radio. Won't take a second."

Relieved, Jessica allowed herself to relax as she listened to the guard's conversation with the patrol car.

"They should get to your place in about five minutes. Wait here until they go inside and make certain no one is there."

Jessica smiled her thanks and the guard continued, seemingly glad to have a little company. "Yes, ma'am, you were very clever not to go inside the house. Never know what to expect from criminals today. Just last week I read where a bunch pulled up a big furniture cleaning van and completely emptied a house." He shook his head. "Of course, by itself that's not too startling, I mean that one is an old trick. But these guys even took clothing and shoes, cut the chandeliers right off the ceiling . . ."

Jessica was spared a further account of the criminal invasion of private homes by the static sound of the radio as the patrol called to tell her they were waiting for her at her garage.

As she pulled up, one of the patrol guards came forward. "Mrs. Martin, I'm Stu Gelsen. My partner and I have checked the house thoroughly, even checked out the crawl space underneath. Whoever was here is gone now."

Jessica felt slightly ill at the realization that someone *had* been inside her home, had invaded her privacy. Her face paled and Stu Gelsen said softly, "Everybody reacts like that, Mrs. Martin. You'll get your bearings in a minute. Would you like to go inside now?"

At the hesitation he saw in her eyes, he added, "We'll be right here beside you. You'll have to go in to see what's missing. And Mrs. Martin, be prepared." His voice softened. "I'm afraid it's quite a mess."

Dreading to see the damage, Jessica swallowed and trailed behind Stu Gelsen, stopping dead in her tracks inside the foyer. It was far worse than she could have imagined.

Furniture was overturned, upholstery slashed, paintings taken from walls, ripped from their frames. Bookcases emptied, volumes tossed onto the floor, spines broken, dust jackets torn.

She felt her legs begin to buckle and Stu Gelsen was quickly at her side, his hands supporting her at waist and elbow.

"Maybe you'd better sit down for a minute." He jerked his head toward his partner, who quickly righted a chair and helped Jessica into it.

"Can I get you a drink? A brandy maybe?"

"No—no, thank you." Jessica's voice was hoarse with shock. "Are all the rooms like this?"

"I'm afraid so, ma'am. We've called the police, they should be here soon to take a formal report and dust for fingerprints. Our jurisdiction doesn't extend beyond checking the house to see if it's safe to enter." He cleared his throat, affected by the shock and pain he saw on Jessica's beautiful face. "I'm afraid you can't touch anything until they arrive."

"I understand," she murmured. "Can I go through the rest of the house?"

"Well," he stammered, "well sure, I mean, it's your house. But, Mrs. Martin, isn't there someone you'd like me to call? Someone you'd like to be with you right now?"

Jessica had to bite the insides of her cheeks to control the tears that threatened to come. There wasn't anyone she could call. Michael was gone, Jeremy was at home with his family. Except for Carol, there was no one Jessica was close enough to call and she wasn't about to disturb Carol at that hour. She shook her head as the police arrived.

Jessica walked them through all the rooms, becoming more and more sickened by the devastation. Everything had been ransacked, yet nothing had been stolen. Her jewelry was heaped on her dressing table, the outsized jewelry box gutted. Her mink coat was thrown on the floor, the lining ripped from the hem. Expensive stereo equipment, televisions, and VCRs were pried open, their electronic guts exposed. She became more and more confused. Who had done this, and why?

The police sergeant shook his head. "Could have been vandals—some wild kids. It happens more and more these days. But somehow, this just doesn't feel like that to me." His eyes scanned the room again. "Kids usually get all liquored up, but look at the bar—it wasn't even touched."

They both stared at the open mirrored shelves, the glasses and bottles all neatly in place.

"Doesn't make sense. If it was vandalism, they'd have trashed that, too."

Jessica had no explanation to offer, and the sergeant continued his musings. "Could someone have been looking for something in particular, Mrs. Martin?"

Jessica racked her brain, but shook her head. Nothing came to her mind.

"Well," he said, "it was just a thought—you know, like in the movies." His voice trailed off as he recognized his weak attempt at humor had failed.

Jessica thought again of the man watching her from the plateau at the cove. But if it had been him, what could he have been looking for in her house? She shivered.

The sergeant raised his eyebrows. "What is it? Do you remember something, Mrs. Martin? Something somebody could have been looking for?"

"No," she said quickly. "Nothing like that. I'm sure I'm just being foolish, Sergeant, but a couple of weeks ago, I thought a man was watching me—maybe following me."

The sergeant frowned. "Did you report it to the police? Give a description?"

"No, I didn't. I mean, I couldn't—I didn't get a good look at him." She shook her head tiredly. "In fact, I'm not even certain anyone was following me. It could have been my imagination."

"Maybe," he allowed. "But still, if you'll pardon my saying so, you're a very attractive woman, Mrs. Martin. And there are all sorts of nuts running around out there today. You can't be too careful."

Jessica's heart began to race at the thought of some maniac hounding her. But she couldn't let herself start thinking that way, not with everything else that had happened to her.

"I'm sure it was nothing, Sergeant. But I will be careful, I really will. Besides, if it was some madman after me, why would he have trashed the house? Why wouldn't he have waited for me to return?"

The sergeant recognized the naked fear in her eyes and decided nothing could be gained by adding to it. "I'm sure you're right, ma'am. It doesn't make sense. Probably what happened is that someone got the wrong house. Probably weren't looking for this place at all."

Jessica smiled gratefully. "I hope you're right, Sergeant."

"Still, if you are living here alone, I don't think it's a good idea for you to stay here tonight. I'm not suggesting whoever did this will be back, but I don't think you'd feel too comfortable here after seeing all this."

"No, I wouldn't. Thank you, Sergeant, for thinking of that."

"Isn't there a relative you could stay with? Someone you'd like to call?"

"No," she said with more emphasis than she intended. "I mean, I don't want to disturb anyone." Her thoughts focused again on the fact that there was no one she could call. "I'll just go to a hotel." She rose unsteadily. "Do you suppose one of your men could stay here until I get a few overnight things?"

"Certainly! No problem. In fact, I'll stay myself. You pack what you need and I'll have the men close the house. As soon as you're ready, I'll drive you to the hotel in your car."

"Oh, you don't have to do that. I'll be fine."

"Nonsense, you've had a shock. You shouldn't be driving tonight. One of my men can follow us and take me back to the station."

Jessica was too fatigued to argue. "Thank you. I'll only need a few minutes."

She hurriedly packed an overnight bag and gratefully handed her keys to the sergeant who drove her to the Beverly Wilshire Hotel. The blasé expression on the doorman's face did not change as he noted Jessica's police escort. Nothing fazed Beverly Hills doormen.

Once inside her suite, Jessica felt a new surge of panic, as if she might faint. The bellboy noticed how pale she looked. "Is there something I can do for you, Mrs. Martin?"

Jessica felt a little foolish, but her uneasiness overcame it. "Yes, yes there is. Look, I've just had a dreadful experience. My home was ransacked and I'm still very shaky. Would you mind going through the suite for me? Check out the rooms, closets . . ."

As if it were the most ordinary request he'd ever heard, the bellboy smiled cheerfully. "Of course I'll check." He opened the closets, looked behind the bar, went on into the bedroom, and repeated the process, finally checking the bath. He returned to the living room, his smile still in place. "All clear. Sorry about your house. Is there anything else I can do for you?"

"No," Jessica said softly, as she reached into her wallet for a twenty-dollar bill. "Thank you, I feel much safer now."

He accepted the bill and bid Jessica good-night, adding she had only to ring if she needed anything. He would be on duty all night.

Jessica bolted and double-locked the door behind him. Shakily, she sank onto the sofa. She knew it was a cliché reaction, but she felt as though she had been physically violated. Nausea flooded her stomach, and her upper lip beaded with perspiration. It was as if someone had stripped her bare; she felt vulnerable, exposed, even here in the safety of her hotel suite. It was the worst feeling she had ever had and she wondered if she would ever again feel totally private, if she could ever return to live in her house. At that moment, she did not think she could.

Chapter 36

Ed Franklin had been back in New York preparing the groundwork for the segment, working blind without Sol Bernstein's input. All he could do without the doctor was research World Vision, combing the company history for any hint of corporate hanky-panky. He couldn't get into the meat of the story until Bernstein arrived. Ed was beginning to get nervous, worried the doctor had changed his mind and backed out. Or worse, that Jessica Martin was really in league with World Vision and had gotten to Bernstein before he left Arizona, persuaded him to destroy the file. His reporter's instincts told him to trust Jessica, but he couldn't be sure.

The first thing to do, Ed decided, was figure out if Sol had actually left Arizona. This time, posing as a young toxicologist who wanted Bernstein to comment on a paper he was publishing, he contacted the doctor's brother in Arizona, saying he understood Sol was vacationing there. But the call proved fruitless. Sol's brother had no idea where Sol was, said he had left the ranch and was probably back in Chicago.

Ed had to know if Bernstein had changed his mind. He'd have to contact Jessica Martin again, see if he could detect anything. He wasn't sure she would accept a call from him, but he had to try.

When she came on the line, Ed spoke quickly. "I'm glad you decided to accept my call, Mrs. Martin. I wasn't sure you would."

"And I'm not sure why I did, but since I have, why don't you get to the point," she said coolly.

"Look," Franklin began on a conciliatory note, "I guess you're still angry because of the way I got into your office to discuss Dr. Bernstein. I wish you could believe my intentions are only to help him."

Jessica was still determined not to reveal anything. "I don't recall you bringing up any specific name when you came to my office," she said. "I only remember you mentioning World Vision and asking if they were a client of mine."

Ed had to hand it to her, she was quick. He hadn't even known Bernstein's name when he'd seen her. "You're right. I didn't mention Dr. Bernstein by name. You have a good memory for details, Mrs. Martin. You'd make an excellent reporter."

Jessica kept her tone cool. "Look, Mr. Franklin. I am quite content with my present career. Now, what do you want? I don't have time to waste chatting."

"Okay, okay," he said quickly. "Don't hang up. I'm *still* trying to get some information. I want to find out if you know the whereabouts of Sol Bernstein?"

Jessica was stunned. Had she lost her mind? She spoke without thinking. "If *I* know? But you—that is, Dr. Roberts said that you . . ."

Ed jumped in. "You called Chem-Tran, too?"

"Well, yes," she admitted hesitantly. "It seemed the best place to start. He'd worked there a long time. I felt sure someone would know where his brother practiced medicine. Dr. Roberts told me about your call and that he'd given you Dr. Bernstein's brother's name and address."

"Then you knew he was in Arizona?" Ed pressed. "You contacted him at the ranch?"

"No, I didn't. What good would it have done? By the time I found out where he was it was too late to warn him about you."

"Warn him?" She was definitely off guard. Ed continued to press. "Why would you have to warn him about me?"

Jessica cursed herself for taking his call in the first place. She just wasn't thinking clearly. She answered in what she hoped was a controlled voice. "What I meant was that I felt he had a right to know a reporter was asking questions," she finished lamely. "But as I said, by the time I found out where he was you were already en route to him."

"Mrs. Martin," Franklin said slowly, "this is beginning to smell funny. I think it's time we leveled with each other. I did see Sol Bernstein and he admitted the whole thing. Told me about the file, the false FDA reports." He waited for the information to sink in, then continued, "Why don't we quit playing games with one another? Unless you have something to hide?"

"How dare you suggest such a thing?" Jessica stormed, genuinely outraged. "What would I have to hide?"

Ed wasn't ready to accept her just yet. "You'd know that better than I would," he answered calmly. "But our tip was that you were involved in this up to your neck."

"That's outrageous!" Jessica was near tears. How in the world had she gotten into this mess—who could think she was involved? *Involved*. She swallowed hard as a frightening thought occurred to her. Was it possible? Her voice shook. "My God, maybe I am involved."

Ed did not miss the fear in her voice, the harsh whisper. "What do you mean, Mrs. Martin?"

"I don't know! I mean, maybe it isn't connected at all, but I think, no, now I'm certain someone was following me about a month ago and then . . ." She paused for breath as the enormity of what she was thinking began to sink in. "My home was broken into."

There was a slight pause. Franklin sighed and cleared his throat with embarrassment. "Uh, Mrs. Martin, about your being followed . . ."

Jessica massaged her temples. Why was she defending herself to this pushy man? "I suppose you don't believe me?"

"Oh, I believe you, Mrs. Martin. I believe you." His tone was sheepish. "Are you by any chance referring to your trip up the coast highway to that hidden beach cove?"

Jessica caught her breath sharply. "Yes, yes I am. But how did you know? I haven't told anyone."

"Mrs. Martin, please don't hang up before I can explain," he pleaded, and Jessica was too taken aback to interrupt him. "I know about it because I was the one who followed you."

Jessica was stunned into angry silence.

"Look," Ed put in quickly. "I know you're angry—more than angry—and I'm very sorry if I frightened you. I didn't think you even saw me. You certainly kept your cool."

"And I suppose that makes it all right?" Jessica replied, tight-lipped with fury.

"No, of course it doesn't make it all right. But you have to try to understand, Mrs. Martin. That was before I got to Bernstein. I was desperate for a lead. Our tipster said you'd try to get Sol to destroy the file. That you'd protect your client, World Vision. I thought you might meet Sol in secret, that's why I followed you."

Jessica wavered between relief that it was Franklin who had followed her and anger at the invasion of her privacy. "Why didn't you identify yourself? Why did you let me think some madman was stalking me?"

Ed Franklin swallowed, his shame evident in his voice. "Because, Mrs. Martin, it became quickly obvious to me that I had intruded on a very private time. I didn't want you to know that I was there. You didn't act as though you were aware of me, so as soon as I thought I could slip away without you knowing it, I left." He paused and took a deep breath. "I do apologize, Mrs. Martin."

Her voice was hoarse. "And if you're so ashamed, why are you admitting it to me now?" she demanded.

"For two reasons. One, I don't want you to be more frightened than you already have been. I don't want you to think someone is stalking you. And two, to tell you I'm sorry I believed that you were in league with World Vision."

But Jessica was in no mood for an apology. "This entire situation becomes more outrageous by the minute! In league with World Vision! I begged Dr. Bernstein to go to the FDA! How dare you—how dare *anyone* suggest I'd condone releasing bad drugs on the market!"

"I'm not suggesting that anymore. Sol told me you tried to convince him to go to the authorities, but he also said you tried to get him to bring the file to your office. It's just that at that time, neither of us was that sure of you."

Jessica was not appeased. "Well, it's you who have gone too far. I don't care what your suspicions were, I'm a private citizen and you are not the police. You had no right to follow me, to break into my home . . . destroy it . . ."

Ed was stunned. "Wait a minute! I admit I followed you, but break into your home? The closest I've ever been to your home is waiting at the bottom of the hill the morning you went to the cove."

"You'd do anything to get information. Why should I believe you?"

"Because it's the truth." Jessica recognized the genuine urgency in his tone. "I didn't break into your home, but since someone did, I think you'd better tell me about it."

"Just why should I tell you?"

"Because, Mrs. Martin, I've had some experience with this sort of thing. I'll explain my reasons to you, but first, you *must* tell me what happened."

"I don't see that it is any of your business."

"But it *is* my business. I'm as involved in this as you are. And you may be in danger. Please, tell me what happened."

Haltingly, Jessica told him about the night she had returned to her wrecked home. Ed Franklin listened without interrupting, and when Jessica finished, he asked, agitatedly, "And you're certain nothing was taken? The police found no clues? No prints, nothing?"

"Nothing. Just as I've told you. The police think it was either the work of vandals or someone who had the wrong house."

"What do *you* think, Mrs. Martin?"

"I don't know what to think!" Jessica fought to stay calm. Was the destruction connected with Bernstein? "What could anyone expect to find in my home? It *must* have been a mistake."

"Mrs. Martin," Ed kept his tone gentle, "I don't want to alarm you any more than I already have. But it sounds to me as if it was a pretty professional job. I don't think it's safe to assume it was a mistake."

"What are you suggesting?" Jessica suddenly knew where he was heading, but she couldn't admit it to herself. It was too frightening.

"I'm suggesting that maybe someone *wanted* you to know what they were looking for—something that could be hidden in upholstery, or inside TV sets."

"You mean . . ." Jessica's panic mounted. "But why would anyone think *I* have the file? And why my home? Why not my office?"

"There are a million *whys,* Mrs. Martin," Ed cut in. "For instance, why didn't they make it look like a burglary? Don't you see, Mrs. Martin? If my suspicions are correct, you're being told to back off. Trashing your house could be meant as a warning for you alone. Maybe World Vision knows Sol Bernstein confided in you."

"But how could they know that?"

"Maybe the same source we got our information from. Our tipster seems to have it in for you. Otherwise why suggest we start our investigation with your firm?" Franklin paused to organize his thoughts. "My producer suspected from the first that there was something more than a concerned citizen at work here. Maybe that person has something against *you*. It has to be someone who knows you *and* knows about the file."

Jessica was stunned. Who knew about the file other than Clarendon and herself? Surely David hadn't made the calls to the "Right to Know" people. Unless . . . because she'd fired him? No, it couldn't be Clarendon. Franklin had to be wrong. "There is no way it could be anyone who knows me. . . ."

"No way." Ed was convinced he was right. "It has to be someone who knows you. And we are going to have to find out who that is. I'm going to level with you, Mrs. Martin. I'm getting worried. Your home was trashed, and Sol . . . Well, when I saw him in Arizona, he agreed to come to New York and let us do the story in conjunction with FDA investigators. He was going to deliver the file to me. But I haven't seen or heard from him since I left. And he's had plenty of time to get here." He heard a sharp intake of breath from the other end of the line. "Look, Mrs. Martin, it's obvious you're straight—you just walked into a hornet's nest. I'd like to apologize again for my suspicions."

Jessica paused. "All right, Mr. Franklin. I accept your apology. I suppose you had sufficient reason to think as you did." Her concern was evident as she continued, "I don't know where Dr. Bernstein is and I never saw the file itself. I do know he is frightened and now, so am I. He spoke of a corporate Mafia. . . ." He could hear the fear in her voice. "My God—you don't think? I mean, surely they couldn't have—"

He interrupted her quickly. "It's too soon to jump to those conclusions, Mrs. Martin. We don't know that anything has happened to Sol. But it's safe to assume the wrecking of your house was a warning meant for you and you alone. They want you to stay out of this. I think it's good advice."

Jessica was too frightened to speak. Ed sighed. "Look, we can work on this together without anyone knowing you are still involved. They don't know who I am. If I hear from Bernstein, I'll call you to let you know he's all right. You do the same. Other than that, please try to stay out of this, and don't discuss it with anyone but me." He was silent again, then added, "And you might put on your thinking cap as to just who it might have been that called us. They seem to know an awful lot about all of this—and about you. If you can figure that out, it could be a big lead."

Jessica numbly agreed and hung up. She sat staring into space. She couldn't believe this was happening. As hard as it was to accept, the only possible suspect that came to mind was David Clarendon. He knew Jessica and he knew the facts about the file. It made her queasy to think it, but he had to be the one. Her only consolation was that after this conversation, Ed Franklin finally believed her. A mutual trust had developed between them and Jessica was relieved they would be working together.

Chapter 37

As Michael lifted his pen to write Jessica, he thought back to the day he and Johnny Bridges had left Los Angeles. He grinned, remembering how as Johnny exited the freeway ramp onto Route 66, he began to sing in an off-key voice:

> *You can go through St. Louie*
> *Joplin, Missouri*
> *And Oklahoma City looks mighty pretty*
> *See Amarillo*
> *Gallup, New Mexico . . .*

"Give me a break, Johnny, it's going to be a long drive," Michael groaned.

Unfazed, Johnny laughed. "You don't like my singing? Hell, it's the secret to my love life—drives my women crazy."

"Thankfully, none of them are traveling with us, so you can cancel the concert." Michael's tone was jovial. Once he'd made his decision to start a new life and they had hit the road, his spirits had lifted. "What the hell was that song supposed to be, anyway?"

"You gotta be kidding," Johnny said in amazement. "You don't know 'Get Your Kicks on Route 66'? That was one of Nat King Cole's greatest hits."

Michael laughed at Johnny's genuine indignation. "Maybe if I'd heard Nat Cole singing it, I would have recognized it."

"I'll ignore that remark," Johnny growled, his eyes twinkling. "Anyway, I know the song and I know I'm on Route 66—the only thing is, I don't have a friggin' clue where I'm supposed to be going. Want to let me in on it?"

"I thought you were such a big adventurer," Michael kidded. "If I tell you now, it'll take all the fun out of it. Don't you want to be surprised when we get there?"

Happy to see Michael cheerful, Johnny said, "You just point me in the right direction."

"You stay straight on course until we reach New Mexico. I'll give you directions after we hit Gallup."

"New Mexico it is."

They drove for the better part of the day, stopping only for a quick lunch and gasoline. They stayed overnight at a roadside motel and headed out early the next morning, reaching Gallup, New Mexico, around noon.

Determined to keep his end of the bargain, Johnny asked no further questions about their destination. He followed Michael's directions and drove past Gallup an additional forty miles. Michael took a sheet of paper from his jacket.

"Okay, be on the lookout for our turnoff. And look sharp; it's not going to be easy to spot it. We want Highway 57."

Johnny kept his eyes peeled. Suddenly it was upon them, the paved off-road lasted for about three hundred yards before it turned into a rutted, narrow dirt road, barely wide enough to accommodate two automobiles. He felt Michael's amused eyes on him, but would not give him the satisfaction of asking where the impossible road led. He knew Michael was enjoying himself for the first time in recent memory, and he was more than willing to go along with the game. He glanced pointedly around the barren, dusty desert land and said drily, "Beautiful scenery. Must get positively overrun during the tourist season."

Michael chuckled and braced himself against the dashboard. The van was bucking wildly over the ruts.

"We probably should have made this leg of the trip on horseback," he said.

"The Lone Ranger and Tonto, huh, Kimo Sabe?"

"Buck up, Tonto. We should be almost there."

Johnny's head bounced against the roof of the car as they hit a particularly deep rut. "Jesus! Almost where?" he blurted.

"Guardado atras Vista," Michael laughed, enjoying Johnny's temporary discomfort.

Johnny feigned shocked amazement. "You don't mean *the Guardado atras Vista!"*

"The very same," Michael answered seriously. "Roughly translated, it means *Hidden from View."*

Johnny again scanned the barren landscape. There was nothing in sight save tumbleweeds and dust. "An apt name for it, from the looks of things. Just when do we reach it? I'm beginning to fear for the tires, not to mention my butt."

"The turnoff is just ahead—right up there."

Johnny's eyes followed the direction Michael pointed and he groaned aloud. The road they were to take looked even worse than Highway 57. "Better hold onto your hat, pardner," he cautioned as he maneuvered the turn. They drove for some ten miles with Michael insisting they were nearly there and Johnny responding with dark, silent looks of disbelief.

Finally, Michael said, "Look, there it is." Johnny slowed the van to a near crawl.

He drove past several small adobe huts, a makeshift cantina of sorts, a few barefoot children, a few mongrel dogs, and that was it. The children and a few old men waved, and guitar music filled the air. Someone was singing a Spanish song but neither of them understood the words.

Johnny turned the van around and drove back to stop in front of the cantina. He got out, stretched his legs, then opened the door and activated the electric ramp for Michael's wheelchair. As Michael wheeled himself down, Johnny noted that no one seemed the least surprised by their arrival, nor paid any attention to the wheelchair. It was as if they had been expected. Johnny searched Michael's face for a clue, but found nothing. Michael was going to play it out to the end.

Refreshments of tacos and ice-cold beer were offered by the cantina owner. After they had eaten, an elderly man came to Michael and handed him a simple but carefully drawn map. Johnny strained to catch a glimpse, but Michael had quickly shoved it in his pocket. He thanked the man, paid for the tacos and beer, and they headed farther into the desert.

Johnny kept a careful eye out for the crude landmarks Michael described for him, and listened as Michael kept up a running but uninformative monologue about what might await them when they reached Deliverance.

As they drove deeper and deeper into the desert, Johnny kept a careful watch on the gas gauge, but Michael seemed unconcerned. Finally Johnny broke his silence. "You keep talking about a surprise when we reach there. I'm wondering *if* we'll reach there. More likely a band of hungry coyotes will get us before we arrive at Deliverance, whatever the hell that is."

But Michael remained silent, his face enigmatic. Johnny let it rest.

It was dusk when they first caught sight of the camp. Johnny's face clearly indicated he thought Michael had gone around the bend as he took in the basic army tents and swirling dust. There was a small wooden sign stuck into the hard-packed earth that read Deliverance. Johnny pointed to it. "Well, Kimo Sabe," he drawled, "not heap big city like Guardado atras Vista, but looks like we have arrived."

He looked at Michael but could not read the sudden change in his expression. He did not laugh or even smile at Johnny's attempt at humor; he simply stared at the encampment with wide eyes. To Johnny it had all the appeal of an archaeological dig. Silent for once, he parked the van next to the largest of the tents, activated the ramp, and helped Michael out of the van.

They waited outside the tent for several long minutes

before the flap was thrown back and a tall, rugged-looking man stepped out.

Deeply tanned, with thick gray hair worn long and curling around his ears, he wore no shirt, and the same gray hair matted his muscular chest. His black eyes were friendly and his greeting cordial.

"Hello," he said, offering his hand. "I am Antonio d' Abrizzio. Welcome to Deliverance." He smiled and bowed slightly from the waist. "And you must be Michael Martin."

Johnny felt his stomach sink. It wasn't an archaeological dig. It must be some sort of religious commune. What the hell had he let his loyalty and friendship for Michael get him into? Michael accepted the proffered hand. "I am Michael Martin. And pleased to meet you. This is my friend, Johnny Bridges. Johnny, Signor d'Abrizzio."

He shook Johnny's hand and said, "No need for formality here. Call me Antonio. It is what everyone does."

"Antonio it is."

Michael eyed Johnny carefully, but could not read his expression. Johnny stood quietly, letting Michael take the lead. But it was Antonio d'Abrizzio who spoke. "Your letter did not give a specific date. We weren't sure when to expect you, but we have your tent ready. Please follow me. You can rest and we can talk later, over dinner."

Johnny retrieved a couple of suitcases from the van and followed Michael and Antonio across the camp to a medium-sized tent. It was clean and spartan: two cots, two bureaus, a small oil stove, a washstand with two tin basins and a pole-hung shaving mirror made up the interior.

"We have a communal shower," Antonio said, "but privacy is no problem. I'll let you get settled in. Dinner is in one hour. The main tent is also the dining hall. We have a good cook, so be prepared to enjoy. Ciao." And he left.

Johnny sat down on one of the cots, his eyes wary, but his tone light. "Who was that masked man, Masked Man?"

Michael grinned. "Guess fun and games are over for a while, huh, Tonto? Let me fill you in."

Michael wheeled his chair over to the cot upon which Johnny sat. During the two years Johnny had been his nurse-

237

companion, they had become good friends, but Michael had never really taken Johnny into his confidence. Now was the time. He needed Johnny's help, but if he was to ask him to stay, Johnny had a right to know exactly what it would entail and why Michael had decided to come here.

"Johnny," he began, "you are a pretty observant guy. I know you've been aware of what has been going on these past two years. The strain between Jessica and myself, how angry I've been."

"I've had some idea," Johnny admitted softly, all glibness gone.

"It had to stop—I had to stop. I was angry for so long, Johnny. I nurtured my anger, my bitterness, nurtured it until it became all-encompassing. Until it became my reason for living." He stared off into space, his voice deep with emotion. "It was hell—hell for both of us, but worse for Jessica. At least I had my anger to feed on. I'm afraid Jessica had nothing." He took a deep breath. This was more difficult than he'd expected. "I had to leave, I had to make a clean break of it, because I knew Jessica never would. She's too loyal, too decent."

Johnny nodded but said nothing. He was as fond of Jessica as he was of Michael and it had been painful to see two such fine people suffer so much.

"I knew I had to be the one to leave but I didn't want just to run away. I'd done enough running away the past two years. I ran away inside my head, inside my heart. Do you understand?"

"I think so, but go on."

"Okay. I'd been thinking of going for a long time. But I didn't know where to go, or what to go to. I knew I couldn't just travel and do the meaningless things retired people with money do. I knew I'd have to have something meaningful if I was ever going to get my act together and start living again."

He frowned, intent on his words. "I thought about it a lot, thought about how much better off Jessica would be—how much better off we would both be. And I knew somewhere in my gut that I would find the right time to go—but I didn't know where I would go." His eyes lightened and his voice took on an edge of excitement as he continued hurriedly. "And then one day I saw an article in the *Architectural Times* on Antonio d'Abrizzio, our host. He's from Milan, also an architect. An architect with a dream—a dream that I once read about and wanted to become a part of. That's what Deliverance is all about. That's what this camp is all about."

He leaned forward, his eagerness apparent. "Antonio is here with a small army of professional volunteers and about twenty-five young people whose most remarkable talent is their belief in mankind and its continuation on this planet. Deliverance is to be a city of the future—a model of what man can accomplish for future generations."

His eyes flashed with conviction and Johnny found himself getting caught up in his excitement. "He has environmentalists, energy conservationists, seismologists, naturalists, all dedicated to creating a totally self-sufficient city. A city powered by natural energy sources—the sun, the wind. There will be experimental planting, grains grown without the use of chemicals. Construction that will withstand earthquakes and other disasters. The needs of mankind will be provided for without screwing up the air or the soil."

Michael had to pause for breath. He hadn't realized just how excited he was at the prospect of being a part of the project, of having the chance to help create something new, something to challenge all his creative skills.

"These volunteers are all people like myself, Johnny. Professionals with the financial wherewithal to give a couple of years of their lives to this project. Leave something on this earth they can point to with pride. I want that too, and this is the one way I can do it. That's why I wrote to Antonio volunteering my services."

"Why all volunteers?" Johnny asked, breaking his silence in his growing excitement.

"Because to make it work, Antonio absolutely refuses to take any funding. He will not answer to any financial authority, won't compromise what he intends to build."

"Makes sense. Where do I come in?"

"You know I need you, Johnny. There's still so much I

can't do on my own, and I want my physical limitations to be as little a hindrance to what I can do on this project as possible. So you would basically be doing the same job you've been doing for the past two years. But I'm sure there would be something you could contribute to the project as well, if you wanted to be a part of it."

Johnny didn't answer right away. Michael knew he was carefully considering what his decision would mean. Finally, Johnny spoke.

"Hell, why not?" he grinned. "I wouldn't mind having a little contribution to the future on my record. Camp living might not be so bad. There's only one thing, though. You *know* I'm not cut out to be a monk, Michael. . . ."

Michael grinned at him. "Gallup is a pretty sophisticated town and it's only a couple of hours' drive from here. I'll bet you can rustle up something in the way of feminine charm."

"Then what say we get on over to the tent, sign up, and chow down?"

Johnny offered his hand and Michael shook it gratefully.

That had all been well over a month ago, and as Michael sat staring at his writing pad, he prayed he could convey all the excitement and fulfillment he felt in his letter to Jessica. He felt a calm sense of peace, certain that what he'd committed himself to for the next two years would be a turning point for him.

He wasn't worried about what would happen when the project came to an end. He'd cross that bridge when he came to it. For now he was content—and he had somehow to get that across to Jessica. Set her mind at ease and yet not raise false hopes. He wasn't going back—not to a marriage that was over for both of them, and not to the life he'd been living since his accident.

With determination, he put pen to paper.

Chapter 38

Jim Steiner paced back and forth outside the door to Jessica's office. He had requested a meeting to discuss the Middle Eastern assignment, determined not to accept it, yet worried it could mean the end of his career with Martin Management. He trusted Carol, but he was far from confident as he knocked on Jessica's door.

Jessica noted the difference in Jim the moment he stepped through the door. Something was missing, something in the way he moved. Then suddenly, she realized he'd dropped his defensiveness. The thrust of his shoulders, the street-fighter stance, were gone. He looked worried.

"Sit down, Jim," she said, indicating a chair in front of the fireplace. "Would you like some coffee?" she asked as she rose to join him. "I'm sure there is still some in the pot."

He shook his head and Jessica took the seat opposite him. "What can I do for you?"

"Jessica," he said, his voice as strained as his body, "I—uh—I'm not quite sure how to put this, but uh—I—look, Jessica," he blurted quickly, anxious to get it over with, "I just can't accept the assignment for Amalgamated's slot in the Middle East. If you want to can me, I'll understand," he went on hurriedly, "but I can't do it. There's just no way."

He'd rushed the words so that Jessica hardly knew how to respond. She tried to keep her tone noncommittal. "Before we talk about canning anyone, why not tell me why it is you can't accept the assignment?"

His eyes held the same look of pain Carol had seen when he'd confided his problem to her. Jessica saw it and decided to let him take his time.

But Jim did not feel comfortable baring his soul to Jessica. He made it short and sweet, his usual style with people he was unsure of. "It's because I'm Jewish. That's all there is to tell you—I can't do it."

Jessica took a deep breath. This was the last sort of problem she'd imagined. She understood his dilemma, but damn, they were so far behind schedule as it was. Still, she'd have to let him off the hook and she'd have to be tactful.

"Jim, I apologize. I should have thought—I mean, I know you're Jewish. I should have asked you if it would be a problem for you." She smiled. "Obviously you don't have to accept the assignment."

The relief on his face was immediate, and Jessica knew she had said the right thing—taken the blame for bad judgment and left him his dignity. "I'm not up on the scheduling right now. Who's on vacation in legal?"

"Marc and Eileen. There's only myself and Bob Henderson until next week."

"Which search is Bob working on?"

"A couple, actually. One for Computron and a couple for law firms."

Jessica thought for a minute, then said, "Okay, this cuts it a little short because of John Adams's time frame, but tell Bob I want you to switch assignments. Have him put everything on hold except Amalgamated. You take over his current work load. We'll have to put on a big push, but I think we can manage it."

Jim was not a man accustomed to being humble, but at that moment, he was. His voice was tinged with emotion despite his effort to control it.

"Jessica—well, I appreciate this. I owe you one! You can

count on me to break my bal—uh, my neck to make up the difference." And saying that, his old attitude seemed to return. "I already talked to Bob. I mean, I had hoped you'd understand. He had no problem with making the switch. He's all right, you know?"

Jessica grinned. "Then it's all settled. I hope you understand my position. I sympathize with your feelings, but I have a business to run, and Amalgamated is a very important client. I cannot pass judgment on their business activities."

Jim nodded his head. "Sure Jessica, I understand. I just gotta respect myself, and this was the first time I've ever been put to the test."

"Good, then everything's settled. In future, Jim, don't wait to tell me if you're uncomfortable about an assignment for whatever reason. There's usually a solution and anticipating a problem up front saves a lot of time."

He rose from his chair and looked at Jessica for a long moment. Then the old grin returned to his face and his shoulders straightened to their normal forward thrust. He turned and quickly left the office.

Jessica remained seated before the fireplace, her mind wandering. What a strange business she was in—all the psychology necessary to keep client, candidate, and recruiter happy. She smiled to herself. She was glad it had happened. Jim's newly displayed sensitivity pleased her. She felt more than ever that he would be a success in the business. If he could care about something deeply, enough to risk losing his job for, he would surely care about the needs of the people he placed. His stock had just risen a good fifty percent in her estimation.

The intercom buzzed. "It's Jeremy Bronson on line two," Carol said.

Jessica rose and returned to her desk. She felt her heart beating faster.

"Jessica," Carol asked, "do you want to take the call?"

"Oh, yes. Certainly, Carol," Jessica replied hurriedly. "I'll pick it up right away."

She seated herself and lifted the receiver. "Hello, Jessica." Jeremy's deep voice caused her an involuntary shiver. "How are you?"

"I'm fine," Jessica lied, her palms suddenly damp. "I'm—I'm managing."

"Now that's something you are getting very good at, aren't you?"

She noted the disappointment in his voice and her shoulders slumped. What the hell was she doing? She had thought long and hard about Jeremy, his family, the complications. But none of her agonizing had altered the fact that Jeremy was right: She was falling in love with him. She wanted to see him, be with him, be held by him. She was tired, frightened, and most of all, she was *lonely*. She just couldn't fight it anymore, and the sound of his voice helped her realize she had made her decision. Her voice strengthened. "No, no, suddenly I'm not so good at that, Jeremy. Not so good at all."

There was only a slight pause before he asked in a hopeful tone, "Are you saying what I think you are?"

Jessica did not hesitate. She needed Jeremy. Enough was enough. "Yes, Jeremy, I'm saying exactly what you think."

His tone grew husky. "When?"

Jessica surprised herself with her boldness. "I can leave right now—can you get away?"

His voice pulsed with happiness. "I've just left."

Jessica smiled shyly as the line went dead.

Chapter 39

Jessica did not miss the quick flicker in Carol's eyes when she announced she was leaving the office for the day. But she didn't let it deter her. If Carol did suspect what was happening, she'd keep her own counsel. She was one person Jessica knew she could trust.

A sense of urgency made Jessica drive faster than usual, and she was downtown in front of Jeremy's building in half an hour. When she rang the doorbell, Jeremy answered immediately.

She stepped inside and removed her suit jacket, draping it over the sofa. When she turned, Jeremy stood before her.

He traced the contours of her face tenderly, then took her into his arms, kissing her hungrily, passionately, possessively.

She found herself unable and unwilling to resist. All doubts melted at his touch, and she returned his kisses with equal hunger. When he lifted his head, his eyes were a mixture of heat and love. He put his hands on the top button of her blouse and murmured, "This time, let me do it, Jessica."

His hands were sure, confident, his eyes bold in their

appreciation as he removed her blouse and bra, exposing the swell of her creamy breasts. Jessica gasped as she became caught up in their mutual desires.

He did not speak, but kissed her gently all over as he continued to undress her. His hands lingered on her breasts, then slowly roamed to cup her buttocks and draw her closer for another passionate kiss of exploration. Jessica felt her legs fail her just as he lifted her into his arms and carried her carefully into the bedroom, placing her across the heavy comforter.

His eyes never left her face as he began removing his own clothing. Jessica felt her own eyes riveted on his muscular physique as he came toward her, sitting on the edge of the bed, running his hands down the length of her body as if to convince himself she was really there, love shining in his eyes.

He lay beside her and as he pulled her body to fit his own, she was amazed she felt no shame, no awkwardness. All she felt was need, need and desire for this virile, exciting man whose own desire mounted by the moment.

"You are so beautiful," he whispered, his hands stroking and exploring her in wonder. She felt her own passion rise, felt herself straining in his embrace, felt her body beg for more of him.

But he would not be rushed. He responded to her throbbing senses with caresses that intensified rather than satisfied her desires. His kisses sent bolts of heat coursing through her body, causing little moaning sounds to escape her lips. She felt herself growing wet, losing control.

She kissed him with an abandon totally new to her and the lunging response of his fiery tongue made her cry out from somewhere deep inside herself. It was give and take in its purest form. Under his sure hands and mouth, Jessica became a woman she did not recognize. At last, silencing her, he lifted her legs and entered her. Together they rode the crest of their passion until with a shuddering, time-stopping thrust, they fell back, exhausted and fulfilled.

They lay quietly side by side, holding hands, unwilling to break the spell. Their breathing slowly returned to normal, and Jeremy turned her to face him, staring deep into her green-flecked eyes. "Hold me, Jeremy," she whispered.

He cradled her to him, softly murmuring endearments. Jessica relaxed, feeling safe and protected for the first time she could remember. Jeremy planted kisses on her forehead, against her closed eyelids, and finally upon her lips. Jessica never wanted it to end. Once again Jeremy's hands began their sure exploration and once again Jessica found herself responding eagerly.

"Jessica," he breathed against her mouth. "That first time was pure heat. But this time, this time is for us."

And it was easy, exquisite loving. A tasting of one another, an exploration their earlier out-of-control passions would not allow. Jessica felt herself near tears of release as his mouth left her lips and began a slow descent down her heated body.

It had been magnificent and Jessica felt the incredible liquidity that comes after totally satisfying lovemaking. Jeremy propped himself up on one elbow and leaned over her, lingering passion in his eyes as he stared at her lovely face. Suddenly, he grinned. "In the movies, someone is always dying for a cigarette about now. I don't suppose that would apply to you?"

Jessica laughed up at him. "Yes! I don't care if I am a cliché, yes! I'm dying for a cigarette."

Still grinning, he wrapped a blanket around his waist and padded into the living room. Jessica felt marvelously alive. Two years of denial and rejection had been a very long time, but Jeremy had ended it for her, ended it gently, tenderly, beautifully.

He returned to the room with a lighter, cigarette, and ashtray. Jessica lit the cigarette and inhaled deeply, her body still singing with release.

"Speaking of clichés, Jessica," Jeremy said as he stroked her hair, "I knew it would be like this—I knew it would be exactly like this."

"But how could you have known? I would never have believed I could be so free—so . . ." She searched for the right word, finally settling for, ". . . so wanton."

He grinned at the old-fashioned term. "I knew because, because . . ." He laughed. "Hell, I don't know *how* I knew. I just did."

"I gave you a pretty hard time. I can't believe how patient you were."

"It's easy to be patient when you love someone. And I do love you, Jessica. My God, darling! You can't imagine how much I love you."

Jessica did not respond. She lay staring at the ceiling for a long moment, a frown creasing her forehead. She sat up and swung her legs over the side of the bed, planting her feet on the floor. She stubbed out her cigarette and reached for a blanket to cover her nakedness.

"Jessica? What is it?" Jeremy asked anxiously. "What's wrong?"

"Nothing, nothing and *everything*," she said. "Jeremy, that was so wonderful, so unbelievable."

"Then what . . . ?"

"I've never felt so frustrated in my life. This is so damned unfair. I'm in love with you, Jeremy. Why do you have to be married? Why does our love have to have a cloud over it? It's unfair. I hate it."

Jeremy did not answer immediately. He wanted to choose his words very carefully; he would not, could not lose her now. He took a deep breath, then said in a quiet, calm voice, "We'll work it out, darling. There has to be a way. We aren't the first people this has ever happened to."

"I don't care about other people!" Jessica was near tears. "Right now, after finally letting myself go, letting myself love and be loved, all I can seem to care about is us. You and me. And I don't see how in hell we can work it out."

"I'll ask Margaret for a divorce," he blurted desperately.

"No! I don't want that, Jeremy," Jessica cried. "Oh, that's not true either. I *do* want that. I want to be able to be with you all the time. But damn! It scares me so. How can we be happy at her expense? What about your children? Jeremy, it won't work."

He took her by the shoulders, his grip firm, his tone intense. "Don't say that, Jessica. Don't say it. It will work

248

out, I'll make it work out. We love one another, you can't just walk away from that."

"I don't *want* to walk away from it." Tears streamed down her face. "It's wonderful to feel love again, wonderful. But it scares me at the same time."

He rocked her in his arms, afraid to speak. He wasn't at all sure how Margaret would react to the thought of divorce, but he couldn't let Jessica know that. He couldn't risk her leaving him, not now.

He cupped her chin in his hand and raised her face. He kept his gaze steady, his voice reassuring. "It will be okay. You've got to believe me, it *will* be okay."

"Oh, how much I want to believe you, Jeremy. How *very* much."

"Then *do* believe me, darling. Believe me."

He knew someone was bound to be hurt by their situation, he had to admit that to himself. But he was determined that that someone would not be Jessica. He pulled her closer and wiped the tears from her cheeks.

"Jessica, I want to make love to you again. Right now, no more talking, not today. This day belongs to us."

Jessica started to protest, but he covered her lips with his own, and as his kiss set fire to her mouth, she knew she had neither the strength nor desire to resist.

Chapter 40

"It's turning out to be a lovely morning, boss." Carol grinned as she took a chair in front of the fireplace in Jessica's office. "Not one problem—not even with Stacey."

Jessica smiled at the barb, but did not comment, and Carol continued. "John Adams called and the meetings are going well with your two men in New York. And Bob Henderson already has a line on a couple of men for the Middle East." Carol's tone softened as she added, "You were damned decent about Jim's dilemma, Jessica."

Jessica smiled away the compliment. "What else?"

"Just one more thing," Carol replied. "As a matter of fact, I'm not sure exactly what it means. That Ed Franklin from 'Right to Know' called yesterday, just after you left the office. He said to tell you . . ." Carol looked at the ceiling, trying to remember his exact words. "Oh yes, he said to tell you the man had arrived with the package so you don't have to worry about it anymore."

Jessica silently thanked the Lord. Everything was turning out all right. "Wonderful!" She beamed at Carol. "I wish I could tell you about it, Carol. But I can't, I promised—not just now. It's something they are working on for a show and it's very hush-hush."

Carol shrugged her shoulders. "Hey, that's okay, boss. I just thought I'd slipped up somewhere—it didn't make any sense to me."

Jessica laughed. "The day you slip up on something, I'm going into retirement. But I'm glad it's been quiet," she added. "I left a lot of work undone yesterday and I'll be glad of the chance to get at it this morning."

Carol took the last sip of her coffee, but not without noting the sudden blush that crept up Jessica's cheeks. She guessed the reason, but said nothing. "I'll hit the road and let you get at it. If you need anything, just buzz me."

Jessica sat back, reluctant to plow into the work on her desk. She hadn't felt so good in a long time. Her body felt renewed. She closed her eyes and relived the hours she had spent with Jeremy, feeling again the touch of his hands, the warmth of his kiss. She was in love—and it made her feel like a teenager, trembling with excitement and fantasy.

They were so marvelous together, like two people reborn. And there was so much to look forward to—all the things they had yet to discover in each other—all the glorious things in life they had yet to share. They had so much in common—their work, their sense of humor, their curiosity. They had the rest of their lives to discover one another, not just a few stolen hours. Jessica smiled, fantasizing about trips with Jeremy, cooking for Jeremy, living with Jeremy . . .

She sat bolt upright, opening her eyes. What the hell was she doing? Jeremy was married—that hadn't changed. And neither had her fears of what the destruction of his marriage could mean. "Damn," she whispered. Why couldn't she just accept things as they were? Why couldn't she believe the old bromides—ones like "you can't break up a happy marriage"? Divorce was commonplace today, so why did it torment her? Wouldn't Jeremy's wife be better off? Jeremy was in love with Jessica; surely a clean break from his marriage would be the best thing?

But Jessica knew that was only half the story, that the pain she would cause was undeniable.

The buzz of the intercom snapped her eyes open. Carol said, "It's that Ed Franklin again. I didn't say you were in. Do you want to talk with him?"

She picked up the receiver, and began talking immediately. "Mr. Franklin, I can't tell you how relieved I was to get your message. What a load off my shoulders to know that Dr. Bernstein is with you in New York. I've been worried sick. It was so kind of you to keep your word and let me know immediately."

There was silence on the other end for a moment, and Jessica asked, "Mr. Franklin? Are you there?"

"Yes," Ed said finally. "I'm here, Mrs. Martin."

"I am sorry for jumping in like that, Mr. Franklin," Jessica apologized. She sat back in her chair. "Please, how can I help you?"

"I don't know that you can. . . ." he said slowly. "But I thought you had a right to know." He hesitated, then said in a monotone, "Sol Bernstein is missing."

All the elation drained away in an instant and suddenly Jessica felt numb. "But," she blurted, "you said—yesterday—you left a message—you said everything was all right. That he had arrived with the package and that I didn't have to worry. Now you say he's missing. . . ." Her earlier mistrust resurfaced. "I don't believe this—you're playing another of your sick little games."

"It's not a game, Mrs. Martin."

"But how? What happened?"

Ed Franklin paused for a moment, then began to recite the chain of events dully. "I got a call from him yesterday saying he was in New York and had the material. He was at the Hotel Madison. He promised to meet me at my office this morning." He breathed deeply, as if the words were painful. "I called you right after Sol's call, but you weren't in the office. I left the message because I thought you'd want to know he arrived safely."

"Then how could he be missing? Are you certain?"

"I'm certain he is missing," he replied. "As to what happened, that's another story. I only know he's gone."

Jessica could not get her lungs to work properly. Why?

Why hadn't he been protected? She could not control her fury. "You promised him protection!" she flung at Franklin. "He trusted you! How could you have let this happen?"

The pain in his voice was unmistakable, but it was lost for the moment on Jessica. "I promised him protection as long as he was within our care. I tried to convince him to come to New York with me while I was in Arizona. He didn't trust me completely, I guess. He insisted on getting to New York by his own means."

"But once he was there," Jessica insisted, "once you knew which hotel he was staying in, you should have had someone there right away! You broke your promise, and now God knows what has happened to him!"

"Hey, wait just a minute!" Franklin put in quickly. "We sent a guard over right after he called me, but when the guard got to the hotel, Sol didn't answer his door. The guard figured he was being extra cautious, so he went to the lobby to call on the house phone, but he got no answer. That's when the guard called me." Franklin sighed. He felt terrible and he knew Jessica Martin was completely panicked. "I went to the hotel immediately, but Sol didn't answer his phone or his door when I identified myself."

Jessica did not comment. Ed continued, "When I got no answer, I went back to the lobby and talked to the desk clerk. He remembered Sol because he listed Arizona as his home—the clerk loves Arizona." Ed's voice rose in frustration. "He said that Sol had gone out. He had checked a briefcase into the hotel safe and about twenty minutes after he'd called me, Sol requested the clerk to remove the briefcase from the safe, signed for it, and left the hotel. The clerk had the check-in and check-out times written on the hotel chart—standard procedure. It only took forty minutes from the time Sol checked into the hotel, called me, reclaimed his briefcase, and left the hotel. I double-checked the time; it all fits." Ed's next words were heavy with concern. "The clerk said he thought there were two men accompanying Sol, but he couldn't be sure, nor could he give any sort of description because he had been busy with new arrivals." Ed's voice caught. "It might be nothing. Sol may just be acting extra cautious, but if something has happened to him, I'll have to live with it the rest of my life."

This time his distress was unmistakable. Jessica relented. "I'm sorry, Mr. Franklin. I'm afraid I got hysterical. I'm sure you tried to protect him." Her voice began to tremble. "That poor man, he knew he was in danger. How did they find him?"

"*We* found him, Mrs. Martin," Ed reminded her. "They may have found him too."

They were both silent for a moment, alone with their private fears.

Jessica closed her eyes and massaged the side of her temple. She could not get the ringing sound of Sol Bernstein's voice out of her mind. "I can't help but feel I'm responsible for this," she said slowly. "If I'd handled it better . . ."

"Stop that, Mrs. Martin!" Franklin advised her. "This is not your fault. If there is any blame, it's mine for not insisting he come with me from Arizona—for not getting to the hotel on time. But placing blame isn't going to help now."

"What *is* going to help?" Jessica cried. "What are we going to do now?"

"*We* aren't going to do anything, Mrs. Martin," Ed insisted. "*I* am going to continue this investigation. They don't know who I am—at least I don't think they do. *You* need have no further part in it." He hesitated for a moment, then added, "At least, not right now—down the line, when I get to the bottom of all this, I'll probably need your testimony. But for now, I want you to stay out of it. *If* they have Sol, they have what they want and you won't be in any further danger. But until we know that for a fact, you have to stay clear of this."

"But there must be something I can do," she pushed.

"If you could only figure out who has it in for you, who planted the tip with us and tried so hard to involve you. If I could pinpoint that person, then I might start getting somewhere!"

Jessica's mind worked quickly. She still found it impossible that David Clarendon would have done such a thing, but he was her only possibility. "Mr. Franklin, only two other people knew about this—at least that's what Dr. Bernstein told me. Paul Mellon, the former regulatory attorney for World Vision, the one Sol told about the file"—she took a deep breath—"and from this office, David Clarendon, the recruiter who placed Dr. Bernstein at World Vision." Her voice became nearly inaudible. "The recruiter I fired."

Ed paused. "Our tip came from a woman," he said finally.

Jessica could not help the relief that came over her. "Then I was right. It couldn't have been someone who knows me, not if it was a woman. I'm the only woman who knows about this."

"Unless . . ." Franklin's tone was reflective. "Unless your David Clarendon had a woman make the call, thinking he wouldn't be connected to it. But I still don't buy it—you said he was as frightened as Mellon. Still, we have to consider everyone."

Jessica's relief quickly dissipated. "It's all such a mystery. I still can't believe it of David. It's a pretty drastic thing to do just to get back at me, and he was absolutely opposed to getting involved. I don't like to think it, but I guess he's the only logical suspect." She hesitated. "What will you do now?"

"Let me worry about that, Mrs. Martin." Ed's tone was firm. "I want you to promise me you'll stay out of this. *I* owe Sol Bernstein. And I will not give up until I find him. Now, give me your word. There's nothing you can do, and I don't want you in any further jeopardy."

Reluctantly, Jessica agreed and they said good-bye. She sat staring into space, her chest heavy with anger and fear. She had a terrible feeling that the worst was yet to come.

Chapter 41

Stacey stood before her bedroom mirror, carefully scrutinizing her reflection. Mirrors did not lie, and she smiled in relief—she looked fantastic. Now, if everything could just go as planned, she thought stonily.

She'd piled her mass of honey-colored hair high atop her head. Soft stray wisps floated around her face and the nape of her neck. She'd taken particular care with her makeup and her turquoise eyes sparkled, the pale peach blusher applied to her cheekbones and temples adding just the right glow to her already lustrous skin.

She'd chosen an azure silk kimono that brought out her eyes and caressed every curve of her luscious body. She knew the combination of innocence and seductiveness was irresistible.

Her efforts at domesticity had been limited to having her favorite French restaurant send over luncheon and chilled wine. Her maid had set the table before the fireplace, which burned with cozy intimacy. Stacey had then given her the rest of the day and evening off. She looked around one last time as the bell rang. Everything was in order and Eric Radner was going to have a very different kind of matinee than he'd envisioned. She needed to get him to make a commitment today, and had pulled out all the stops to make it happen.

As she opened the door, she was gratified by the quick look of approval in his eyes. He handed her his coat, noted the table set for lunch, and casually seated himself on the couch rather than heading straight for the bedroom.

His eyes were amused, his face smugly possessive. "You look good enough to eat, Stacey."

Ignoring the fact that he'd never availed himself of that opportunity, Stacey smiled. "Believe it or not, there are other things on the menu besides myself today," she said softly. "I thought I'd surprise you with a fancy lunch."

Eric's eyes remained amused, his voice slightly mocking. "And made it all with your very own little hands, I'll bet."

But Stacey was too sharp for that. He knew she was no hausfrau. "You lose, sweetie," she smiled. "I don't cook, have never cooked, and never plan to cook. But I do dial a telephone remarkably well." She pointed to the table. "The feast you are about to enjoy comes directly from L'Escargot—and you'd damn well better enjoy it, because it cost me a fortune."

"Which you will no doubt write off as a business expense," Radner laughed. "Ah, Stacey, you are one pisser of a woman."

Deciding he was being complimentary, Stacey crossed to the table and poured two glasses of wine. Joining him on the couch, she handed him a glass, then sat back, allowing the silk of the kimono to strain against her full breasts.

She smiled, her voice warm and sexy. "Actually, I just thought you'd like a little something extra today."

"Stacey, my girl," Radner said matter-of-factly, "I don't like to fuck on a full stomach, and I'm not much of a man for extras. I like to get exactly what I came for." He drained the wineglass in one gulp, then continued, "I don't like surprises—*any* kind of surprises. You know why I'm here, and it's not for some damned fancy French lunch."

He plunked the wineglass down on the table, saying, "Now, suppose you tell me what you're really up to so we can get down to the main event."

There it was: the slight narrowing of the eyes, a sudden cold alertness in them that Stacey found slightly unnerving, even though she'd seen that look before. Maybe it wasn't going to go quite as smoothly as she'd planned. He wasn't going to have a full belly and a bottle of wine to mellow him out, make him more receptive. But she had to see it through—had to go for it. She was desperate, and Stacey wasn't used to feeling desperate.

"I don't know why I try to fool you, Eric," she said, keeping her tone light. "Okay, you're right, there is something else. I want to talk to you about something important and I wanted to do it in a romantic way, over luncheon and French wine."

"I'm a scotch man myself," he retorted. "And romance is for the movies, so why don't you just spit it out?"

Jesus, he was cold. They could have been discussing business. She forced herself to stay calm, keeping her tone soft, slightly breathless.

"Eric, a girl can't just 'spit out' her feelings, as you put it. I want to talk about us. We've been meeting like this for months now—and it's been wonderful," she hastily added. "But a girl can't help but wonder—I mean, just where are we going, Eric?"

He returned her gaze for a moment, then pointedly looked at his watch. "If we're going to stay on schedule, we're going to the bedroom."

Stacey was only thrown for a moment. "That isn't funny, Eric."

"It wasn't meant to be funny. I never kid around. I repeat, you have something on your mind, just spit it out."

Stacey hadn't expected violins and flowers from Eric, but she hadn't anticipated him being this callous. She'd always thought she managed him pretty well. Still, she had to keep trying. She made her tone injured. "All right, Eric, if that's the way you want it. Yes, there's something on my mind." She took his hand in hers, her eyes soft. "You must know by now that I'm in love with you. That I want to be your wife."

Eric didn't hesitate. He withdrew his hand and shook his

head. "Sorry, honey, you've got the wrong guy. I told you going in, I'm not the marrying kind."

"I know you did, Eric. You didn't play any games with me. And at first, it seemed enough, I mean, it was exciting, fun—I didn't count on falling in love with you. . . ."

Eric allowed his amusement to show in his face, but he kept his tone civil. "Well, that's very nice, Stacey. But it doesn't have to change anything. We can go on just the way we have been."

Stacey felt the beginning of panic. He had to marry her and if she couldn't get him to do it by just telling him she loved him, she would be forced to go to phase two. She would have to admit she was pregnant. A fact she had saved as a surprise.

"Yes, Eric," she said sincerely. "Ordinarily I'd agree with you—no need to change anything—but . . ." She allowed her voice to trail off.

"But?" Eric snapped, his antennae automatically raising.

"But things are no longer the same," she said demurely, lowering her eyes for a moment before smiling at him. "We are going to have a baby, Eric. I'm pregnant."

He smiled and for a second she felt a jolt of relief. But his words took her aback. "I think you're a little mixed-up there, Stacey. *I* am not the least bit pregnant. If you are pregnant, then *you* are going to have a baby. *We* have no such plans."

Stacey was stunned. She'd been sure of his ego, sure it would be thrilling that a man of his age could have sired a child by a beautiful young woman like herself. Didn't all men want little reproductions of themselves? "Eric, I don't understand! It's your child!" she insisted. "My God, I thought you'd be thrilled. A child—maybe a son to share your accomplishments, a son to look up to you."

"Nice thought, honey," he interrupted, "but no dice." He laughed. "I don't even like kids—never did. They get in the way, cause too many problems." He leaned back comfortably. "I think you'd better line up a nice accommodating doctor. Of course, I'll take care of the expense, you can't write that tab off." He chuckled in appreciation of his humor.

She could not believe what she was hearing. "Eric." She allowed her eyes to tear. "Are you suggesting an abortion?"

"Unless they've changed the name of the procedure, I sure as hell am."

Stacey felt her panic mount. She could not accept what he was saying. She had to keep trying.

"Eric," she pleaded, "I don't want an abortion. I want the baby—our baby. I want to belong to you, I want us both to belong to you." She paused for breath, then rushed on. "Surely I mean something to you?"

He did not answer and his stony silence made Stacey realize he *didn't* care—baby or no baby, he wasn't interested. She was determined not to give in—not yet. She could always abort the child if he insisted. She softened her tone.

"Eric, if I don't mean anything to you," she began, "then why do you continue to come here? Why let me hope, let me believe we would eventually make a commitment to one another? Why let me fall in love with you?"

His cold laughter startled Stacey. "Jesus, you can do better than that! Cut the crap!" he said harshly. "You're not in love with me—if you're in love with anything it's Radner Enterprises and all that goes with it." He scowled. "You disappoint me, Stacey. I gave you credit for more brains. You've always seemed a pretty good negotiator in the past."

"Eric," she cried, "this isn't something to negotiate. I do love you. Why else would I be carrying your child?"

"Because, my dear, you took me for an aging fool," he answered calmly. "You thought I'd be thinking with my cock instead of my brains. Thought I'd come apart at the seams with thoughts of a little Eric Radner. *That's* why you are carrying my child—if it is my child."

"Of course it's your child!" she fired back at him, her nerves raw. "How dare you suggest it isn't?"

"Dare? Look, Stacey, learn a lesson from this, a lesson for the next guy. You made a mistake. I thought you were pretty sharp, but you outsmarted yourself. You blew this one, honey."

"Eric, what are you talking about?" she demanded, although she was beginning to realize what was coming. "I got pregnant, it happens. I'm happy about it, and I was sure you'd be happy too." The crazy thing was that Stacey *had* been sure the child would please him. That the unexpected, unplanned-for pregnancy would turn out to be a bonus.

"Knock off the happiness crap, Stacey," he replied. "You're right about one thing, though. You *got* pregnant. This is the twentieth century and you're a big girl who's been around the track a bit. If you're pregnant, then you got pregnant deliberately." The look he gave her was one of disgust. "It was a stupid stunt, kiddo, and I ain't buying it."

Stacey began to tremble with frustration. Her pregnancy was an accident, she had taken precautions and she had no idea how it had happened, what had gone wrong. But she had not deliberately become pregnant. It had never occurred to her that she couldn't get Eric to propose to her through her charm and beauty alone. She hadn't needed pregnancy! She had genuinely believed he would be thrilled about the baby. She had misread the man completely and it was a bad sign, but she wasn't finished yet.

"You're wrong, Eric. It wasn't deliberate—but it *did* happen. I *am* pregnant with *your* child." Her eyes were steady as she met his accusing gaze. "I didn't try to trick you with the baby, Eric. I didn't."

"The hell you didn't!" Eric insisted, then grinned wryly. "Too bad, Stacey. You should have been more patient. You should have waited awhile longer."

"Waited for what? More insults? More accusations?"

"For time to change my mind, Stacey." His expression was ironic. "For a little time to change my mind about marriage."

Stacey's head reeled. He had sworn never to marry—was he playing a game with her? Was there still a chance? "Then you do care for me?" she whispered.

"I think *care* is a little strong, Stacey," he replied coolly. "But *if* I had decided to change my mind, you would have done. That's about the best I can offer, you would have *done* had I decided to take a wife." He laughed. "Hell, you're beautiful and I *thought* you were smart. You sure as hell would never have bored me." He crossed his legs and leaned back against the sofa. "I'm getting a little old to be chasing tail and I admit, the thought of marrying you did cross my mind once or twice. And the file was almost complete." He shook his head. "Oh well, that's the way it goes. I guess it's for the best that you didn't wait it out."

Stacey thought she was losing her mind. What file? "Eric, I may be obtuse, but I don't know what you're talking about. What file?"

"You disappoint me more by the minute. You really can't be that naive. I'm talking about the Stacey Dawson file. Surely you don't think I'd approach the thought of a possible marriage with any less caution than I would a business acquisition?" He smiled without warmth. "Had I decided to marry you, you would have been just another acquisition. Before I buy—and make no mistake, Stacey, I knew I would be buying you—before I buy I check out the merchandise. And with the exception of one little incident, you were shaping up as pretty acceptable merchandise."

Stacey was livid with herself—she should have known he would check her out. But to what "little incident" was he referring? She'd had lovers, but he'd known she was no innocent. She had to know. "Eric, if you have a file on me, I want to know what's in it. What incident are you talking about?"

Eric smiled his cobra smile, completely at ease. "Sure, kid, no reason not to tell you. Hell, you didn't do much more than any other good-looking young woman has done. Nothing too worrisome, nothing too unusual. Just that one little thing that was distasteful at first, a possible tendency . . . but since it wasn't repeated, I discounted it as youthful curiosity."

He was making her frantic. What incident—what "possible tendency"?

"You know, Stacey," he said, "you'd better learn to cover your tracks, learn how to handle sticky situations better." He chuckled drily. "It's a dumb move to make enemies in this world just because you're through with someone. The world is too small for that luxury." He paused, then looked directly at her, saying, "The incident I'm referring to happened in Georgia at one of your conventions. Surely you knew I'd check out your behavior at those conventions! Remember Dr. Kosnovitch?"

Stacey felt the color drain from her face. She'd almost forgotten it herself. How in hell did he find out about that?

"I can read your mind, Stacey. Never mind how I found out," he went on. "I can find out just about anything I really want to know. You treated that poor old dike badly. You behaved like a teenage cock-tease who gets a finger fuck in the backseat of a car, then runs inside to Mommy, while some poor bastard has to be content with smelling his finger and beating his meat."

Stacey felt faint.

Radner went on unsparingly. "You made that old woman mad, Stacey—she was only too happy to tell my investigator about your little romp in the hay. It's all there in the file." He waited for a moment to see if Stacey would say something, but she said nothing and he continued. "Still, like I said—it was only a one-time thing according to all reports. I wasn't worried about coming home to find my wife in bed with another woman. It wasn't big enough to write you off as a possibility, Stacey." He sighed. "If you'd only had a little more patience, you might have had it all. Everything you wanted."

Stacey had never felt so trapped. She was furious at her own helplessness and at Eric for being so powerful he could dump her without a second thought. Damn it, he couldn't! She was a fighter and he couldn't back her against the wall. She had counted on becoming his wife and she wasn't about to give it up easily. She had her *own* information file, and he had shown her the perfect way to use it; he'd outsmarted himself. If he forced her hand, she'd show him just how much he had underestimated her.

"Okay, Eric," she said with a calmness she did not feel, "so you know all about me and were considering marriage anyway. Are you telling me just because I'm pregnant all that has changed? I'm still the best damned merchandise you'll ever find." She sat up, adjusting her kimono around her. "You think of me as an acquisition—okay, let's negotiate. I want to be Mrs. Eric Radner. If the child, *your* child, is a problem, I'll have the abortion."

"Sorry, honey," he chuckled. "I'm not interested. You tried to con me, play me for a sucker. That kind of action is habit-forming. I don't like it. But cheer up, you'll do better next time." His chuckle turned into a sneer. "Hell, think of this as a good lesson. You're still young enough to get a man. Just don't make the same kind of dumb mistake—not if you want to play with the big boys. Getting knocked up is small potatoes." He rose from the couch.

Stacey had never been more vulnerable, more at risk in her life, and she was afraid. He was forcing her to use the only weapon she had.

"Eric," she said firmly. "I don't think we're quite finished with this discussion." Her voice was a command. "Sit down!"

He looked at her, anger glinting in his eyes. Eric Radner was not accustomed to taking orders. "I think I've said all I have to say, Stacey. You tell me how much money you need for the doctor and I'll send it to you."

"We can talk about that later, Eric. What I want to talk about now is the Pythons."

For the first time since his arrival, Stacey caught a glimmer of concern in Eric's eyes. She knew she had him by the balls, but he didn't—not yet. Still, the mere mention of the baseball team he so desperately wanted had made him pause, and Stacey was suddenly no longer afraid. She was, in fact, going to enjoy cutting the son of a bitch down to size. Enjoy *her own* power.

He tried to brush it off. "Don't worry, kiddo. There's no hard feelings. I'll still give you a box seat."

Stacey's voice was calm, casual. "That's very generous of you, Eric. I only hope you'll be in a position to do that."

This time, he made no effort to conceal his concern. He sat back down on the couch, facing her. "Now just why in hell wouldn't I be in that position, Stacey? What game are you trying to play this time?"

She would not be rattled. She was in the driver's seat and she was going to come out on top. She smiled sweetly and sipped her wine before saying, "You know, Eric, since you told me of your plans to buy the Pythons, I've gotten very interested in baseball. After all," she shrugged, "I did plan on being your wife and I wanted to be well informed so that we could enjoy your new toy together."

She paused, enjoying the tense, wary expression on his face. She had him and she knew it. "Big business, baseball. And what a cozy little club the National League is. Quite a fraternity. Just like one big happy family."

"What the hell are you getting at, Stacey?"

"Now, Eric," she replied. "Relax, take your own advice, be patient. I've been doing a lot of homework and I've learned quite a bit about what's involved in acquiring a league franchise—it isn't just having the money, you know," she said coldly. "Did you know there has to be majority acceptance by the other franchisers before a man can buy a team? And further," she smiled wickedly, "the morals clause—now that one, sweetheart, is a biggie. And no way around it either."

Eric was silent, his face strained.

Stacey pressed on. "Good old baseball. America, the 'Star-Spangled Banner,' Mom's apple pie. Have to be as pure as the driven snow for baseball, Eric." She paused. "There was that Max Arno, you must remember him—the man who tried to buy the Mustangs? What was it, three, four years ago? Poor old Max just didn't get that majority vote. Seems he had a few skeletons in the closet, couldn't quite get by the morals clause. I don't exactly know what those skeletons were, but they sure scared hell out of the League—enough to cost him that majority vote. Such a shame . . ." She clucked sympathetically. "Of course, those things probably happen all the time—could happen anytime."

"Okay, Stacey," Eric said sharply. "Knock off being cute. What the hell are you implying?"

"I'm not *implying* anything," she replied innocently. "It was in all the papers, public knowledge. He didn't get the franchise—poor old Max Arno . . ."

"What the hell does Max Arno have to do with me?" he interrupted. "You tell me what the hell you're getting at!"

"I'm getting at a deal, Eric. A business deal—pure and simple." Her voice was cold, secure. "I get what I want and you get the Pythons. It's as simple as that."

"You're an even dumber broad than I thought!" Radner spat at her. "There are no skeletons in my closet, Stacey. Not a single one. My attorneys know what's involved in getting the franchise. They already checked me out—I'm Mr. Clean. I'll get that majority vote and you'll get nothing. Understand me? You'll get nothing!" His fury caused his hands to tremble. "You stupid cunt! Do you think this is how it's played in the big leagues? Do you think you have anything to blackmail me with? You have nothing! You've made another stupid mistake, kiddo."

Stacey laughed. She felt giddy. He was the one who was stupid and he had even given her the idea. She took his hand and placed it on her stomach. "Your attorneys didn't know about this. I'd say I have *something*. Wouldn't you, Eric?"

He jerked his hand away as if it had been burned.

"If you won't marry me," she went on, "I'll have to think of my child, won't I? Our child? I'm just a helpless young woman who believed the big industrialist when he promised marriage." She frowned in mock disapproval. "And look at him now, trying to force me into an abortion, trying to make me murder my baby. . . ."

Radner struggled desperately for control. Every muscle in his body was tensed, ready to spring as he listened to her.

"I'll have to file a paternity suit, won't I, Eric?" She smiled. "I'm sure the Right-to-Lifers will back me up, probably even finance my legal fees." She kept her smile in place. "The press will eat it up."

Her voice was pitched low and easy and her eyes glittered. "And of course I'll win in court. The blood tests will be positive. This *is* your child, Eric. I'm not so sure you can count on that majority vote. I'm not sure —"

The force of the blow snapped her head backwards. He grabbed a fistful of hair and jerked her up from the couch. He hit her again and again, swearing he would kill her. Stacey was so caught up in the excitement of winning that she scarcely felt the blows until the one to her stomach doubled her in half, her head snapped up and connected with Eric's fist and she fell to the floor, knocked unconscious.

For a moment, Eric stood staring stupidly down at her. He felt panicked—she looked so white, so still. He forced himself to pick her up and lay her on the couch. Her lip was bleeding and her right eye was already turning a dark blue. But she was breathing—thank God! She was breathing.

He began to pace; he didn't think he'd hit her that hard. She was just knocked out. But what the hell should he do? He couldn't leave—he couldn't predict what she'd do when she came to. She might call the police—he couldn't have that. What the hell should he do? He should call someone, but who? Who could he trust?

Suddenly it came to him: There was only one person he could call, only one person he could involve in this. He raced across the room and dialed Jessica Martin's number. He waited for what seemed an eternity before she came on the line.

Chapter 42

Carol sifted through the stack of mail on her desk for the second time. The envelope was not there. She rose from her desk and headed for the reception room.

Mary Ann Thomas smiled as Carol reached her desk. "Hi, Carol."

"Mary Ann, I seem to be missing an envelope that was sent Air Express to Jessica. I have the receipt that you signed, but I don't have the envelope. Do you remember accepting it?"

"Yes, I do. It was just this morning. Oh, I think I know what happened. I think I might have gotten it mixed up with Stacey's mail. I was sorting everything when she rushed out of here."

Carol raised her eyebrows. "Rushed out?"

Mary Ann frowned. "Yeah, she didn't say anything. Just tore out of here. But she looked like someone who had just gotten some really bad news."

"I hope nothing terrible has happened," Carol said. "You never know with Stacey."

"That's for sure," Mary Ann agreed. "Want me to go get the envelope? I'm sure I mixed it in with her mail."

"No," Carol said, "don't bother. You stay at your desk

268

and I'll get it. Just have Jessica's calls put directly through to her. She'll let you know if she wants to accept them or not."

Even though she knew Stacey wasn't in her office, Carol knocked before entering. She silently swung the door open, wrinkling her nose at the lingering odor of Stacey's over-powering perfume.

Walking quickly to Stacey's desk, she riffled through a stack of unopened letters when she heard Mary Ann announce that Eric Radner was calling for Jessica—urgent. Carol started to remind Mary Ann just to put Jessica's calls through when she heard Jessica answer that she'd be with him in a few seconds.

Carol frowned. Jessica sounded terribly upset.

What was wrong? And just as she was about to ask, she realized she shouldn't be hearing Jessica's voice, or Mary Ann's either. Stacey's intercom had not buzzed.

She stood rooted to the spot, listening in disbelief as Jessica picked up the receiver in her office.

"Yes, Eric," Jessica said. Carol recognized the panic in her voice. "What can I do for you?"

There was a momentary silence before Carol heard Jessica ask in a surprised voice, "Come to Stacey's home? But why? What's happened?"

More silence. Damn! Hearing only one side of this conversation was frustrating.

Jessica said, "Eric, calm down. All right, if you say it's that urgent, I'll come right away. But I do wish you could give me some idea of what's going on . . ."

Another pause.

"All right," Jessica said resignedly. "I'll get there as soon as traffic will allow."

Carol heard her hang up the phone.

What could have gone wrong with the intercom system that Carol could hear Jessica's conversation in Stacey's office? She'd have to get Mary Ann to call the telephone repair and . . . "Wait a minute," she said. "What's this?" At the base of the telephone, near the back wire, was a tiny button. She'd never seen a telephone with that sort of attachment. What . . . and then it hit her.

"Jesus! It's a bug," she gasped. Somehow, Stacey had bugged Jessica's office.

Carol stared in anger and amazement at the offensive gadget. Hard to spot, but there it was. The on-off control. Obviously, Stacey had forgotten to turn it off.

Carol quickly left the office, closing the door behind her and heading as fast as she could to Jessica's office. She rushed in without knocking.

Jessica looked up, startled. Carol never came in without knocking, and her face was ashen. "Carol, what's wrong? You look so white."

Carol caught her breath before answering. "I'm surprised I'm not scarlet. I'm seeing red!"

Jessica felt something uneasy begin to stir in her stomach. "Tell me, Carol," she said quietly.

"Jessica, I just heard you agree to go to Stacey's house at the request of Eric Radner."

"But why has that made you so angry?" she asked, bewildered. "I don't know what's happened or why Eric is even at her house—but it shouldn't make you angry that I'm going. He is a client, and she is an employee."

"Jessica." Carol's voice was now calm. "I heard your side of the conversation while I was in Stacey's office."

Jessica was still dazed from Ed Franklin's call and the news that Sol Bernstein was missing. The implication of what Carol was saying eluded her. "You just heard me talking on the telephone while you were in Stacey's office?" she repeated numbly.

Carol nodded. "I was looking for a letter for you mistakenly placed with Stacey's mail when I found it. You can come see the little bastard for yourself—it's attached right to her phone. I don't know where it's attached in here," Carol finished.

Suddenly Jessica understood. She gasped and her eyes grew huge. "Carol, are you saying that my office has been bugged? And that Stacey . . ."

"You got it, boss," Carol said in disgust. "This time that little bitch has gone too far. This is too damned much!"

Jessica sat staring at Carol. The whole morning had been too damned much. "I want to see it. Let's go to Stacey's office."

"Come on, I know right where it is. It blends into the color of the phone almost exactly. If you weren't looking for it, you'd never spot it."

Jessica followed Carol out of the door and down the corridor to Stacey's office. Carol went right to the phone and pointed out the tiny button.

Jessica felt sick to her stomach. Suddenly, her head echoed with Ed Franklin's statement: "Our tip came from a woman." It had been Stacey who had tipped the "Right to Know" people. Stacey who'd caused this whole ugly mess. Stacey must have monitored all her calls—all of them. The nausea spread. Could she also have heard Jessica agree to meet Jeremy at his apartment? She felt her anger mount. Was Stacey planning to blackmail Jessica—Jessica and Jeremy? She could no longer kid herself—Stacey was capable of anything. But why?

"Carol," she said, "get a locksmith over here immediately. You keep the new keys with you until I get back. Then we'll try to figure out how to dismantle this thing."

"When you get back?" Carol's tone was incredulous. "Do you mean you're still going to her house? After knowing about this?"

"Of course I'm going!" Jessica replied, anger making her voice hard. "Now more than ever, I'm going. I have to know what she's up to."

Carol thought for a moment before saying, "Jessica, maybe that's not such a good idea. Mary Ann told me Stacey left here this morning looking as though she'd heard some very bad news. You don't know what you could be walking into."

Jessica had a pretty good idea of the "bad news" Stacey had heard. She must have heard Ed Franklin's call—must have heard that Dr. Bernstein was missing and could be in serious danger—and Stacey was responsible.

"Don't worry about me, Carol," she said firmly.

"How about if I go with you? You shouldn't go alone—no telling what that little bitch has cooked up. And Eric Radner, too. Something smells rotten."

"Thanks, but I'll go alone. I'd rather you were here, taking care of things, I don't want anyone else to know about this."

Carol sighed. "Okay, but promise you'll be careful. And if I don't hear from you by quitting time, I'm coming out there."

"I'll be okay, Carol," Jessica reassured her. "Stacey is up to something all right, but I'm not in any physical danger. Radner is there, and I want to know *why!* I'll check in as soon as I can."

Chapter 43

Jessica forced herself to drive slowly as her car wound around the twisting curves of Coldwater Canyon Drive. Stacey's house was at the very top of Mulholland Drive and Jessica winced as the road narrowed and twisted as she made the turn off the canyon.

She reached the top and pulled onto the dirt road that led to the isolated house. Parked in front was Stacey's Mercedes SL, Eric Radner's Silver Cloud Rolls Royce, and a dark gray Chrysler sedan Jessica did not recognize.

She parked her car next to the Rolls and was about to get out when the front door of Stacey's house opened and a man exited carrying a small black medical bag. The man gave her a cursory glance, got into the Chrysler, and backed down the dirt road.

Jessica felt her pulse begin to race. As she got out of her car, she found her legs were trembling. She paused for a moment until she felt steadier, then walked up the steps and rang the bell.

Eric Radner answered the door. He looked disheveled and there were blood spots on his shirt front and lapels. At the sight of the blood, Jessica's heart raced with new fear.

"Eric," she managed, "what on earth is going on?"

"Get inside," he urged. "We can't talk out here."

With mounting fear, Jessica stepped into the foyer. Eric raced ahead of her and Jessica followed him into the living room. She noted with alarm a chair overturned and the shards of a broken wineglass on the coffee table. Stacey was not in sight.

"Eric," she demanded, "where is Stacey?"

Eric whirled to face her, his skin flushed, a pulse beating in his temple. "Now, don't get hysterical on me! Stacey's fine. Sit down and I'll explain —"

"I will not sit down!" Jessica interrupted angrily. "I want to know where Stacey is and what's going on here."

"She's in her bedroom, but she's—"

Jessica did not wait for him to finish. She headed quickly down the hall, Eric close on her heels. She hesitated outside the bedroom door, then quickly turned the knob and stepped inside. She was unable to suppress a gasp as she looked at Stacey's battered face. Her right eye was a swollen purple mass and there was a bandage covering her lower cheek. "My God," she whispered. Stacey did not move and Jessica turned shocked eyes to Radner.

"She's all right," he snapped. "My doctor gave her a sedative—she'll sleep for quite a while."

Jessica returned her gaze to Stacey, relieved to see that she was breathing evenly. "What happened, Eric?" she managed.

"She got what she asked for, that's what happened," Eric answered, glaring at Stacey's inert form. He turned and left the bedroom. Jessica looked at Stacey for a long moment, then quietly returned to the living room where Eric Radner sat sipping a glass of scotch. He looked up as she entered.

"Pour yourself a drink, Jessica. I think you're gonna need one."

"I don't want a drink," Jessica hissed. She fished inside her purse and found her cigarettes, quickly lit one, and inhaled long and deep. She stared at Eric.

"Who did that to Stacey?"

"She did it to herself—at least she brought it on herself."

He took a hefty swallow of scotch. "Don't look so damned worried—she'll be okay."

Jessica was astounded by his coldness. It was obvious he had beaten Stacey. "She didn't look okay to me, Eric."

"I told you, stop worrying. My doctor took care of her. Besides, that kind of alley cat always lands on her feet."

This was ridiculous. What the hell was she doing there? It was none of her business. Still, she had to know what was going on, if only to protect herself.

"Eric, I insist on knowing what happened and why you called me here."

"What happened is that little bitch tried to trap me into marriage by getting herself knocked up." He spat the words. "Well, nobody traps Eric Radner into anything. Nobody!"

Jessica swallowed hard. She should have listened to Carol. She should never have come to Stacey's. She forced her voice to sound calm. "Stacey is pregnant?"

"Not anymore she isn't," Radner sneered, "My doctor said she lost the kid."

The contempt Jessica felt turned to nausea, and she inhaled deeply to hold down the sick feeling. "Eric, I don't know anything about this, but if what you say is true, it's disgusting. You're a man of the world. You must know there are alternatives to beating her half to death."

"Of course I know that!" he shouted. "I offered to pay for an abortion. But that's not good enough for the little gold digger. She's after big game—she wants to be Mrs. Eric Radner, and I wouldn't buy it!"

Jessica was repulsed. It was all so sordid. "Stacey wanted to have her baby?"

"Her baby! Don't let her con you with her little maternal act, Jessica. When I told her no dice to marriage, when I told her she couldn't trap me into that bag, she said if the kid was a problem she'd get rid of it."

He rose and paced the room. "When I still wouldn't buy it, she threatened a paternity suit. Threatened to go to the press. Hell, she might have even talked to Peter Ueberroth . . ."

"Who?"

"Peter Ueberroth—the baseball commissioner! That's who! Don't you get it yet, Jessica? She goddamned threatened to cost me the majority vote of the National League!" He was out of control. "She goddamned threatened my baseball team!"

A child miscarried—a woman badly beaten—and all Radner could rave about was a baseball team. Jessica crushed out her cigarette and rose from her chair, grasping her handbag tightly. She made no attempt to conceal her disgust. "I find this whole situation despicable. But none of it has anything to do with me. I'm leaving."

She walked toward the foyer, but Eric's words stopped her cold. "I wouldn't leave so fast if I were you, Jessica. Not if you care about your consulting firm."

She turned back to face him. "What does any of this have to do with my firm?"

"At this point, maybe nothing," he answered coolly, thinking fast. He couldn't let her go, he needed her help. "But if you don't stick with me through this, if you don't get that little bitch to see the light, your firm will be in it up to your very pretty little ears."

Jessica was speechless. How could he try to trap her in this mess? Or had Stacey somehow twisted something she'd heard through the bugging device into something that might damage her?

She forced her voice to sound calm. "Eric, there is no way you can involve Martin Management in this. And there's no way I can help you convince Stacey to forget about this. I'm afraid you're on your own." She finished in what she hoped was a tone of finality.

"Like hell I am!" he bellowed. "You'd better sit down, Jessica!"

She remained standing, hoping he wouldn't see the fear in her eyes.

"Jessica." There was no mistaking the menace in his voice. "If Stacey takes this thing public, if she spoils my chances at the one dream of my life, I'll personally ruin both of you. I'm a powerful man. She picked the wrong person to play games with. If she persists, I'll accuse you of running a high-class call-girl service through your consulting firm—I'll smear your name in so much media mud you won't be able to leave your house."

Jessica stared at him in disbelief.

He continued, more vehement than ever, "And I'll make it stick, Jessica. You can bet on it! I have plenty of friends in high places. There won't be a corporation in the world that will do business with you. You'll be finished." He paused briefly, looking at her intently. "I'll swear you set me up with Stacey, and I'll get others to swear I'm not the only one." He smiled icily as he said, "Now, don't you think you ought to sit down?"

Eric's tone was now friendly, persuasive. But it was no less deadly in intent, and Jessica knew it.

"Of course, I wouldn't like to do that to you, Jessica. All you have to do is help me with Stacey. Make her see the stupidity of her stunt."

"Eric," she began, masking her nervousness with contempt, "that is the most disgusting, vile threat imaginable. And there's not a way in the world you could make such an accusation stick."

"Well now, Jessica," he smiled, "I didn't exactly say I would get it to stick legally, but I will get it made public far and wide and the damage will have been done. So if that bitch tries to take me down, I'll take both of you with me. It's up to you."

"But, Eric," Jessica argued, "how am I supposed to convince her to be reasonable? I'm the last person she'll listen to. You have no idea how much Stacey resents me. I've only just begun to find out myself."

"I don't expect you to do it on your own, Jessica. I'm a fair man. Before she tried this stunt, Stacey and I had some good times together. It might surprise you to learn that I was even considering marriage before this crap. I'm willing to negotiate, make some sort of financial settlement with her." He shrugged. "Hell, I've got nothing but money. You help me convince her it would be in her best interest and we'll all come out of this smelling like a rose."

Jessica massaged her temples, trying to think clearly.

"You find out what she wants." Eric's voice rang with assurance. He knew he had won—Jessica had no choice. "As long as it isn't marriage," he continued, "we can work it out." He headed for the door. "You call me by tomorrow at the latest." Then, as an afterthought, "My doctor left pills and instructions on the table over there." And he was gone.

Jessica sat quietly staring into space. She felt ill, suddenly aware of the stale French luncheon on the table before the fireplace. She rose, walked to the telephone, and dialed the office. Carol was on the line at once and agreed to come right over. Jessica hated to involve her, but she knew she had to trust someone; the doctor's instructions for the pills were one every four hours. They would have to give them to Stacey in shifts.

When she hung up the telephone, she began to clear away the remains of the luncheon, piling everything into the kitchen sink, unable to stomach the heavy, sour odors.

She returned to the living room and crossed to the bar, pouring herself a generous snifter of brandy. She stepped to the fireplace and stirred the coals, turning the logs with the poker until the fire caught, introducing a welcome warmth into the suddenly cold room. She took a seat and stared unseeingly into the flames. She was furious at being caught in the ugly situation between Stacey and Eric, but she was also determined that she would not be their victim. Nothing and no one was going to wreck the business that she alone had made successful. She'd fight them both, all the way to the mat.

Chapter 44

Carol arrived at Stacey's house and was ushered in by Jessica, who still held the brandy snifter in her hand. Carol glanced at the snifter, then the angry flush in Jessica's cheeks. She spoke in her usual ironic tone. "Any more where that came from?"

Jessica nodded and indicated the bar. Carol poured a snifter of brandy and turned back to Jessica.

"Let's sit down, Carol," Jessica offered. "Here by the fireplace."

Over brandy, Jessica told Carol everything, from the very beginning—Michael's departure, her love affair with Jeremy, ending with Stacey's threat to Radner and his consequent threat against Jessica. When she had finished, she leaned back tiredly, saying, "And that's about it, Carol. The whole story."

She smiled. "You know, Carol, you really are a terrific listener. You didn't interrupt me once."

Carol shrugged. "You tell a pretty direct story."

"Well, I wish that was the end of the story, Carol. But I'm afraid we've just begun. I know Stacey will carry out her threat against Radner and that will leave me up the proverbial creek." Jessica stared into the fireplace. "Unless Rad-

279

ner can come up with something outside marriage that will satisfy her."

Carol could no longer contain her anger. "That damned little bitch!" she spat. "You're right, of course, she *will* do it and Radner will do anything to cover his own buns. What do we do now?"

For the first time that day, Jessica's smile was not forced. The friendship and affection Carol offered without question was heartwarming. "I hated to involve you, Carol. But there was no one else I could trust."

"Hey, boss or no boss, we're friends first."

"That we are, Carol." Jessica thought for a minute, then suggested, "Maybe Stacey will consider a financial settlement. She'll gain nothing by going public. It's the only thing I can think of."

"I think the little bitch will take the money and run for the hills. Radner won't have a thing to worry about, other than explaining it to his tax man."

"Maybe Radner won't have to worry," Jessica said slowly. "But I still do. Don't forget, Jeremy is still a married man with a family. Nothing has been worked out yet, and Stacey could cause a lot of grief."

Carol stifled her anger. The situation called for a clear head. She looked at Jessica and smiled. "We've got an ace up our sleeves, too. It's illegal to bug an office or a telephone. That gives us some bargaining power."

Jessica's face brightened. "You're right! I hadn't thought about that. I guess I'm not thinking too clearly about anything lately." And as quickly as her face brightened, it turned grim. "Everything seemed to happen so fast—Michael gone—Dr. Bernstein missing and probably in terrible danger—the company threatened, and I . . ." She swallowed the lump in her throat. "Oh, Carol, I'm in love with Jeremy and I don't know what's going to happen. He's been married for sixteen years. And even if it isn't my fault, even if I didn't cause the breakup, I don't know if we'll ever be free to marry—if his wife will even consider a divorce."

Carol was quiet. Having survived a bad marriage herself, she was hard-pressed to see the importance of marriage to

Jessica. She used her most mischievous voice. "So? You and Jeremy will be lovers instead of man and wife. Sounds more fun to me anyway—the Katharine Hepburn and Spencer Tracy of the corporate world." Her grin was contagious.

Jessica responded with a little laugh. "Something like that, I guess. I know it's old-fashioned, but I can't help it, Carol. I'm really in love with him and I want more than that to our relationship, and so does Jeremy." She sighed. "But you're right, of course. Things will all work out somehow."

"I'm certain of it," Carol reassured her. "When do you plan to talk to Stacey?"

"Tomorrow morning, I guess," Jessica replied with a tiny yawn. She was worn out. "The doctor doesn't expect any problems. The pills are mild tranquilizers and there are painkillers if she asks for them."

"Look, you're exhausted. Why don't you let me spell you tonight—then you can come back in the morning? I'll be able to open the office after you get here."

Jessica hesitated, but with her usual insistence, Carol made it hard to say no. Finally, Jessica went back to the Beverly Wilshire Hotel, still unable to move back to the wreckage of her home.

When Carol let Jessica back in the next morning, she was relieved to see that Jessica seemed less strained. Her eyes had some of their old fight in them, and she seemed ready to tackle what lay ahead.

Carol was pretty tired herself, but greeted Jessica cheerfully, silently promising herself she would get in a quick nap at the office during lunch hour.

"How's Stacey, Carol?" Jessica asked, just a hint of concern in her tone.

"She's awake, and she's all right. She looks like hell—he must have really worked her over," Carol answered with an expression both of satisfaction and revulsion. "She wasn't too thrilled to see me here—asked if the whole damned office was waiting outside to take turns."

Jessica nodded glumly. It sounded as if Stacey was in fighting form.

"I offered to make her some breakfast, but all she wanted was coffee," Carol said. "There's plenty in the pot—would you like a cup?"

"I'll get some later, Carol." Jessica took off her coat. "Have you told her I was coming?"

"Yeah, I told her." Carol sounded worried. "She's ready for a fight, Jessica. I don't know if I should go to the office or stay here in case you need me."

"You go to the office," Jessica urged. "This one can't be avoided and I'm the one who has to handle it."

Carol gathered up her purse and said, "Just remember one thing, Jessica—she doesn't fight fair. Don't let anything she says get to you."

Jessica felt a sudden surge of affection for Carol. "I'll remember that." She walked with her to the door. "I'll call you later at the office."

When Carol was gone, Jessica stood in the living room trying to gather her composure to walk into Stacey's bedroom. She finally knocked on the door.

"I'm awake," Stacey responded, her voice thick.

Jessica entered the room and stood in the doorway for a moment. The two women regarded one another warily—two fighters in the ring sizing each other up.

Jessica was appalled at what she saw. Stacey's black eye was swollen nearly shut and her lower lip was puffed, perhaps slightly scarred. Jessica suddenly remembered the huge signet ring Eric Radner wore and shuddered at the thought of it ripping into Stacey's face. Without thinking, Jessica murmured, "Oh, Stacey, your face."

Stacey glared through her unswollen eye, her voice still thick as she tried to form the words around her bruised lip. "So I won't enter the Miss America Contest."

Jessica ignored the sarcasm. "How do you feel?"

Stacey shrugged. "I'll live. Look, I don't imagine this will be quick, so why don't we get right to it?"

"Do you want to start, or shall I?" Jessica asked.

"I don't give a damn who starts it, I'm the one who's going to finish it!"

282

"Stacey." Jessica fought for control. "Let's try to be civilized."

Stacey's voice remained hard. "I can't be civil if you're planning on one of your asinine lectures."

"I don't think a lecture would cut it, Stacey." Jessica felt the grip on her anger slipping away. "Not after the rotten stunts you've pulled. The trouble your actions have caused—"

"My heart breaks!" Stacey interrupted her. "Listen, Jessica, you might have been in a position to take that tone with me in the past, but I know better now. You're as big a whore as I'll ever be!" She sat up in bed, pulling the sheet around herself. "At least I don't pretend—all your martyrdom over poor suffering Michael, everyone believing you were some kind of saint! Nobody knew you were getting it on with Jeremy Bronson."

"Stacey, my relationship with Jeremy Bronson is none of *your* damned business! How you found out about it is *my* business!"

She did not miss the slight darkening of Stacey's eyes. "You got it, Stacey. We found the bug. Evidently you forgot to turn it off in your rush yesterday morning."

Stacey was shaken but determined to bluff it through. "So you found the bug. What are you going to do about it?" Her smile was mocking. "It looks to me like we're at a standoff. You know I bugged your office and I know you're fucking Jeremy Bronson. We both keep our mouths shut—no harm done."

"No harm done? Stacey, your meddling may have put a man's life in danger! An honorable, innocent man! I know you heard my conversation with Ed Franklin yesterday morning—you know Dr. Bernstein is missing! And it's your fault!"

Stacey's face paled slightly, but still, giving an anonymous tip wasn't illegal. And she was damned if she'd let Jessica lay any guilt trips at her door. "Bullshit! If he's in danger, it's his own fault! He should have gone to the FDA! I did what was necessary—someone had to do the right thing."

Jessica's anger nearly overwhelmed her. "Don't try to play the concerned citizen with me, Stacey. Even Ed Franklin didn't buy it. You tipped him about Dr. Bernstein to damage me in some way. You've caused unspeakable grief just to harm me. Why in hell didn't you just resign? Why did you go on working for me if you have something against me?"

"Because quitting wouldn't have brought you down," Stacey said with deadly calm. "You don't seem to be getting the message, Jessica. I hate you and all you stand for. I've had enough of your kind of condescension to last me a lifetime. I intend to destroy you and Martin Management Consultants along with you!"

"That's why you installed the bug? Because for some twisted reason, you hate me?"

"Give the lady a cigar!" Stacey laughed. "It would have worked too, Jessica. If Eric hadn't lost his cool, hadn't got so damned scared about his fucking baseball franchise." A crafty look came into her eyes. "You'd never have caught me—you're not smart enough. Nobody is smart enough to catch me."

"Listen to yourself, Stacey," Jessica said, frustrated. "We *did* catch you—don't you see? Carol found the bug *before* Eric called me here. For God's sake, Stacey, you didn't have to resort to all this . . . why didn't you come to me, talk it out? I would have tried to help you—"

"Cut the shit, Jessica!" Stacey snarled, unwilling to listen. "There isn't a shovel big enough for it. I'm alone! Just as I have been all my life. I do what I do to survive. I don't need your crumbs—I'll make it and you can't stop me."

"I can try to reason with you, if you'll just listen to me."

"No thanks!" Stacey said stonily. "I'll manage on my own, I always have. Now, you get the fuck out of here—I've had enough of this. We have nothing more to talk about."

Jessica reached into her pocket for a cigarette. Lighting it, she said coldly, "On the contrary, I'm afraid we have a lot to talk about. Obviously you're finished at Martin Management, but whether you like it or not, Eric Radner has appointed me to bargain with you, so you're stuck with me."

Stacey laughed harshly. "Sweating through his silk shirt, is he? Well, there's still nothing to talk about. I've told him what I want—if I don't get it, I'm calling the cops. I'm going to accuse him of murder. I'm going to swear out a complaint against him for the murder of my child!" she finished triumphantly.

"Stacey, there is no way Eric is going to marry you. He's made that perfectly clear. And for the life of me, I can't imagine why you'd even want that any longer." She shook her head. "Look at what he did to you. Your life would be hell. . . ."

"That may be, but it would be a secure hell—I'd be somebody! For once!"

"Secure? How?" Jessica asked incredulously. "Because you'd bear his name? Think about it—he's a ruthless man. Even if he did marry you, he'd dump you without a cent. He'd find some trumped-up charge and with his power he'd make it stick. You won't gain a thing by forcing him into marriage. Don't be a fool. Consider your options."

And she *was* thinking—Jessica could almost see her mind working. She prayed for the right words to persuade Stacey. The last thing she wanted to do was let Stacey know that Eric was blackmailing her. All Stacey would need to hear was that she could hurt Jessica and her company by destroying Eric's reputation.

Warily, Stacey finally said, "And what options are you talking about? What did Eric offer?"

"Nothing specific. That is, he said he was a reasonable man and would make a financial settlement with you. But," she continued firmly, "he said he would *never* marry you, no matter what you did. He wants to know what you want."

"But you already know what I want, don't you, Mrs. Jessica Martin? I want what you have. I want respectability . . . prestige. I want *Martin Management Consultants!*"

Jessica drew back as if Stacey had slapped her. Stacey was undeniably disturbed, and clearly her hatred of Jessica and what she stood for far outweighed her own need for survival. There was no reasonable settlement that would satisfy Stacey. Jessica decided to play it cool and aloof, intimidate Stacey. "Martin Management Consultants is not for sale, Stacey."

It worked. She saw in Stacey's eyes that she was afraid of Jessica. Jessica's poise and confidence were a threat.

"Then you tell him I want my own firm. I'll still put you out of business—you just watch me," Stacey said with false bravado.

Jessica took the first relaxed breath of the morning. She feared no competition, from Stacey or any other recruiter. She was too good at what she did, too well entrenched within the corporate world to be overthrown. But she knew she couldn't let Stacey think it was that easy. She had to make her eager for the battle she was about to propose.

"Oh, Stacey," she laughed. "Do you think for a moment you scare me? I'd like nothing better than to compete with you. In fact, I'd relish the chance."

She rose and looked down at Stacey, propped against her pillows. "You'd better think this over before I call Radner. There's an old saying—'be careful what you ask for because you just might get it.' Are you sure this is what you want?"

Stacey grinned maliciously. "Nice try, Jessica. But you don't fool me—you're scared shitless. And you have every right to be. You know I'll wipe up the floor with you." She was practically licking her lips. "I'll take away every account you have. I'll steal every recruiter. I'll even have the good sense to hire David Clarendon—you were a fool to lose him, but then, that's typical of you. You ought to learn there's no room for emotions in business." She shifted her position on the bed. "No, you don't fool me with your petty little challenge. Yes! That's exactly what I want," she concluded. "I want my own firm and I want the money to finance it!"

Jessica held back her elation. Stacey had taken the bait—now maybe the whole mess could be put to bed. She kept her tone bemused. She couldn't afford to drop her pose until everything was signed, sealed, and delivered. "Okay, Stacey," she said, "but I warn you, I'll fight you to the mat."

"The phone is right beside you, Jessica." Stacey pointed. "Call Radner and tell him what I want and what it's going to cost him," she commanded imperiously. "I want one million dollars—tax-free. And I want it in my bank by tomorrow afternoon—deposited to my personal account."

Jessica was stunned. Without thinking, she blurted, "A million dollars? Are you mad? He'll never go for it."

"Oh yes, he will," Stacey chuckled. "I know Eric—he wants his new Tinkertoy set. A million dollars to Eric Radner is a spit in the ocean. But to me, it's a bomb planted right in your office." Her eyes narrowed. "I'm going to beat you, Jessica. And I'll spend every cent of the million to do it."

Jessica was both astounded and panicked. She knew how wealthy Radner was reputed to be—but a million dollars! Still, she had to try. She forced a grin and reached for the telephone. "You know, Stacey, this is going to be the most fun of my career."

She dialed the private number Radner had given her and he came on the line at once. "Eric," she said, "I've just finished talking to Stacey—she's decided to deal. She wants one million tax-free and she wants it in her account by tomorrow afternoon."

Jessica listened in amazement to Eric's voice on the other end of the line. She sensed how tense Stacey was, but did not look at her, afraid her astonishment would show on her face. When he'd finished, Jessica could say only, "Yes, yes of course I'll tell her," and hang up.

She turned back to face Stacey, who was now leaning comfortably against the pillows. She looked confident and casual, but Jessica knew she was bursting with anticipation. "You've got your deal, Stacey. The money will be in your bank by tomorrow afternoon."

"I kinda thought it would be." Stacey smiled. "What is it you are supposed to tell me?"

"Oh, the arrangements for the money to be deposited. Eric's attorney will be here tomorrow afternoon at one o'clock. He'll have some papers for you to sign. Papers in which you will admit to having tried to blackmail Eric Radner. Papers in which you will state there never was a child and that you did not miscarry—that there was no beating." Jessica kept her tone even, her distaste covered. "Papers in which you will admit you have no claim against Eric Radner, never did have such a claim, and will never make such a claim in the future. There will be a notary public here to witness your signature."

"Wait up just a minute," Stacey interrupted. "How do I know the money will be in the bank after I sign the papers? Does he think he can trick me so easily?"

Jessica had to swallow bile. Eric wasn't letting her off the hook just yet. "Eric will meet me at your bank at one o'clock. He'll hand me a cashier's check made out in your name. Who is the president of your bank?"

"Harry Baumberg."

"Fine. The minute I deposit the check to your account, Mr. Baumberg will telephone you to confirm it's valid. Then you'll sign the papers." Jessica took out a cigarette and was surprised to see her hands still trembling as she lit it. "I gather you know Baumberg well enough to recognize his voice?"

"I do," Stacey replied.

"Then I assume everything is satisfactory?"

"Oh, more than satisfactory. Eric even gave me a bonus—*you* have to deposit the money *I'll* use to ruin you. It's really rich." She laughed. "Well, Jessica, I can't say it hasn't been fun."

Jessica took a long drag on her cigarette before she replied. Stacey stretched lazily, her eyes never leaving Jessica's face.

"I don't think we're quite finished, Stacey. I can think of nothing I'd like better than meeting you in the marketplace. But there is the little question of your having illegally bugged my office." She let the steel show in her voice as she went on. "Nothing can be done about the damage you've already caused." She swallowed hard to get past the sudden lump in her throat. "What guarantee do I have that you won't try to blackmail me the way you tried to blackmail Eric?"

Stacey laughed derisively. "Because you no longer have a goddamned thing I want! I never heard anything really important, Jessica," she said coldly and glanced at Jessica shrewdly. "But that isn't what's worrying you, is it? You're afraid I'll spill the beans about you and Bronson. That's it, isn't it?"

"The thought crossed my mind, Stacey."

"Who the hell would care about you two?"

"His wife and children, to begin with."

"Well, don't let it worry you!" Stacey said. "I'm going to be too busy shoving my success down your aristocratic throat. I don't give a good goddamn who you fuck! I've got what I want now. But, if it will make you feel better, have Eric's man draw up a letter stating I bugged your office—that'll protect the wife and kiddies. Have him add that I stole the master computer code from your office. That ought to be enough to hold over my head."

Jessica's eyes widened in shock. She hadn't even considered that in addition to installing the bug, Stacey had gone through her private files.

Stacey laughed again. "Don't panic, Jessica. I didn't have time to use it. Just change your codes and your precious files will be safe." She stuck out her hand mockingly. "Do we have a deal or not?"

Jessica stared at the outstretched hand for a long moment. Did she really have any choice? At last she said, "We have a deal." Ignoring Stacey's hand, she turned and walked to the bedroom door. "Well, Stacey," she said as she opened it, "I think that wraps things up. Good luck with your firm."

Stacey laughed until tears rolled down her bruised face. It was several moments before she was able to gasp out the words to Jessica's departing back. "See why I'll beat you, Jessica? You actually mean it when you wish me luck!"

Jessica would not dignify the remark. She left Stacey's house without another word.

Chapter 45

Jeremy Bronson eased his car into the circular driveway of his Pacific Palisades home. The sun glanced sharply off the lead-glass window. It was a beautiful house, solid, secure—just like the lives that were lived inside. Jeremy knew that this serenity was about to be shattered, had known since his wife's uncharacteristic telephone call requesting his presence at lunch when the children would be in school. He also remembered this was the housekeeper's day off. Margaret obviously wanted to talk with the assurance of privacy.

His stomach muscles tightened. Somehow, his wife must have picked up on his involvement with Jessica. Her intuition surprised Jeremy. He'd been very discreet—had he underestimated her?

In any case, she had requested, no, had politely insisted he be home for lunch. In a way it was a relief. There seemed no point in delaying what was to come. He left his car and headed up the walk, letting himself in through the massive double doors. The foyer was empty. "Margaret?"

"In the living room. I thought we might have a drink before lunch."

That was also uncharacteristic. Margaret rarely drank more than a glass of sherry before dinner. He headed down the hallway, then entered the French doors to the living room. Margaret was seated before the fireplace, where a pitcher of martinis, a bottle of sherry, and two glasses rested on the table in front of the ivory-silk couch.

"Well," he began hesitantly, "this is a nice touch. You know I love a good martini before lunch."

"I hope it will be good. I'm never sure of the vermouth."

Jeremy took the seat opposite her. He knew Margaret would have prepared it exactly as he liked it—the gin would have been refrigerated, the martini pitcher chilled, rinsed with vermouth, emptied, and the cold gin poured at just the right velocity so as not to bruise the liquor. She would have prepared the martini as she did everything—perfectly.

He smiled appreciatively as he took his first sip. "As usual, just right." He looked at her over the rim of his glass. She had drawn her ash-blonde hair into a gentle knot at the nape of her neck. She wore, as usual, very few cosmetics, and her dress was a simple, pale yellow linen, her shoes buff-colored pumps. She could have posed for a picture in *Town and Country* magazine—the perfectly groomed executive wife.

She smiled tentatively, then, as if she had made a decision and was determined to carry it through, she added, "I hope my call hasn't disrupted your schedule too much?"

"No," he assured her quickly, recognizing her nervousness. "As a matter of fact, you saved me from a deadly dull meeting with Frank Griffin. You remember him, head of personnel?" She nodded. "It's the damnedest thing with Griffin; no matter how often we have lunch, or where we have it, he always orders exactly the same thing. Always. I get so involved waiting for him to slip up and get a little adventurous, I usually forget what the hell we are supposed to be meeting about."

Margaret's laugh was forced. "Margaret," his voice was gentle, encouraging. "We could sit here and make small talk, but I know you have something on your mind. What is it?"

She fidgeted with the stem of her glass, then placed it on the tray, barely tasted. Her voice was wary, and she did not meet his eyes. She focused her gaze on the mantel above the fireplace, the photographs of their two children staring silently back at her. "I'm not sure just how to begin, but, Jeremy . . . this time it's different, isn't it?"

Jeremy knew what she meant but wanted to hear how she saw things. "What is different, Margaret?"

"This isn't just a diversion, is it, Jeremy?" She was not quite pleading, but he could sense that she was hoping against hope her intuitions were wrong. Jeremy did not respond, and Margaret quickly rushed out the words. "This woman means something to you, doesn't she?"

It was Jeremy's turn to reflect. He shifted his position and took another sip of his martini. Certainly he didn't want to hurt Margaret more than he had to, but he didn't want to play games, either. He knew how much courage it had taken for her to bring this up.

"Yes, Margaret, she does," he said as gently as possible, yet he could see his admission had already wounded her. She said nothing and he continued, "I don't know how you knew, but yes, this time it's different."

"How different?" The pain in her eyes made his heart lurch. "Are you in love with her?"

He hadn't thought Margaret would be this hurt. He'd been so certain that as long as her life-style was secure, but then . . . how could she know her security was not threatened, that he would always provide for her and the children? He knew she cared for him, but for such a long time their relationship had been that of two friendly companions he hadn't expected the mingled pain and fear in her eyes. He ached for her, but knew he had to be truthful.

"I could deny it, Margaret, but I won't. Yes, I am in love with her, very much in love with her."

"I see," she said softly. She did not look at him, kept her eyes glued on the photographs of their children. "I was rather afraid that would be the answer—I've suspected for some time now."

"But how, Margaret?" Jeremy thought he'd managed to hide his newfound happiness until he could find a way to break it to her gently. "What made you realize that this was serious? I've been discreet, I thought—I'd never do anything to hurt you deliberately."

She smiled, a sad but patient smile. "Jeremy, I know I'm no ball of fire as a woman—I've always known my limitations. But I *am* a woman, and women's intuition really isn't something to scoff at." She picked up her glass of sherry, but she did not sip it. "We've been married for over sixteen years. I know our relationship is—uh—unorthodox. But even though you haven't shared my bed in a long time, you are still my husband." She smiled ruefully. "Perhaps because we *haven't* shared a bed for so long, it has given me a better perspective on you—maybe I can be somewhat more detached than most wives. I'm very sensitive to your moods, Jeremy."

Once again he felt he had underestimated her. "And have my moods been so different?"

"Oh, quite. Even the children have noticed. In fact, I'm not certain I'd have had the courage to bring this up if the children hadn't mentioned it. It was their remarks that made me face up to the fact that this—I, well—that this was something we had better talk about."

He digested that for a minute before asking, "How have my moods changed?"

"You've been happy, Jeremy. Really happy—something you haven't been for a long time. Oh, I daresay you've been content as it were, sustained by your work, the children, the peaceful life we lead. But you haven't been happy." She smiled at the mention of their children. "Bobby said he thought you were getting younger, Melissa said your walk is bouncy." Again she smiled, but with a touch of irony. "You *do* have a spring to your step lately, Jeremy."

"I'm sorry if I've been obvious, Margaret. . . ."

"One shouldn't have to apologize for happiness. It's too rare a commodity."

He didn't know how to respond. If only she'd throw a tantrum, play the aggrieved wife. He didn't know how to deal with this cool poise . . . unless—was she going to attempt some sort of reconciliation? He prayed not, it was far too late for that.

"Margaret, if it's the children's security that worries you . . ."

"Obviously that is a part of my concern, Jeremy. I love our children dearly, as of course do you. But please don't invest me with qualities I don't possess. Of course I am concerned for their security, their happiness. But I am not entirely selfless." She paused and sipped her sherry. "I am also concerned about myself—my security, my happiness. Marriage to you and the life-style we lead are all I really know, all I've ever really wanted, actually. This woman is a threat to all of that, isn't she?"

Jeremy's instinct was to deny it—he intended to make certain of Margaret's financial security and that of his children. But he could not deny that their life-style would change. When he was silent, Margaret exhaled sharply, as if for the first time since she'd called him. Jeremy knew she was fighting to control her emotions, and he gave her great credit for the effort it cost her.

She looked at him pensively before asking, "Would you think me totally plebeian if I asked you about her? I don't want to know who she is," she hurriedly added, "or any of the intimate details—just the type of woman she is."

For a moment, her request threw him. He hadn't been prepared to discuss Jessica. Yet he suddenly felt that Margaret had a right to know what kind of woman it took to make him fall in love, make him want to end a marriage of over sixteen years. She had the right to know it wasn't some sexy, empty-headed young thing.

"She's a wonderful woman, Margaret," he said, stopping himself before adding that under different circumstances, Margaret would have liked her as a person. "She lost her husband," Jeremy said carefully. "We have known one another about three years, but we've only been together for a short time. As I've said, she is a wonderful woman and would not be unfaithful to her husband. . . ."

His voice trailed off. He'd been certain assuring Margaret that Jessica was quality would help—that sort of thing was so important to her. And she *had* asked. Yet he realized it had exactly the opposite effect he'd intended. She said, with uncharacteristic acidity, "How admirable, Jeremy. Marital fidelity *is* an impressive virtue. A pity she could not extend it to include *my* marriage."

Jeremy simply did not know how to respond. What did she want to hear? This was a side of Margaret he had never seen. Yet what the hell did he expect? She was human.

She rose and walked to the French windows, gazing out on the sparkling lawn. She held her shoulders proudly, her spine erect. Jeremy could not help but admire her dignity. When she spoke, the bitterness was gone, but she did not turn to face him.

"Jeremy, I know I could have been a better wife to you. I've always known my limitations and that's the reason I have never confronted you before. You've been, as you say, discreet. You've saved me from embarrassment and I've always been grateful for that." She laughed, but there was no mirth in the sound. "I'm afraid I've been something of an ostrich, Jeremy. I've buried my head in the sand. I wouldn't—couldn't—allow myself to consider that this could happen. That something, that a diversion, could turn into . . ." She was unable to complete the sentence. "I thought there were certain safety factors in our marriage that would prevent this. The children, your career, our mutual respect for one another. Foolishness—utter foolishness. You *did* try to tell me, Jeremy. I've only my own complacency, only myself to blame."

"Margaret," he said brokenly, "you've been a good wife, you mustn't think otherwise. We have different needs, that's all. I don't hold you to blame, Margaret," he finished lamely.

She turned to face him. "I'm certain that somewhere down the road I'll be able to take comfort in that, Jeremy. But not now."

He silently cursed himself. Nothing he could say was going to make it easier for her, and he was only beginning to realize how right Jessica had been. Margaret was hurting—badly. She did love him, for all the lack of passion between them. In her own way she loved him, and he did not know how to ease the pain he was causing her.

Margaret returned to her seat on the ivory sofa and

poured fresh sherry into her glass. She laughed sadly. "The heart is a very complicated thing, Jeremy. At the moment mine is struggling with so many different feelings. I'm totally miserable for myself, but I am also grateful that someone has been able to give you the happiness I was not capable of. Madness, I know, but perhaps you can understand?"

At his nod, she continued, "Please don't think I'm being a martyr. I can't think of anything more repugnant. But I *do* care for you, I always have. I can't seem to bring myself to resent your being happy, not after all these years."

"Margaret, I know you care, you've always cared. Ours hasn't been a bad marriage, you've made me happy in many ways. I *know* you tried—believe that, because it is true."

"It's decent of you to say that, Jeremy. And if it is true, I'm glad. But it doesn't change the fact that you are in love with another woman. A woman whose needs apparently match your own. A woman who can make you totally happy. Even sixteen years of my good intentions can't stand up against all that."

She swallowed and Jeremy caught a glimpse of tears in her eyes, but she sat up straight and composed her expression into the "stiff upper lip" of her English heritage.

"Jeremy, I am not prepared to discuss divorce."

"But I haven't asked for a divorce. I—"

"No, you haven't," she cut in. "Not yet. But you are in love with this woman. How long do you think it will be before you do ask for your freedom? How long before she asks it?"

"Margaret, I know all this is a shock, I know it's painful for you—for both of us. But don't jump to conclusions. She would *never* make that kind of demand—she would *never* break up a home, disrupt our children's—"

"Jeremy!" For the second time she allowed her frustration to come through. "I'm trying to be as civilized as possible, but you aren't making it any easier by your constant reference to this woman as a—as a paragon of virtue. Maybe she really is—frankly, I don't give a damn! I may have driven you into her arms by my complacency, but please, spare me a litany of her sterling qualities."

Jeremy was completely out of his depth. Margaret was seesawing between hurt and fury. He didn't know what to say. He stared at her numbly.

Some of the anger left her eyes at his pathetic expression and she smiled, an almost tender smile. She reached over and covered his hands with her own.

"You look like such a little boy, all of a sudden. Very like Bobby when he feels caught between what he wants and what he knows he is forbidden to have. But you are not a little boy, Jeremy. You are a grown man. What on earth did you think my reaction would be? What did you think we would do in this situation?"

He shook his head. Margaret was right—he *was* caught.

Margaret sighed and withdrew her hand. "Well, I've thought about it, Jeremy. I've been able to close my eyes to certain things in the past, because they never meant anything to you. I knew that. But even I am not stoic enough to ignore this."

Jeremy started to interject, but Margaret raised her hand in caution.

"As I said, Jeremy, I am not ready to discuss a divorce. I may never be ready for that; I don't know. But I do have some pride left. I really don't think I can stand by and 'bite the bullet,' as they say in American cowboy films. This wound calls for a little stronger anesthetic."

Jeremy's heart thudded; he was terrified of saying the wrong thing, of making things even worse. Tentatively he said, "What do you suggest? If it would make it easier for you, I could move into the company apartment. . . ."

Her shoulders slumped in resignation, but she shook her head. "I don't know if that is such a good idea. I don't want the children upset—not yet. They really don't suspect anything. I've given this some thought. After all, I rather suspected I'd learn this—this involvement was different. The school semester is over in just two weeks. I think a trip home to England might be the best solution for now. Mother and Father are getting on, and the children love England. I won't have to make any explanations right away."

A new fear, one he hadn't thought of: the children—his

children—separated from him. "How long would you be gone, Margaret?"

"That really isn't for me to say, is it, Jeremy?" She met his gaze with firm resolve. "It will be up to you to decide if this newfound love of yours is forever. If it is . . ."

"Then what?" he pressed.

"Then we'll just have to see, won't we, Jeremy?"

"But the children, Margaret. You aren't saying you would deny me the right to see my children?"

"I'm not saying anything other than what I've said. I'm suggesting this as the best thing to do at the moment. If after a while, you feel you can't live without this woman, well, we'll have to discuss that at the time. I do have my pride, Jeremy. I won't force you to stay married to me, not if you are certain you no longer want me as your wife. But I can't stay here while you find that out. I really couldn't bear that."

Jeremy's heart was leaden. The children were such a joy in his life, and he knew he had been a good father—they needed him as well. The thought of not seeing them for a long time was nearly unbearable. England! It was so far away—it hadn't occurred to him Margaret would want to return to England. Yet why not? Why should she stay in Los Angeles, answer all the inevitable questions, make all the hollow excuses?

His eyes went dark with pain. He hadn't thought any of it through, he'd only thought of his love for Jessica. Jessica had known it would be this rough—why hadn't he believed her? Mentally he shook his head—even if he had believed her, it would have changed nothing. He loved Jessica, loved her totally, and there was nothing he could do about it. His eyes implored Margaret, but he could not read her expression.

Margaret's tone was weary. "Jeremy, I would never deny the children the right to see their father. They don't deserve that, and I suppose if truth be known, neither do you. But good Lord, what were you thinking? Do you consider me such a marshmallow I would simply smile my wifely smile and say, 'of course dear, whatever makes you happy?' Passionate feelings are not limited to the bedroom, Jeremy. I may not know how to demonstrate them, but I have other feelings, very strong feelings. Surely you didn't think having this great love you've found would be without any cost to you whatsoever?"

"I'm afraid I didn't think, Margaret," he admitted sadly. "I'm afraid I only felt."

This time, she did not try to stop the tears that coursed her silken cheeks. "I'll need time, Jeremy. Time to sort this all out."

He nodded, but could not speak. She returned her gaze to the French windows.

"I'll make arrangements for the trip, Jeremy. In the meantime, perhaps it might be best if you *do* take some things and stay at the apartment for the next two weeks. I can tell the children you're away on business. After we've left for England, you can come for the rest of your things and arrange for the house to be closed up until—until we get things settled between us."

Jeremy's heart constricted at the thought of his children leaving without his saying a proper good-bye, of how terribly he would miss them. And yet in fairness he knew that Margaret was being more than generous. She hadn't said she would *never* give him a divorce, and she had promised she would not keep him from seeing his children. His heart ached, for himself, for his boy and girl, but it ached the most for the gallant woman who stood before him. He got to his feet. "Margaret, I wish I could tell you how sorry I am it all turned out this way."

"And I wish, Jeremy," she said through muffled tears, "that I could wish you both happiness. But I can't. It hurts too much."

He stood quietly watching her for several minutes. Then, realizing there was nothing more to say, he turned and left the living room, his home, and his marriage.

Chapter 46

Carol sipped her herbal tea. Things had settled down and the office routine was back to normal, with only the continued lack of information on Dr. Bernstein's whereabouts clouding Jessica's life. Carol had felt good until half an hour ago, until the express-mail letter had arrived. The letter Carol had to give to Jessica before she left for the day. The letter she now held in her shaking hands.

Damn! If only she had X-ray vision, if only she could see through the thick linen envelope to what was written on the pages inside. What might this letter do to Jessica's newfound sense of well-being?

A glance at her watch put an end to that speculation. It was well past closing time, and Jessica would be leaving soon to keep her appointment with Ed Franklin. She rose from her desk and slowly made her way to Jessica's office.

"Hi," she said, trying to keep the concern from her voice and eyes.

"Carol." Jessica frowned. "What are you still doing here? I thought you left an hour ago."

"Oh, yeah, well," she stuttered, "as long as you were staying late, I thought I'd do some catch-up work myself." Her smile was false and Jessica knew it.

Jessica's voice was as tentative as her smile. "Is there something wrong, Carol?"

"Why do you ask?"

"Because I know you too well."

Carol softly laid the envelope on the desk. "This came by express mail."

Jessica's eyes widened as she recognized Michael's bold penmanship. She swallowed and closed her eyes for a moment. Then she looked up at Carol's worried face. Her hands began to tremble. She looked back down at the envelope and finally found her voice.

"Thank you, Carol." She took a deep breath. "It's late, you go on home now. Don't worry about me, I'll be fine."

Carol started to protest, but did not trust herself to speak. She nodded her head in agreement, turned, and left the office.

It was some time before Jessica could bring herself to pick up the envelope and unseal the flap. Unconsciously she held her breath as she slipped the pages free and began to read.

It was as if Michael himself were in the room, so vivid were his descriptions. His enthusiasm leapt off the pages and Jessica could actually envision Deliverance rising from the dust of the New Mexico desert. She could actually see Michael, Johnny Bridges, and Antonio d'Abrizzio, all of the people involved in the project and Michael's new life.

She found herself alternately smiling in amusement at Johnny's outrageous sense of humor as Michael related Johnny's antics, and weeping with a peaceful happiness at Michael's renewed commitment to life.

Michael wrote, "Life compensates if we allow it." Maybe that was the answer, maybe that was what everyone had to do—*allow life*.

Jessica read the letter several times. As before, she could not find a false note with which she could question or deny his newfound peace and contentment. Michael had found himself, she could not doubt it.

For the first time in a very long time, Jessica's tears were those of joy and relief. She sat at her desk and allowed the last vestiges of pain and doubt to leave her body, heart, and mind.

Finally, her eyes dry, she folded the pages together and slipped them back into the envelope. She lifted Michael's photograph from the desk and held it next to her heart for a very long time. Then she rose and walked to her office wall safe and spun the combination dial. With a last, long look, she carefully placed the photograph and his letter inside. She closed the door and reset the combination lock. Retrieving her purse from her desk, she left her office.

As Jessica entered the reception room, she stopped. Carol was sitting on the edge of the desk, her face a mask of concern.

Jessica smiled. "Thank you, Carol. Thank you for waiting—thank you for so *very* much."

The relief in Carol's eyes bespoke such genuine friendship, Jessica again felt tears threaten.

"Everything all right?" Carol's words were thick, her own eyes misty.

"Yes." Jessica smiled. "Everything is just fine."

A broad grin halved Carol's face and her voice returned to normal. "Then what say we blow the joint, boss?"

Jessica laughed and arm in arm the two women left the building.

Chapter 47

It was one of those rare cold and rainy nights in Los Angeles. As Ed Franklin rode the elevator to Jessica's floor in the Beverly Wilshire Hotel where she had continued to live after the break-in of her home, he wondered how he would find the right words to tell her the news that would devastate her.

He had come to respect Jessica Martin, respect and admire her for her courage and sensitivity. He was sorry he hadn't met her under different circumstances.

When Jessica answered the door, Ed could not miss the worry in her green-flecked eyes.

"Can I offer you a drink, Mr. Franklin?"

"You can," Ed nodded. "Scotch, no ice. And please, don't you think you could call me Ed by now?"

Jessica smiled her agreement, indicating a pair of wing chairs in front of the fireplace.

Ed stared into the crackling fire and again hoped for the right words. Jessica handed him his drink and took the chair opposite him, the crystal of her wineglass reflecting the flames of the fire.

They were silent for a moment, then Jessica said, "You have bad news for me, don't you, Mr. Fran—uh—Ed?"

Ed took a large swallow of scotch, met Jessica's gaze, and admitted, "I'm afraid so. That's why I wanted to meet you here—away from your office." He faltered for a moment. "Why I flew to Los Angeles. I felt I should tell you in person—in private."

Jessica was unable to speak. She knew what was coming, and she did not want to hear it.

"We've both been expecting it—still, it's rough." His voice was hoarse, and he cleared his throat. "Sol's dead, Jessica. I'm sorry but there's no way to soften the blow."

Jessica closed her eyes. Ed Franklin was right—there was no way to soften it. Nor was there any way to halt the quick surge of guilt that coursed through her. She forced herself to open her eyes and look at Franklin.

"When?" she whispered. "How?"

Ed sighed. "They found him four days ago. As to how, the police list it as a robbery-mugging. They found him under a bridge in Central Park."

Jessica set down her wineglass, suddenly nauseated. Ed recognized her pain and determined to say it all quickly. His timidity wasn't helping her.

"It was a single blow to the head. The coroner said he died instantly, that he hadn't suffered." The inadequacy of his last remark embarrassed Ed, but he quickly rushed on. "He had no identification—he had been stripped clean—no wallet—no jewelry, nothing."

"But then, you—how . . ." Jessica's eyes were huge.

"My card. The card I had given him in Arizona. He had it inside his sock. They missed it. The police called me to identify him."

Jessica nodded her head dully. "Then it's all over? The police know everything? About the file? World Vision?"

"No," Ed said emphatically. "I didn't tell them. I made up a story as to why he had my card." Ed leaned forward, his voice taking on a new urgency, sudden life. "Look, Jessica, there's more, something I haven't told you—the reason I didn't come here as soon as I knew about Sol, something I wasn't sure I would tell you."

Jessica walked to the windows, looked out at the rain-streaked sky. Did she want to know more? Dr. Bernstein was dead—she had failed him. She couldn't stop now. She owed it to Dr. Bernstein to stay in until the finish. She had to know everything.

"Tell me the rest." She turned to face Ed. "I think by now you know you can trust me."

Ed regarded her in silence. He *did* trust her.

"You're right, Jessica. But this mustn't go beyond this room. Not until I tell you otherwise."

Jessica nodded.

"I didn't tell the police because I was determined to continue the investigation. Even with Sol dead, I knew I'd be able to expose the bastards. I've learned one very important thing in my years as a reporter—an investigation never rests on one single person. Someone else knows, someone else *always* knows. I knew I'd be able to find that someone, so I kept quiet about the investigation." He indicated his empty glass. "Mind if I help myself to a refill?"

"Of course not," Jessica answered mechanically. "Please do."

Busying himself at the bar, Ed continued the narration. "I figured I still had Paul Mellon. I could shake him enough to crack. And I also intend to find out who tipped us—follow that up."

"Wait," Jessica interjected. "I've found out who she is—she can't help you."

Ed raised his brows and Jessica filled him in on Stacey, convincing Franklin she knew nothing more than she'd overheard through the bug in Jessica's office.

Ed returned to his seat. "Well, it's not the most bizarre twist I've ever heard, and it sure answers a lot of questions. Okay," he allowed, "hands off that aspect. It's no longer important anyway. It was just a loose end."

"I'm sorry I interrupted you, Ed. But you had to know. Tell me the rest, please. Why doesn't the tipster matter anymore?"

"Because I don't need her. I don't even need Paul Mellon. Not now anyway, not until they are brought to trial."

"To trial?" Jessica's eyes widened. "I don't understand—what did you find?"

For the first time since his arrival, Ed smiled at Jessica, some of the tension leaving his eyes and the set of his mouth.

"*I* didn't *find* anything—and neither did World Vision." He leaned back in his chair as he warmed to what he was about to tell Jessica. "A week before they found Sol's body, I received a small package at my office. There was no name, no return address, just my name and the word 'Personal' printed on the wrapper. It didn't surprise me, we get a lot of anonymous mail. Anyway, when I opened it, I found two keys—those odd-shaped little keys for public storage lockers."

His eyes shone. "There were no identifying marks, nothing to give me a clue as to where the lockers they would open were located. Just ordinary locker keys with the locker numbers on them."

Jessica was tense with curiosity, but determined not to interrupt again.

"I was intrigued, but didn't give it too much thought. As a matter of course, I put one of our investigators on it—I was too concerned with Sol's disappearance to start thinking about another story." He sighed. "By the time the police called me about Sol, I was so sickened over his death, I just forgot all about the keys."

Suddenly he smiled and his eyes glinted. "But our investigator hadn't, Jessica. And just two days ago he came to my office to give me his report. The keys were for lockers number A-2 and B-7 at La Guardia Airport. He had located the lockers, but hadn't opened them. The keys had been mailed to me personally, and he thought I'd want to check them out." He shook his head. "I almost decided to pass the task on to him. I wanted to tie everything up and get to Los Angeles to tell you about Sol. But something kept nagging at me. A-2 . . . B-7 . . . those initials—those numbers . . ."

It hit Jessica, and she gasped. Ed grinned in appreciation. "You *are* quick, Jessica. I told you you'd make a great reporter. A-2 as in Analil-2 and B-7 as in Baromide-7." He laughed. "I broke every traffic regulation in the book getting to La Guardia and those two lockers. And, as you have already guessed, the file was there, in two parts, with detailed notes from Sol on how to break down the scientific data." His voice deepened with sudden emotion. "Sol sent me those keys, Jessica—and he trusted I'd figure out what they were for."

Jessica could scarcely absorb what she was hearing. "But I don't understand. If he was coming to meet you, why put the files in a public locker? Why mail you the keys?"

Ed rolled the glass of scotch between his hands. "Because Sol was a lot sharper than we gave him credit for. Once he'd made his decision, he wasn't going to take a chance on World Vision getting their hands on the file."

Jessica shook her head, still confused. "But the men at the hotel—the briefcase Sol had with him . . ."

"I can't be certain, Jessica, but I've been thinking a lot about Sol Bernstein. His discovery of the false test results, his step-by-step notes for me, a layman, on how to break down the very complicated toxicological data in the file. He was truly a brilliant man—with a very complex mind.

"We have no proof that World Vision was behind Sol's disappearance or his death. Not yet. But if it was World Vision who took Sol from the hotel—who took his briefcase—I think they got a dummy version of the file. I think Sol outsmarted them."

As Jessica digested his words, she could again hear the desperate voice of Sol Bernstein echoing in her head. Tears stung her eyes and her voice was thick.

"And it cost him his life."

For a moment, Ed could not respond. He knew his next words would be crucial to Jessica Martin's ability to accept the tragedy.

"Yes, it did, Jessica. Sol risked his life and he lost it. But in so doing, he may have saved countless others."

Jessica's head jerked up. She stared at Ed Franklin, his features blurred by her tears. Her mind was not working fast enough. Ed hurried on.

"Think about it, Jessica. We have the real file—we will be able to expose them, put a stop to those drugs." His tone became animated. "Don't you see? World Vision thinks they're in the clear. They think they have the real file. If they doubted it, they wouldn't have killed Sol."

"But what if it was a duplicate file? What if Dr. Bernstein made two of them?" Jessica was desperate to believe Ed, but her fears were still very strong.

"I don't think so." Ed shook his head. "I think Sol was too sharp for that. But even if World Vision got a duplicate, *we* still have the original. We can still nail them! They have no way of knowing what we have and they'll relax. We *will* nail them." He locked his gaze with Jessica's, his voice fervent. "Sol Bernstein did not die in vain, Jessica. I'll get the bastards, you have my word on it."

Jessica nodded her head. She believed him, she knew he wouldn't quit. "Ed," she asked softly, "what about his family? His wife? Have you talked to her?"

"Yes," he said dully. "I contacted her aboard the cruise ship. She and the children will exit at the next port and fly home to make the arrangements."

Needing to know, yet dreading what she would hear, Jessica asked. "How did she take it, Ed? Is she all right?"

"Jessica, she is a remarkable woman. I'm sorry you didn't meet her. Her name is Bess and she is as fine and brave in her way as Sol was in his."

"How do you mean?"

"Well, she is devastated by her loss—I'm not negating the pain she is in. But, Jessica, she is not bitter. She's proud of what Sol did. She said she would have expected nothing less from him."

Jessica fought against the lump that had formed in her throat. "What will become of her and the children? Do you know their financial situation?"

"No, not yet. I didn't want to get into it until she has had a chance to get her grief under control. But," he continued in a serious tone, "you can be sure that if there are financial problems, 'Right to Know' will take care of them. Also, once we expose those bastards, once we've proven their involvement, I'm going to strongly urge her to file a lawsuit against World Vision."

Jessica was able to smile. "If there is anything I can contribute . . ."

"That won't be necessary, Jessica. The coffers of 'Right to Know' are pretty full. We'll take care of her, I promise you."

There seemed nothing more to be said, and they both got to their feet. Ed did not hesitate to put his arms around Jessica in an embrace of shared sorrow and friendship. He held her for a moment, then broke free and walked to the door. Before leaving the suite, he said quietly, "I'll be in touch." It was enough.

Over dinner in her suite, Jessica told Jeremy about Stacey and Radner's blackmail attempt, the tragedy of Sol Bernstein's death, and the good news of Michael's letter. Jeremy then told her of his conversation with Margaret and that she intended to leave for England. They sat quietly sipping brandy, absorbed in their own thoughts. Finally, it was Jeremy who broke the silence.

"Personally, I'd like to murder Radner." He was still smarting over Jessica's keeping Radner's threat against her a secret from him. But they had already gone over that argument during dinner and he knew he should not pursue it. Jessica was proud she had handled it on her own. He said with concern, "And I think Stacey sounds unbalanced. Frankly, I don't know why you aren't worried she'll come after you again."

"Well," Jessica conceded, "obviously I can't be one hundred percent sure. But at least I have the letter she signed admitting what she did, all of it."

He shook his head in caution. "I wouldn't consider that letter much protection. With her devious mind, she could find all sorts of ways to cause you trouble without it being traced back to her."

"I've thought of that. But what else can I do? If I brought charges against her, it would all become public knowledge. It wouldn't do any good and it might hamper Ed Franklin's investigation." She stared into the fireplace. "It's odd, but I'm not really worried anymore. I think Stacey will try to fight it out with me in business—it's become an obsession with her. She's incredibly bright, Jeremy, and one of the best recruiters I've ever encountered. I even think she'll give me a run for my money. I think she'll become a success." She smiled quickly at his raised eyebrows. "Oh, I don't fear her competition, I know where I stand. Besides, there's plenty of room in the search field for competent people. If I were to be honest, now that the ugliness is past, I think I'm almost looking forward to meeting her head-on."

"Well, I'd be lying if I said I was looking forward to it." He shook his head. "I can't believe all you've gone through in such a short time."

"It's been rough," Jessica agreed. "But I think the worst is over."

Jessica leaned back against the couch. She felt good, ready for whatever life might bring next.

Jeremy watched her for a moment, then spoke. "It would appear that most of the loose ends are tied up. All but one."

"What's that, darling?" Jessica's alarm showed in her eyes.

"Well, you say Michael is content, that he's found what he wants to do. But Margaret . . . Jessica, I realize now just how much I want to protect you, how much I want to take on anyone who causes you trouble, to have the right to do that. But Margaret hasn't given me any definite answer. I have no time frame. It could be a very long time before she is ready for divorce, before I can ask you to be my wife."

Jessica stared into his eyes; he looked so worried, so sad. But a sudden memory struck her and she was unable to suppress a giggle. Jeremy drew back and stared at her. "Now, just what in hell do you find to giggle about at a time like this?"

"It was something Carol said. She said marriage wasn't all that important. She said we could be the Katharine Hepburn and Spencer Tracy of the corporate world."

"What?" Jeremy cried in mock horror, leaping up from the couch. "You'd better tell Carol she needs her eyes checked. Spencer Tracy indeed! It's perfectly obvious I'm the Cary Grant type."

"Cary Grant, is it? Well, who does that make me?"

He looked at her with a devilish leer and began advancing toward her. Laughing, Jessica began backing up, not immediately aware he was heading her toward the bedroom, his mock English accent making her laugh all the harder.

"Aaah! Judy—Judy—Judy . . ."

And then they were in the bedroom, falling into one another's arms, their embraces broken only by the occasional spasm of happy laughter, until their passion took full hold and everything else was forgotten.

Epilogue

Jessica sat at her desk, a line of concentration creasing her forehead as she went through the stack of mail Carol had opened. A sealed envelope on the top caught her attention.

It was marked "Personal and Confidential," a small, invitation-sized envelope. Jessica took her silver letter opener from the desktop holder and slit through the blood-red seal on the envelope flap. She slid the thick vellum card from the opening and read:

> MISS STACEY DAWSON IS PLEASED TO ANNOUNCE
> THAT SHE WILL BE IN HER NEW OFFICES LOCATED
> AT 8400 WILSHIRE BOULEVARD, 15TH FLOOR
> BEVERLY HILLS, CALIFORNIA 90212
> DAWSON MANAGEMENT CONSULTANTS
> SERVING YOUR EVERY RECRUITING NEED.

Jessica stared at the announcement for a long moment before she threw back her head and released a very unladylike laugh.

"Okay, Stacey," she offered to her empty office, "you 're on!"

DESTINY
By Sally Beauman

'The most talked about novel in years'
Daily Mail

'She brings a brilliant compulsion to her writing'
Company

'Will make publishing history . . . one hurtles through the pages'
Daily Mail

'Will probably find more readers than the greatest contemporary literature'
The Age, Melbourne

'Intelligently written and plotted'
Prima

'All the right effects in the right order'
The Times

'An international blockbuster'
Sunday Times

'A compelling and gripping read'
Look Now

'A gripping tale of love and gems in strange places'
Elle

'A go-for-it tale of our times'
City Limits

'Not for the coy reader'
Irish Times

0 553 17352 9

A SELECTED LIST OF NOVELS
AVAILABLE FROM BANTAM BOOKS